MUDDY MAX

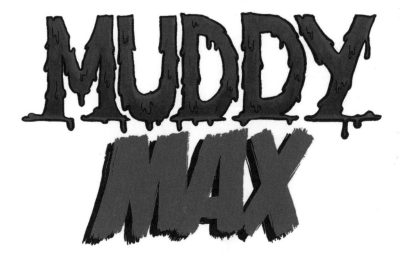

"*Muddy Max* takes that eternal struggle between kids and parents—whether to play in or stay out of mud puddles—and turns it into an epic tale full of secrets and superpowers and one very important lesson: Don't eat mud. It's earthworm poop."

—Matthew Holm, co-creator of *Babymouse* and *Squish*

"What happens when genius-writer Elizabeth Rusch and super-artist Mike Lawrence get together? A book you won't be able to put down—or wash off! Not only does *Muddy Max* ooze adventure, it can also teach all of us something about bravery, science, and earthworm poop."

—Bart King, author of *The Big Book of Superheroes* and *The Big Book of Gross Stuff*

The Mystery of Marsh Creek

Written by
ELIZABETH RUSCH

Illustrated by
MIKE LAWRENCE

Andrews McMeel
Publishing

Kansas City • Sydney • London

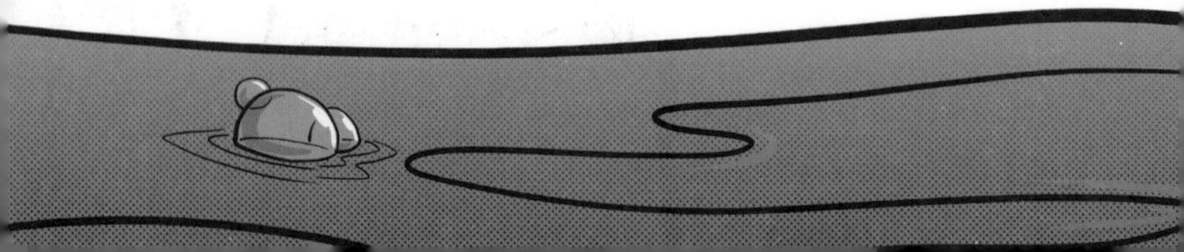

CONTENTS

PART 1

THE PROBLEM WITH MUD

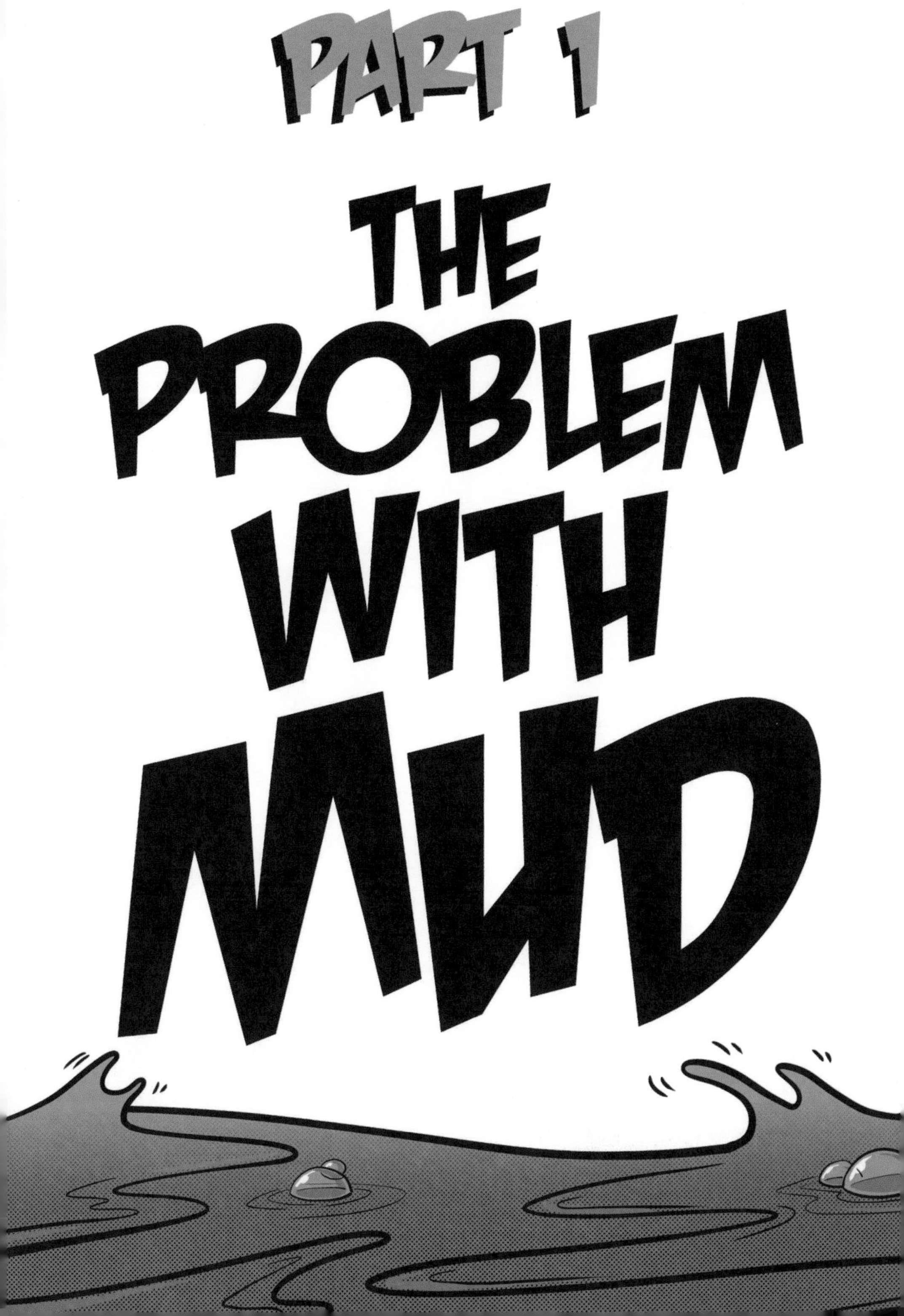

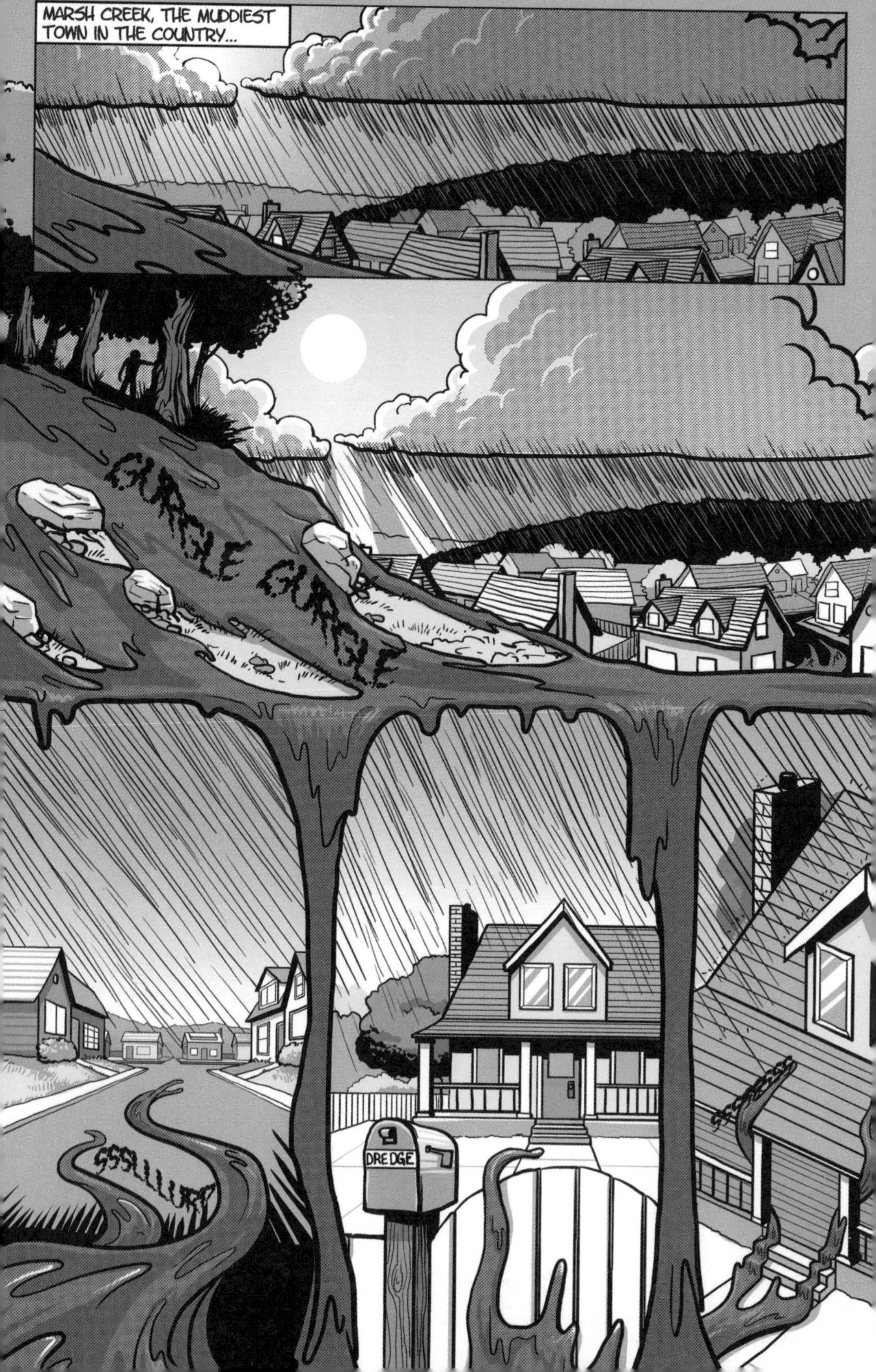
MARSH CREEK, THE MUDDIEST TOWN IN THE COUNTRY...
GURGLE GURGLE
SSSLLURP
DREDGE

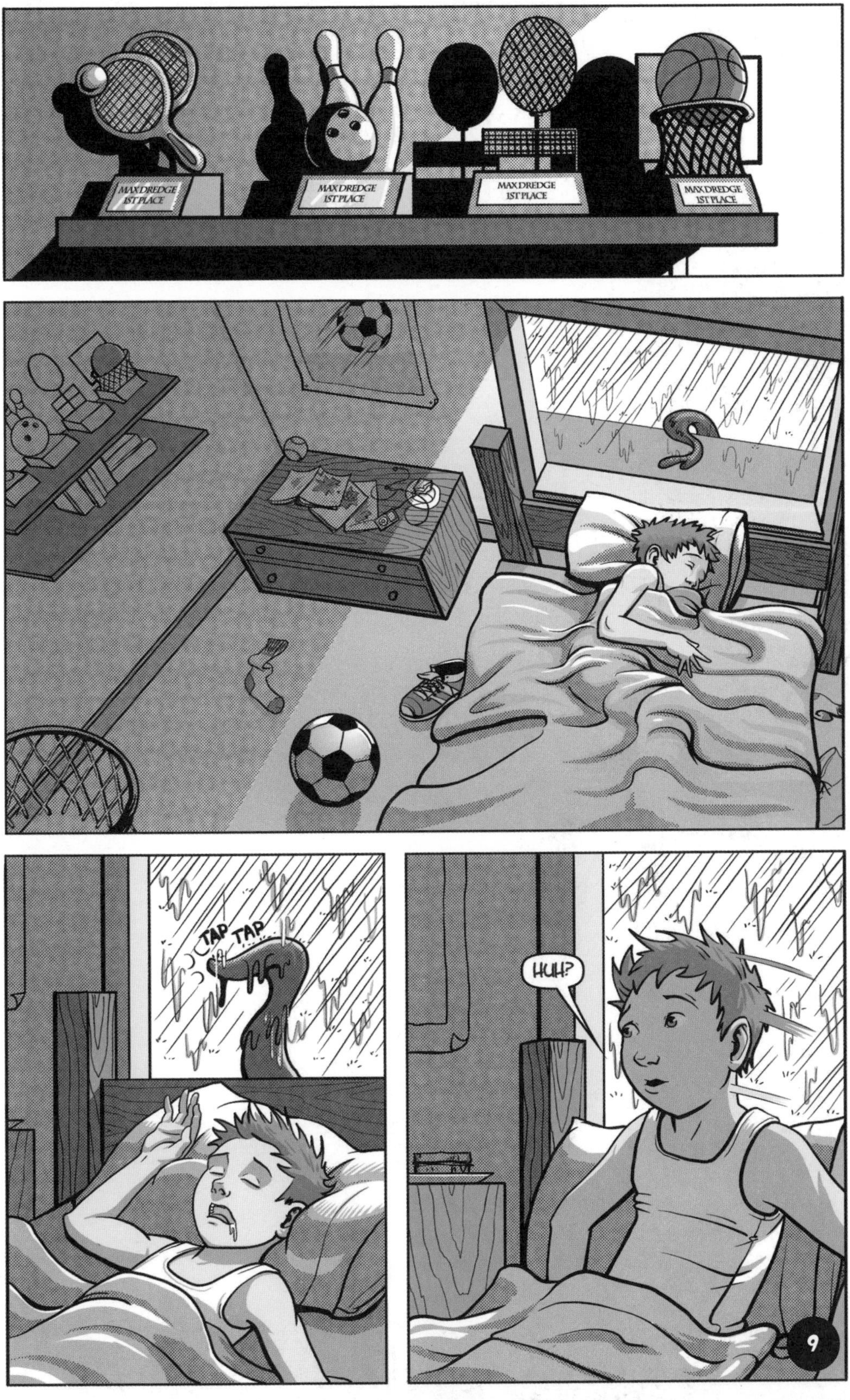
MAX DREDGE 1ST PLACE
MAX DREDGE 1ST PLACE
MAX DREDGE 1ST PLACE
MAX DREDGE 1ST PLACE
TAP TAP
HUH?

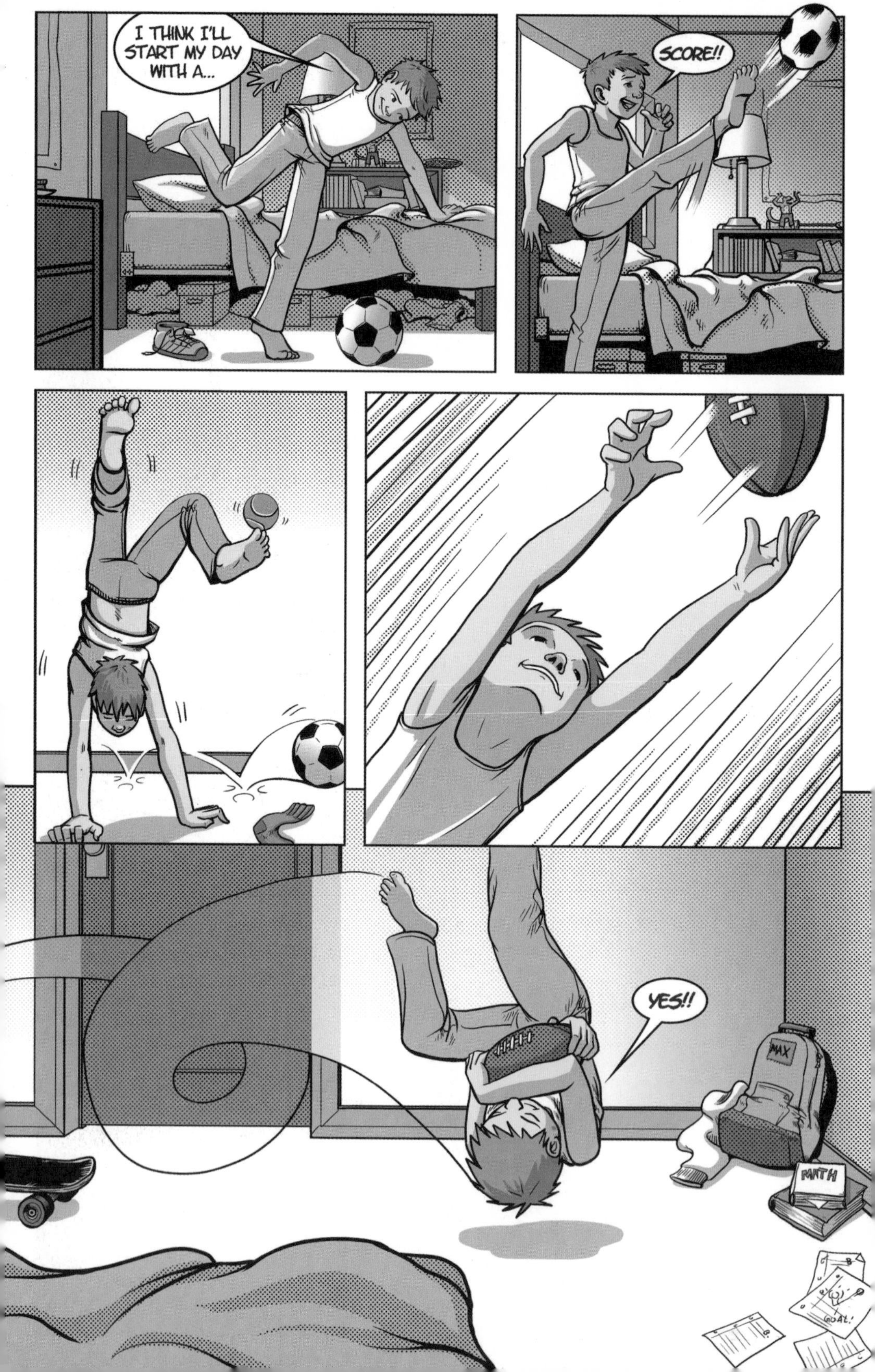
I THINK I'LL START MY DAY WITH A...
SCORE!!
YES!!
MAX
MATH
GOAL!

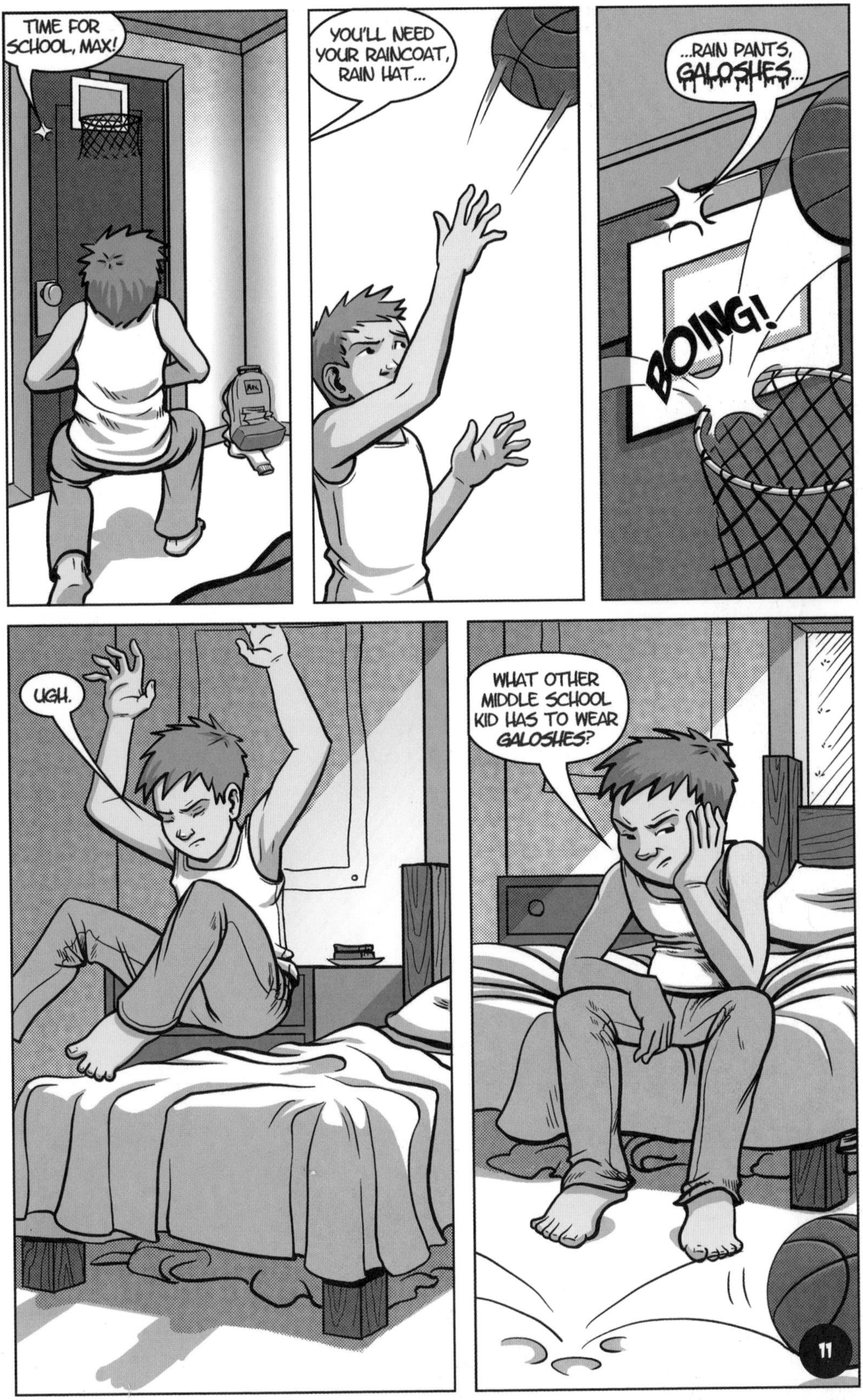
TIME FOR SCHOOL, MAX!
YOU'LL NEED YOUR RAINCOAT, RAIN HAT...
...RAIN PANTS, GALOSHES...
BOING!
UGH.
WHAT OTHER MIDDLE SCHOOL KID HAS TO WEAR GALOSHES?

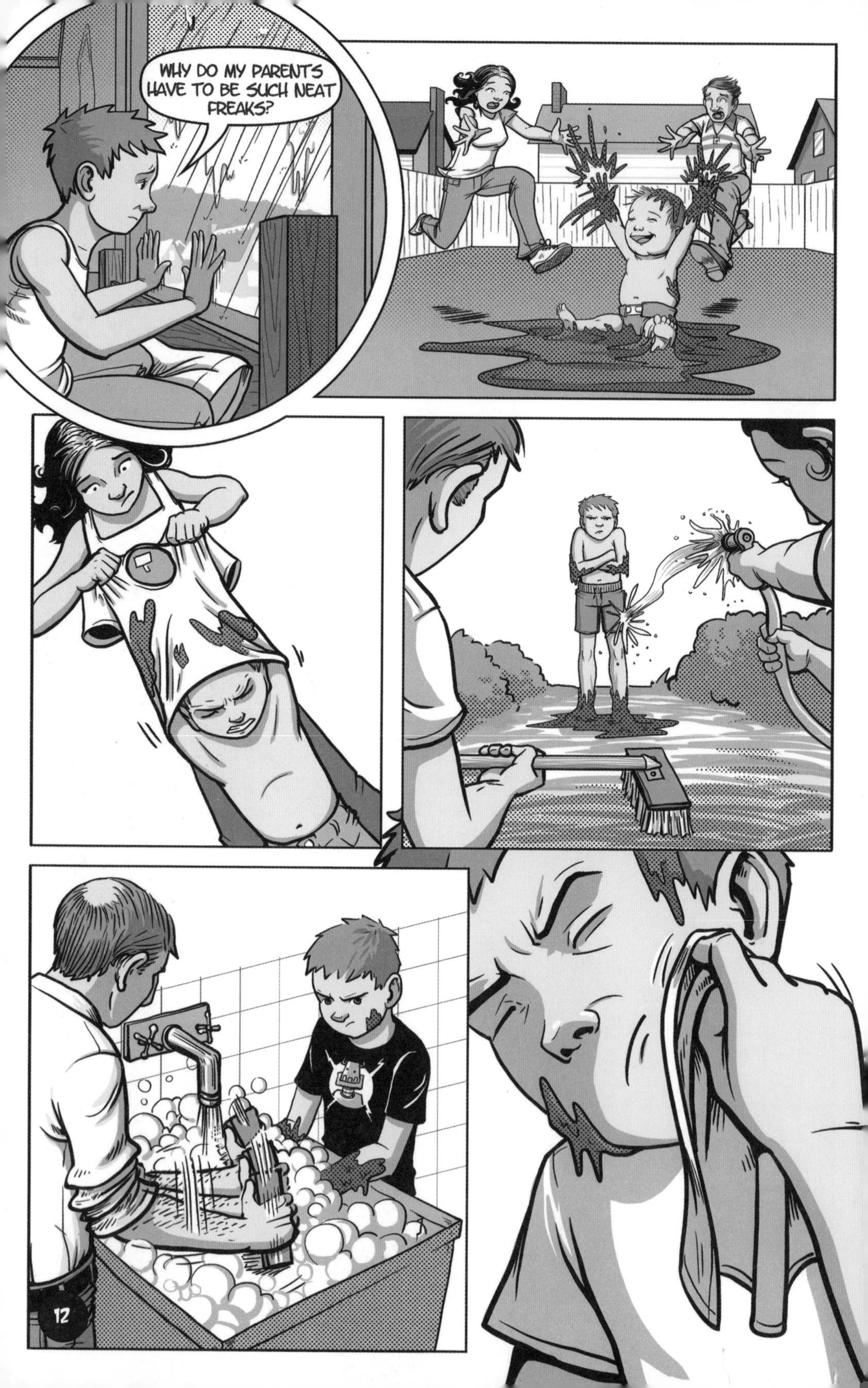
WHY DO MY PARENTS HAVE TO BE SUCH NEAT FREAKS?

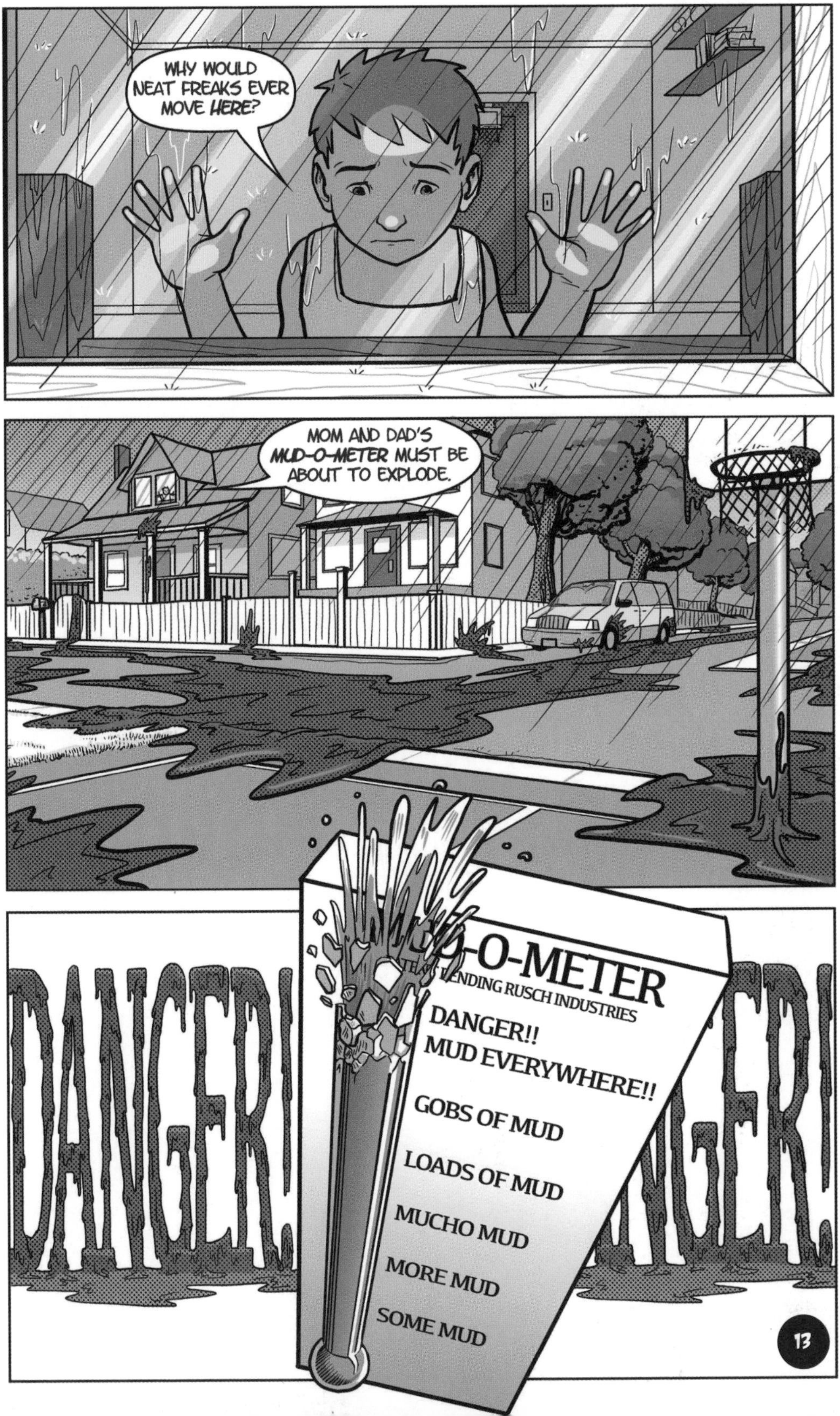
WHY WOULD NEAT FREAKS EVER MOVE HERE?
MOM AND DAD'S MUD-O-METER MUST BE ABOUT TO EXPLODE.
DANGER!
-O-METER
ENDING RUSCH INDUSTRIES
DANGER!!
MUD EVERYWHERE!!
GOBS OF MUD
LOADS OF MUD
MUCHO MUD
MORE MUD
SOME MUD
GER!

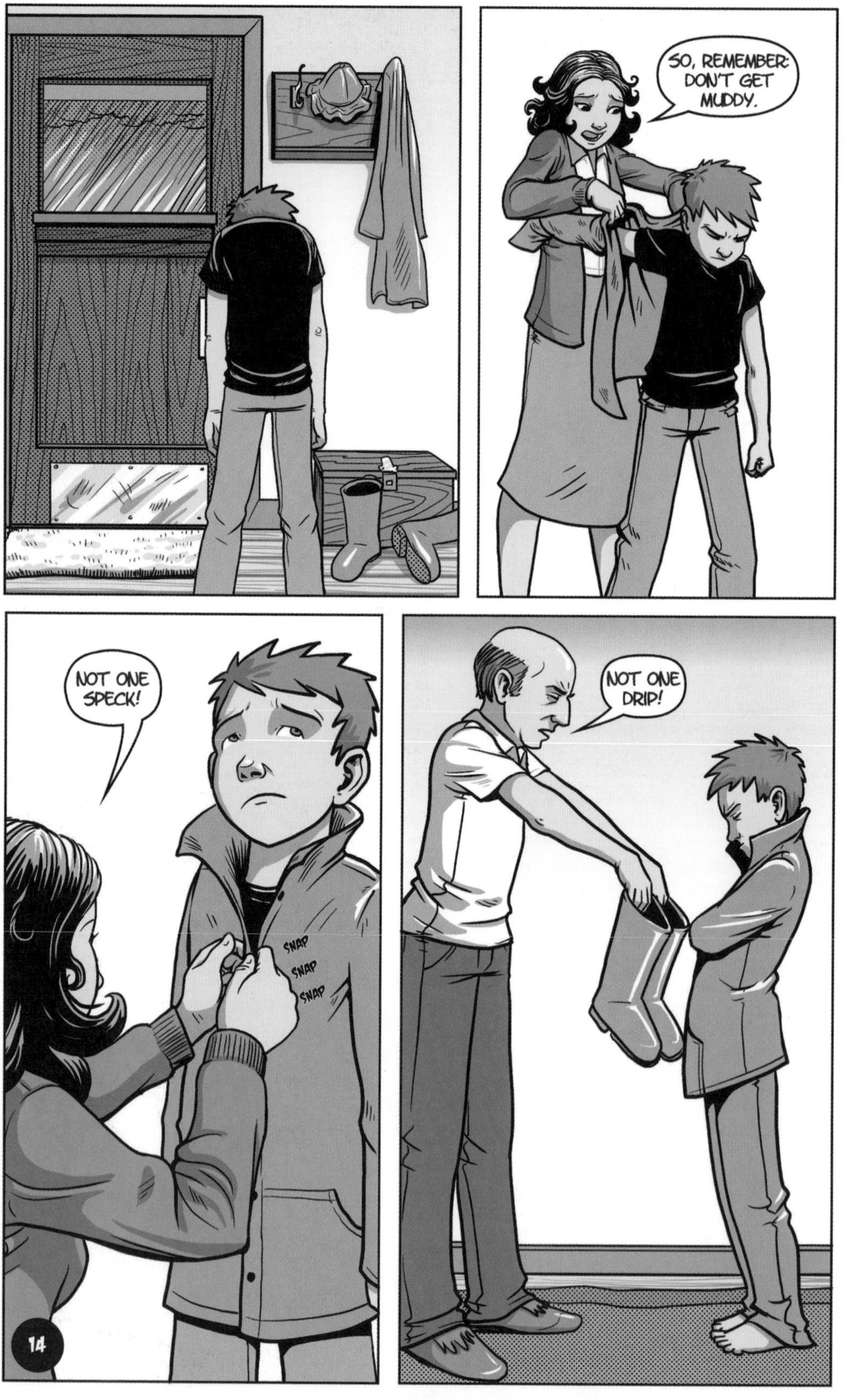
SO, REMEMBER: DON'T GET MUDDY.
NOT ONE SPECK!
SNAP
SNAP
SNAP
NOT ONE DRIP!

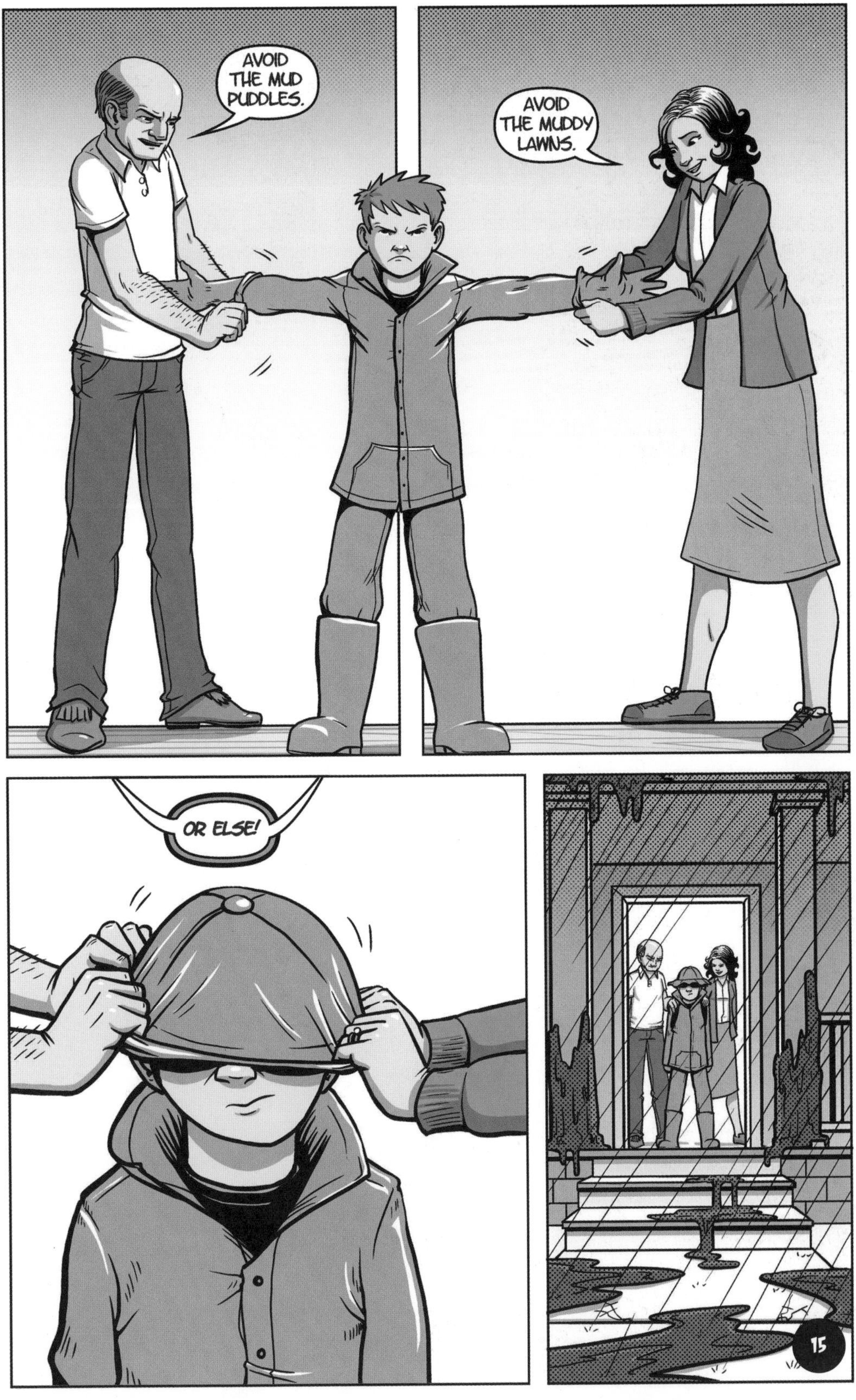
AVOID THE MUD PUDDLES.
AVOID THE MUDDY LAWNS.
OR ELSE!

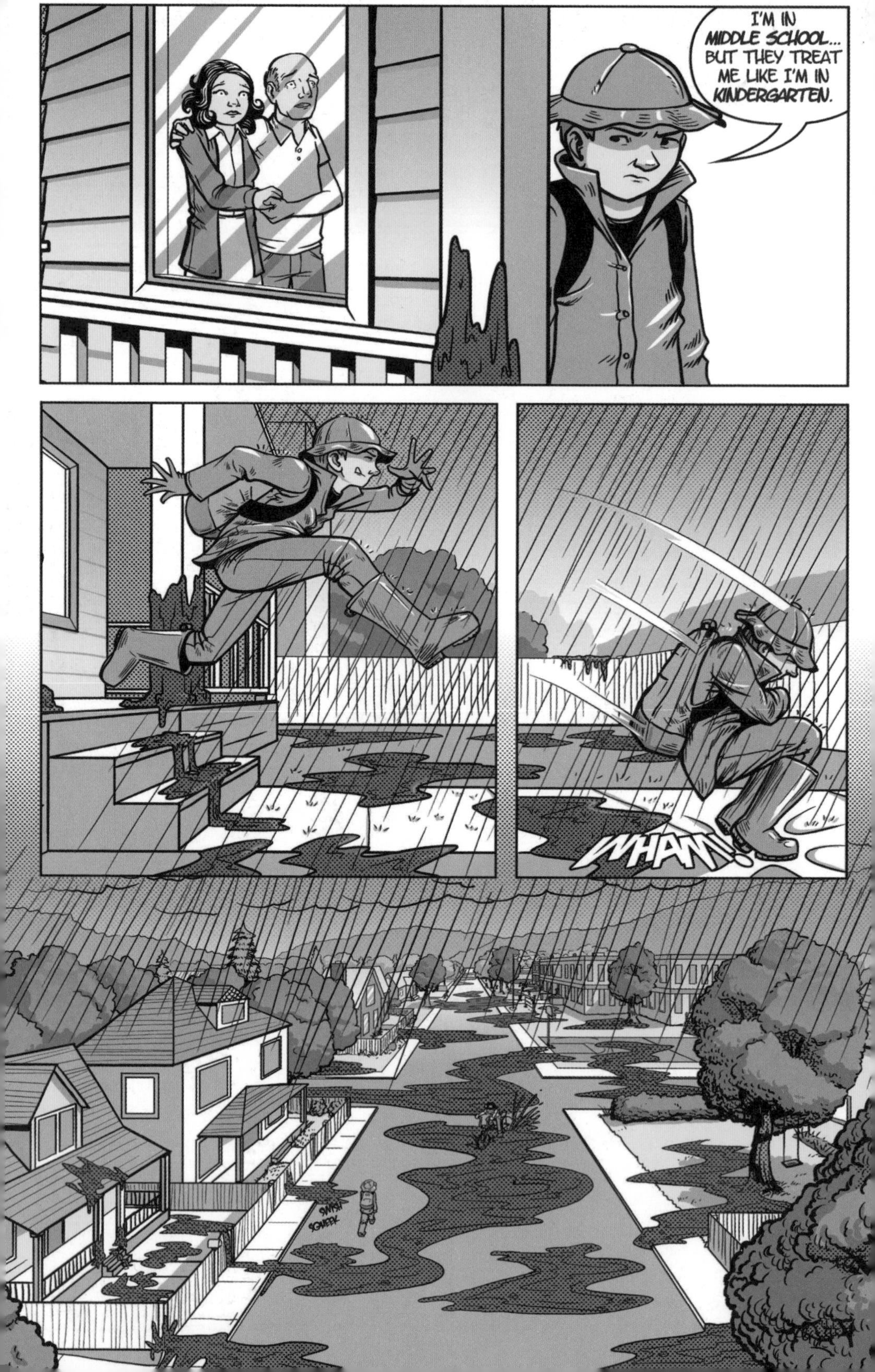
I'M IN MIDDLE SCHOOL... BUT THEY TREAT ME LIKE I'M IN KINDERGARTEN.
WHAM!
SWISH
SQUEEK

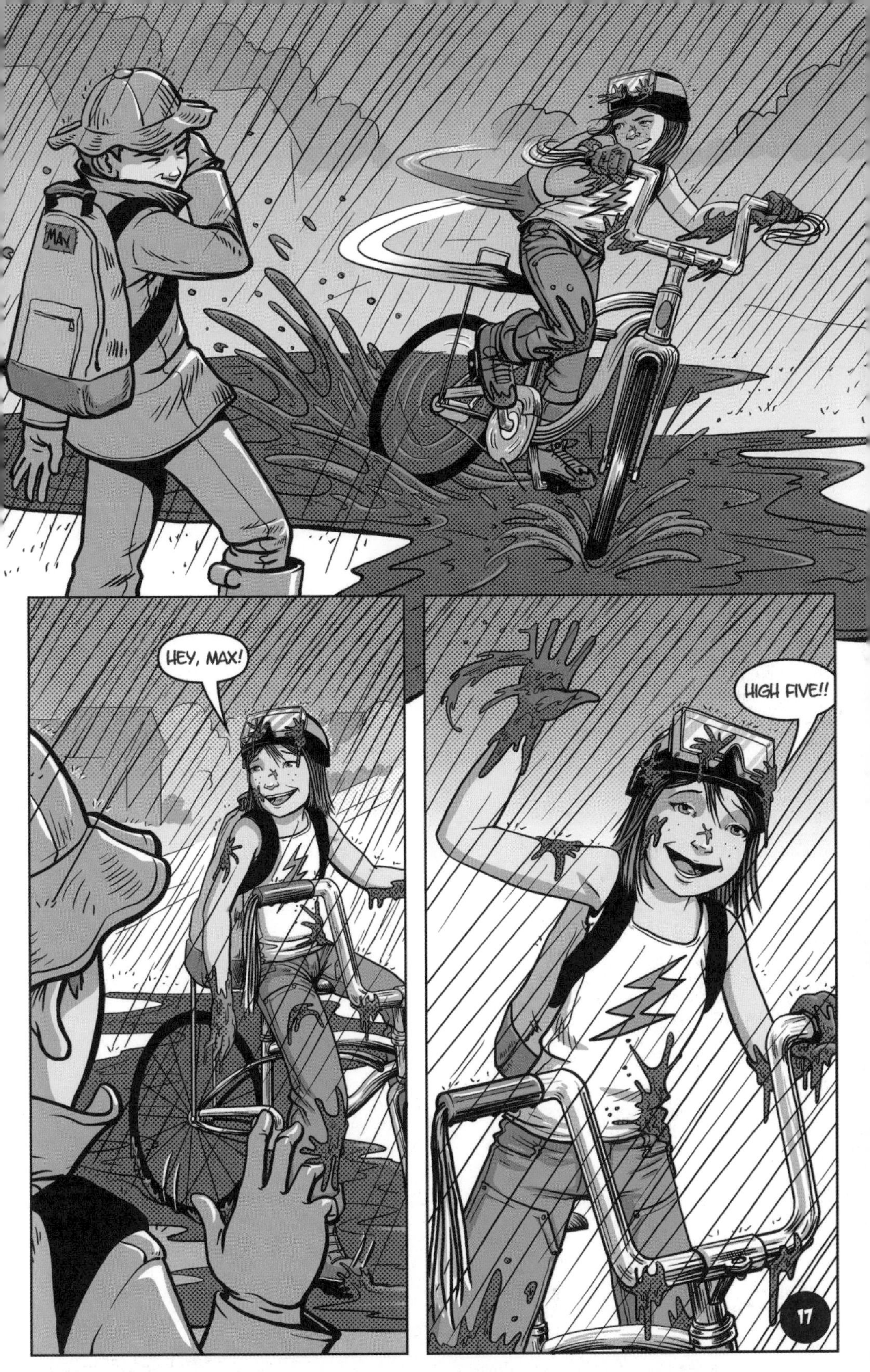
MAX
HEY, MAX!
HIGH FIVE!!

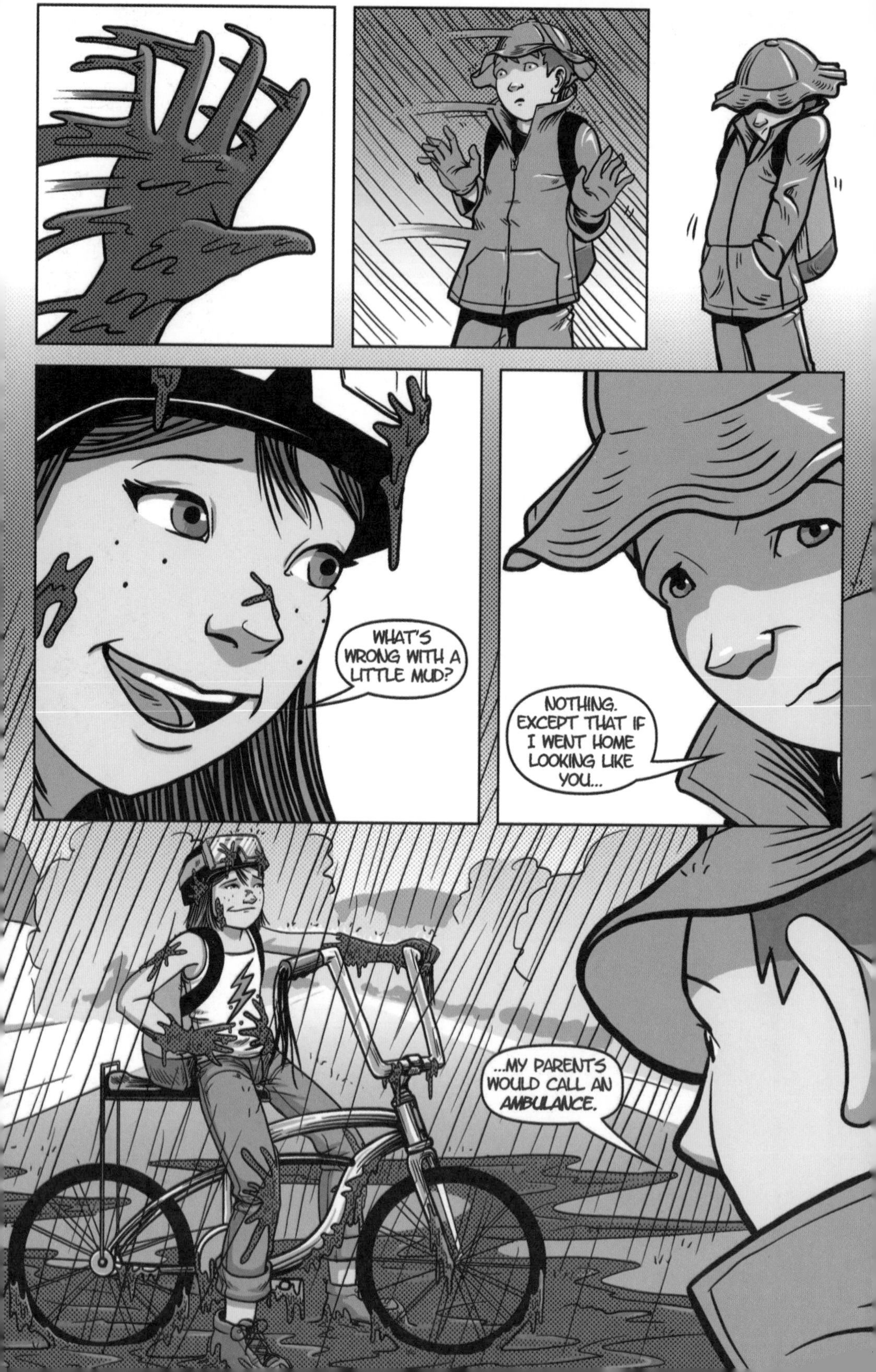
WHAT'S WRONG WITH A LITTLE MUD?
NOTHING. EXCEPT THAT IF I WENT HOME LOOKING LIKE YOU...
...MY PARENTS WOULD CALL AN AMBULANCE.

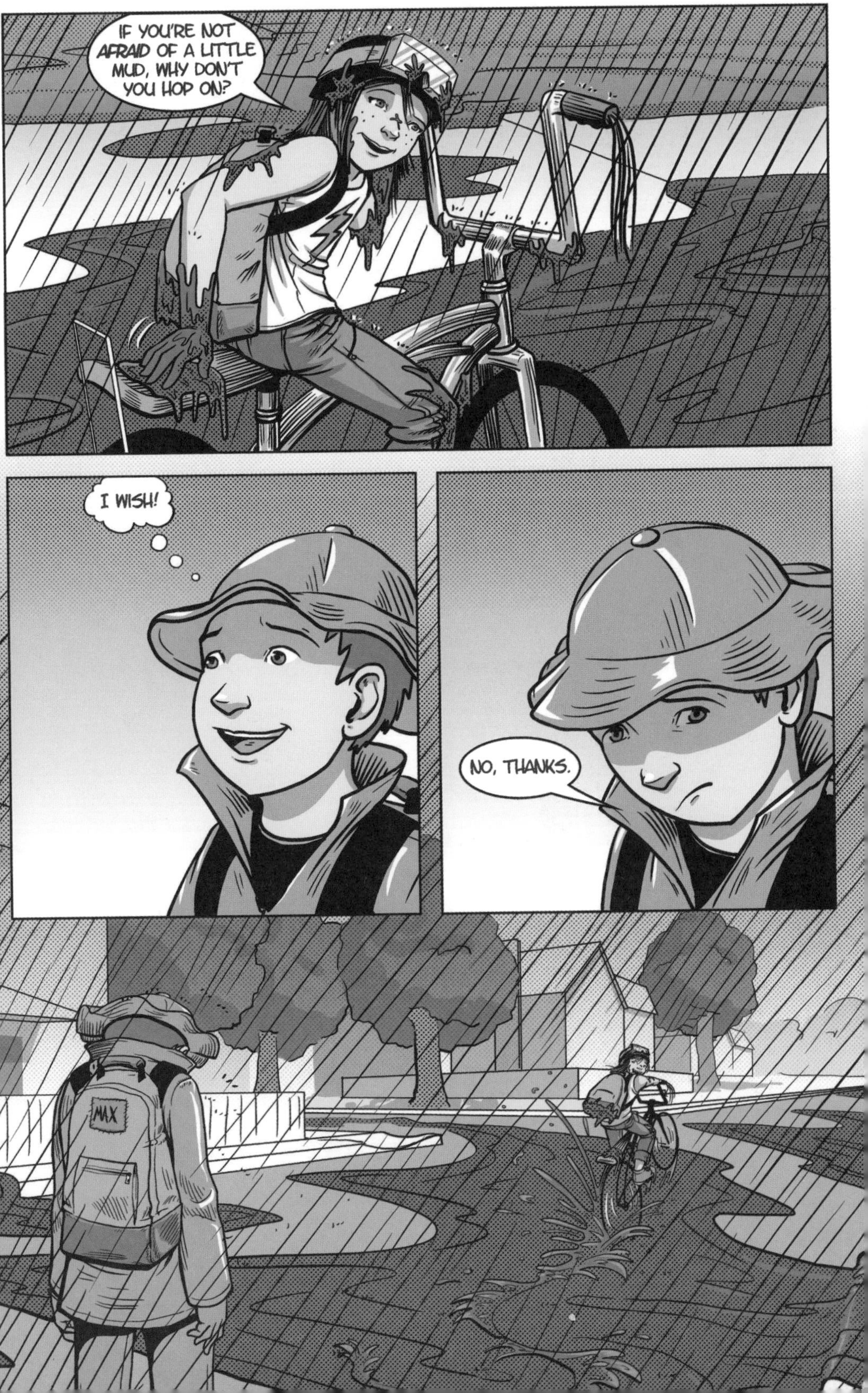
IF YOU'RE NOT AFRAID OF A LITTLE MUD, WHY DON'T YOU HOP ON?
I WISH!
NO, THANKS.
MAX

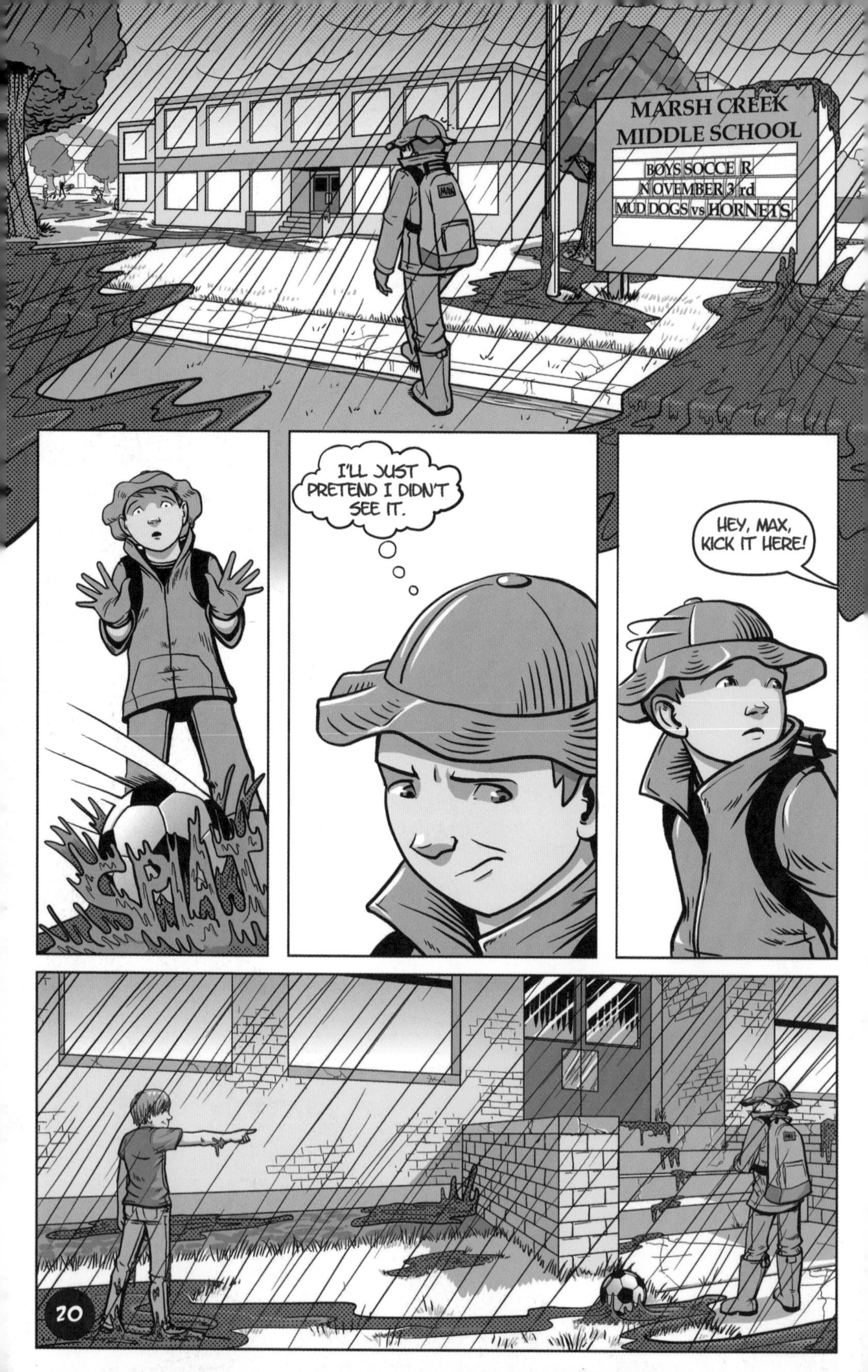
MARSH CREEK
MIDDLE SCHOOL
BOYS SOCCE R
N OVEMBER 3 rd
MUD DOGS vs HORNETS
SPLAT
I'LL JUST PRETEND I DIDN'T SEE IT.
HEY, MAX, KICK IT HERE!

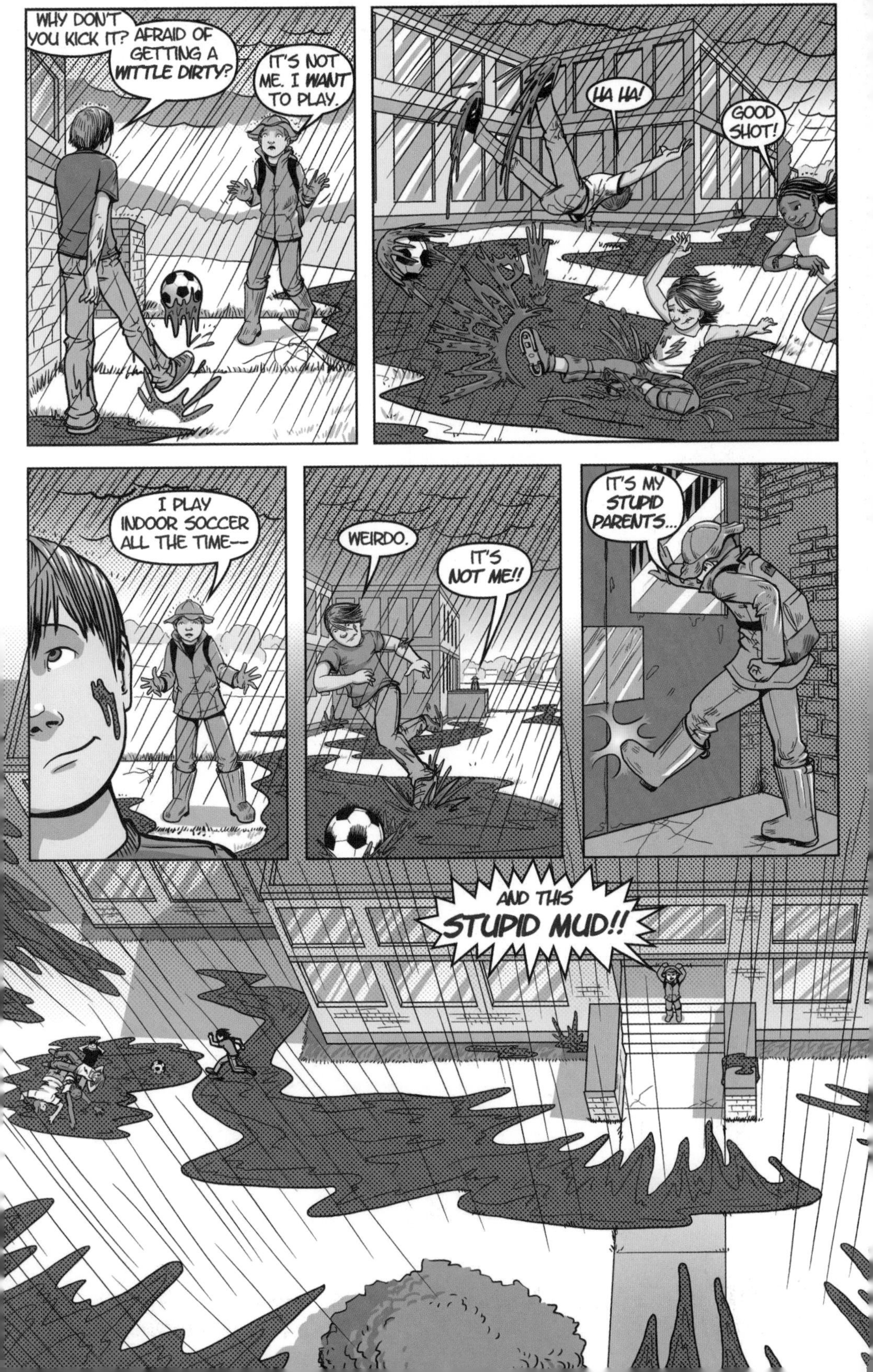

WHY DON'T YOU KICK IT? AFRAID OF GETTING A WITTLE DIRTY?
IT'S NOT ME. I WANT TO PLAY.
HA HA!
GOOD SHOT!
I PLAY INDOOR SOCCER ALL THE TIME--
WEIRDO.
IT'S NOT ME!!
IT'S MY STUPID PARENTS...
AND THIS STUPID MUD!!

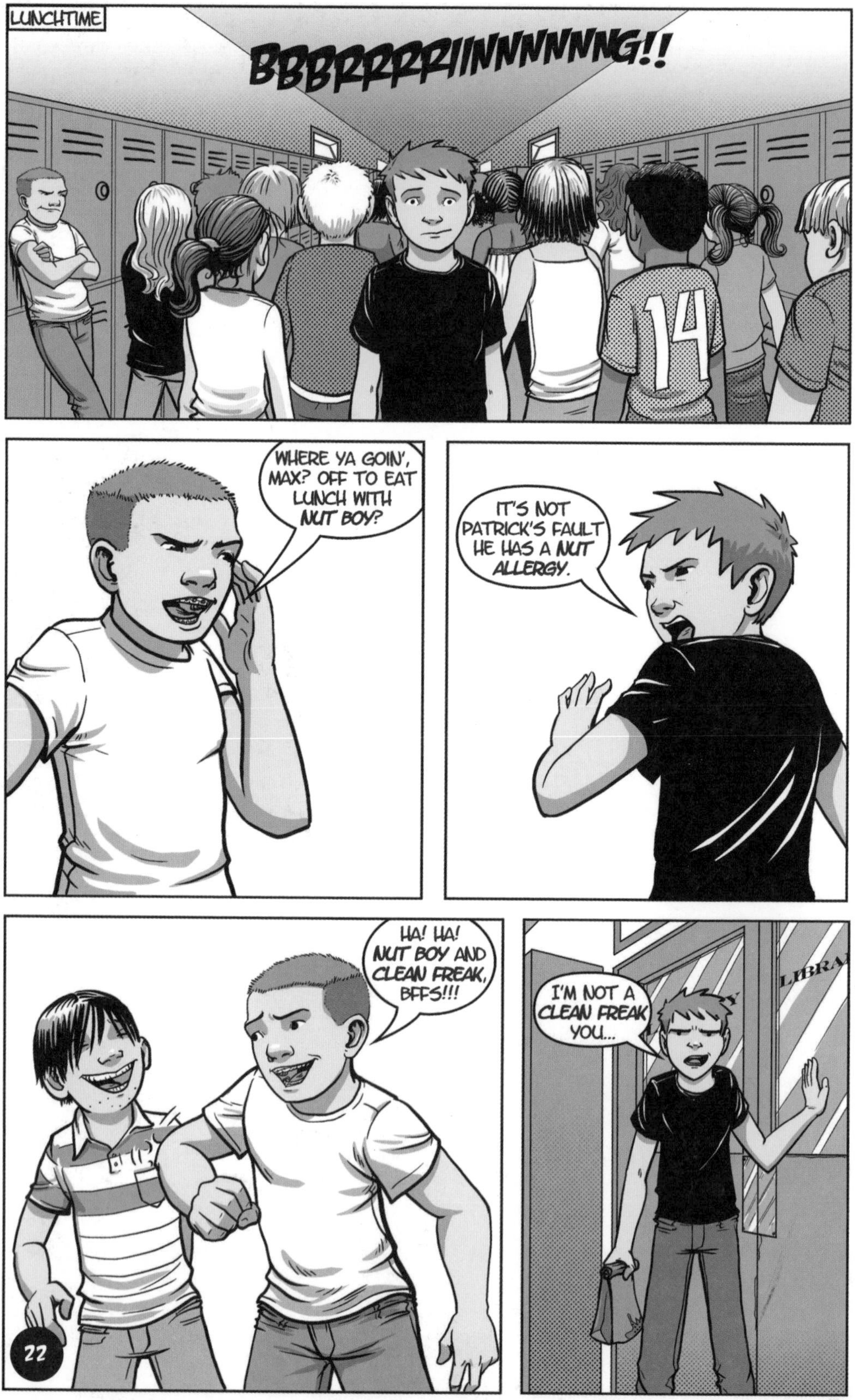
LUNCHTIME
BBBRRRRIINNNNNNG!!
WHERE YA GOIN', MAX? OFF TO EAT LUNCH WITH NUT BOY?
IT'S NOT PATRICK'S FAULT HE HAS A NUT ALLERGY.
HA! HA! NUT BOY AND CLEAN FREAK, BFFS!!!
I'M NOT A CLEAN FREAK YOU...
LIBRA

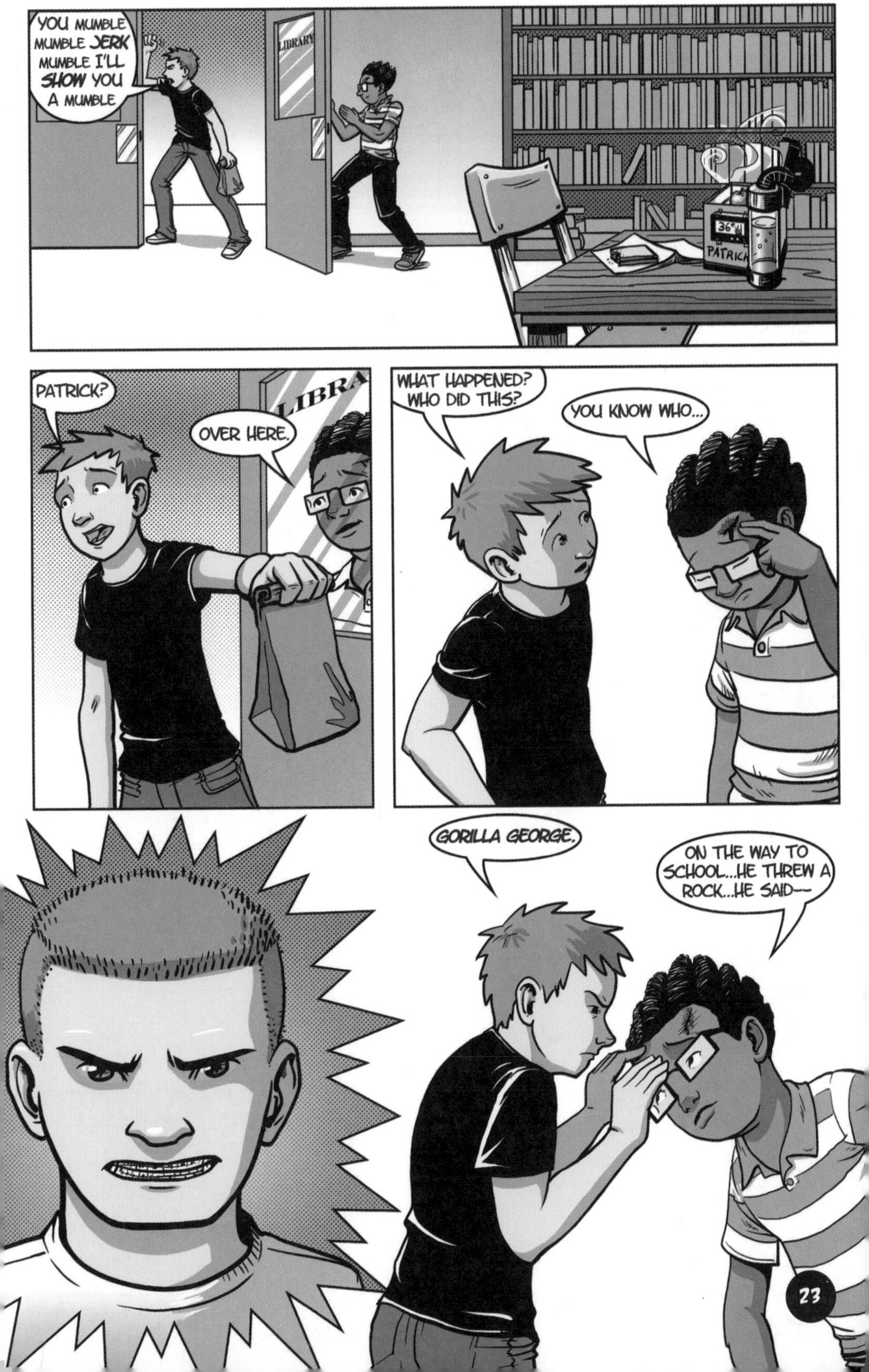
YOU MUMBLE MUMBLE JERK MUMBLE I'LL SHOW YOU A MUMBLE
LIBRARY
36°
PATRICK
PATRICK?
LIBRA
OVER HERE.
WHAT HAPPENED? WHO DID THIS?
YOU KNOW WHO...
GORILLA GEORGE.
ON THE WAY TO SCHOOL...HE THREW A ROCK...HE SAID--

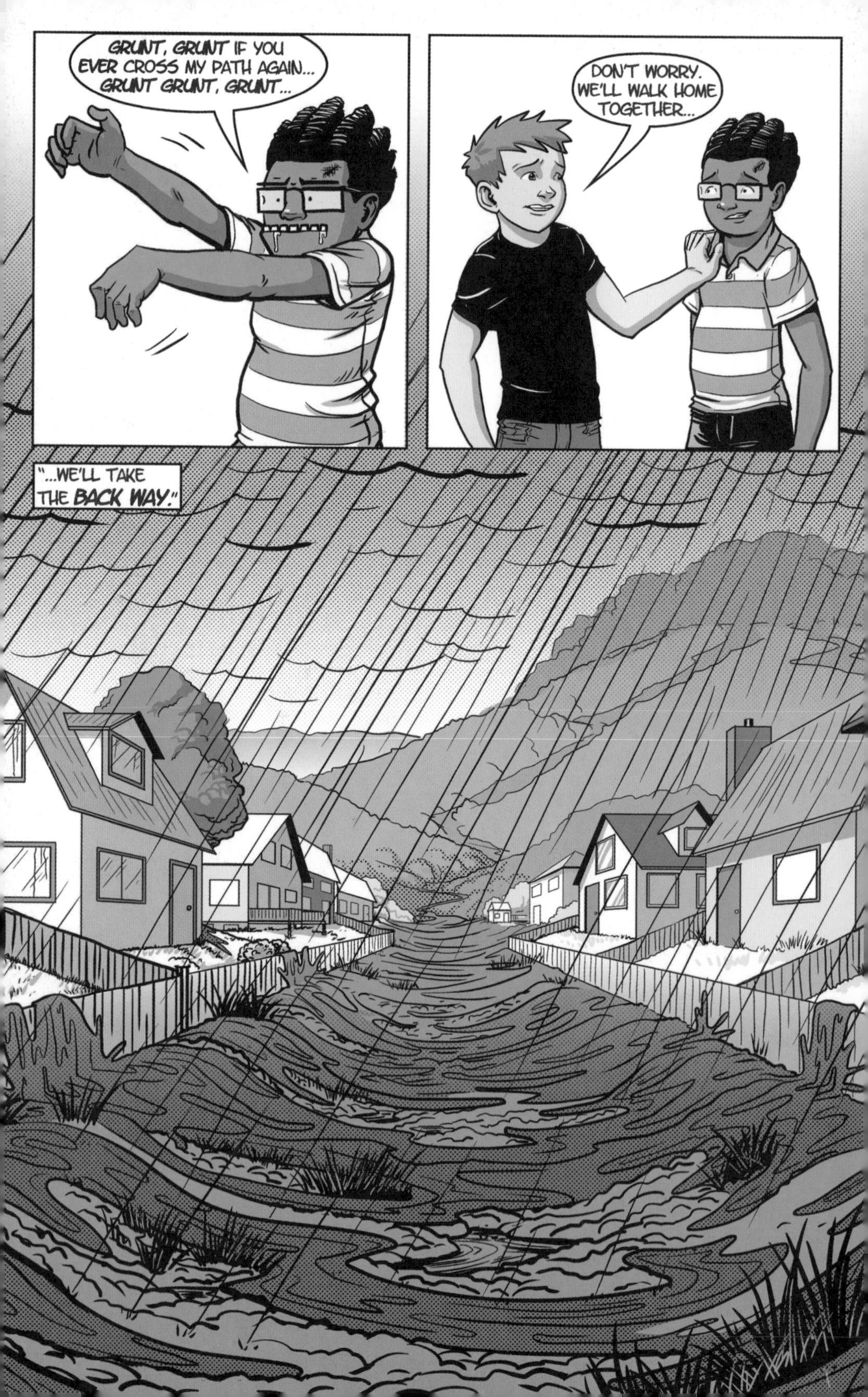
GRUNT, GRUNT IF YOU EVER CROSS MY PATH AGAIN... GRUNT GRUNT, GRUNT...
DON'T WORRY. WE'LL WALK HOME TOGETHER...
"...WE'LL TAKE THE BACK WAY."

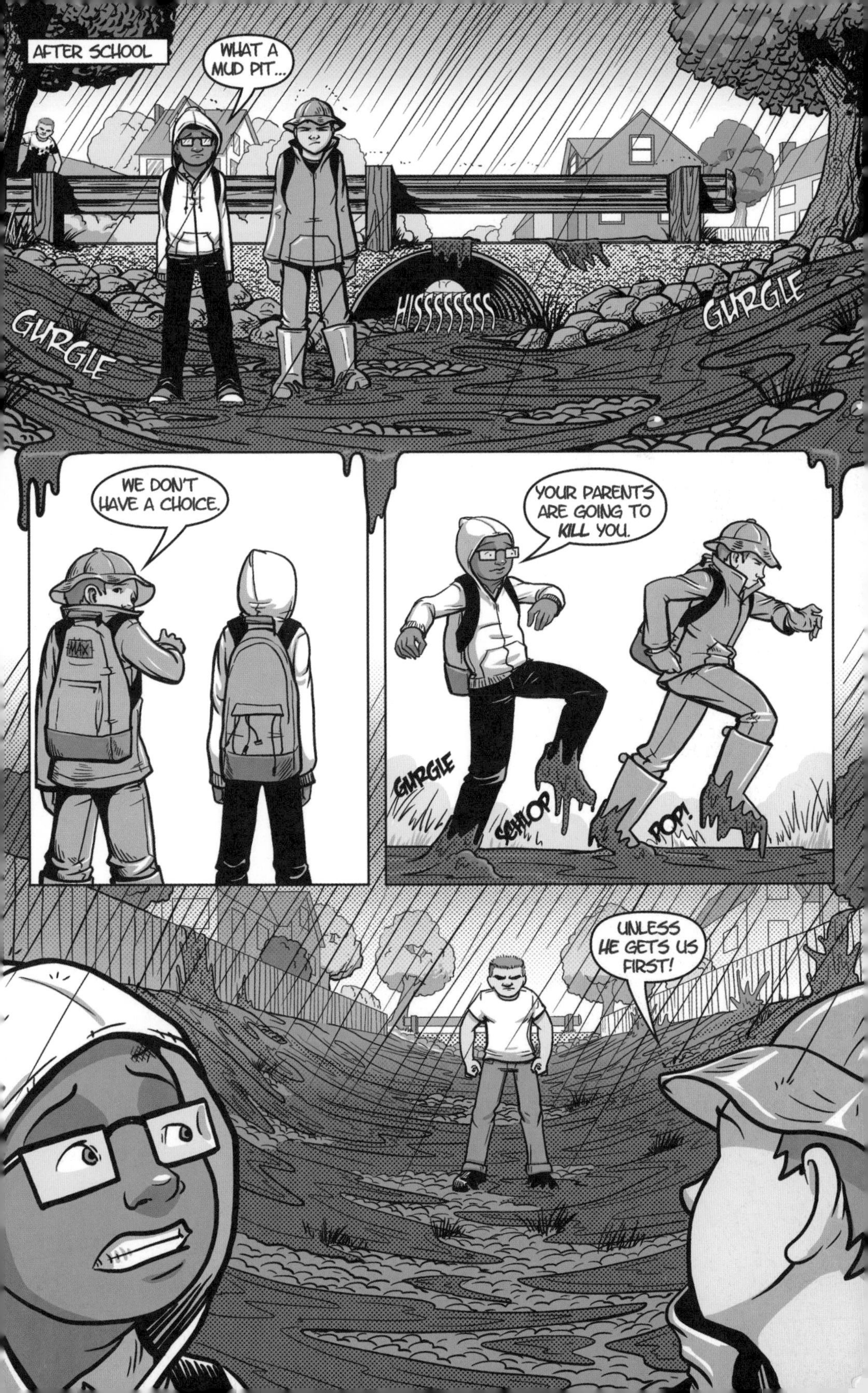
AFTER SCHOOL
WHAT A MUD PIT...
HISSSSSSSS
GURGLE
GURGLE
WE DON'T HAVE A CHOICE.
MAX
YOUR PARENTS ARE GOING TO KILL YOU.
GURGLE
SCHLOP
POP!
UNLESS HE GETS US FIRST!

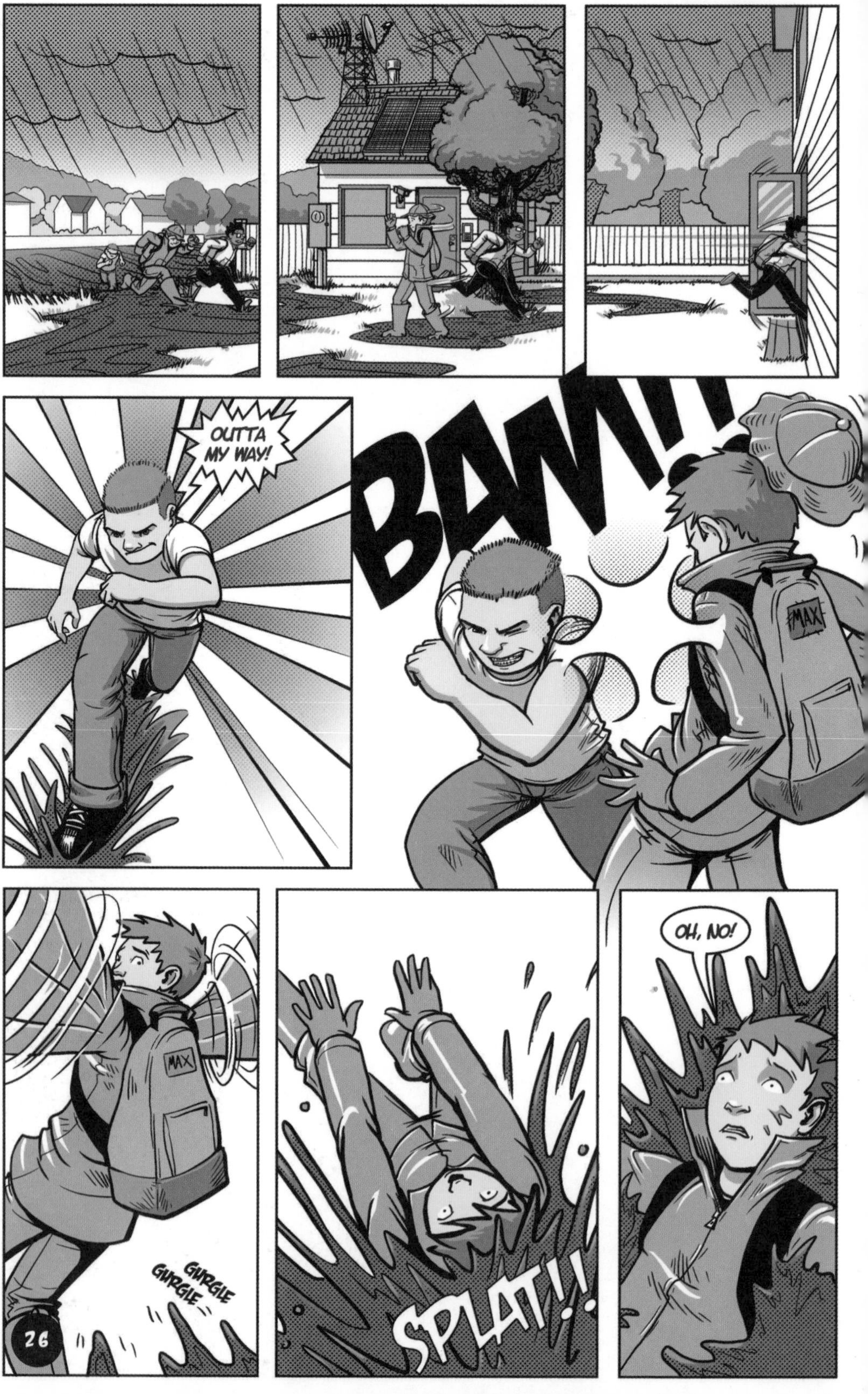
OUTTA MY WAY!
BAM!!!
GURGLE GURGLE
SPLAT!!
OH, NO!

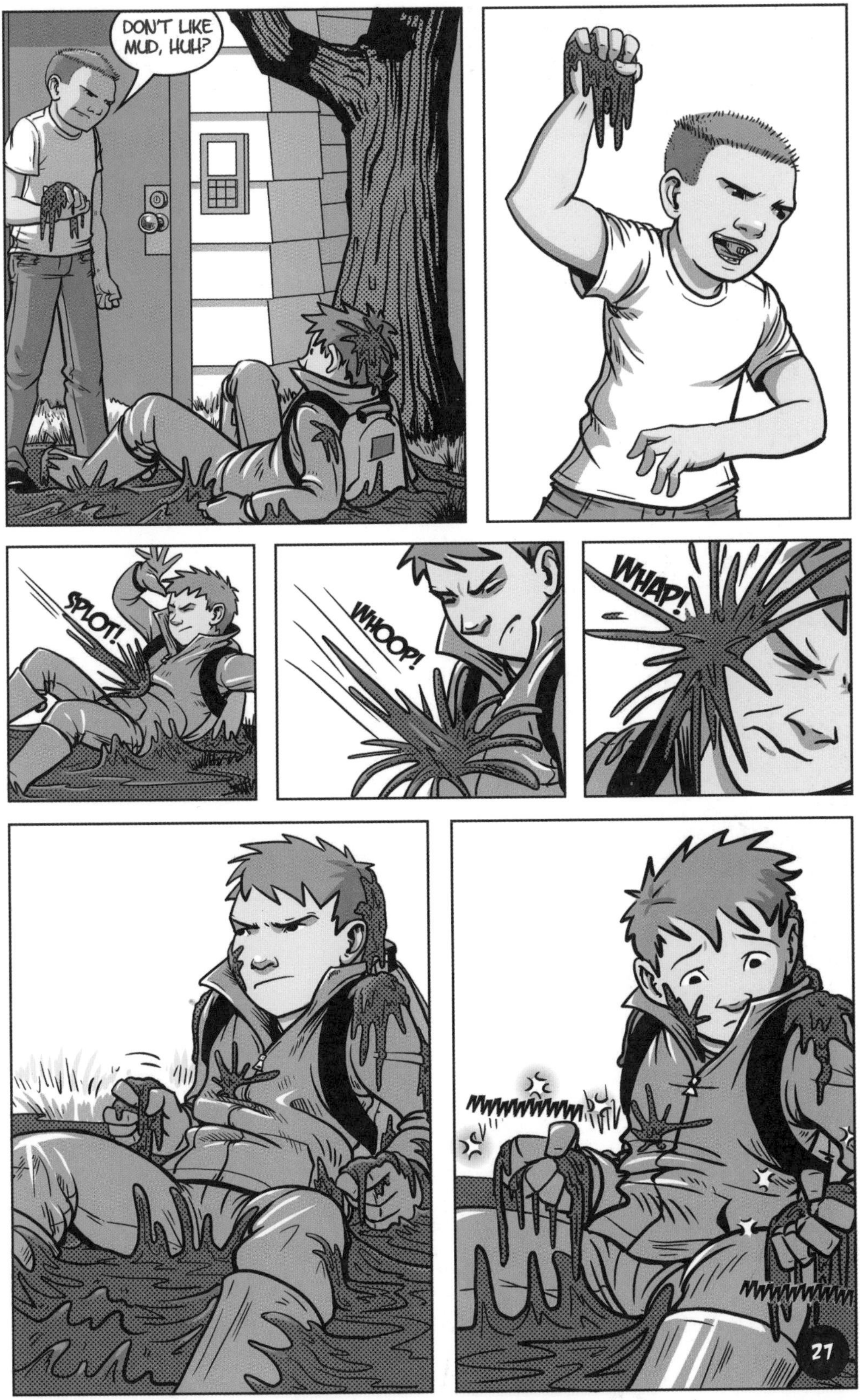
DON'T LIKE MUD, HUH?
SPLOT!
WHOOP!
WHAP!

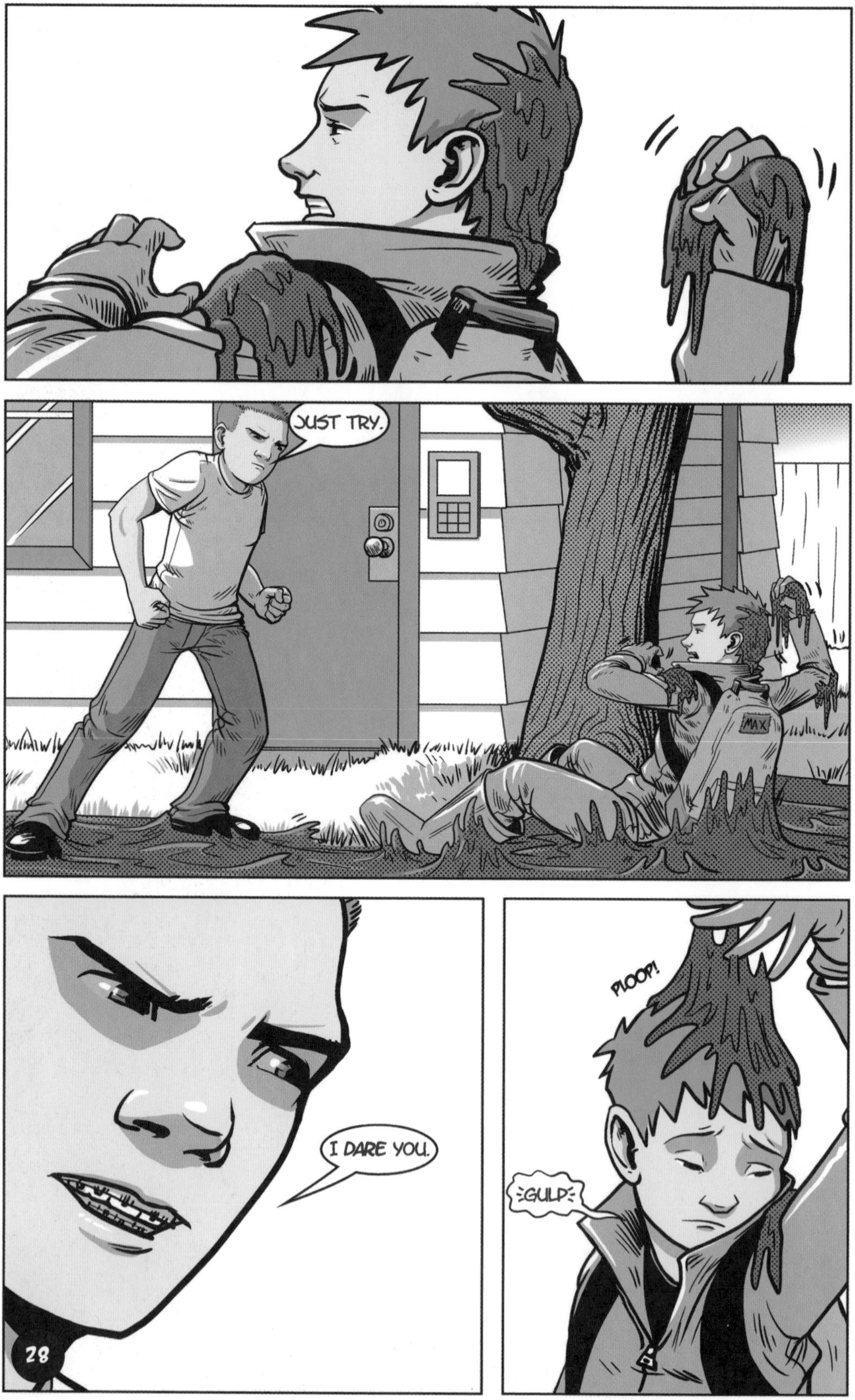
JUST TRY.
MAX
I DARE YOU.
PLOOP!
GULP

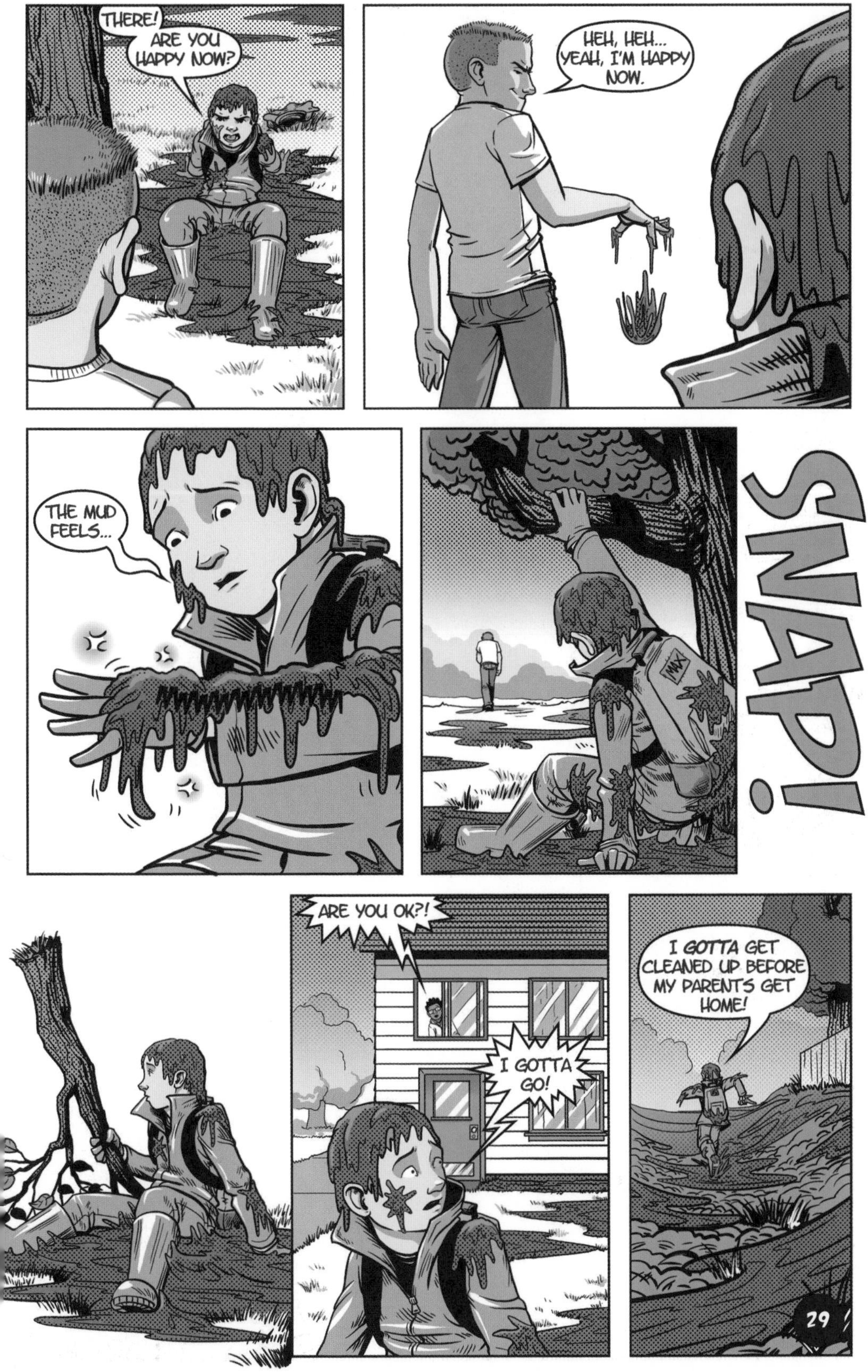
THERE!
ARE YOU HAPPY NOW?
HEH, HEH... YEAH, I'M HAPPY NOW.
THE MUD FEELS...
SNAP!
ARE YOU OK?!
I GOTTA GO!
I GOTTA GET CLEANED UP BEFORE MY PARENT'S GET HOME!
MAX

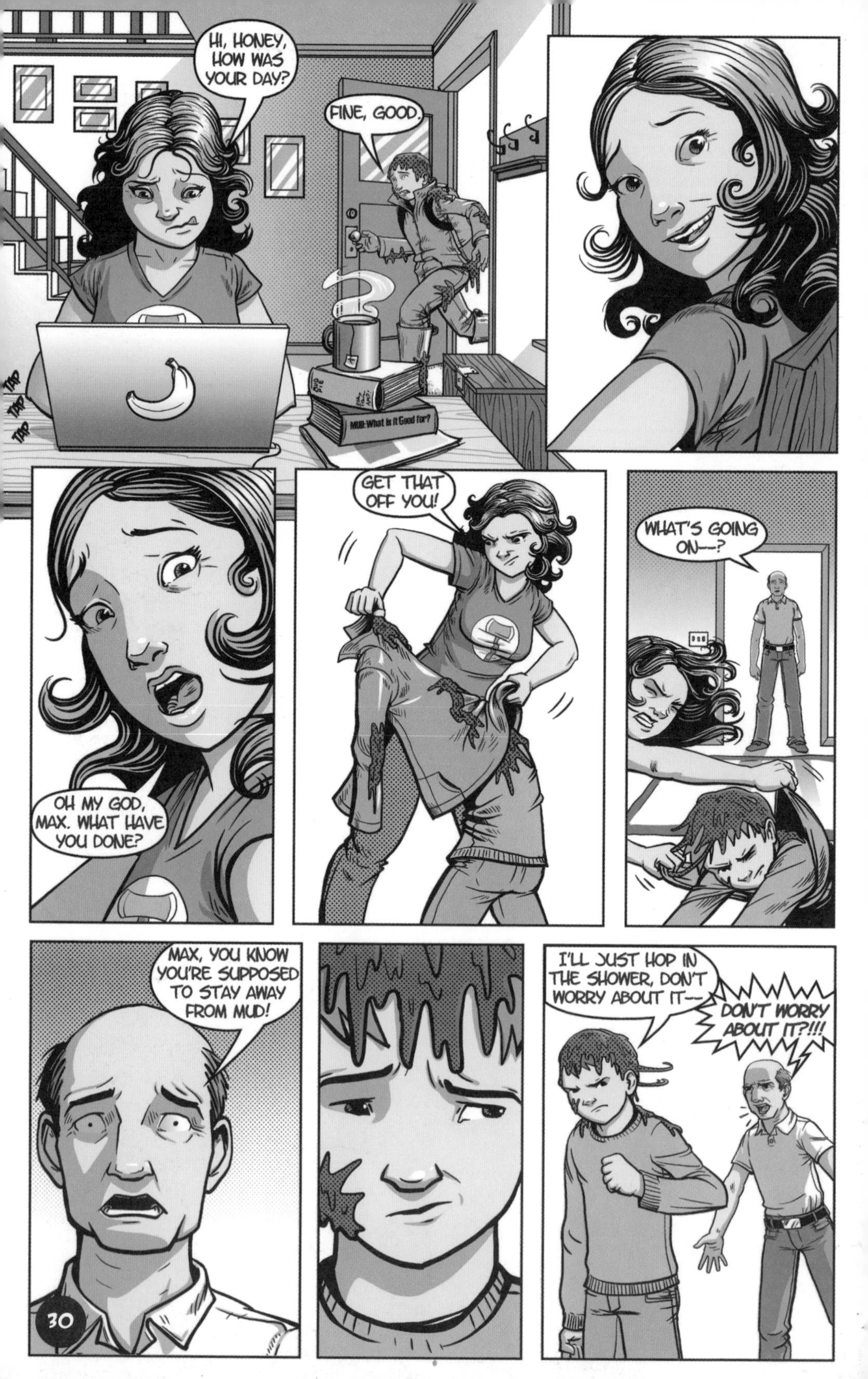
HI, HONEY, HOW WAS YOUR DAY?
FINE, GOOD.
TAP TAP TAP
MUD: What is it Good for?
OH MY GOD, MAX. WHAT HAVE YOU DONE?
GET THAT OFF YOU!
WHAT'S GOING ON--?
MAX, YOU KNOW YOU'RE SUPPOSED TO STAY AWAY FROM MUD!
I'LL JUST HOP IN THE SHOWER, DON'T WORRY ABOUT IT--
DON'T WORRY ABOUT IT?!!!

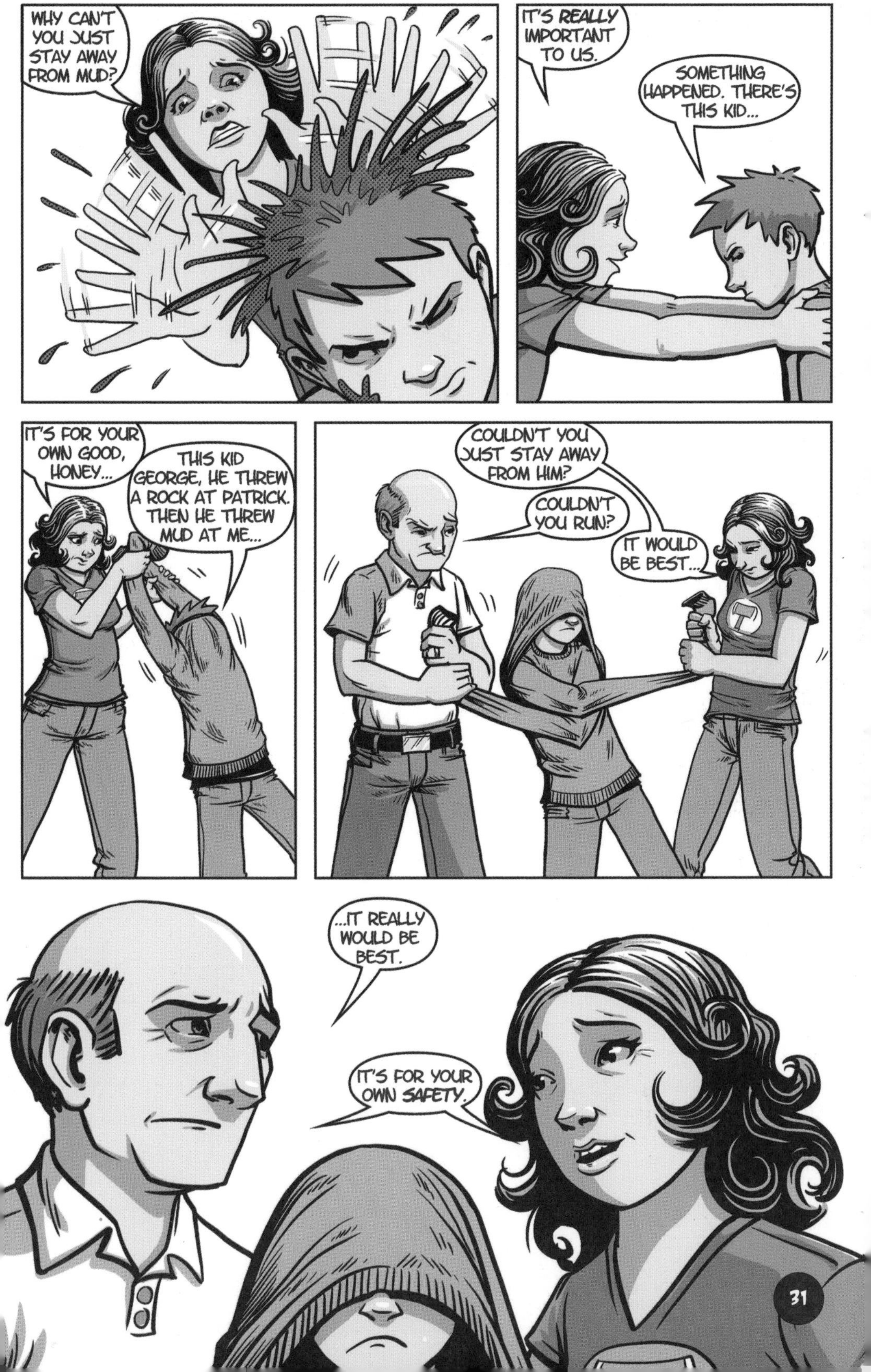
WHY CAN'T YOU JUST STAY AWAY FROM MUD?
IT'S REALLY IMPORTANT TO US.
SOMETHING HAPPENED. THERE'S THIS KID...
IT'S FOR YOUR OWN GOOD, HONEY...
THIS KID GEORGE, HE THREW A ROCK AT PATRICK. THEN HE THREW MUD AT ME...
COULDN'T YOU JUST STAY AWAY FROM HIM?
COULDN'T YOU RUN?
IT WOULD BE BEST...
...IT REALLY WOULD BE BEST.
IT'S FOR YOUR OWN SAFETY.

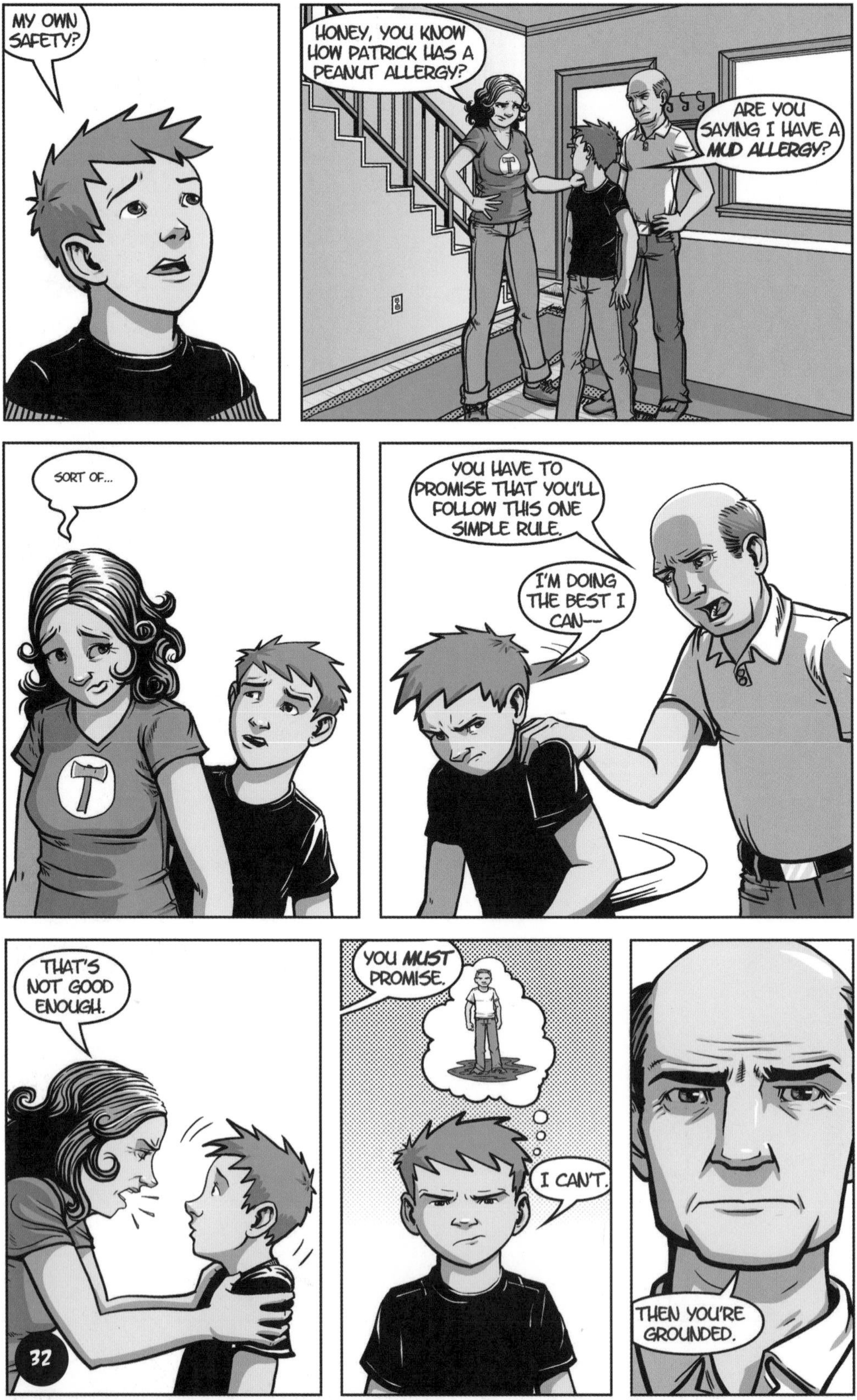
MY OWN SAFETY?
HONEY, YOU KNOW HOW PATRICK HAS A PEANUT ALLERGY?
ARE YOU SAYING I HAVE A MUD ALLERGY?
SORT OF...
YOU HAVE TO PROMISE THAT YOU'LL FOLLOW THIS ONE SIMPLE RULE.
I'M DOING THE BEST I CAN--
THAT'S NOT GOOD ENOUGH.
YOU MUST PROMISE.
I CAN'T.
THEN YOU'RE GROUNDED.

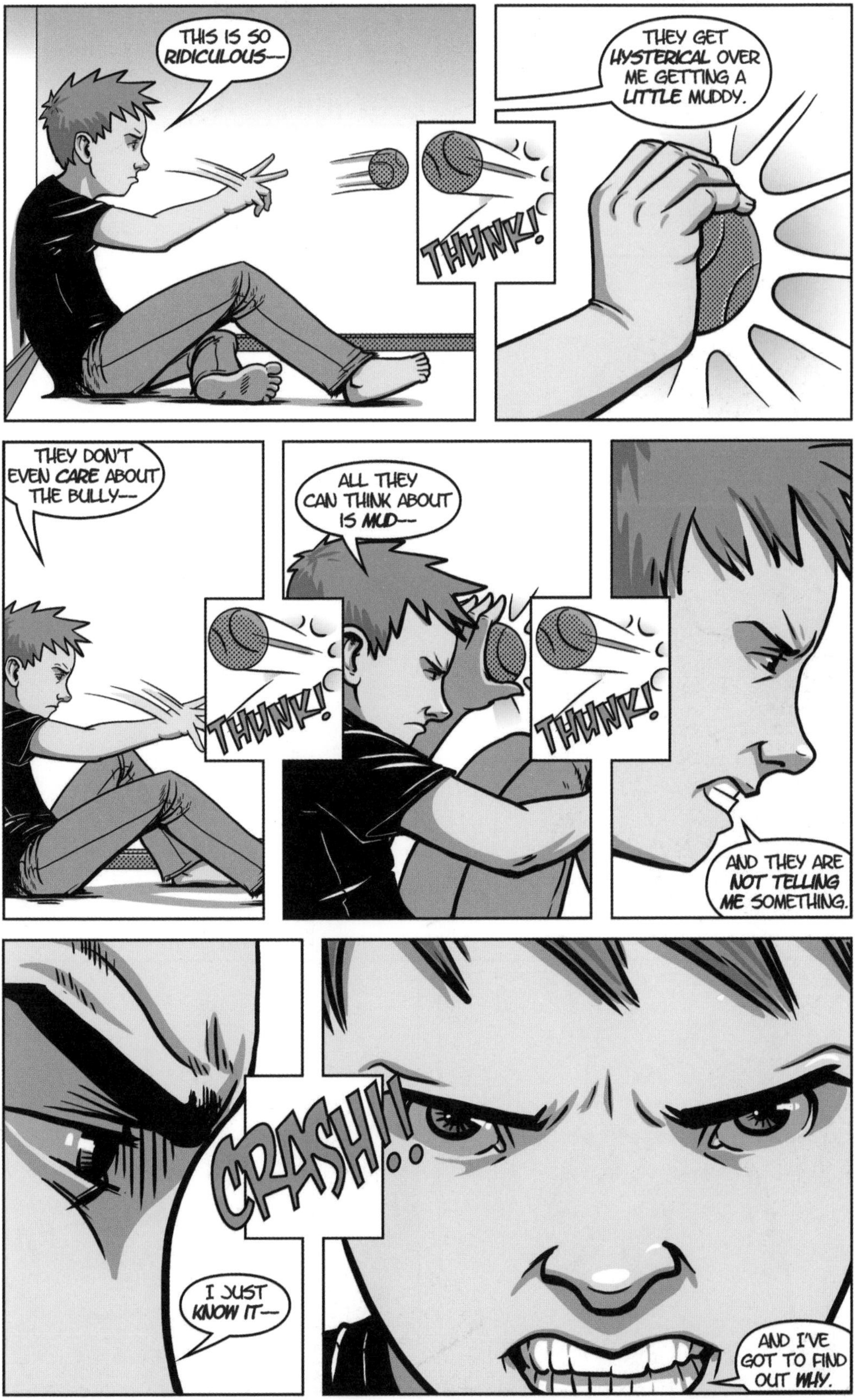
THIS IS SO RIDICULOUS--
THEY GET HYSTERICAL OVER ME GETTING A LITTLE MUDDY.
THUNK!
THEY DON'T EVEN CARE ABOUT THE BULLY--
THUNK!
ALL THEY CAN THINK ABOUT IS MUD--
THUNK!
AND THEY ARE NOT TELLING ME SOMETHING.
CRASH!!
I JUST KNOW IT--
AND I'VE GOT TO FIND OUT WHY.

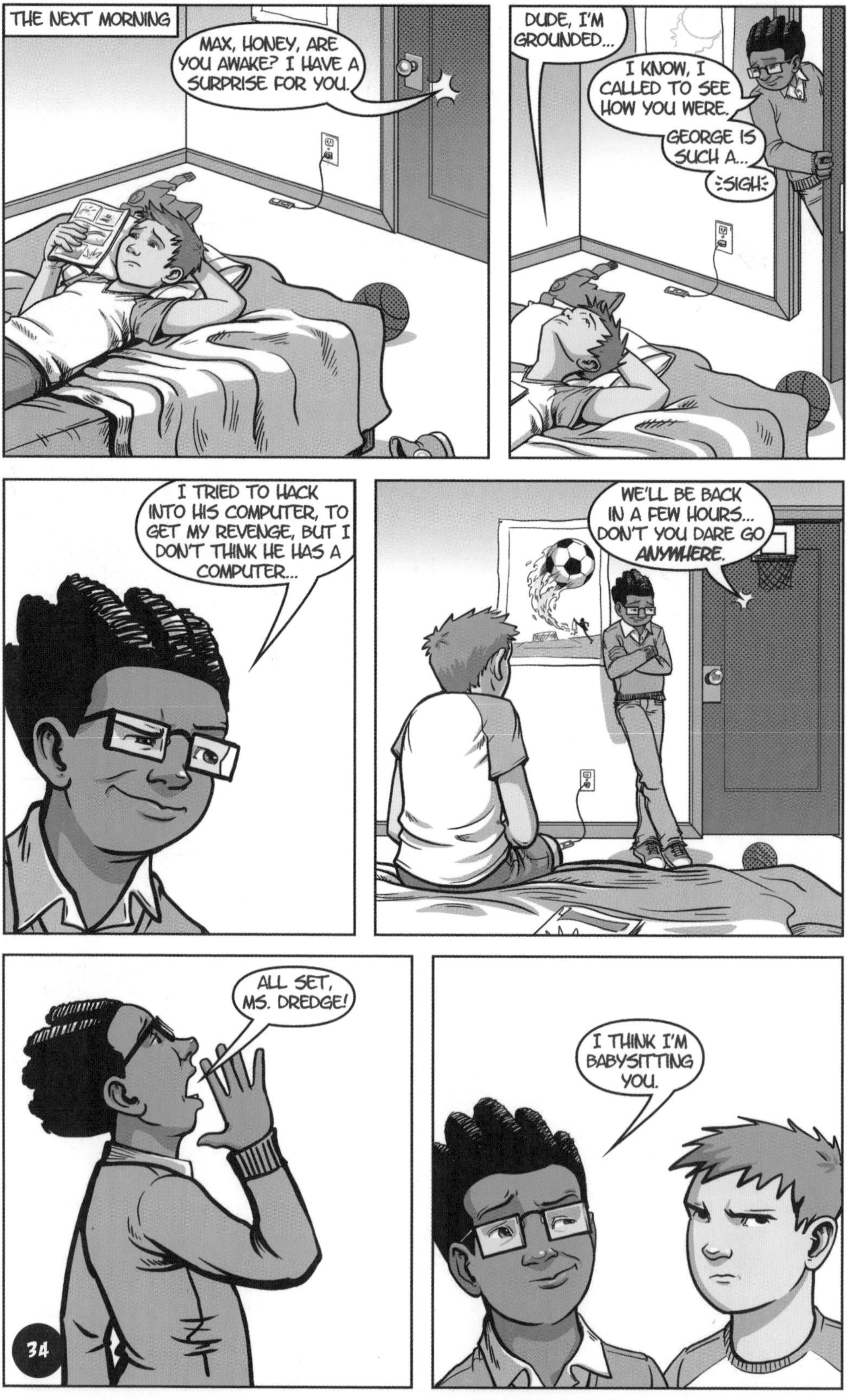
THE NEXT MORNING
MAX, HONEY, ARE YOU AWAKE? I HAVE A SURPRISE FOR YOU.
DUDE, I'M GROUNDED...
I KNOW, I CALLED TO SEE HOW YOU WERE.
GEORGE IS SUCH A...
SIGH
I TRIED TO HACK INTO HIS COMPUTER, TO GET MY REVENGE, BUT I DON'T THINK HE HAS A COMPUTER...
WE'LL BE BACK IN A FEW HOURS... DON'T YOU DARE GO ANYWHERE.
ALL SET, MS. DREDGE!
I THINK I'M BABYSITTING YOU.

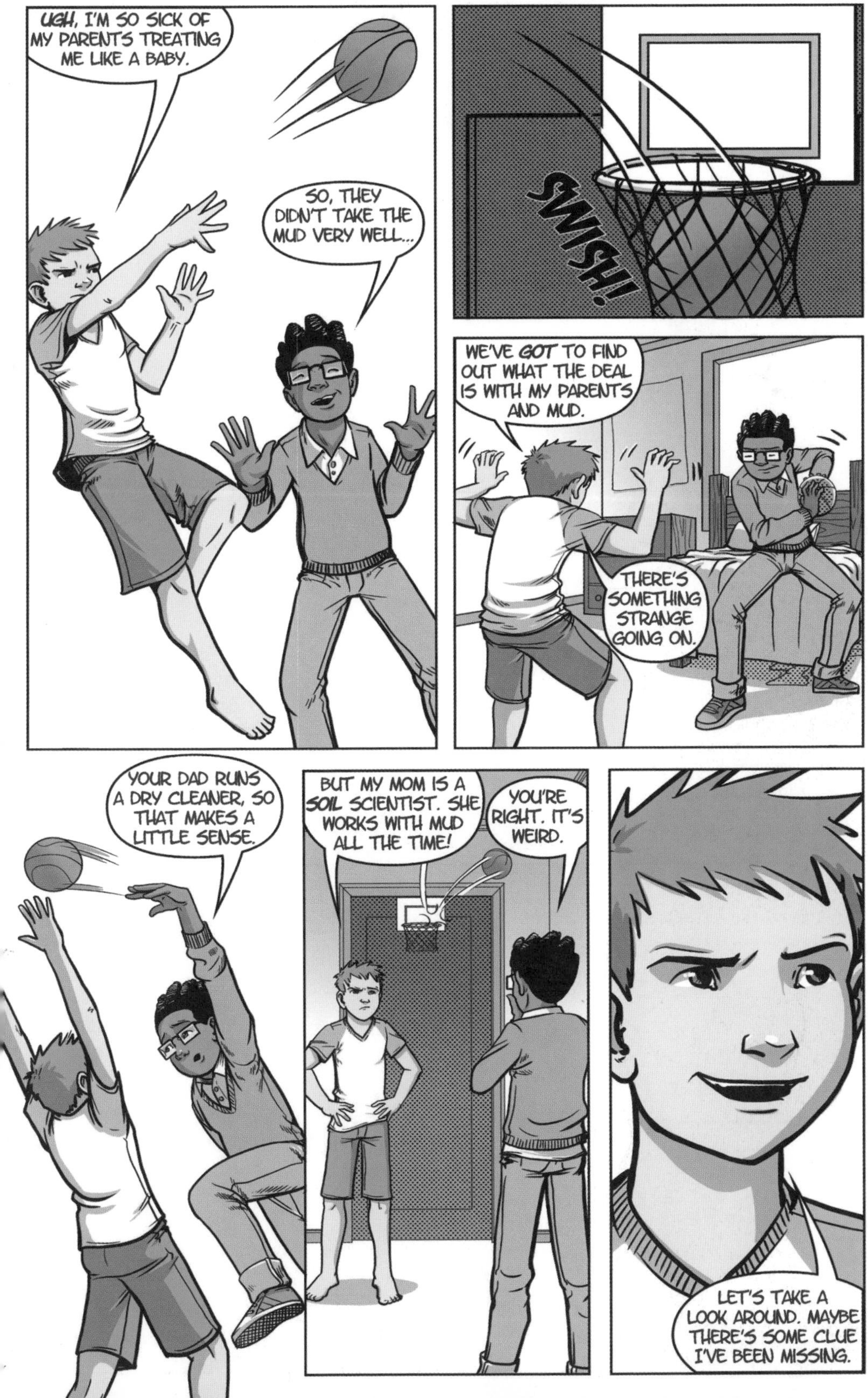
UGH, I'M SO SICK OF MY PARENT'S TREATING ME LIKE A BABY.
SO, THEY DIDN'T TAKE THE MUD VERY WELL...
SWISH!
WE'VE GOT TO FIND OUT WHAT THE DEAL IS WITH MY PARENTS AND MUD.
THERE'S SOMETHING STRANGE GOING ON.
YOUR DAD RUNS A DRY CLEANER, SO THAT MAKES A LITTLE SENSE.
BUT MY MOM IS A SOIL SCIENTIST. SHE WORKS WITH MUD ALL THE TIME!
YOU'RE RIGHT. IT'S WEIRD.
LET'S TAKE A LOOK AROUND. MAYBE THERE'S SOME CLUE I'VE BEEN MISSING.

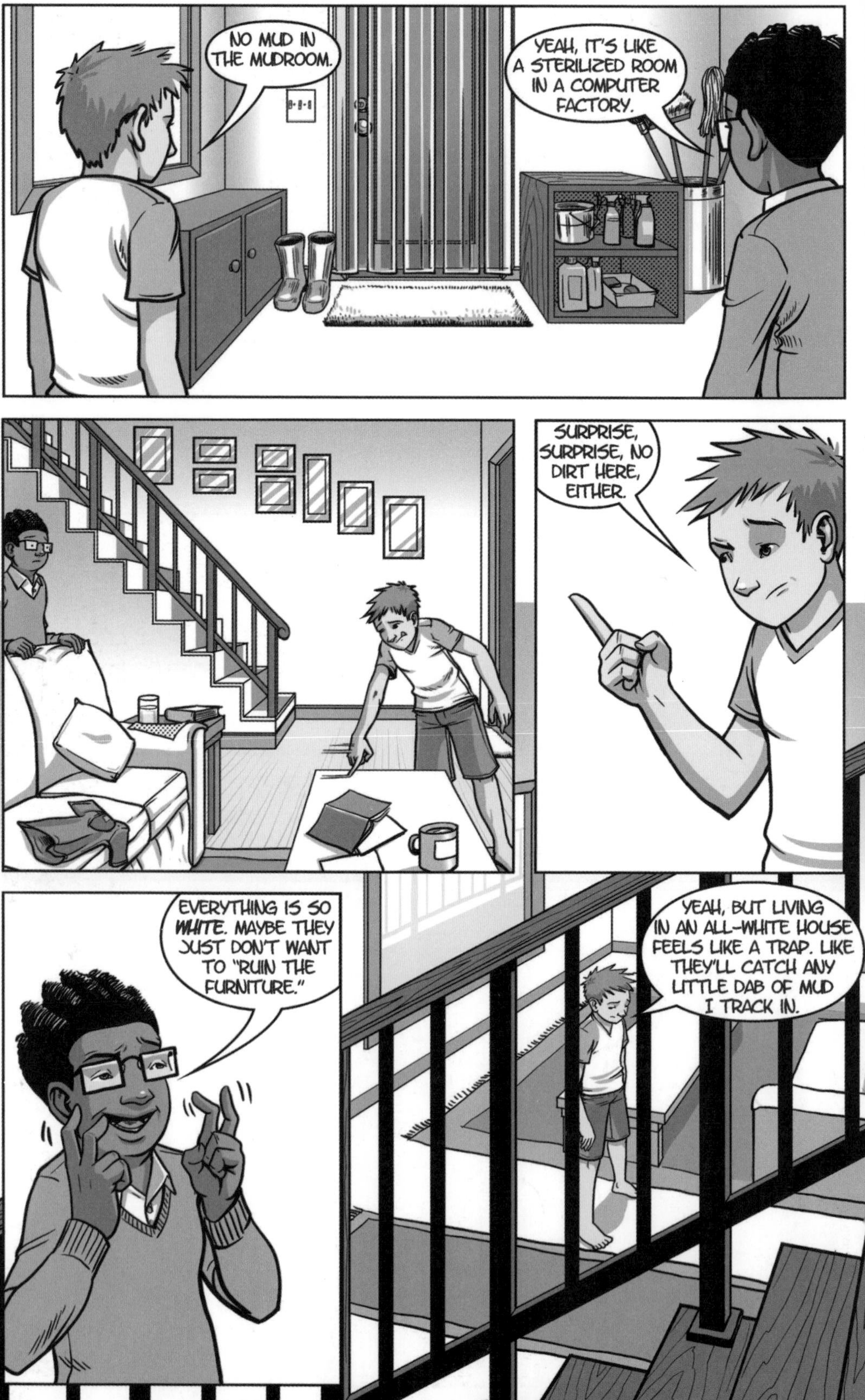
NO MUD IN THE MUDROOM.
YEAH, IT'S LIKE A STERILIZED ROOM IN A COMPUTER FACTORY.
SURPRISE, SURPRISE, NO DIRT HERE, EITHER.
EVERYTHING IS SO WHITE. MAYBE THEY JUST DON'T WANT TO "RUIN THE FURNITURE."
YEAH, BUT LIVING IN AN ALL-WHITE HOUSE FEELS LIKE A TRAP. LIKE THEY'LL CATCH ANY LITTLE DAB OF MUD I TRACK IN.

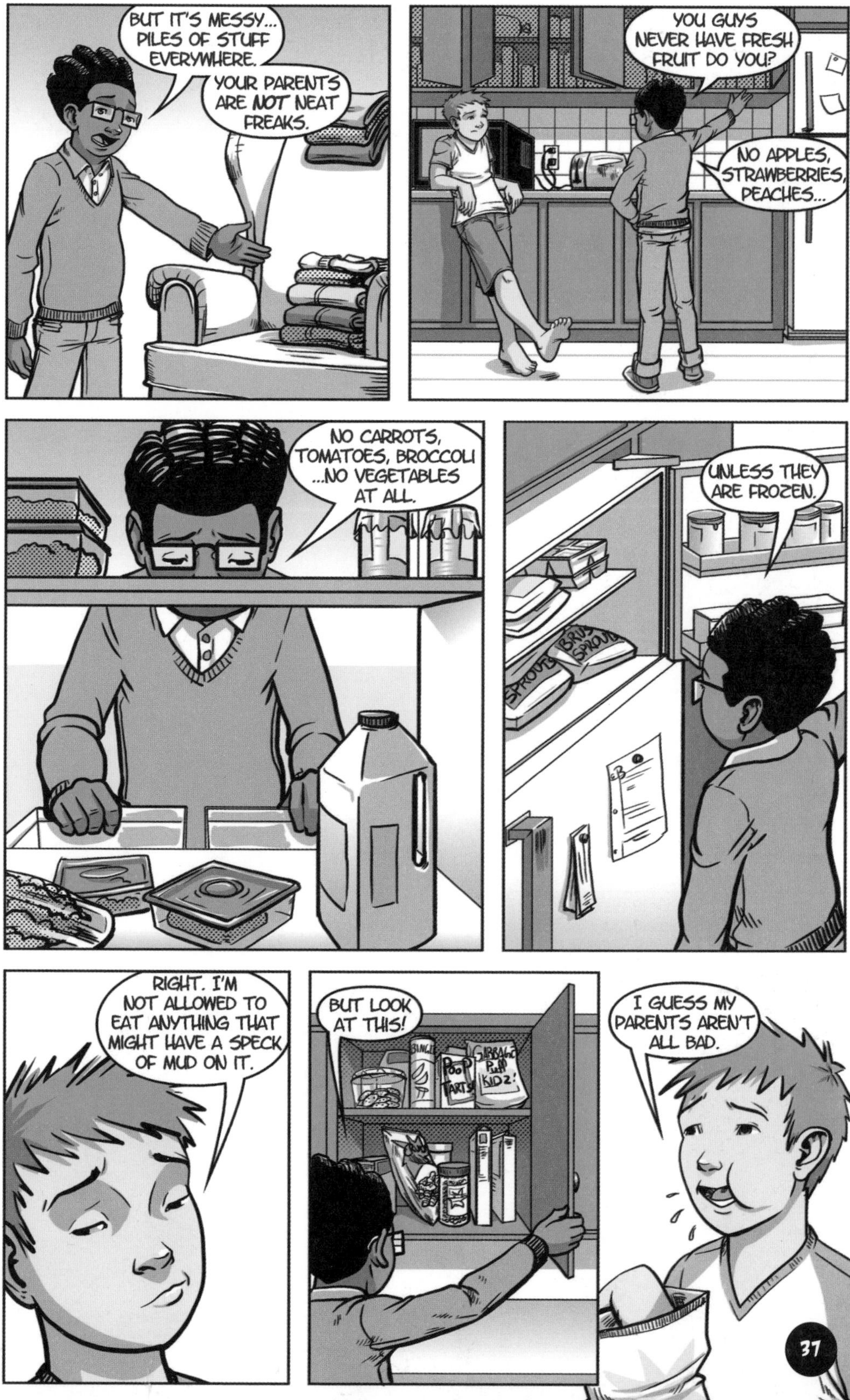
BUT IT'S MESSY... PILES OF STUFF EVERYWHERE.
YOUR PARENTS ARE NOT NEAT FREAKS.
YOU GUYS NEVER HAVE FRESH FRUIT DO YOU?
NO APPLES, STRAWBERRIES, PEACHES...
NO CARROTS, TOMATOES, BROCCOLI ...NO VEGETABLES AT ALL.
UNLESS THEY ARE FROZEN.
SPROUTS
BRUS SPROUTS
RIGHT. I'M NOT ALLOWED TO EAT ANYTHING THAT MIGHT HAVE A SPECK OF MUD ON IT.
BUT LOOK AT THIS!
BINGLE
POOP TARTS!
GARBAGE PAIL KIDZ!
I GUESS MY PARENTS AREN'T ALL BAD.

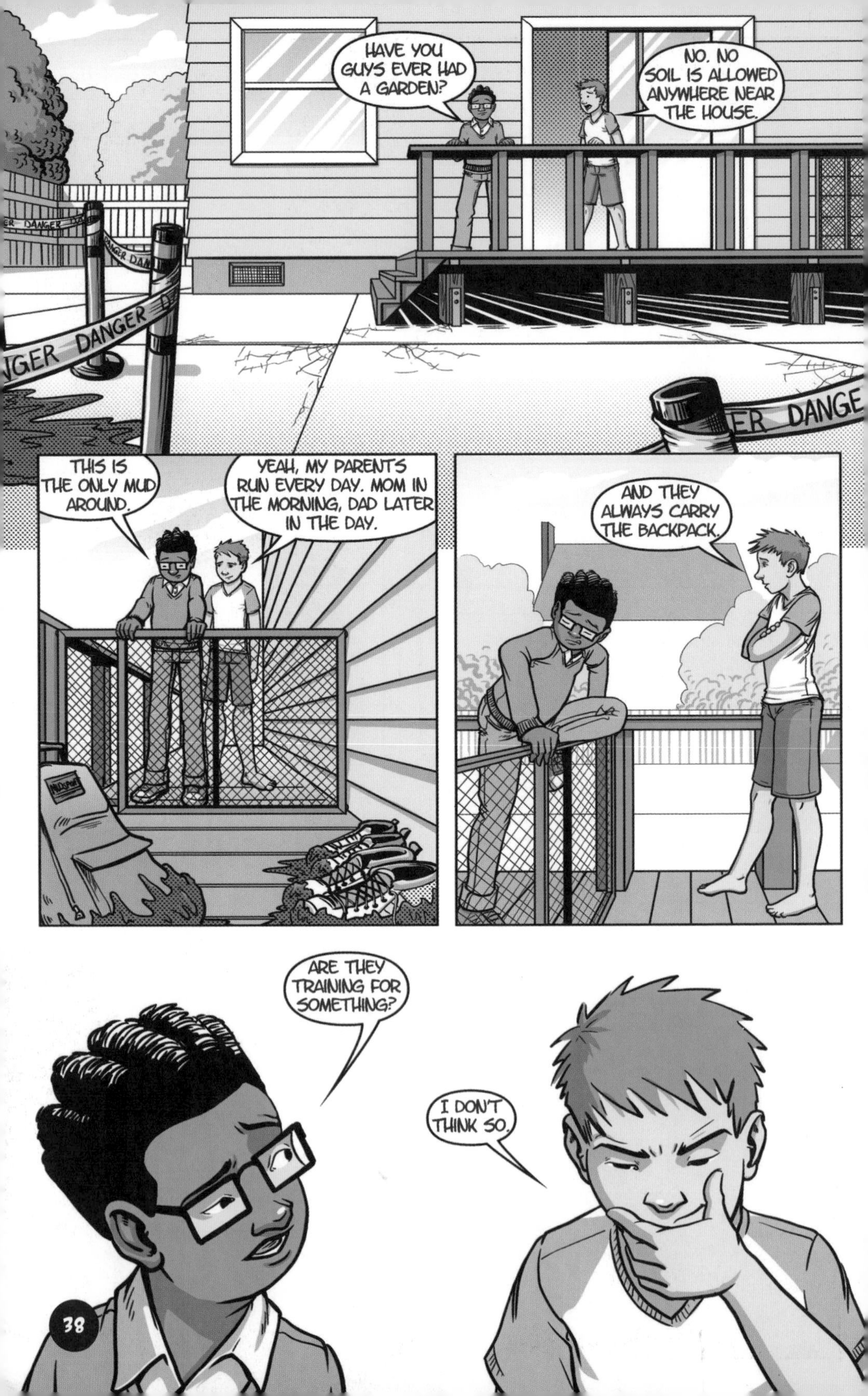
HAVE YOU GUYS EVER HAD A GARDEN?
NO. NO SOIL IS ALLOWED ANYWHERE NEAR THE HOUSE.
DANGER
THIS IS THE ONLY MUD AROUND.
YEAH, MY PARENTS RUN EVERY DAY. MOM IN THE MORNING, DAD LATER IN THE DAY.
AND THEY ALWAYS CARRY THE BACKPACK.
ARE THEY TRAINING FOR SOMETHING?
I DON'T THINK SO.

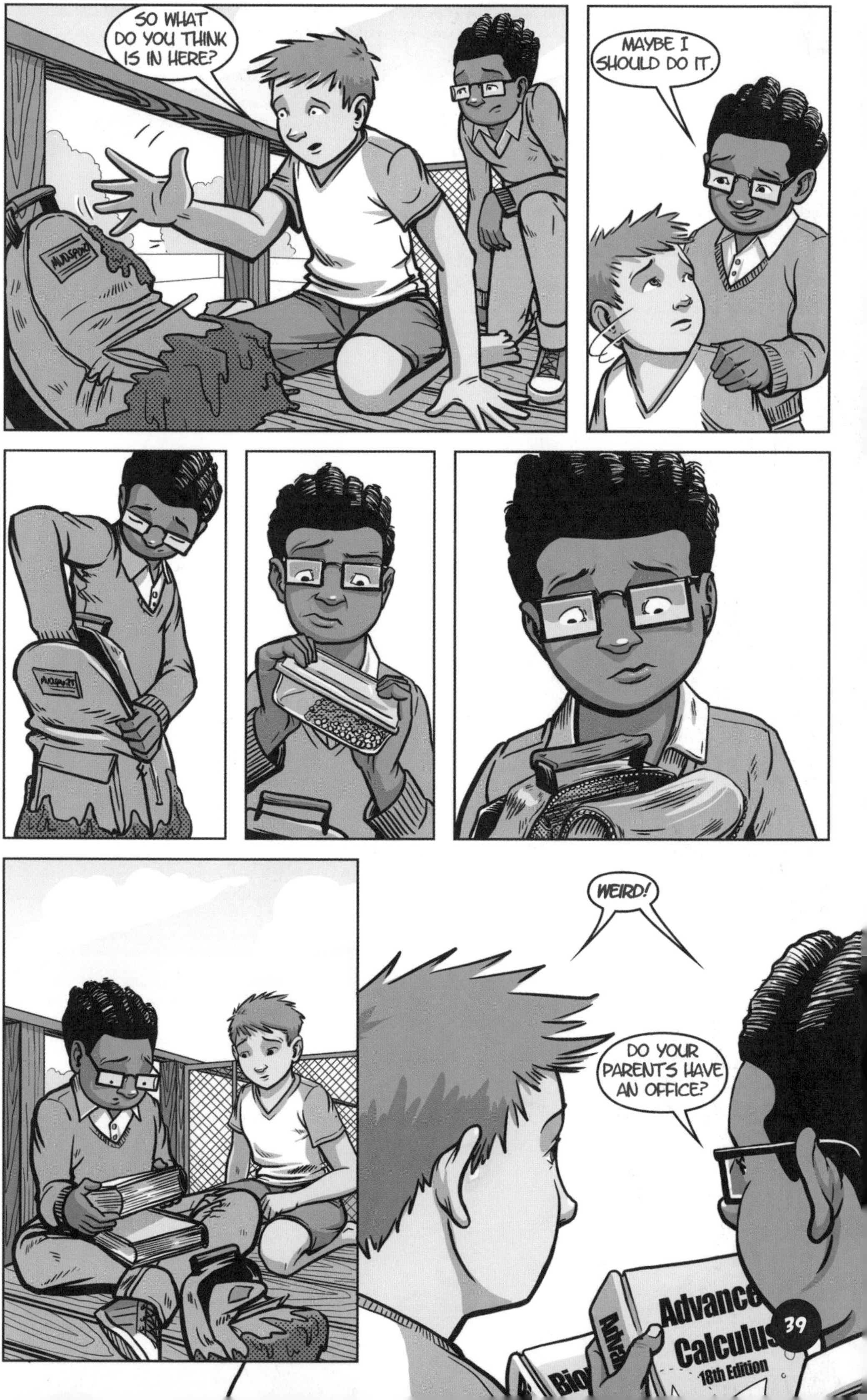
SO WHAT DO YOU THINK IS IN HERE?
MAYBE I SHOULD DO IT.
WEIRD!
DO YOUR PARENT'S HAVE AN OFFICE?
Advance
Calculus
18th Edition

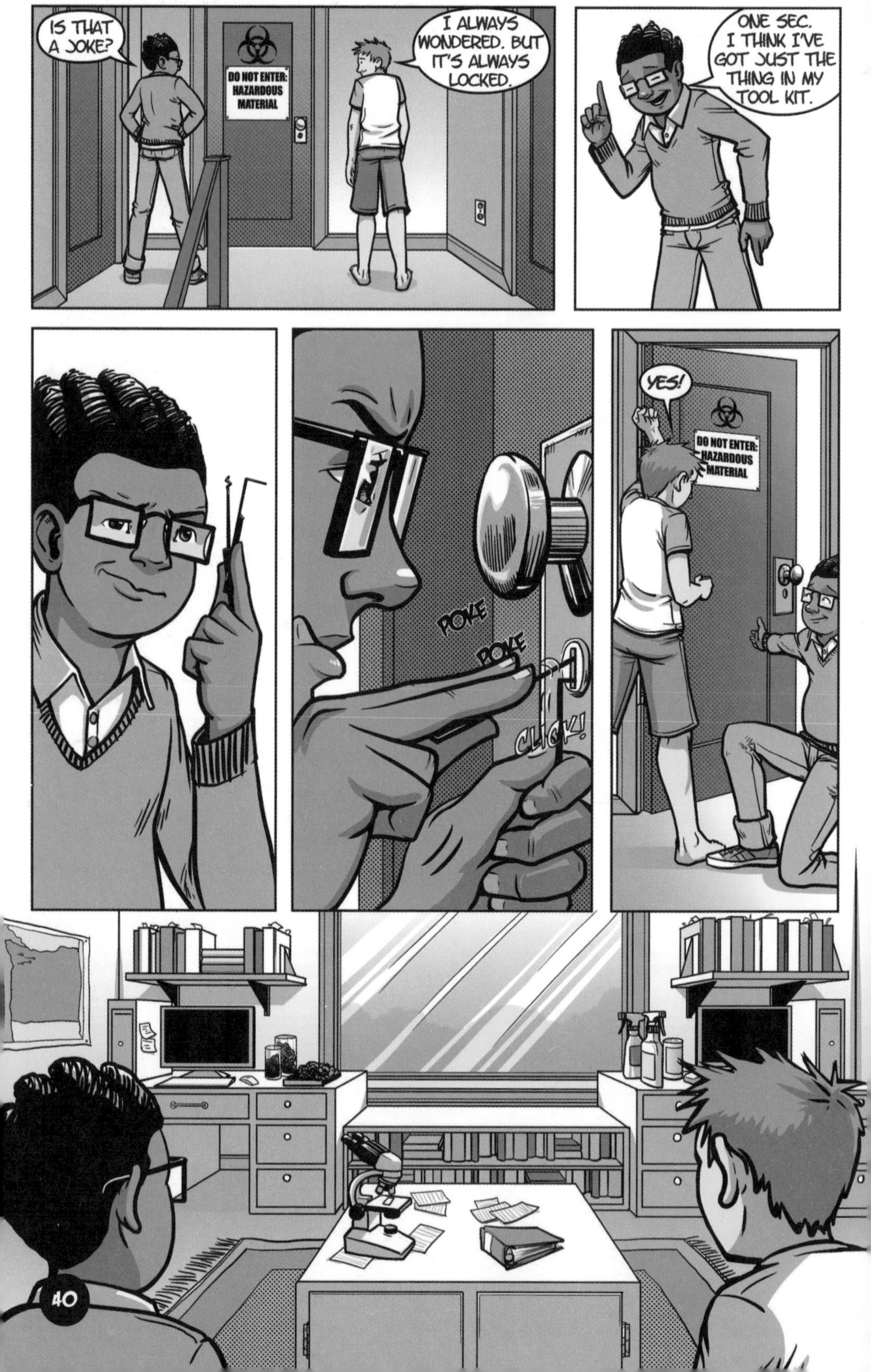
IS THAT A JOKE?
DO NOT ENTER: HAZARDOUS MATERIAL
I ALWAYS WONDERED. BUT IT'S ALWAYS LOCKED.
ONE SEC. I THINK I'VE GOT JUST THE THING IN MY TOOL KIT.
POKE
POKE
CLICK!
YES!
DO NOT ENTER: HAZARDOUS MATERIAL

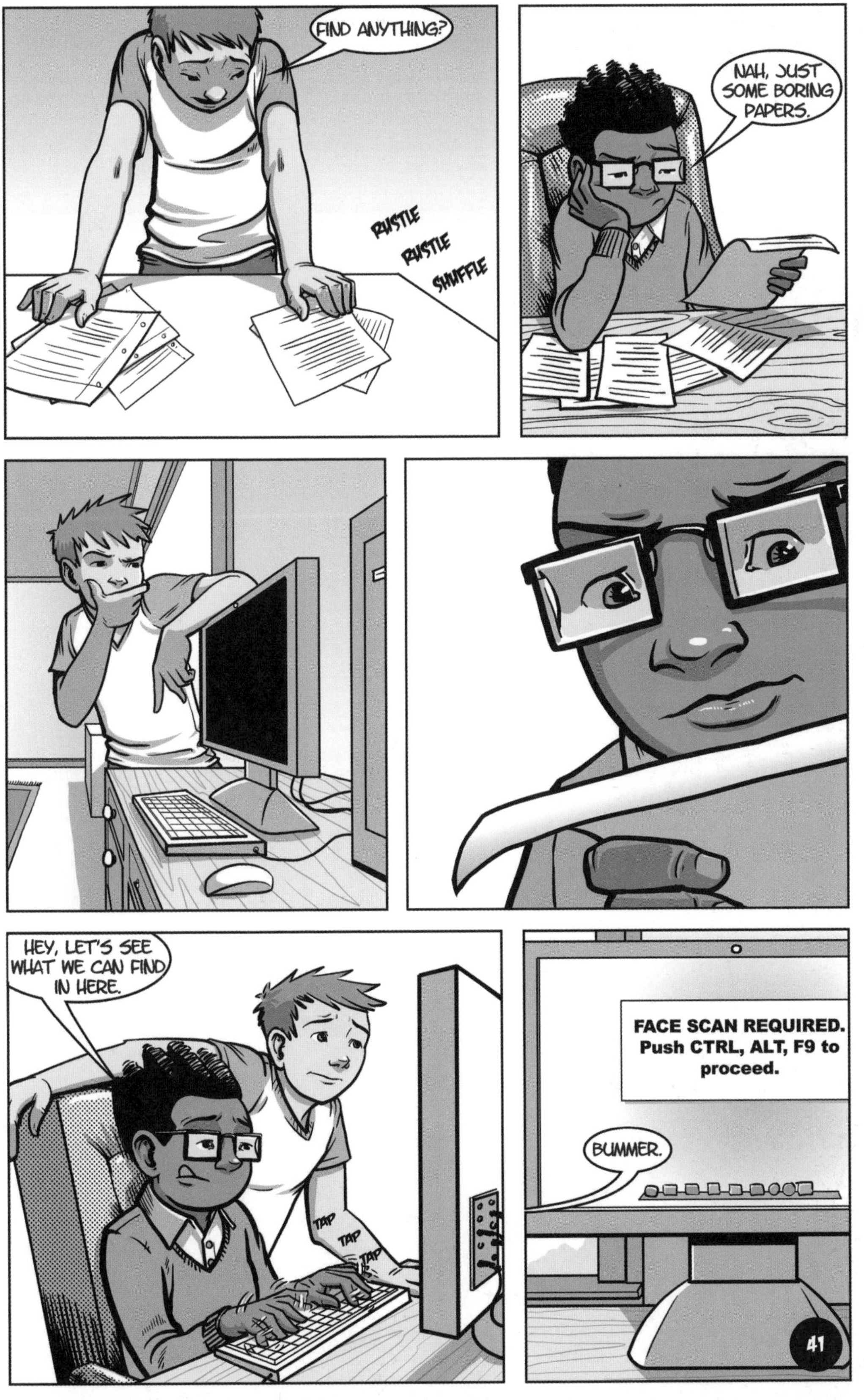
FIND ANYTHING?
RUSTLE
RUSTLE
SHUFFLE
NAH, JUST SOME BORING PAPERS.
HEY, LET'S SEE WHAT WE CAN FIND IN HERE.
TAP
TAP
TAP
FACE SCAN REQUIRED. Push CTRL, ALT, F9 to proceed.
BUMMER.

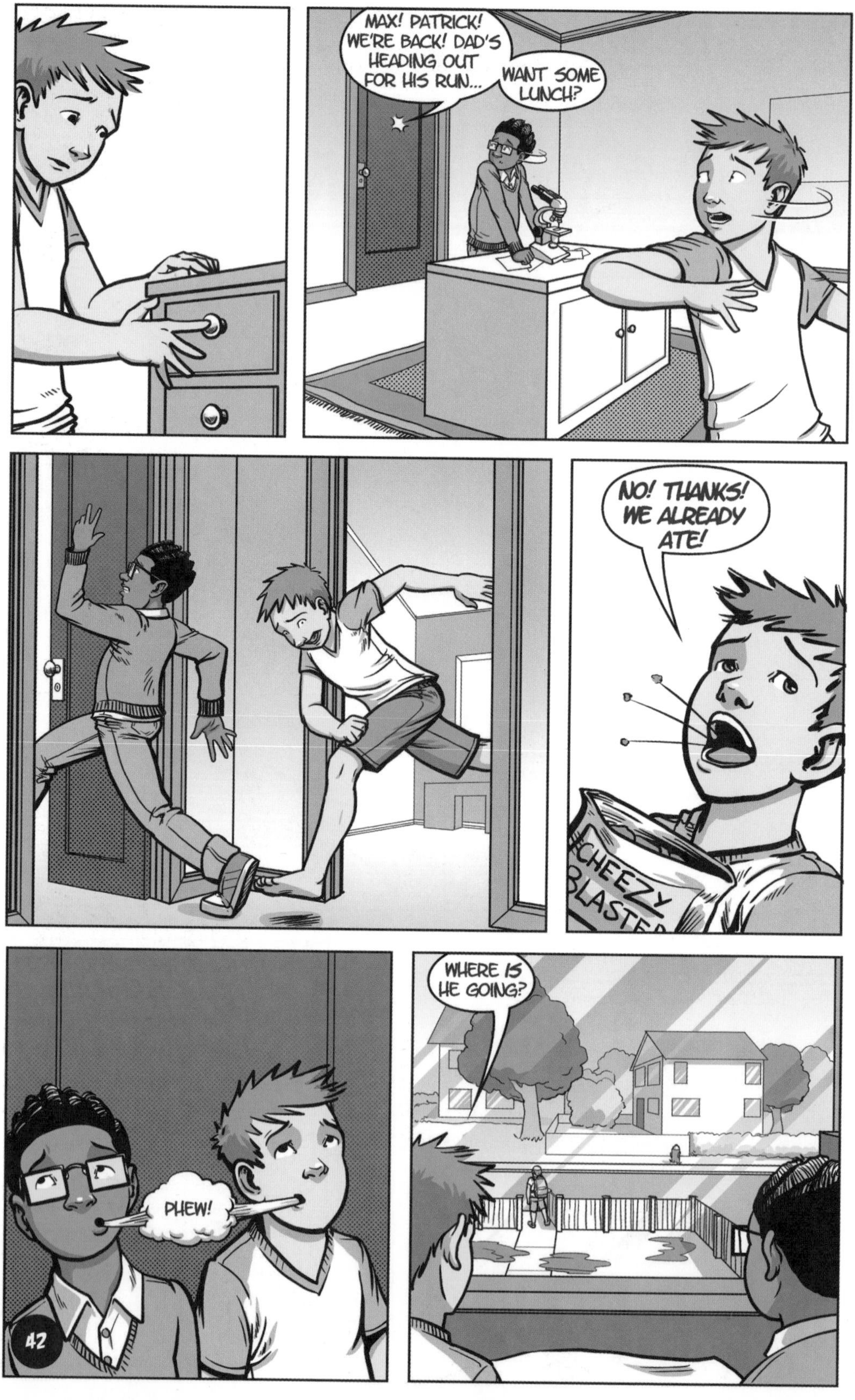
MAX! PATRICK! WE'RE BACK! DAD'S HEADING OUT FOR HIS RUN...
WANT SOME LUNCH?
NO! THANKS! WE ALREADY ATE!
CHEEZY BLASTE
PHEW!
WHERE IS HE GOING?

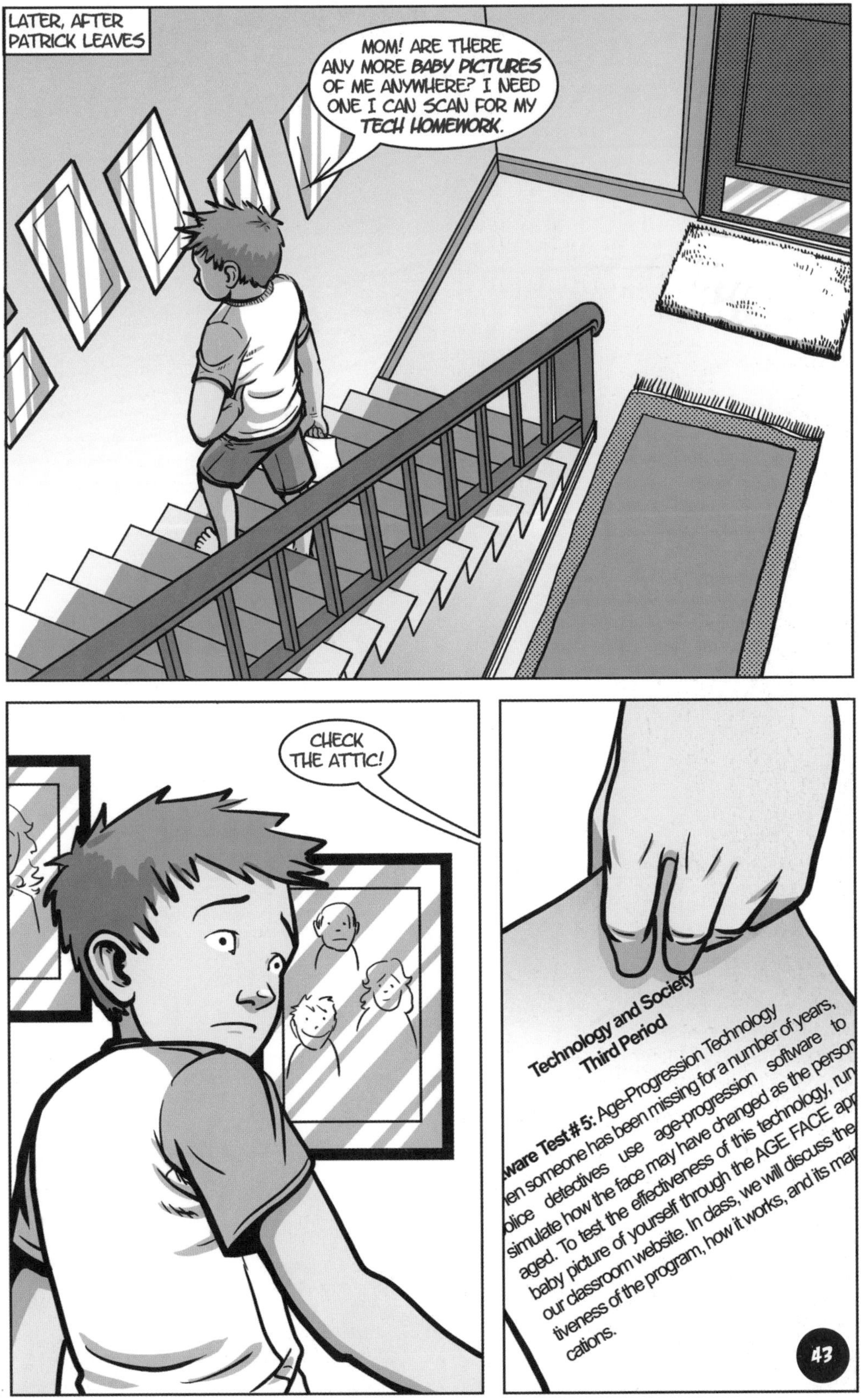
LATER, AFTER PATRICK LEAVES
MOM! ARE THERE ANY MORE BABY PICTURES OF ME ANYWHERE? I NEED ONE I CAN SCAN FOR MY TECH HOMEWORK.
CHECK THE ATTIC!
Technology and Society
Third Period
ware Test # 5: Age-Progression Technology
en someone has been missing for a number of years,
olice detectives use age-progression software to
simulate how the face may have changed as the person
aged. To test the effectiveness of this technology, run
baby picture of yourself through the AGE FACE ap
our classroom website. In class, we will discuss the
tiveness of the program, how it works, and its ma
cations.

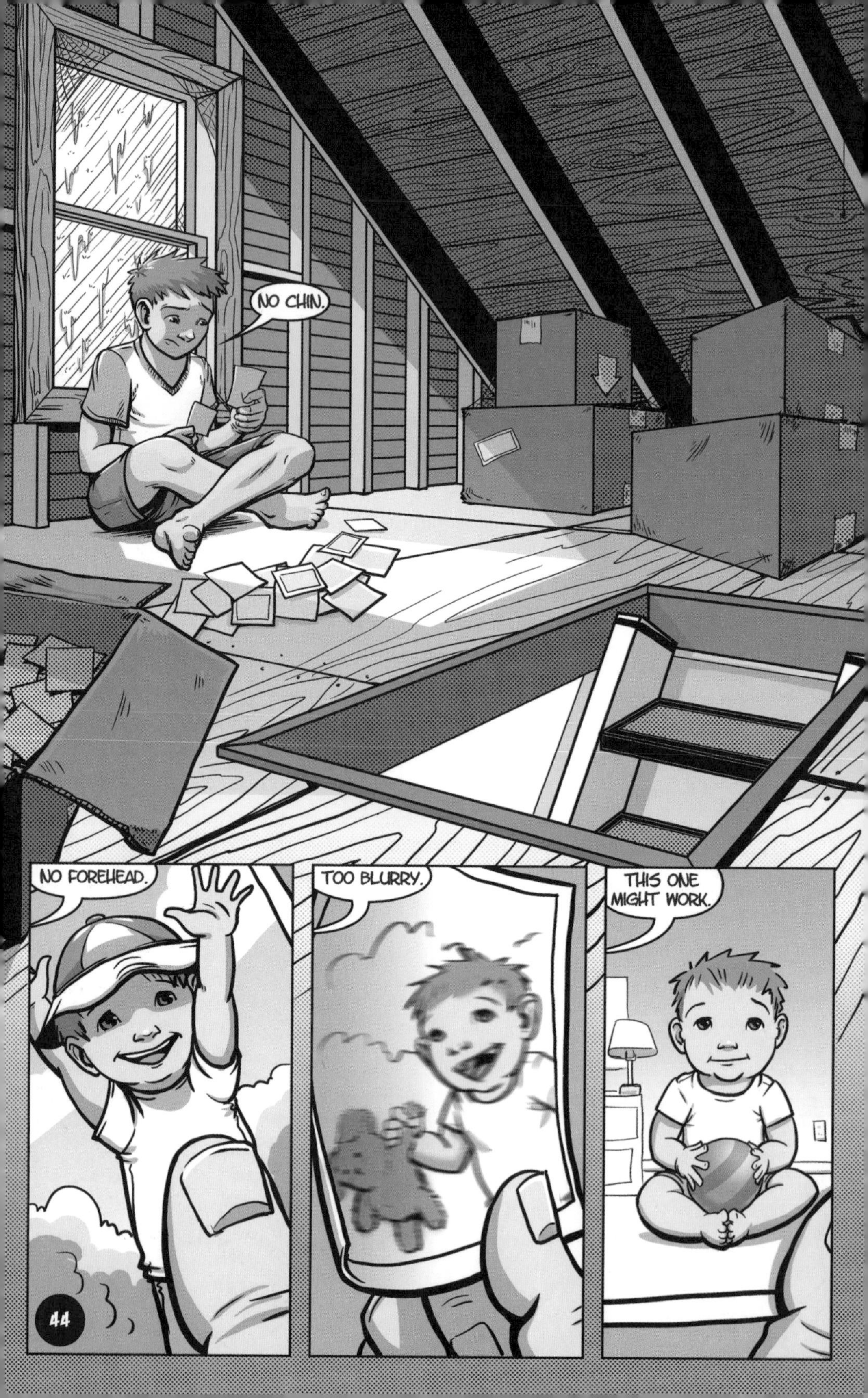
NO CHIN.
NO FOREHEAD.
TOO BLURRY.
THIS ONE MIGHT WORK.

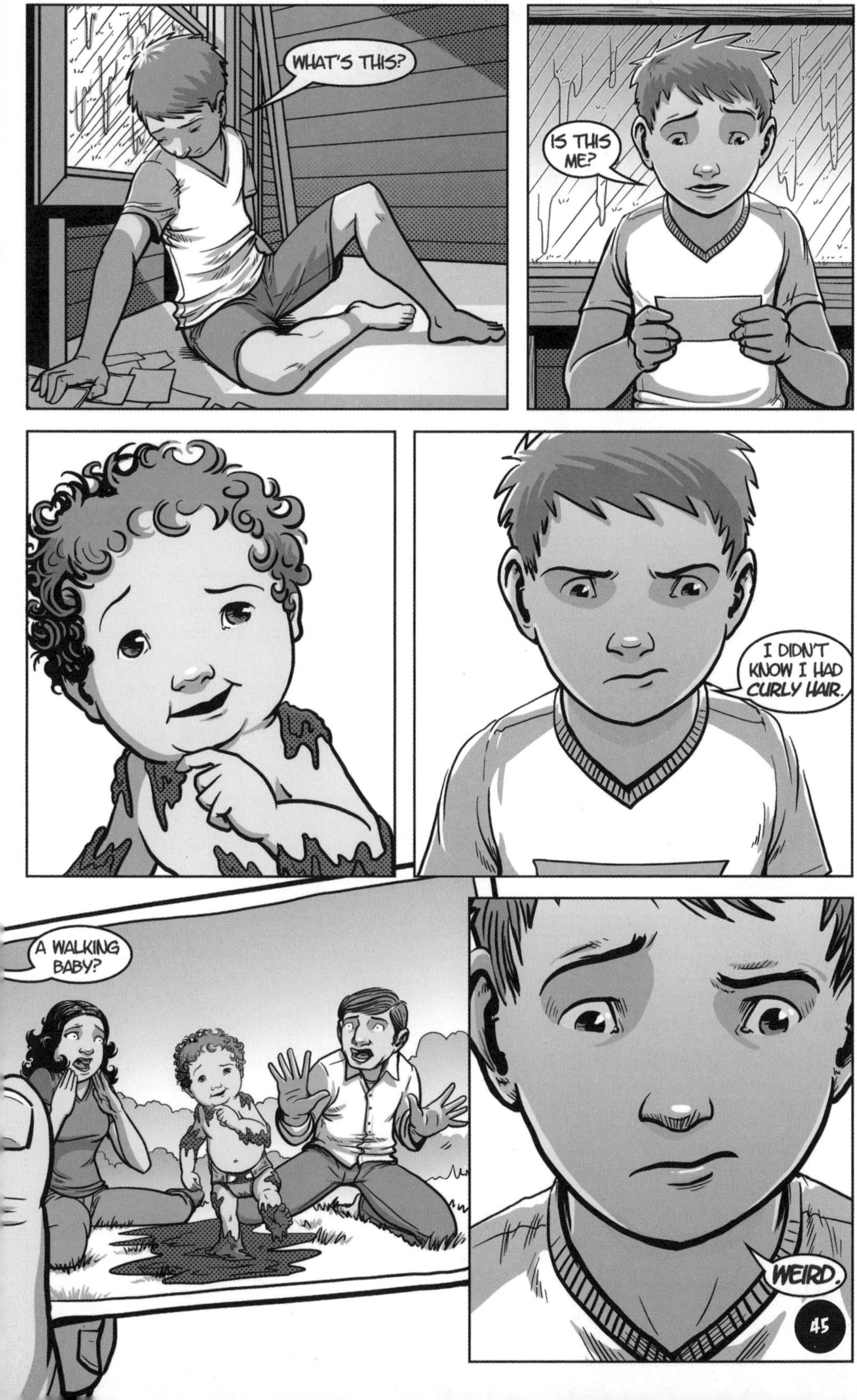
WHAT'S THIS?
IS THIS ME?
I DIDN'T KNOW I HAD CURLY HAIR.
A WALKING BABY?
WEIRD.

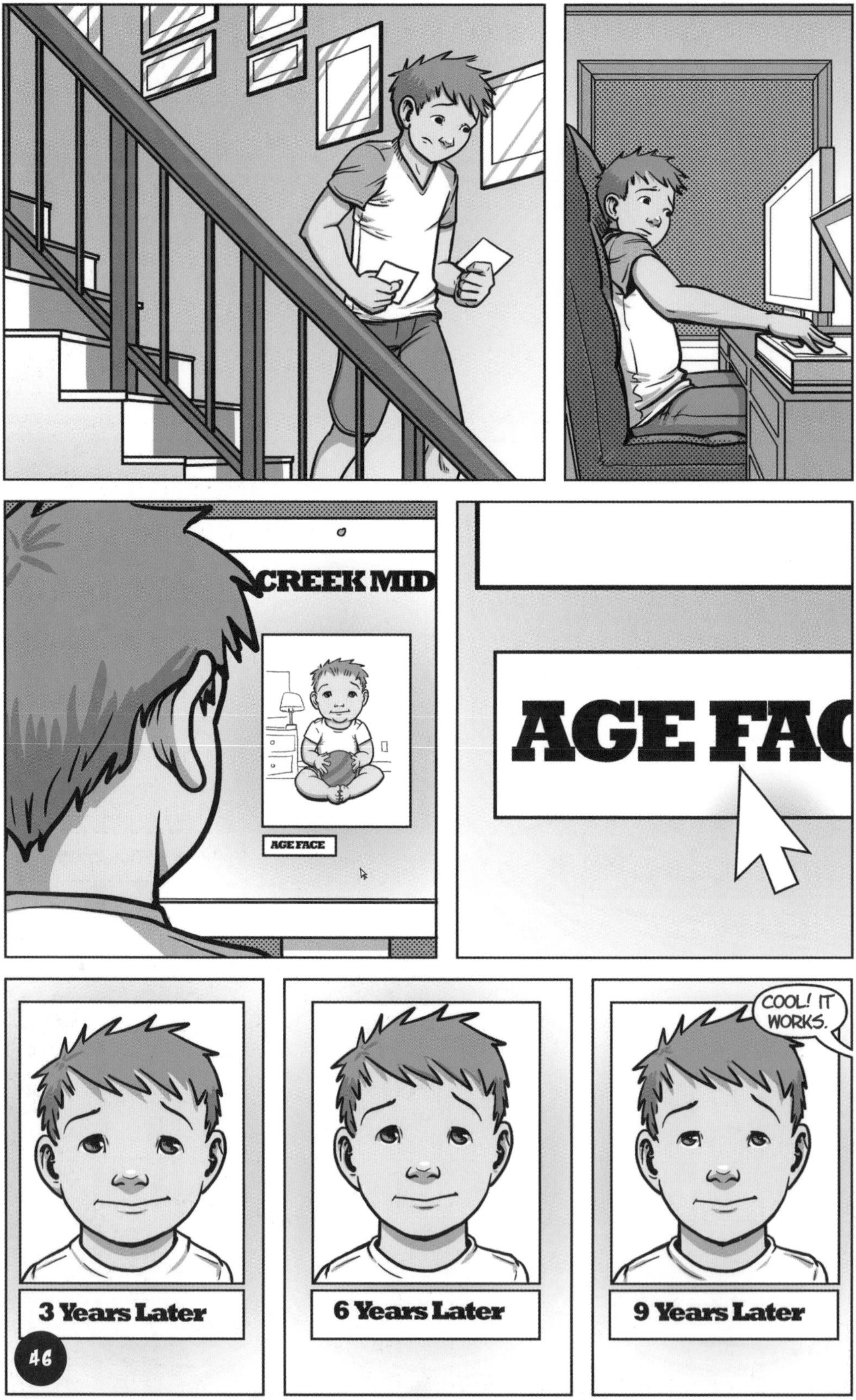
CREEK MID
AGE FACE
AGE FAC
3 Years Later
6 Years Later
9 Years Later
COOL! IT WORKS.

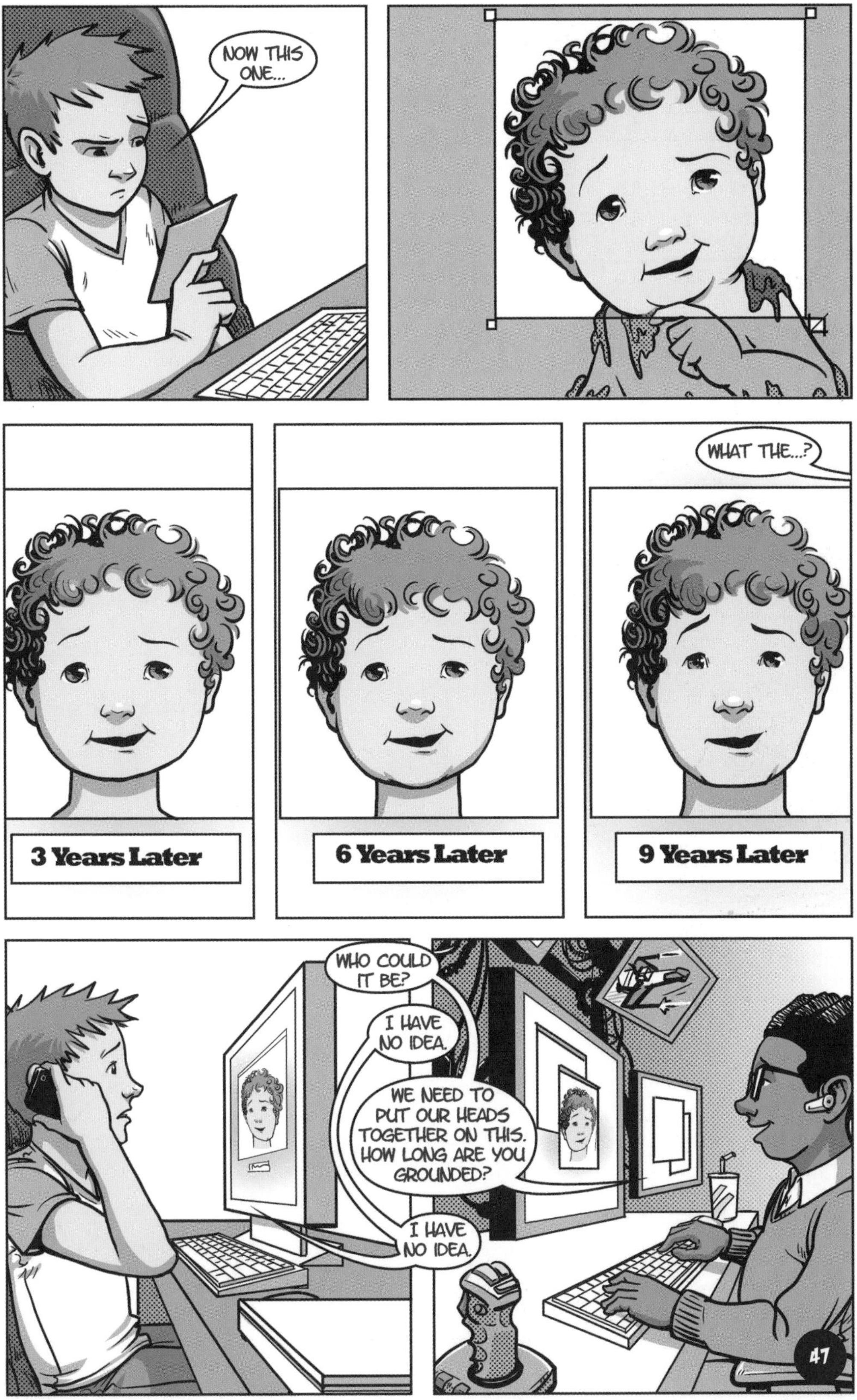
NOW THIS ONE...
3 Years Later
6 Years Later
WHAT THE...?
9 Years Later
WHO COULD IT BE?
I HAVE NO IDEA.
WE NEED TO PUT OUR HEADS TOGETHER ON THIS. HOW LONG ARE YOU GROUNDED?
I HAVE NO IDEA.

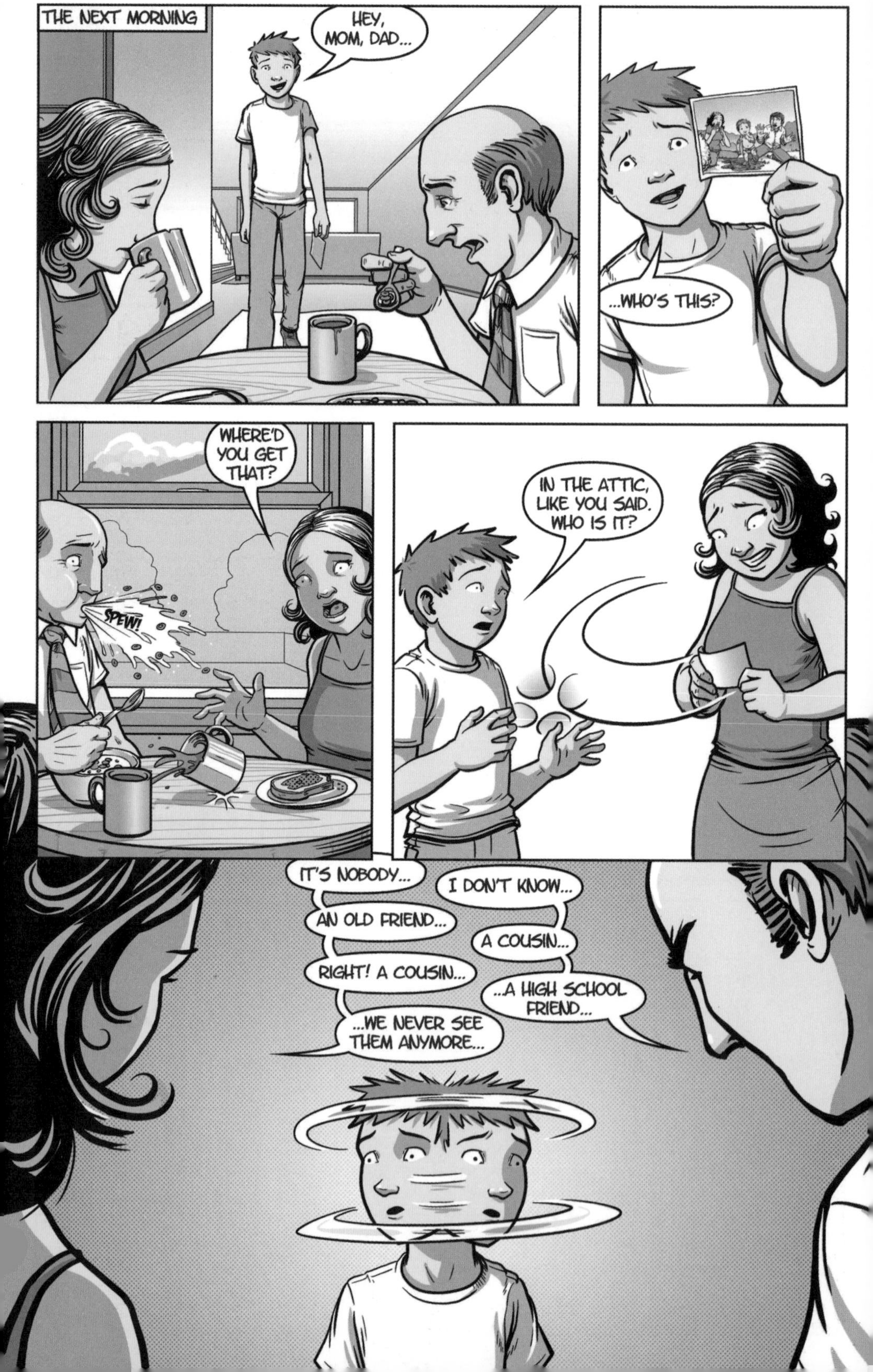
THE NEXT MORNING
HEY, MOM, DAD...
...WHO'S THIS?
WHERE'D YOU GET THAT?
SPEW!
IN THE ATTIC, LIKE YOU SAID. WHO IS IT?
IT'S NOBODY...
I DON'T KNOW...
AN OLD FRIEND...
A COUSIN...
RIGHT! A COUSIN...
...A HIGH SCHOOL FRIEND...
...WE NEVER SEE THEM ANYMORE...

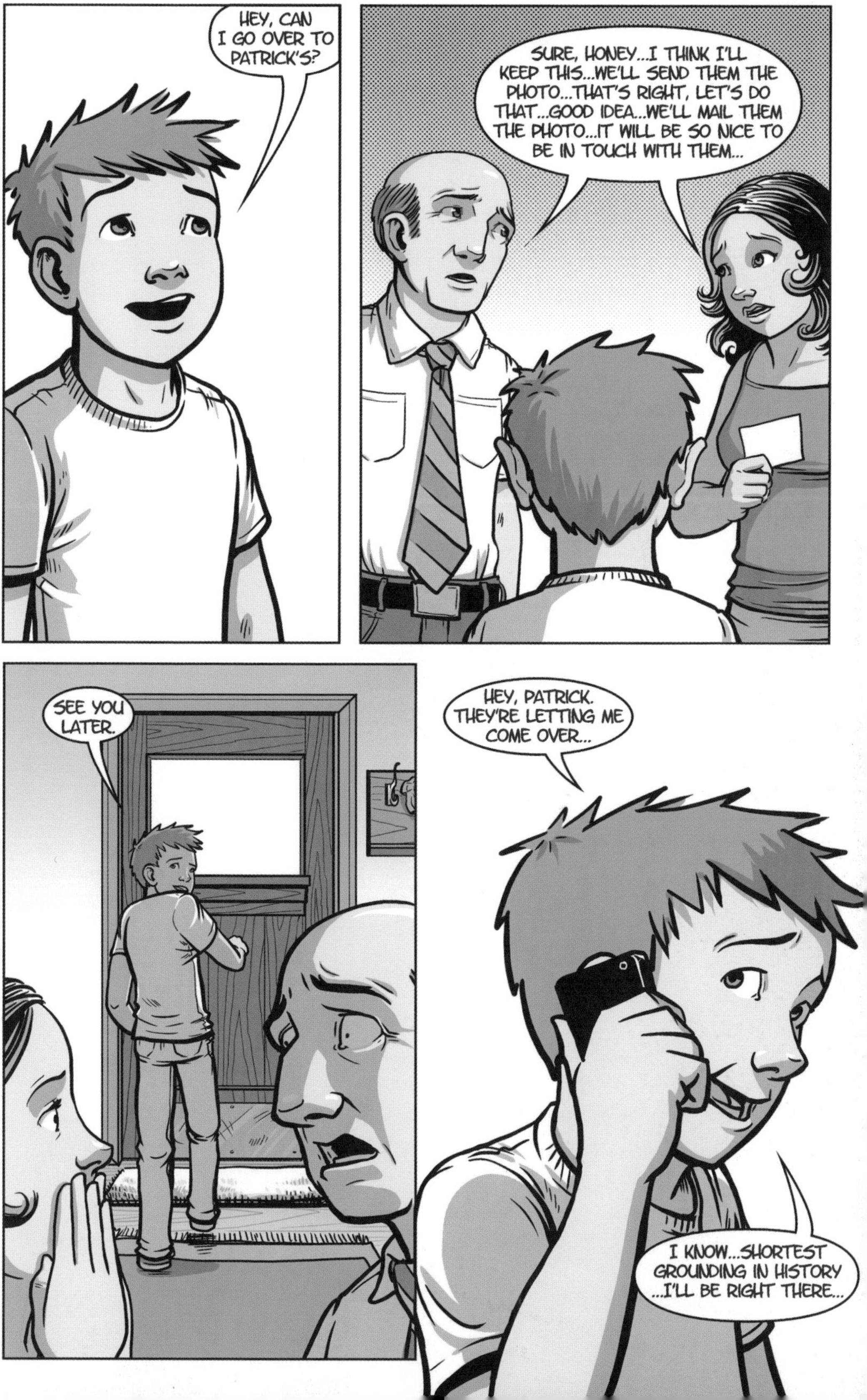
HEY, CAN I GO OVER TO PATRICK'S?
SURE, HONEY...I THINK I'LL KEEP THIS...WE'LL SEND THEM THE PHOTO...THAT'S RIGHT, LET'S DO THAT...GOOD IDEA...WE'LL MAIL THEM THE PHOTO...IT WILL BE SO NICE TO BE IN TOUCH WITH THEM...
SEE YOU LATER.
HEY, PATRICK. THEY'RE LETTING ME COME OVER...
I KNOW...SHORTEST GROUNDING IN HISTORY ...I'LL BE RIGHT THERE...

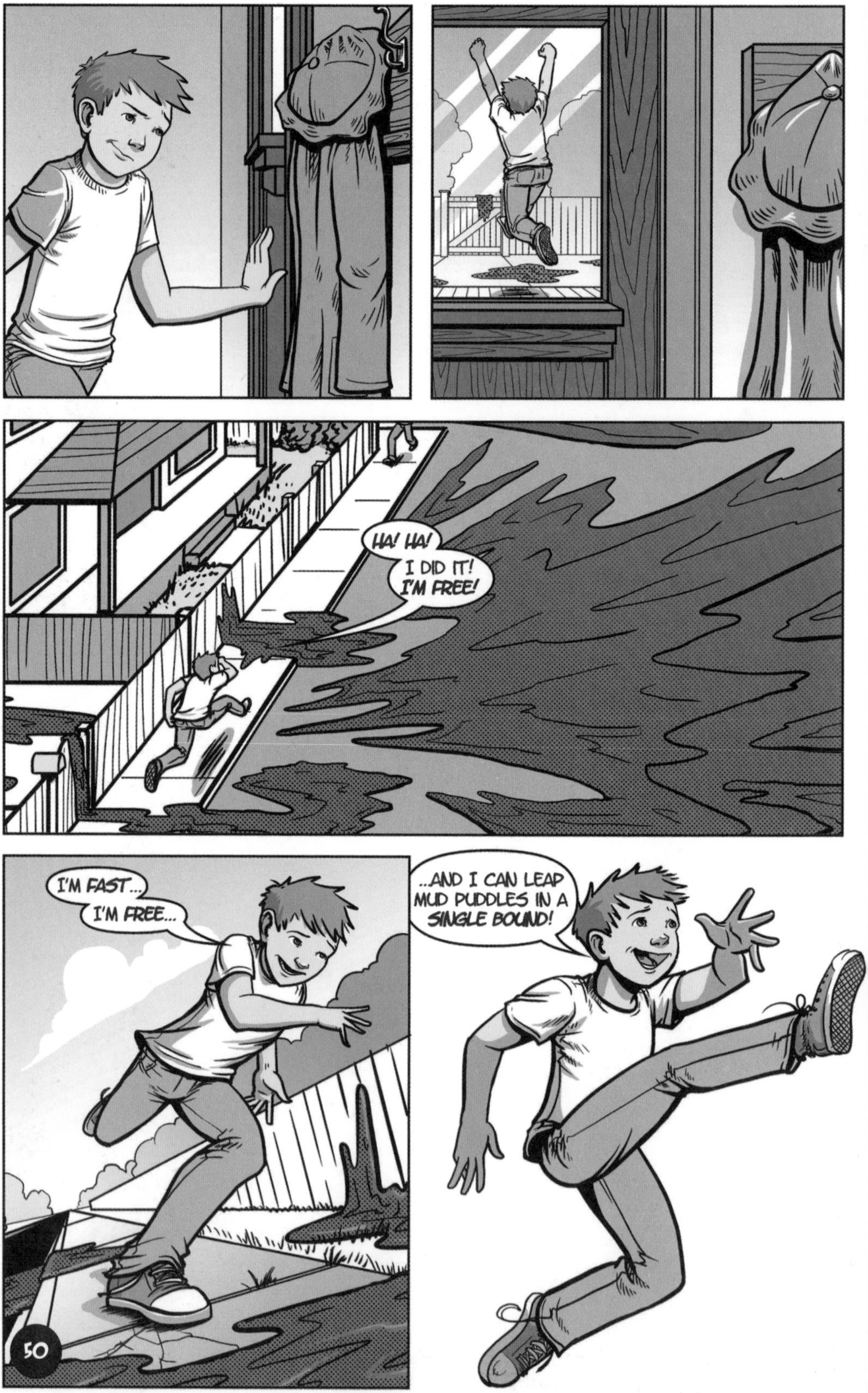
HA! HA!
I DID IT! I'M FREE!
I'M FAST...
I'M FREE...
...AND I CAN LEAP MUD PUDDLES IN A SINGLE BOUND!

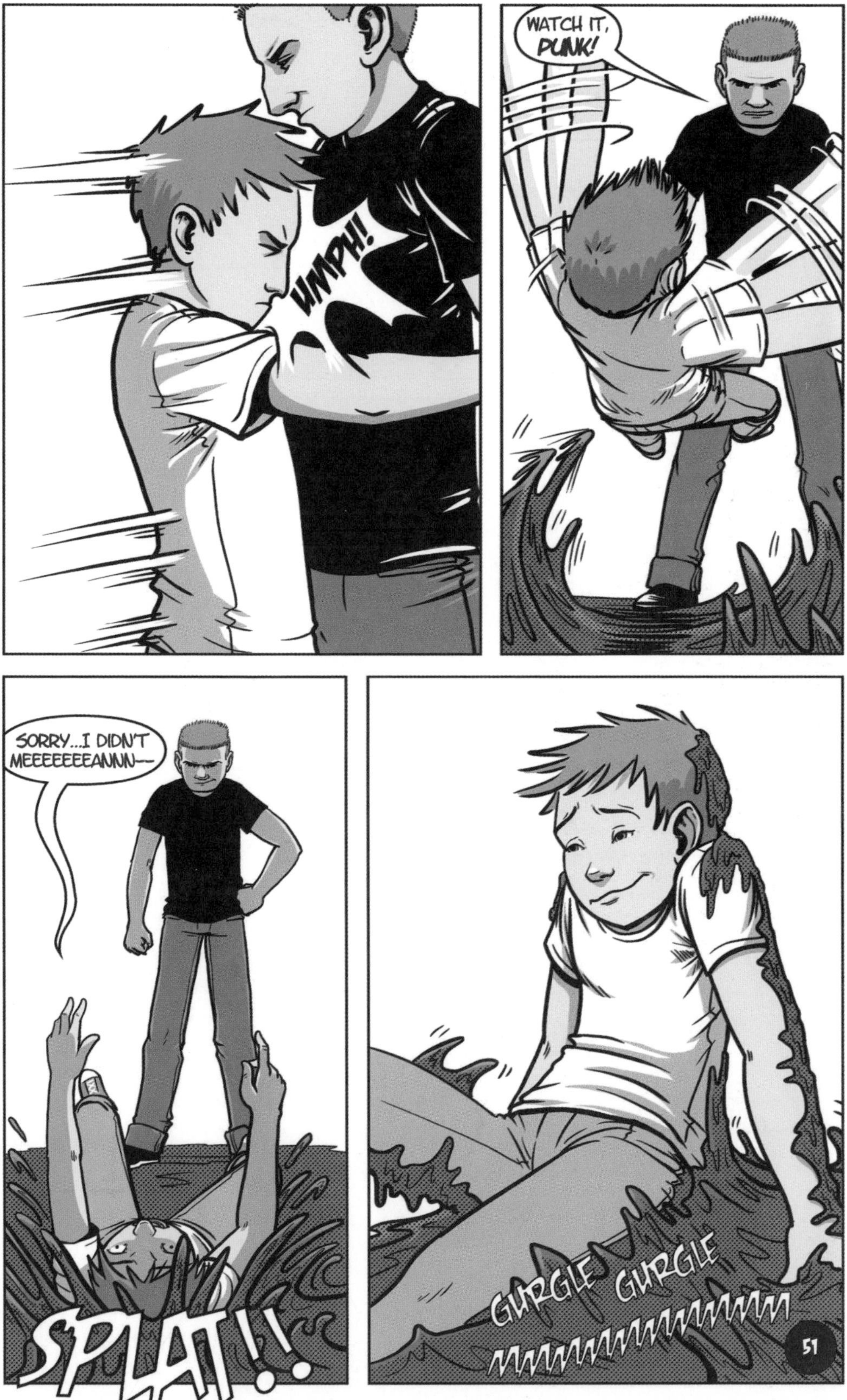
UMPH!
WATCH IT, PUNK!
SORRY...I DIDN'T MEEEEEEEANNN--
SPLAT!!
GURGLE GURGLE
MMMMMMMMMMMMMM

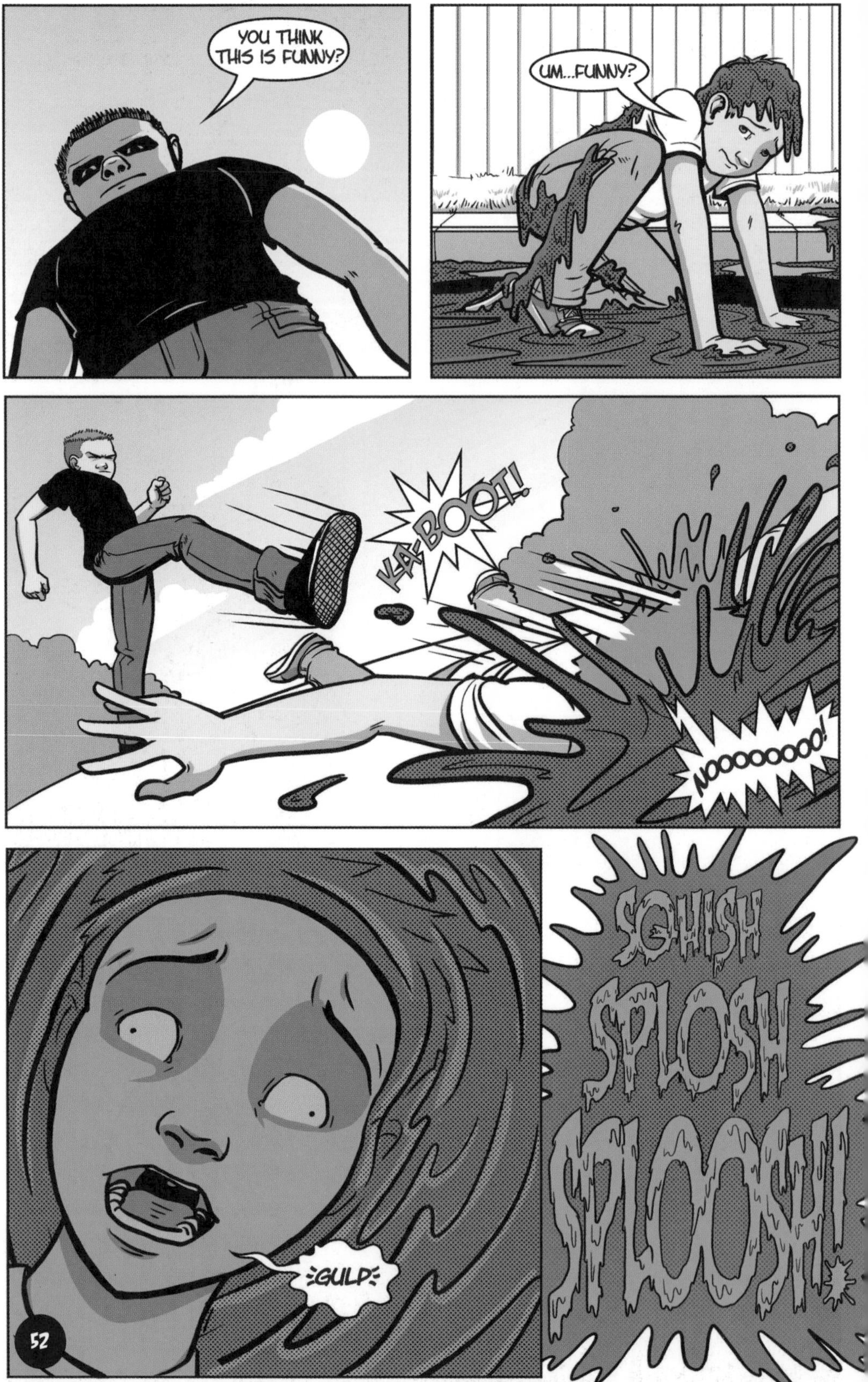
YOU THINK THIS IS FUNNY?
UM...FUNNY?
KA-BOOT!
NOOOOOOOOO!
SQUISH
SPLOSH
SPLOOSH!
GULP

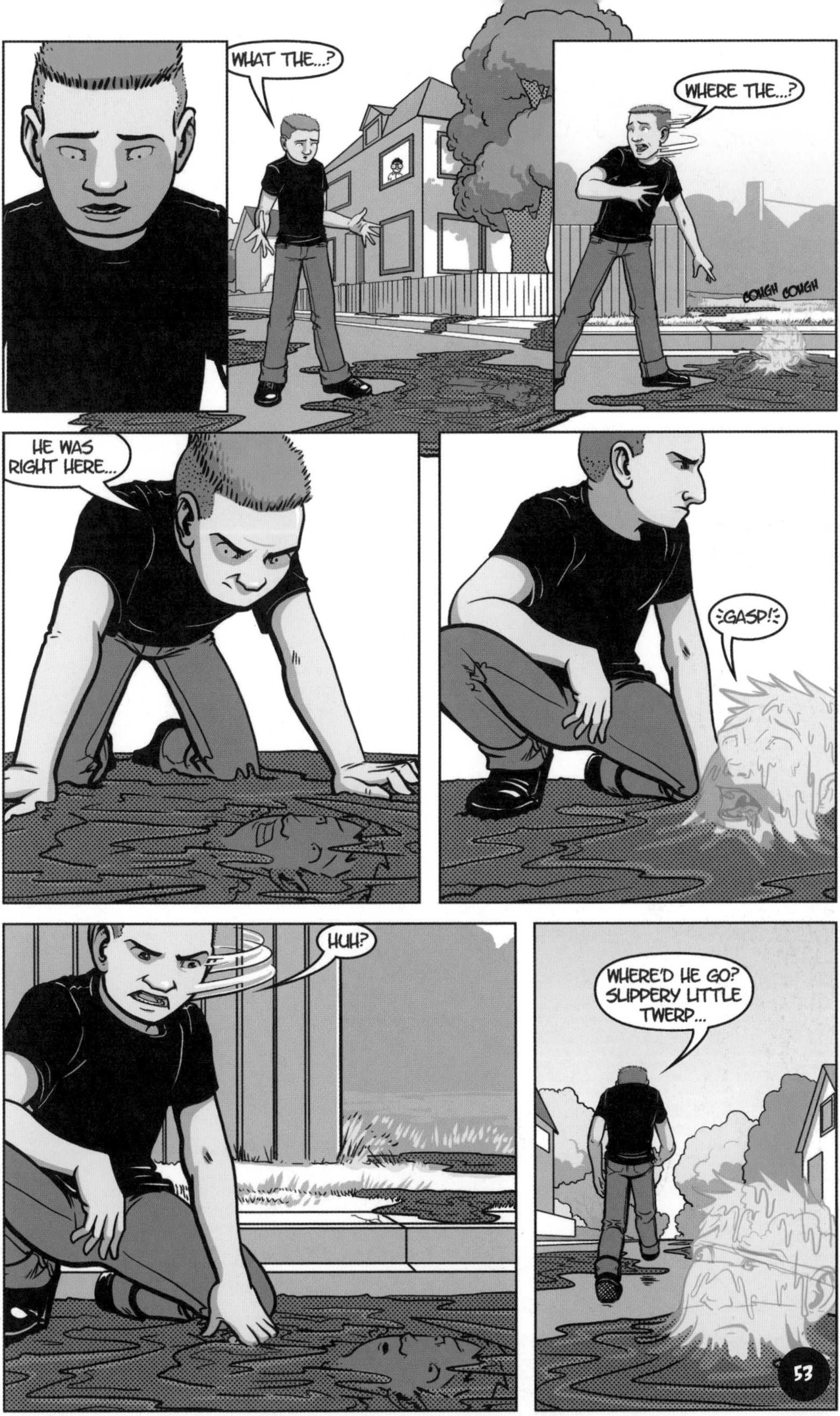
WHAT THE...?
WHERE THE...?
COUGH COUGH
HE WAS RIGHT HERE...
GASP!
HUH?
WHERE'D HE GO? SLIPPERY LITTLE TWERP...

PART 2

THE MARVELS OF MUD

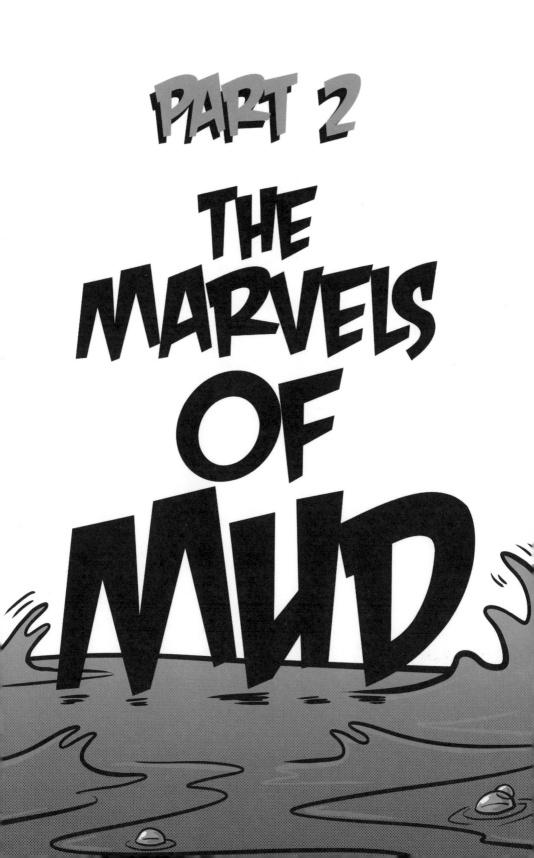

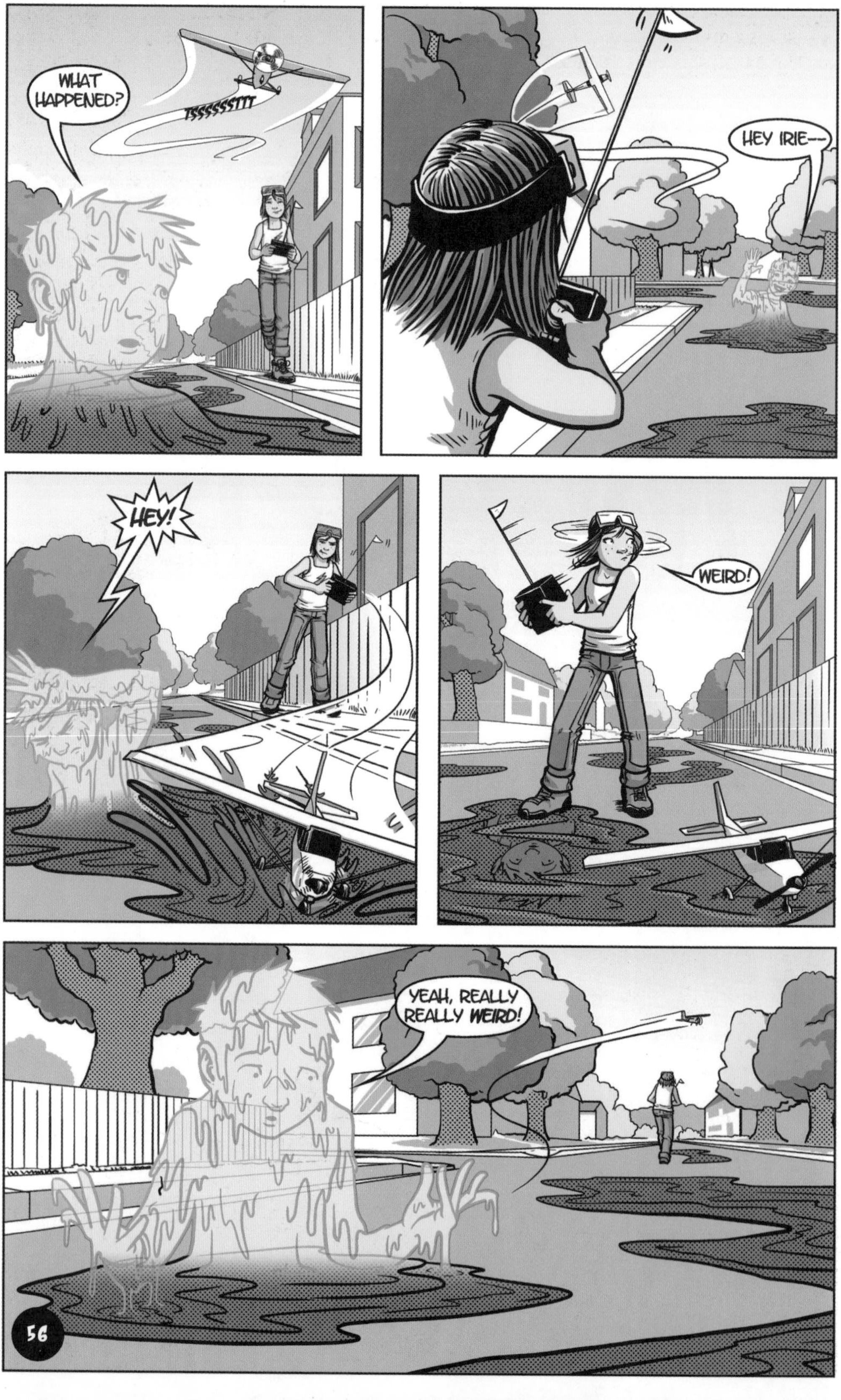
WHAT HAPPENED?
TSSSSSSTTT
HEY IRIE--
HEY!
WEIRD!
YEAH, REALLY REALLY WEIRD!

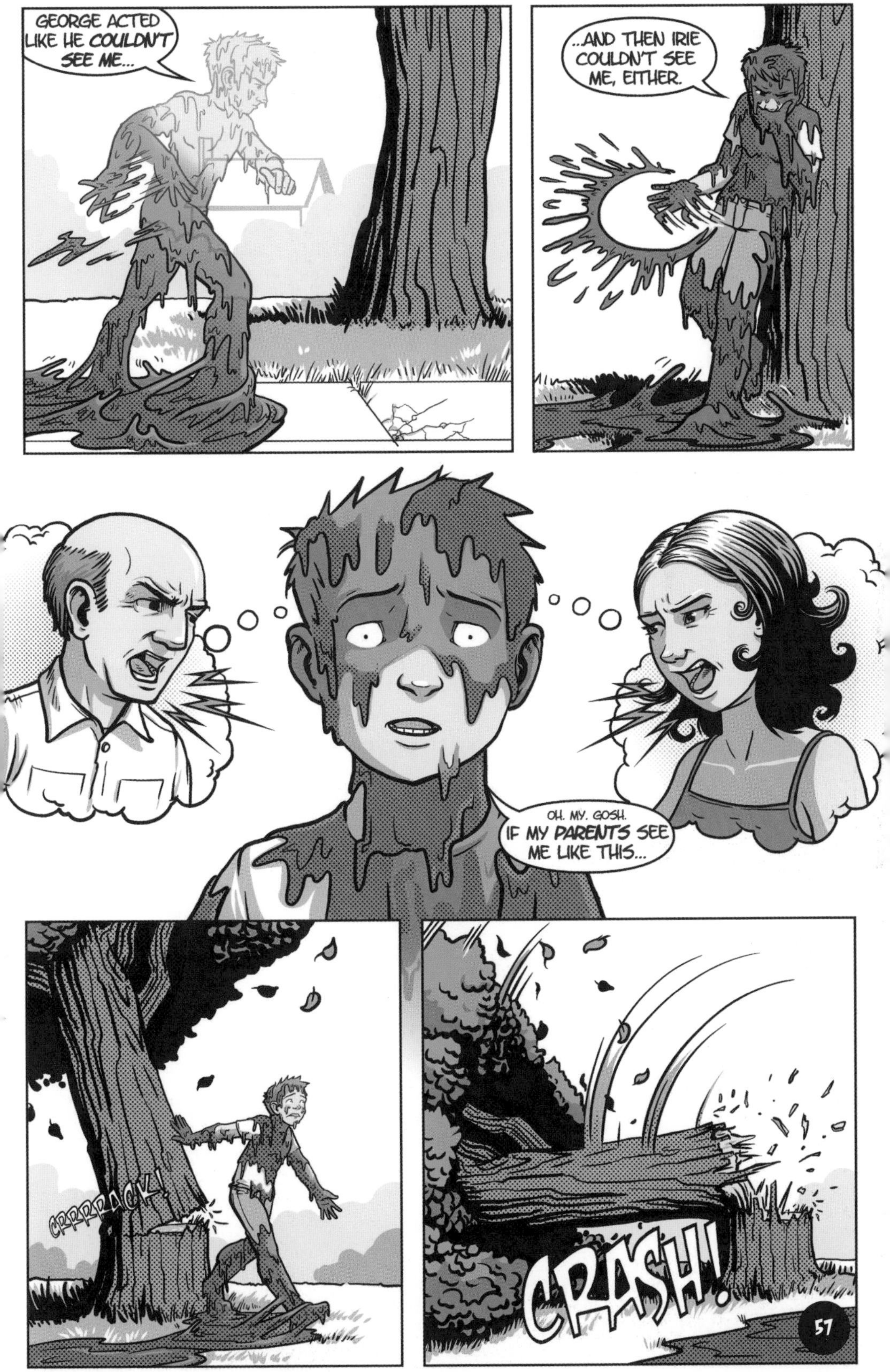
GEORGE ACTED LIKE HE COULDN'T SEE ME...
...AND THEN IRIE COULDN'T SEE ME, EITHER.
OH. MY. GOSH.
IF MY PARENTS SEE ME LIKE THIS...
CRRRRACK!
CRASH!

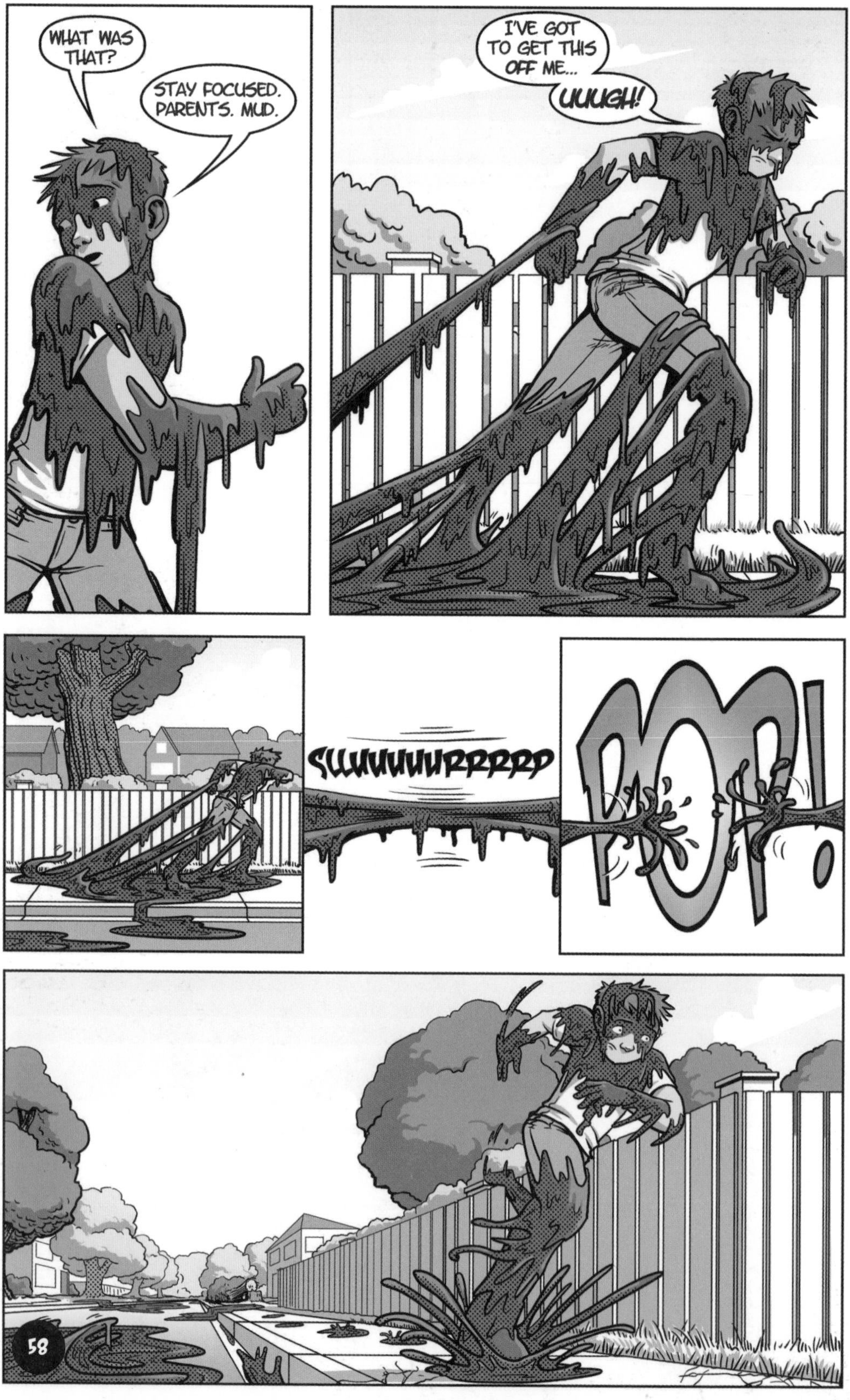
WHAT WAS THAT?
STAY FOCUSED. PARENTS. MUD.
I'VE GOT TO GET THIS OFF ME...
UUUGH!
SLLUUUUURRRRP
POP!

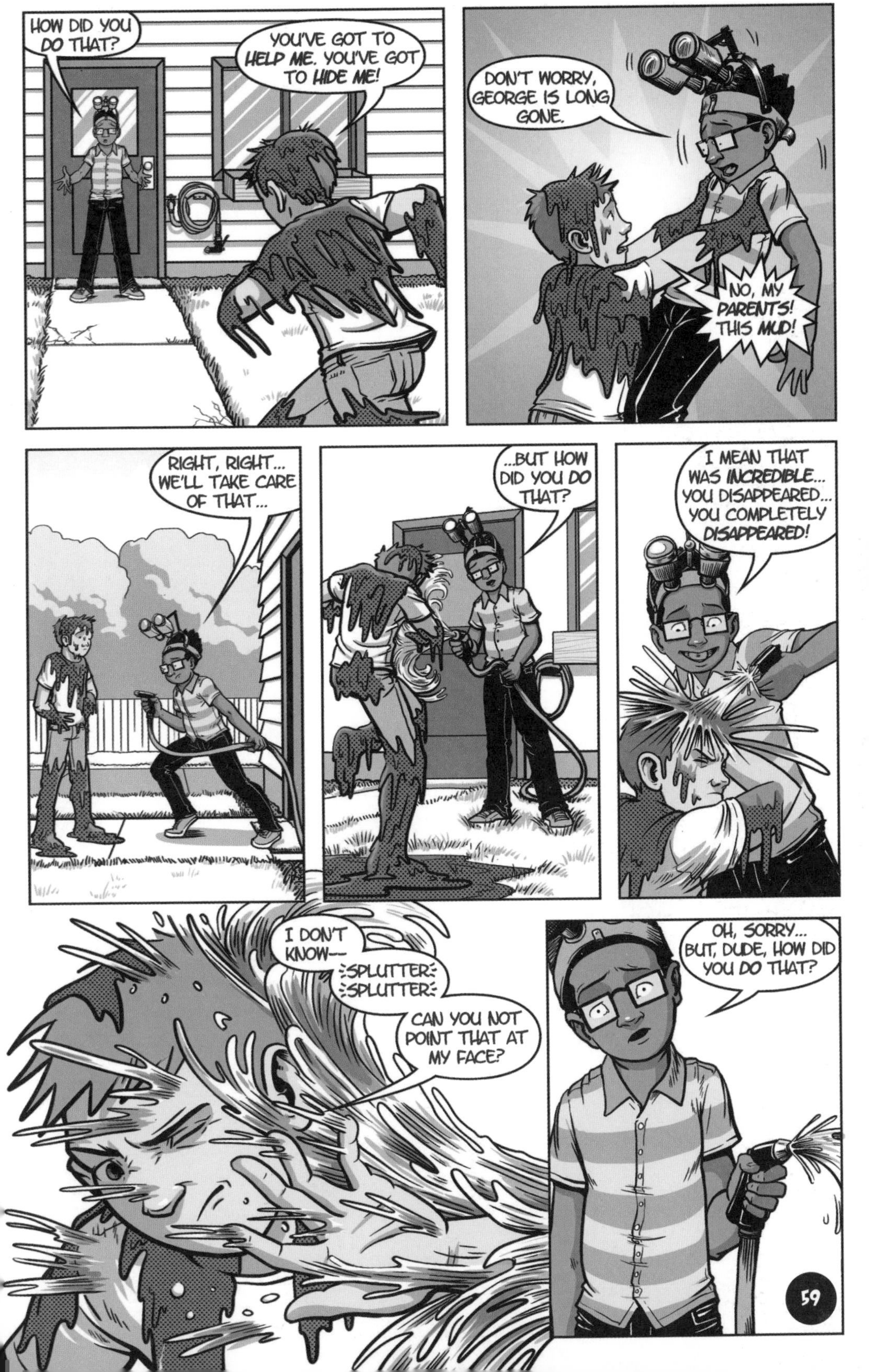
HOW DID YOU DO THAT?
YOU'VE GOT TO HELP ME. YOU'VE GOT TO HIDE ME!
DON'T WORRY, GEORGE IS LONG GONE.
NO, MY PARENTS! THIS MUD!
RIGHT, RIGHT... WE'LL TAKE CARE OF THAT...
...BUT HOW DID YOU DO THAT?
I MEAN THAT WAS INCREDIBLE... YOU DISAPPEARED... YOU COMPLETELY DISAPPEARED!
I DON'T KNOW—
SPLUTTER SPLUTTER
CAN YOU NOT POINT THAT AT MY FACE?
OH, SORRY... BUT, DUDE, HOW DID YOU DO THAT?

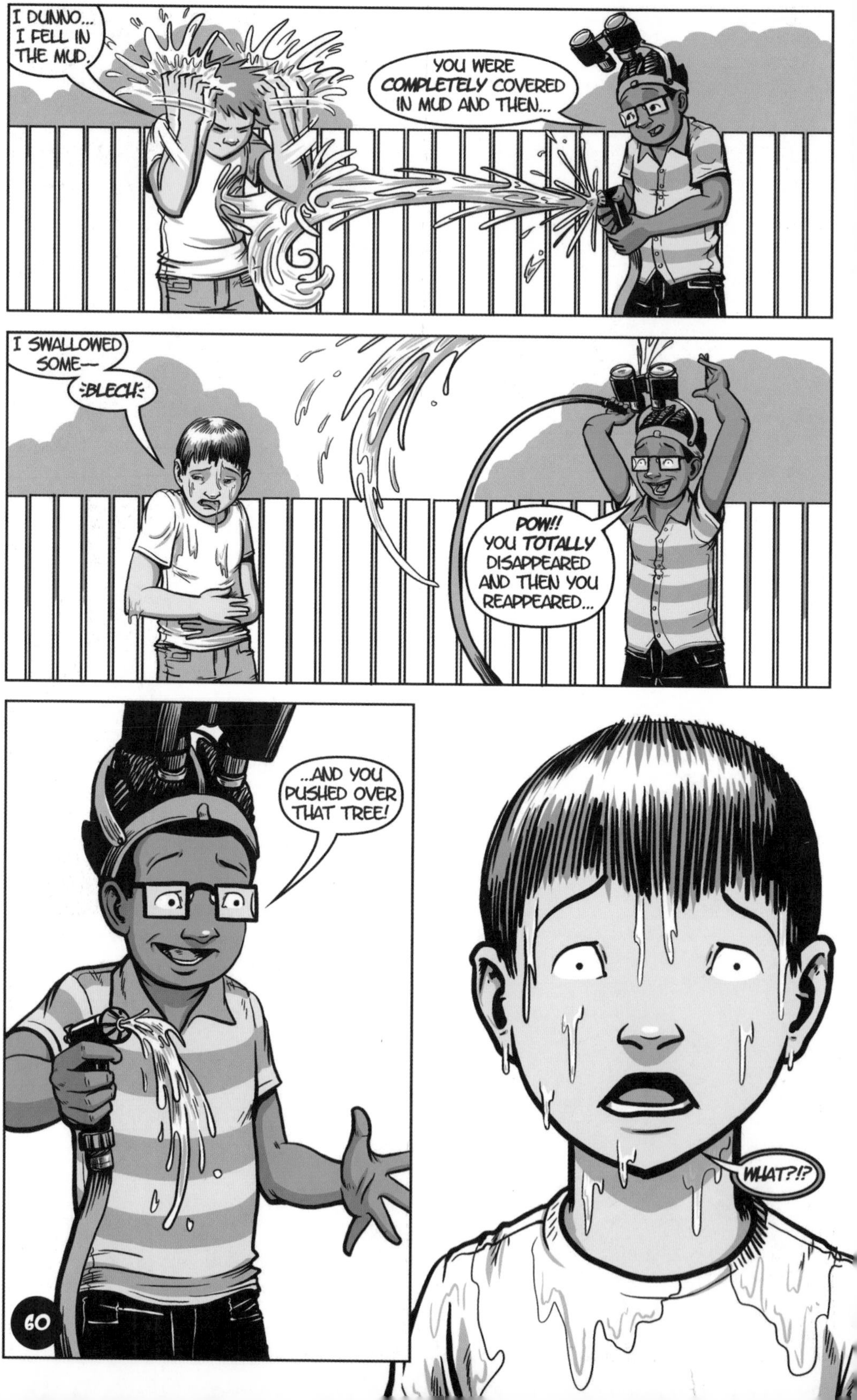
I DUNNO... I FELL IN THE MUD.
YOU WERE COMPLETELY COVERED IN MUD AND THEN...
I SWALLOWED SOME--
BLECH
POW!! YOU TOTALLY DISAPPEARED AND THEN YOU REAPPEARED...
...AND YOU PUSHED OVER THAT TREE!
WHAT?!?

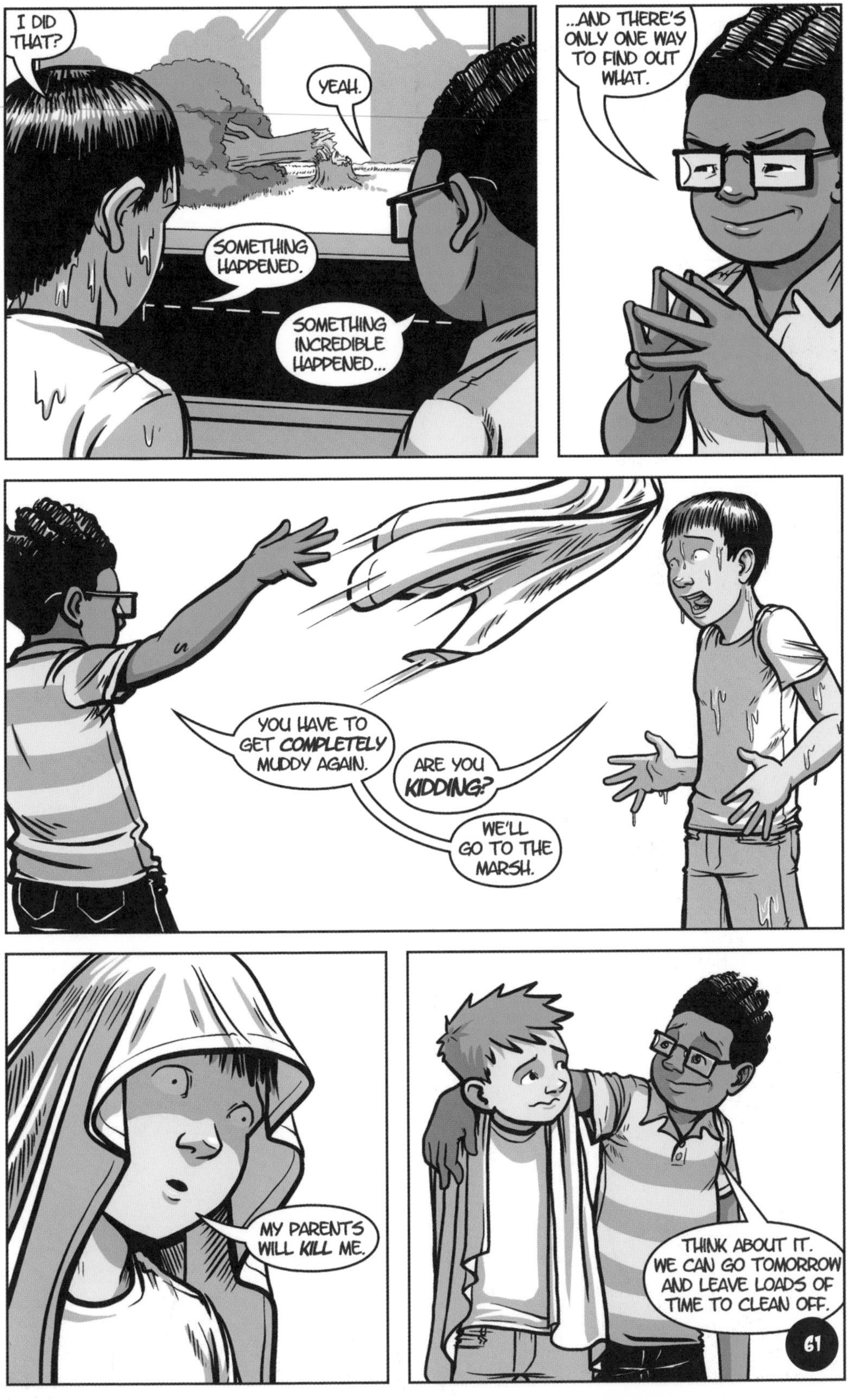
I DID THAT?
YEAH.
SOMETHING HAPPENED.
SOMETHING INCREDIBLE HAPPENED...
...AND THERE'S ONLY ONE WAY TO FIND OUT WHAT.
YOU HAVE TO GET COMPLETELY MUDDY AGAIN.
ARE YOU KIDDING?
WE'LL GO TO THE MARSH.
MY PARENTS WILL KILL ME.
THINK ABOUT IT. WE CAN GO TOMORROW AND LEAVE LOADS OF TIME TO CLEAN OFF.

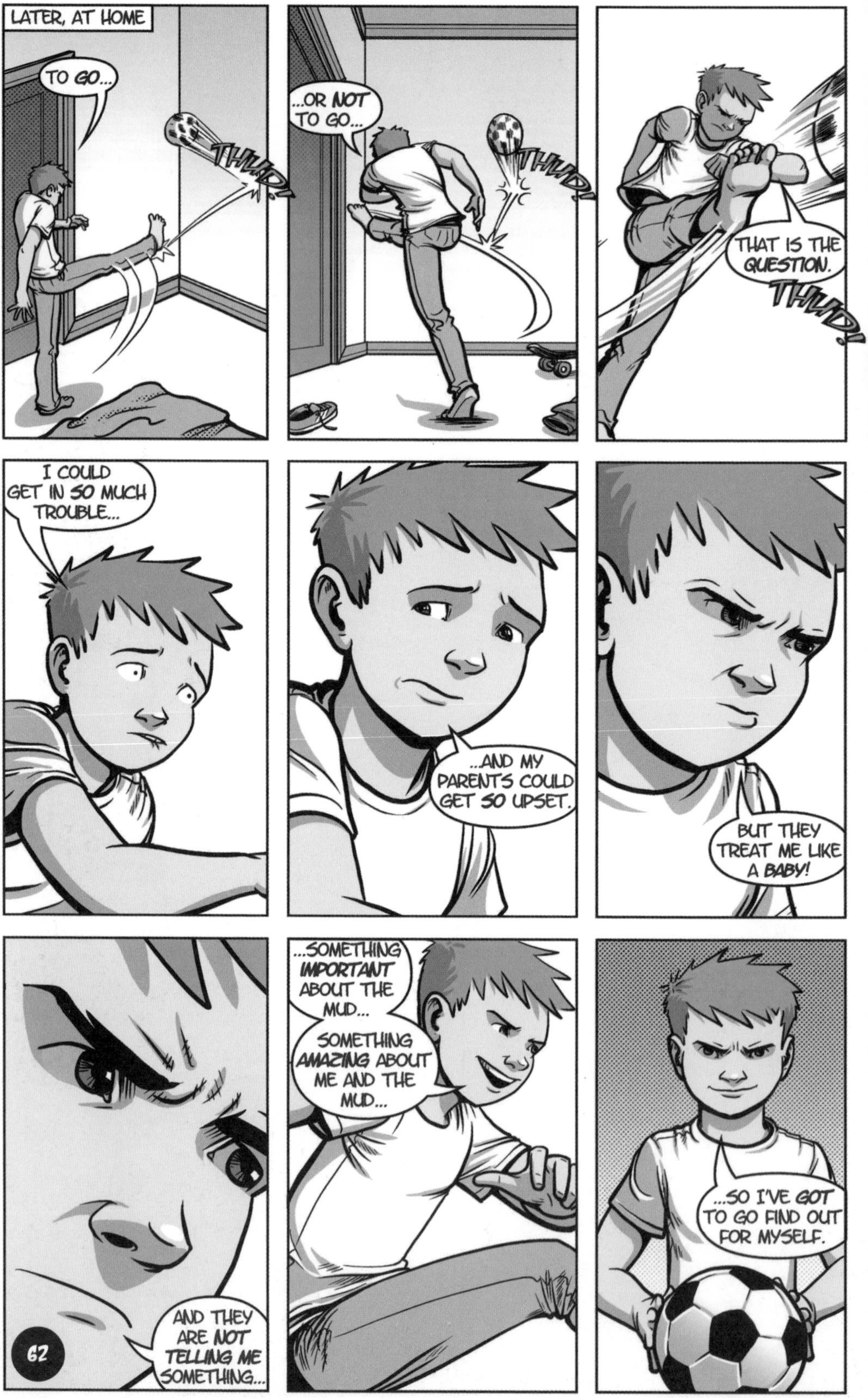
LATER, AT HOME
TO GO...
THUD!
...OR NOT TO GO...
THUD!
THAT IS THE QUESTION.
THUD!
I COULD GET IN SO MUCH TROUBLE...
...AND MY PARENTS COULD GET SO UPSET.
BUT THEY TREAT ME LIKE A BABY!
AND THEY ARE NOT TELLING ME SOMETHING...
...SOMETHING IMPORTANT ABOUT THE MUD...
SOMETHING AMAZING ABOUT ME AND THE MUD...
...SO I'VE GOT TO GO FIND OUT FOR MYSELF.

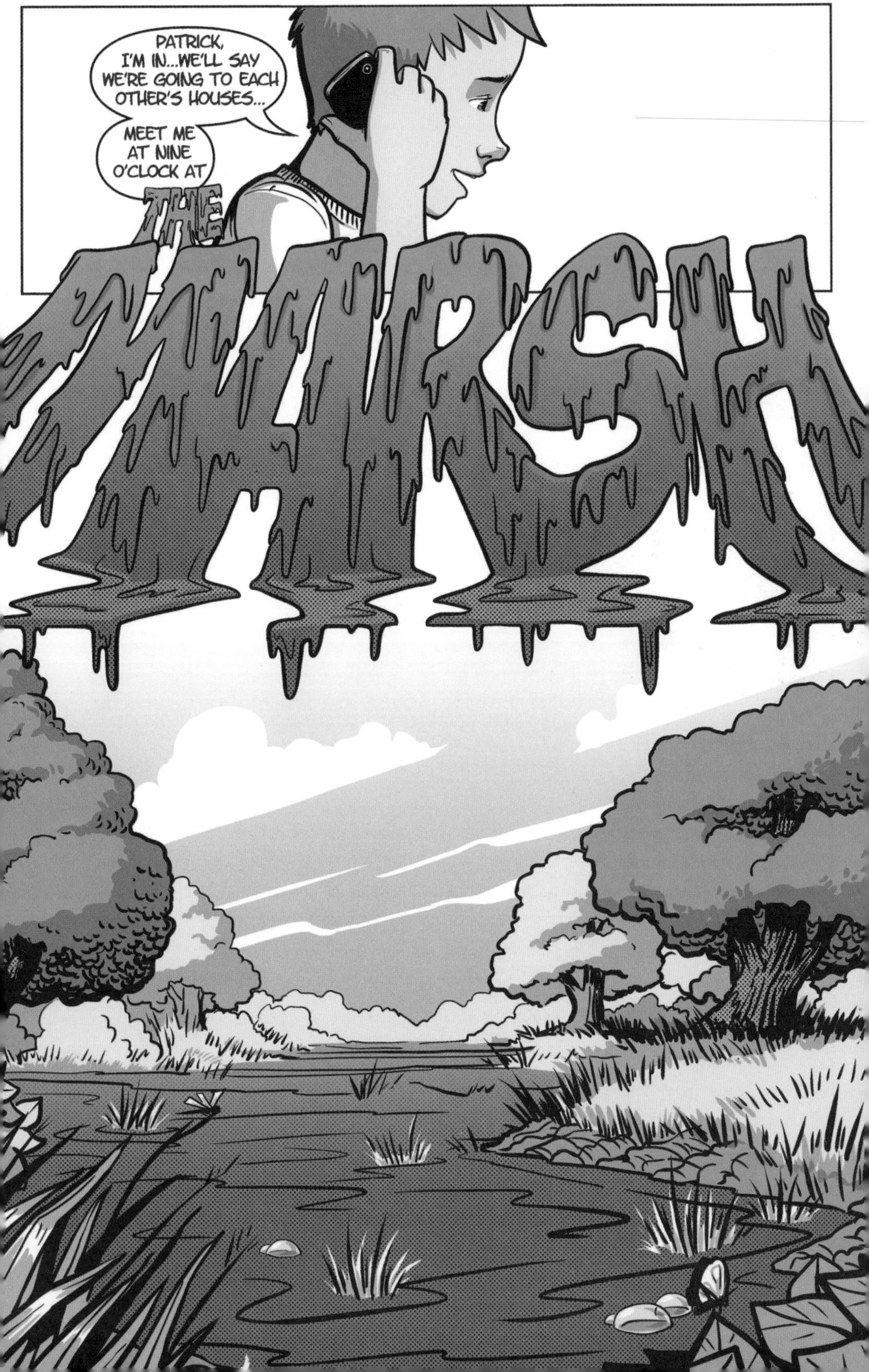
PATRICK, I'M IN...WE'LL SAY WE'RE GOING TO EACH OTHER'S HOUSES...
MEET ME AT NINE O'CLOCK AT
THE MARSH

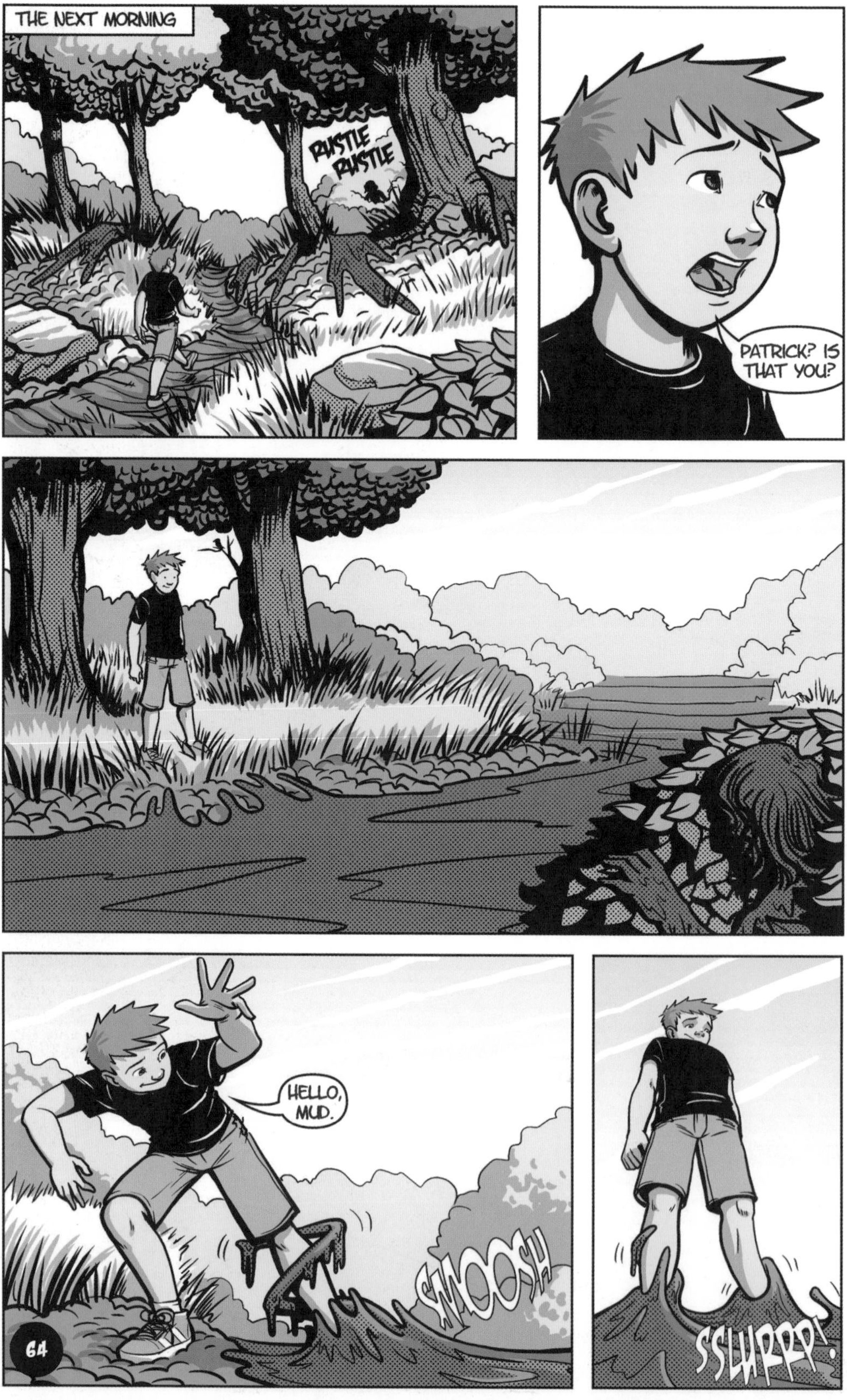
THE NEXT MORNING
RUSTLE RUSTLE
PATRICK? IS THAT YOU?
HELLO, MUD.
SMOOSH
SSLURRP!

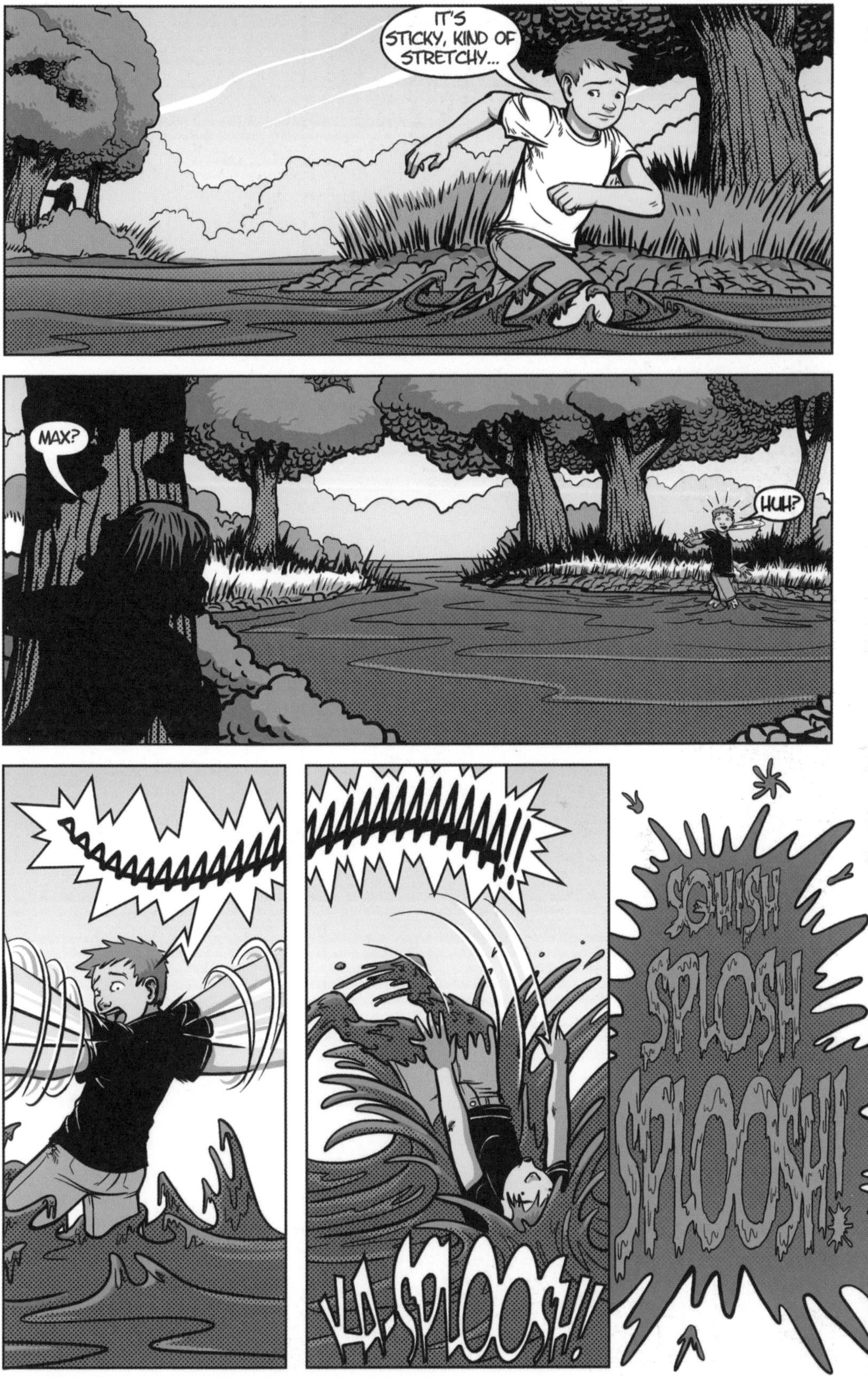
IT'S STICKY, KIND OF STRETCHY...
MAX?
HUH?
AAAAAAAAAAAAAAAAAAAAAAAAAAAAA!!
SQUISH
SPLOSH
SPLOOSH!
KA-SPLOOSH!

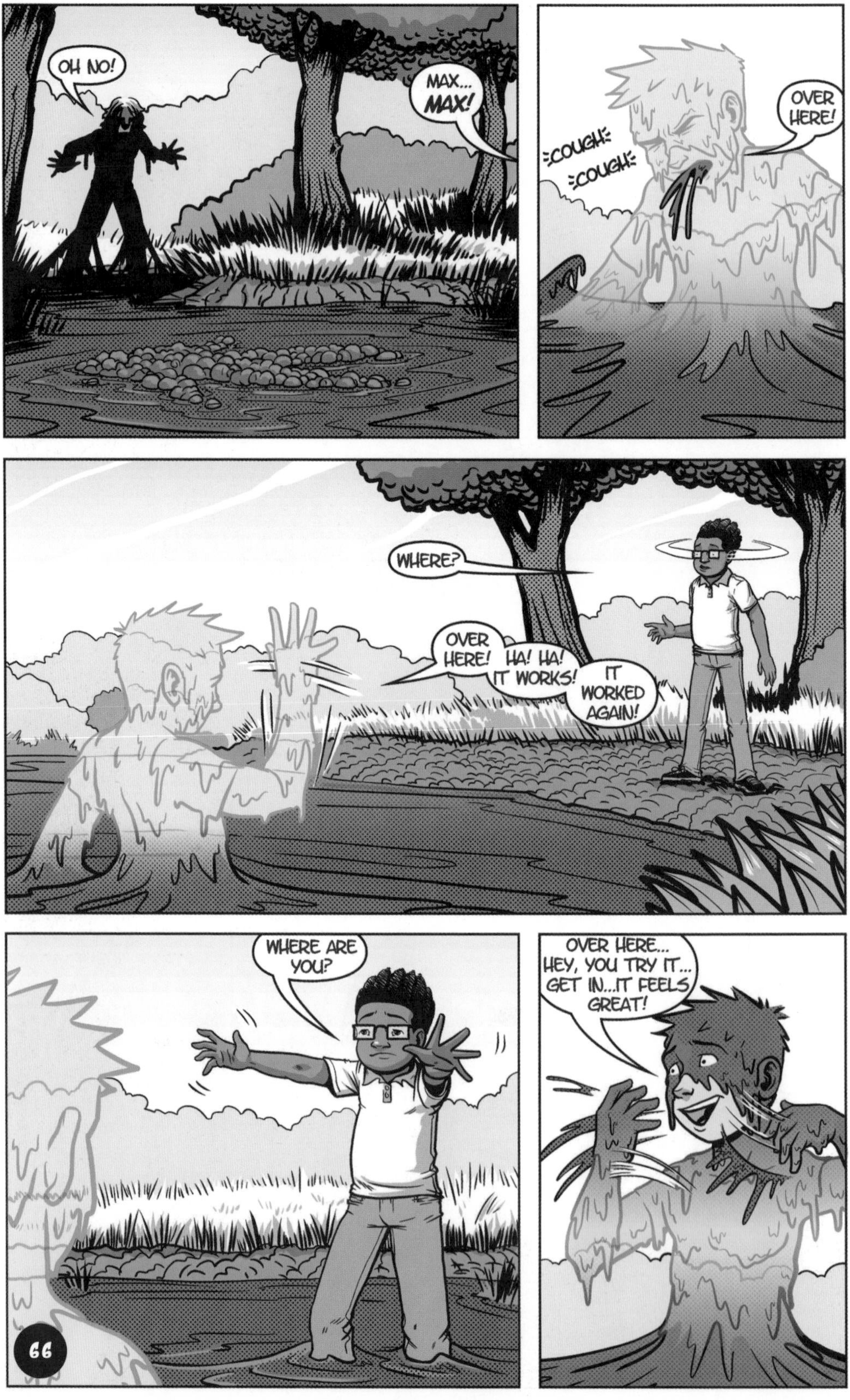
OH NO!
MAX... MAX!
OVER HERE!
COUGH
COUGH
WHERE?
OVER HERE!
HA! HA! IT WORKS!
IT WORKED AGAIN!
WHERE ARE YOU?
OVER HERE... HEY, YOU TRY IT... GET IN...IT FEELS GREAT!

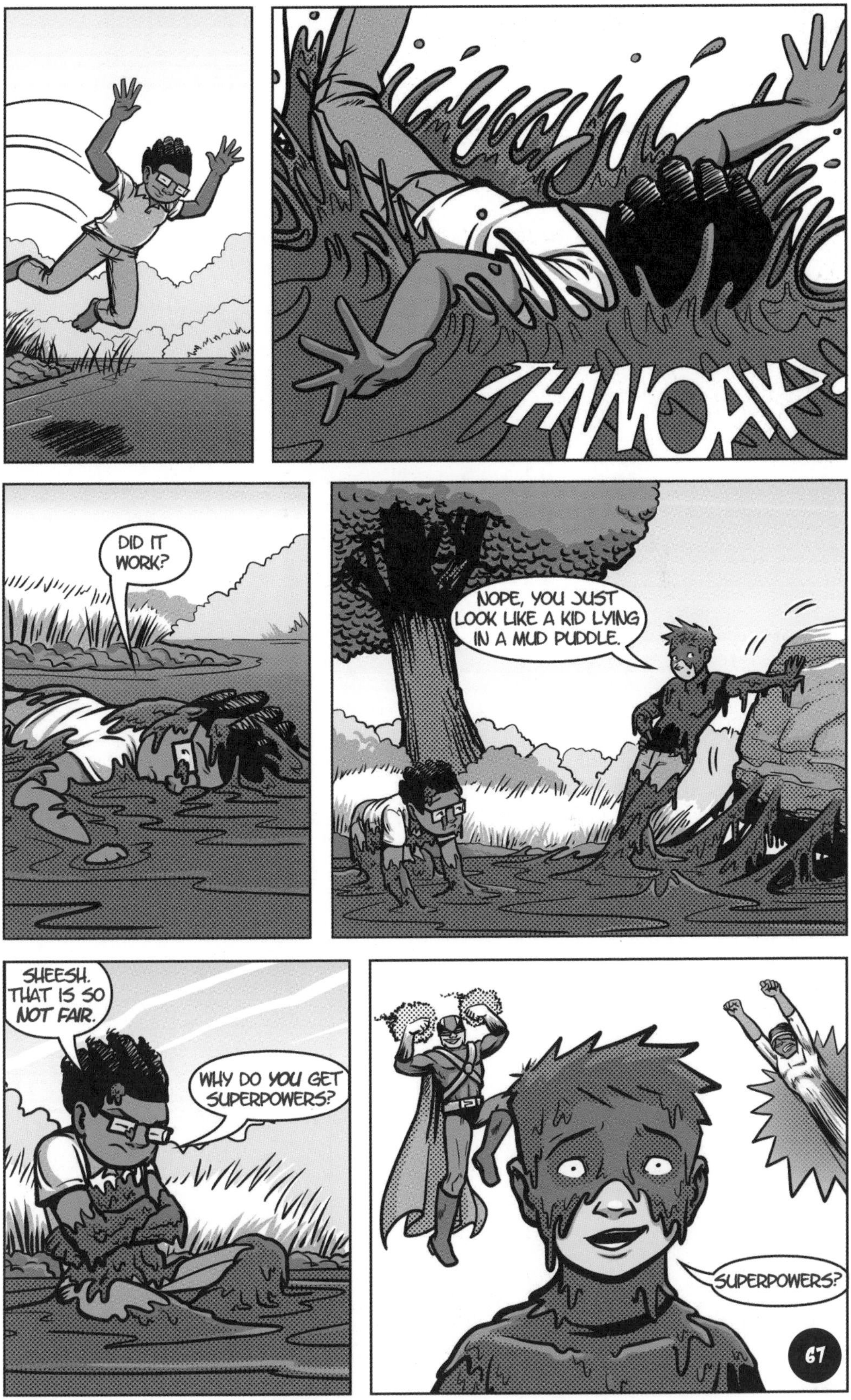
THWOAK!
DID IT WORK?
NOPE, YOU JUST LOOK LIKE A KID LYING IN A MUD PUDDLE.
SHEESH. THAT IS SO NOT FAIR.
WHY DO YOU GET SUPERPOWERS?
SUPERPOWERS?

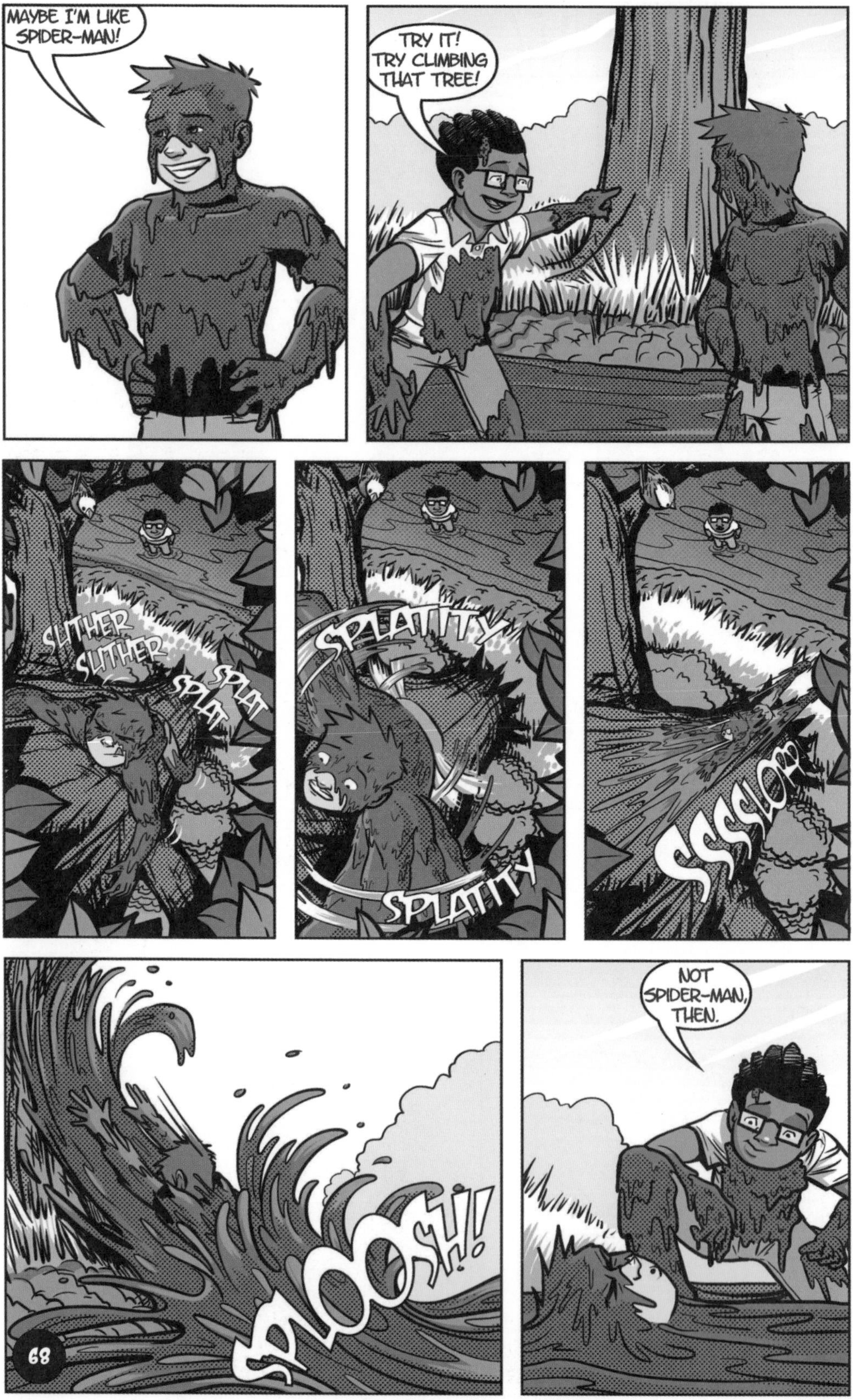
MAYBE I'M LIKE SPIDER-MAN!
TRY IT! TRY CLIMBING THAT TREE!
SLITHER SLITHER
SPLAT SPLAT
SPLATITY
SPLATITY
SSSSLORP
SPLOOOSH!!
NOT SPIDER-MAN, THEN.

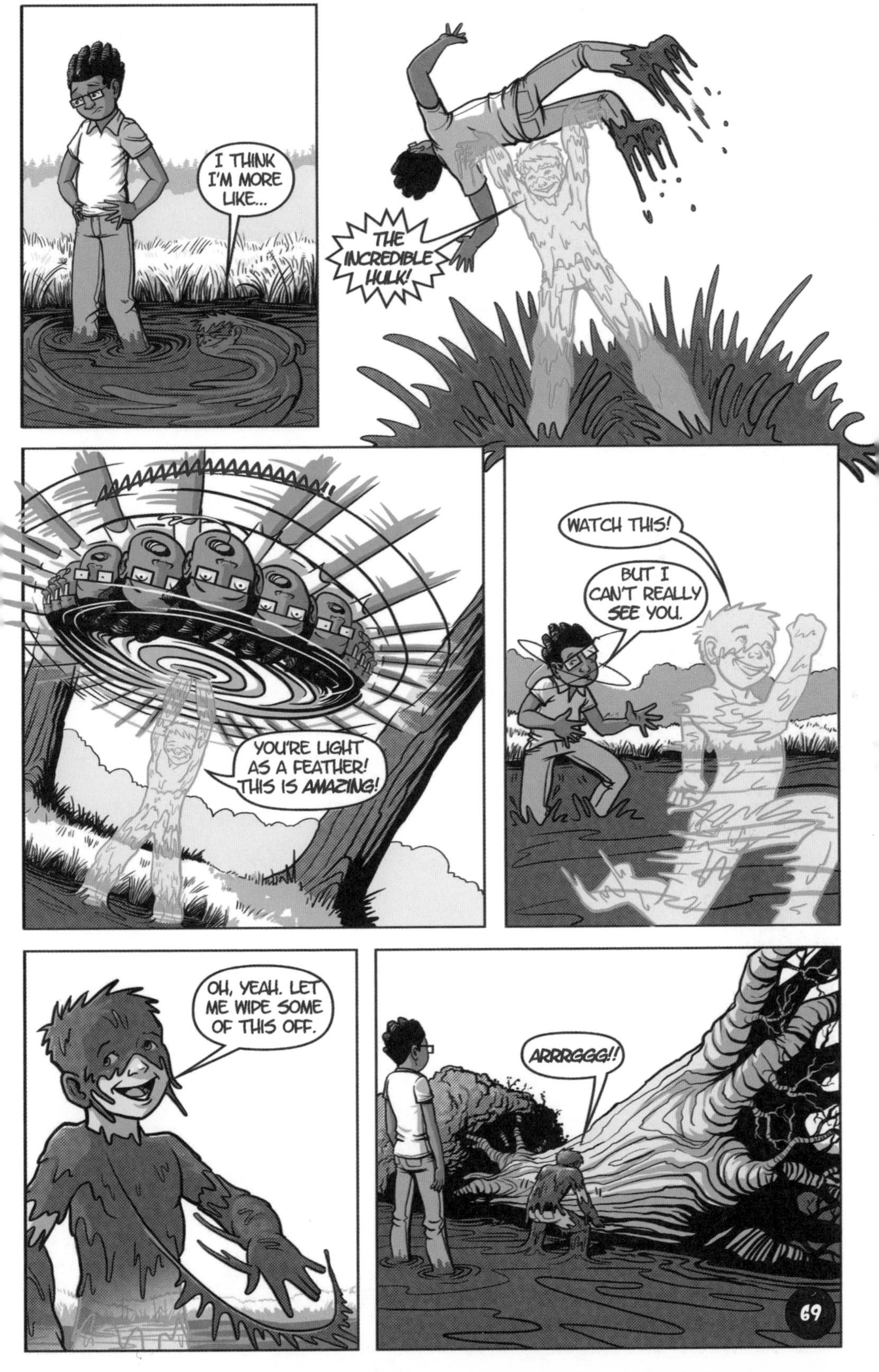
I THINK I'M MORE LIKE...
THE INCREDIBLE HULK!
AAAAAAAAAAAAAAAAAAA!
YOU'RE LIGHT AS A FEATHER! THIS IS AMAZING!
WATCH THIS!
BUT I CAN'T REALLY SEE YOU.
OH, YEAH. LET ME WIPE SOME OF THIS OFF.
ARRRGGG!!

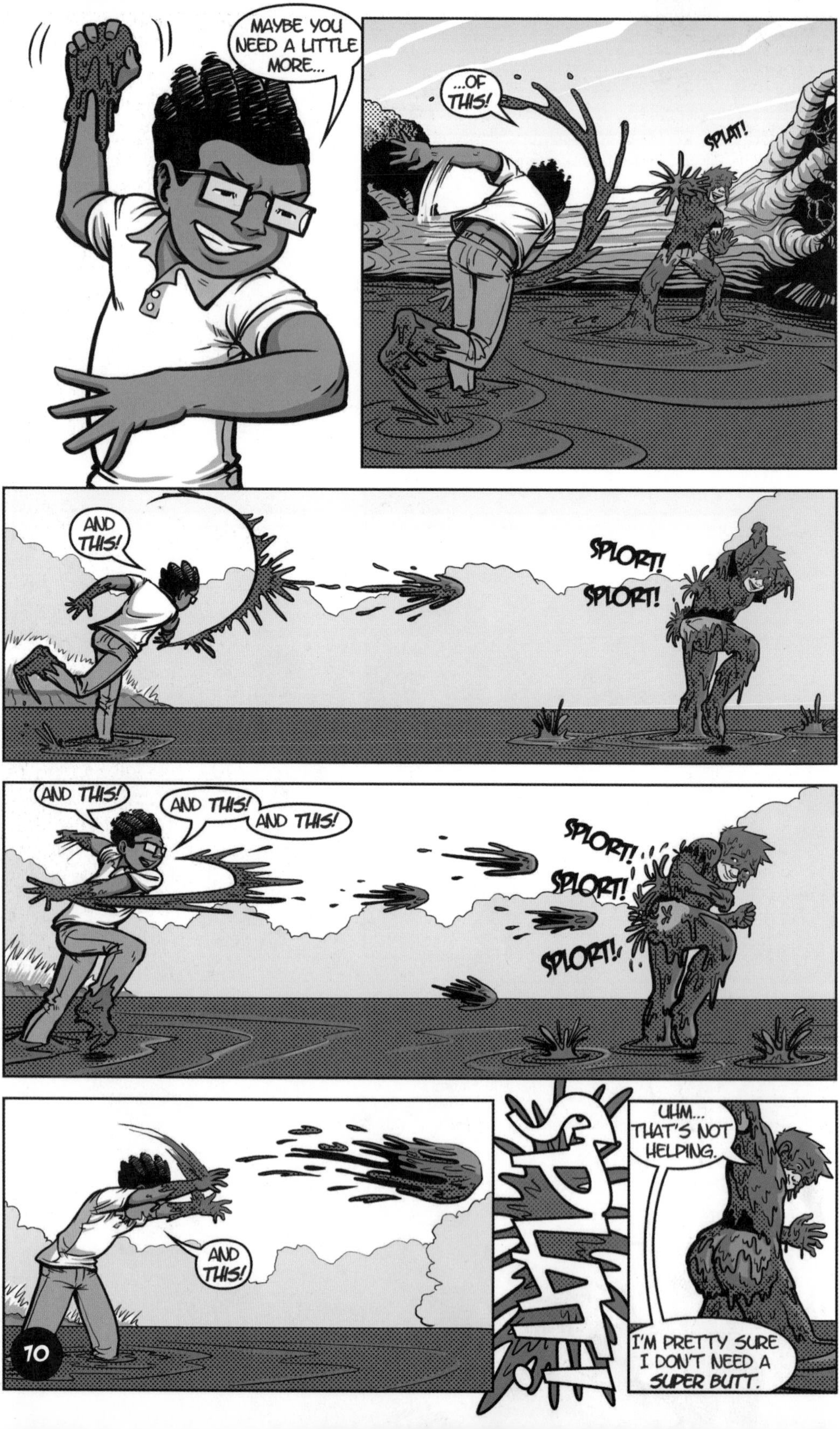
MAYBE YOU NEED A LITTLE MORE...
...OF THIS!
SPLAT!
AND THIS!
SPLORT!
SPLORT!
AND THIS!
AND THIS!
AND THIS!
SPLORT!
SPLORT!
SPLORT!
AND THIS!
SPLAT
UHM... THAT'S NOT HELPING.
I'M PRETTY SURE I DON'T NEED A SUPER BUTT.

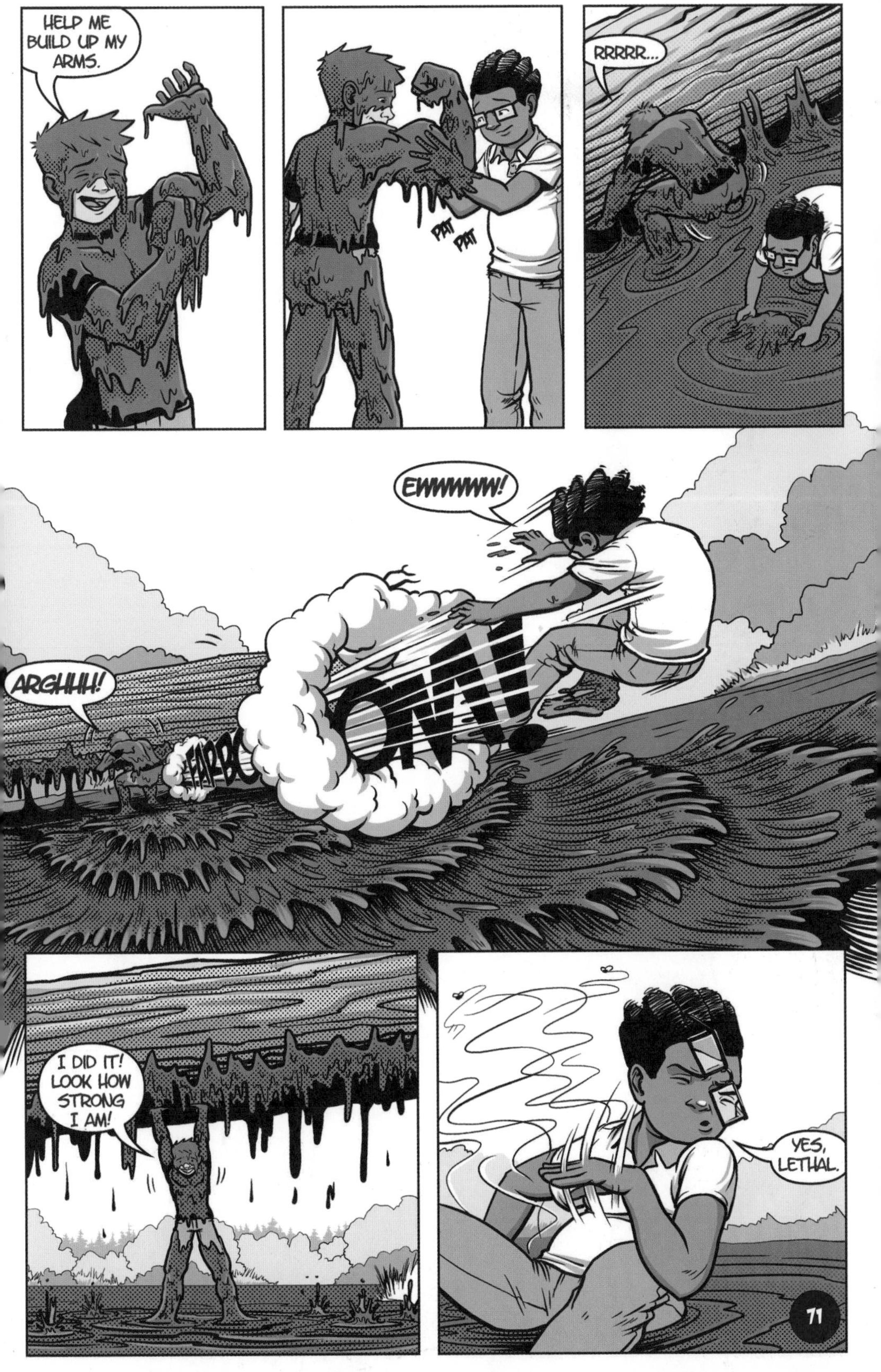
HELP ME BUILD UP MY ARMS.
PAT PAT
RRRRR...
EWWWWW!
ARGHHH!
FARBOOM!
I DID IT! LOOK HOW STRONG I AM!
YES, LETHAL.

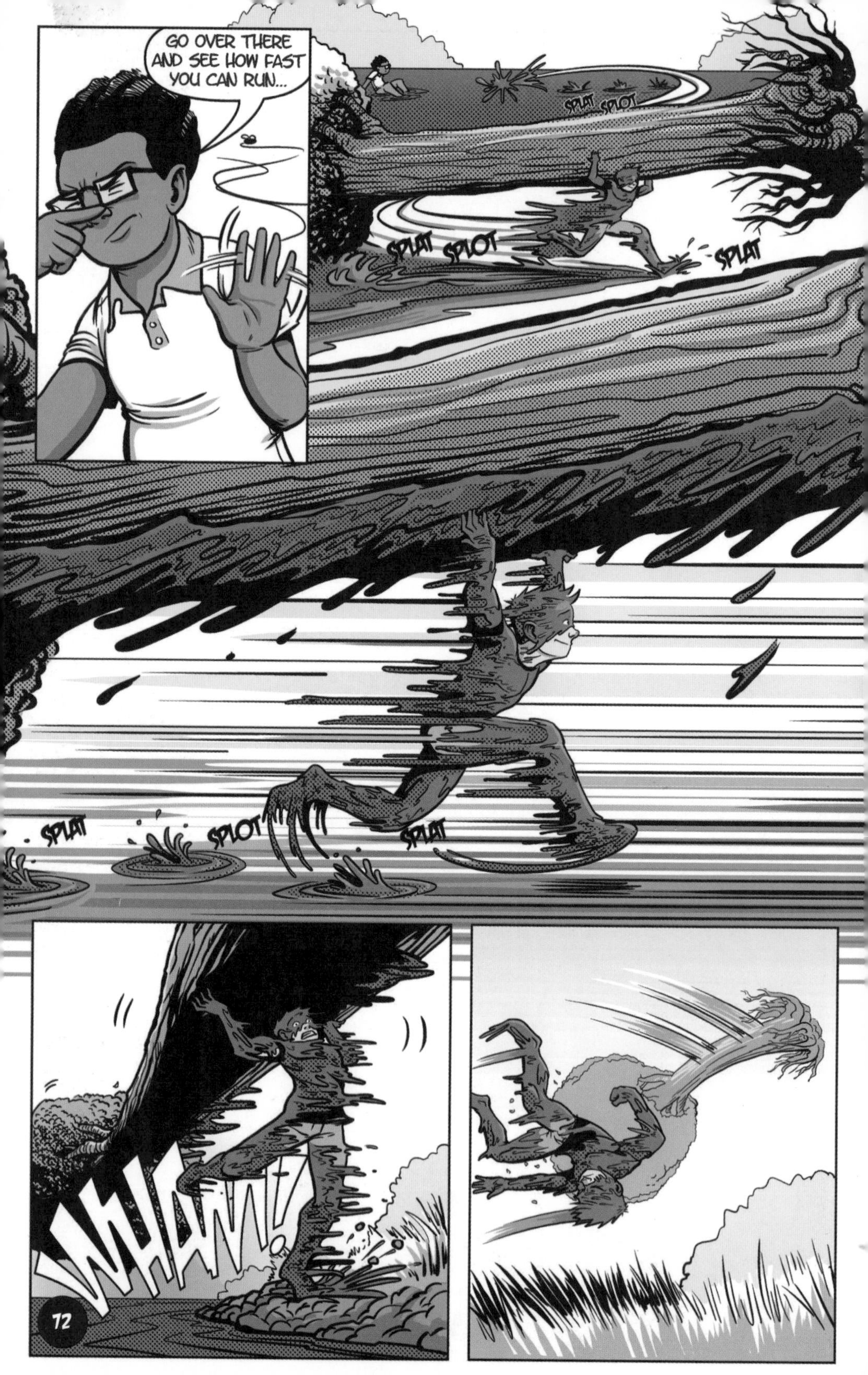
GO OVER THERE AND SEE HOW FAST YOU CAN RUN...
SPLAT
SPLOT
SPLAT
SPLOT
SPLAT
SPLAT
SPLOT
SPLAT
WHAM!

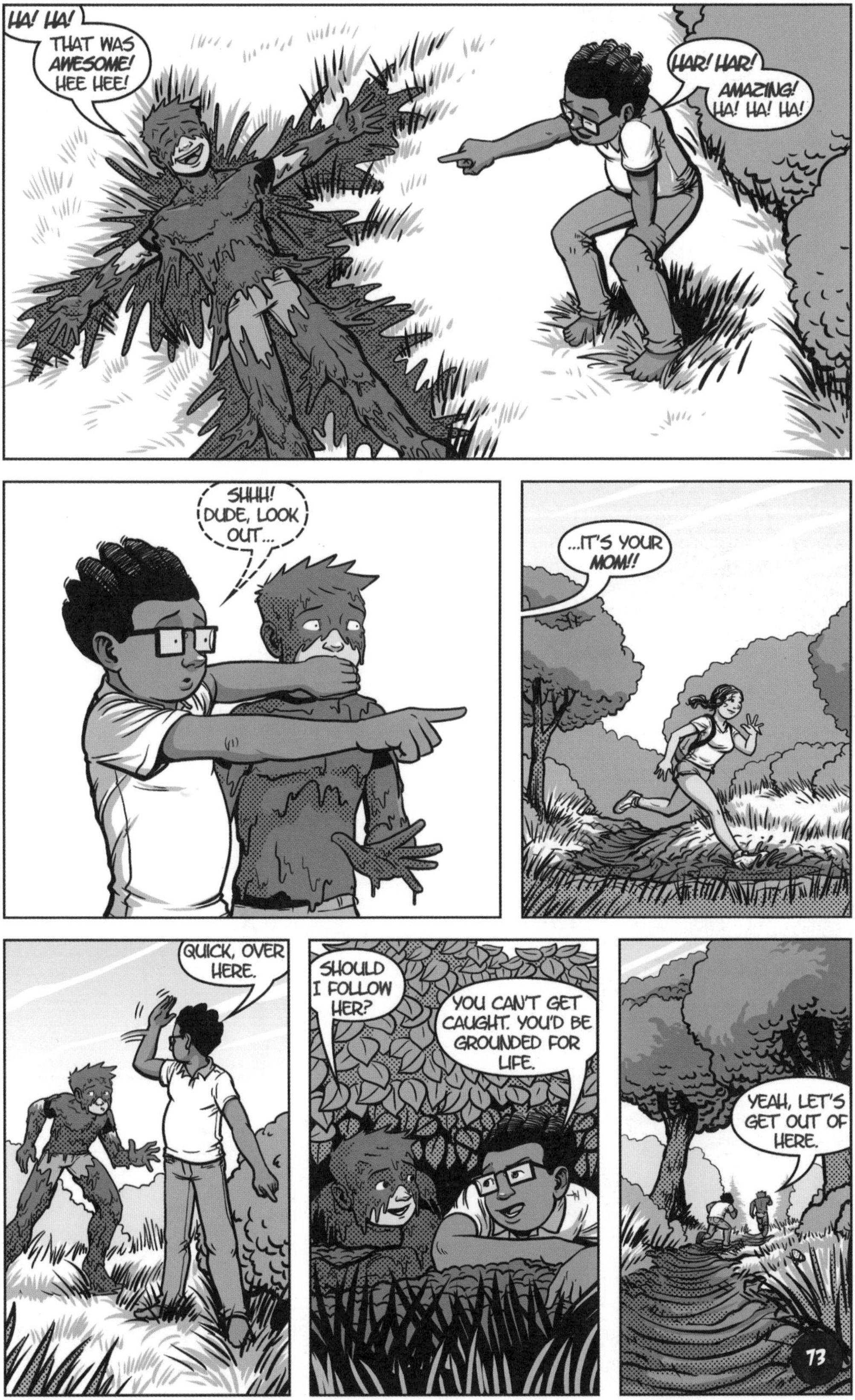
HA! HA!
THAT WAS AWESOME! HEE HEE!
HAR! HAR!
AMAZING! HA! HA! HA!
SHHH! DUDE, LOOK OUT...
...IT'S YOUR MOM!!
QUICK, OVER HERE.
SHOULD I FOLLOW HER?
YOU CAN'T GET CAUGHT. YOU'D BE GROUNDED FOR LIFE.
YEAH, LET'S GET OUT OF HERE.

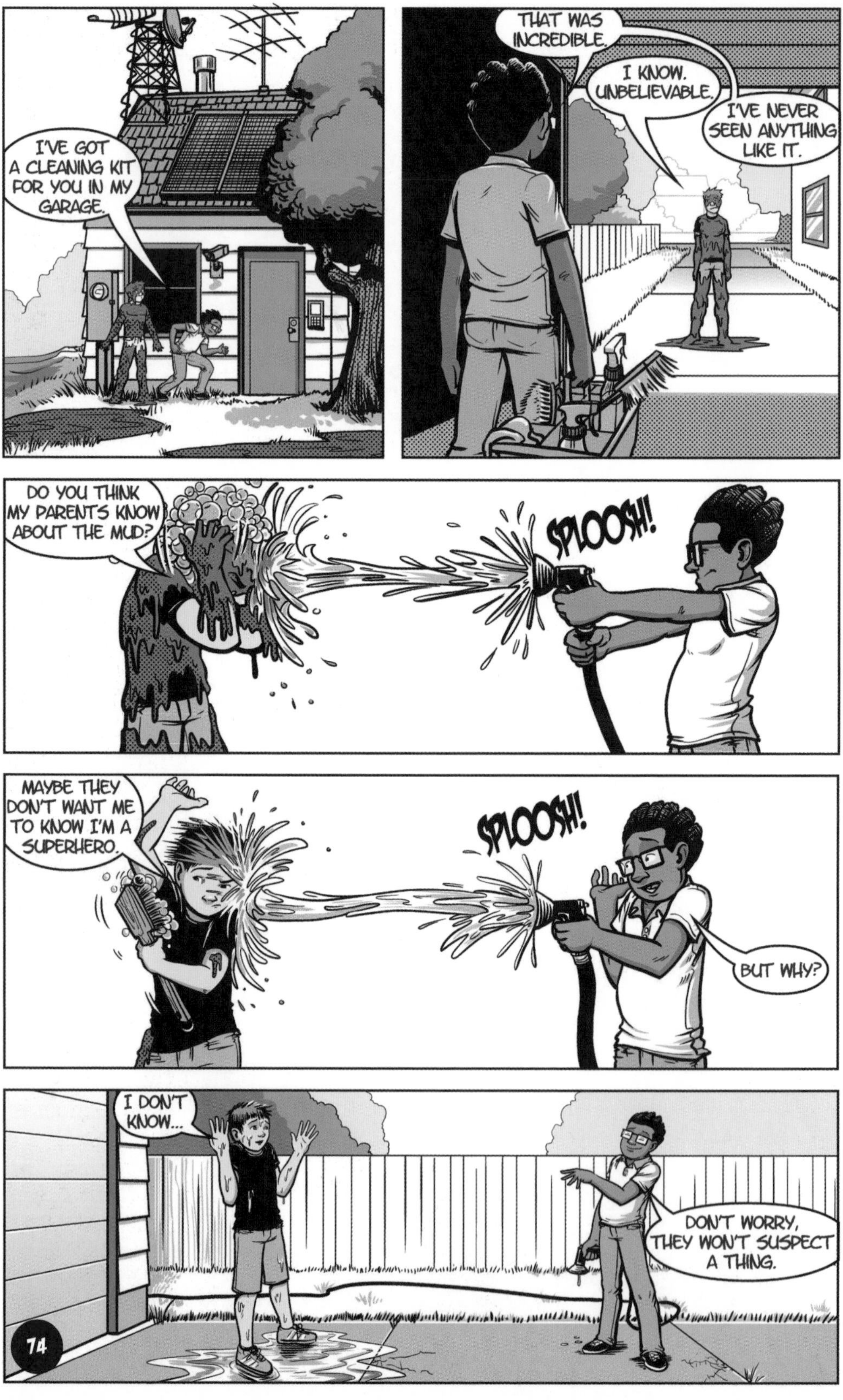
I'VE GOT A CLEANING KIT FOR YOU IN MY GARAGE.
THAT WAS INCREDIBLE.
I KNOW. UNBELIEVABLE.
I'VE NEVER SEEN ANYTHING LIKE IT.
DO YOU THINK MY PARENTS KNOW ABOUT THE MUD?
SPLOOSH!
MAYBE THEY DON'T WANT ME TO KNOW I'M A SUPERHERO.
SPLOOSH!
BUT WHY?
I DON'T KNOW...
DON'T WORRY, THEY WON'T SUSPECT A THING.

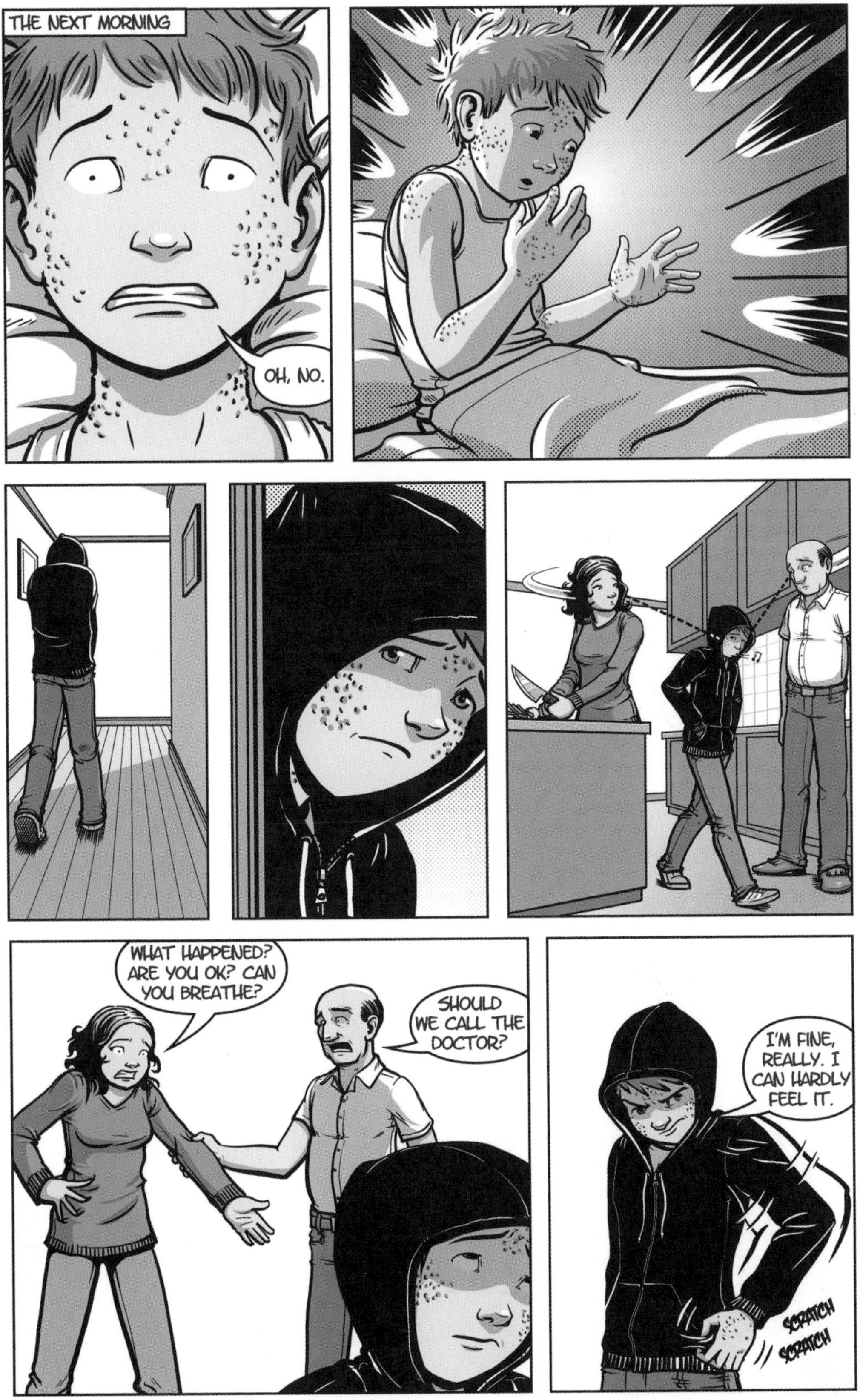
THE NEXT MORNING
OH, NO.
WHAT HAPPENED? ARE YOU OK? CAN YOU BREATHE?
SHOULD WE CALL THE DOCTOR?
I'M FINE, REALLY. I CAN HARDLY FEEL IT.
SCRATCH
SCRATCH

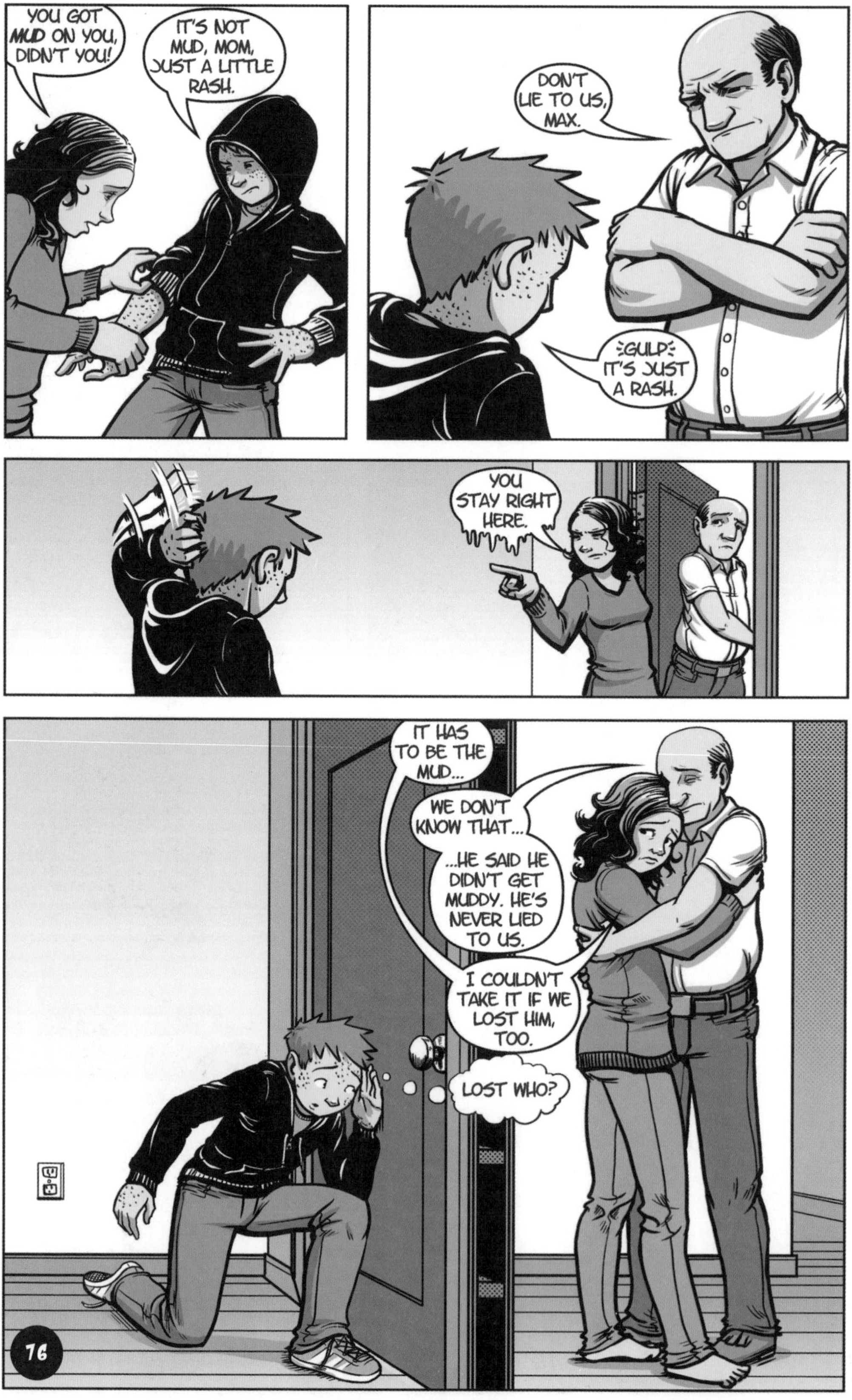

YOU GOT MUD ON YOU, DIDN'T YOU!
IT'S NOT MUD, MOM, JUST A LITTLE RASH.
DON'T LIE TO US, MAX.
GULP IT'S JUST A RASH.
YOU STAY RIGHT HERE.
IT HAS TO BE THE MUD...
WE DON'T KNOW THAT...
...HE SAID HE DIDN'T GET MUDDY. HE'S NEVER LIED TO US.
I COULDN'T TAKE IT IF WE LOST HIM, TOO.
LOST WHO?

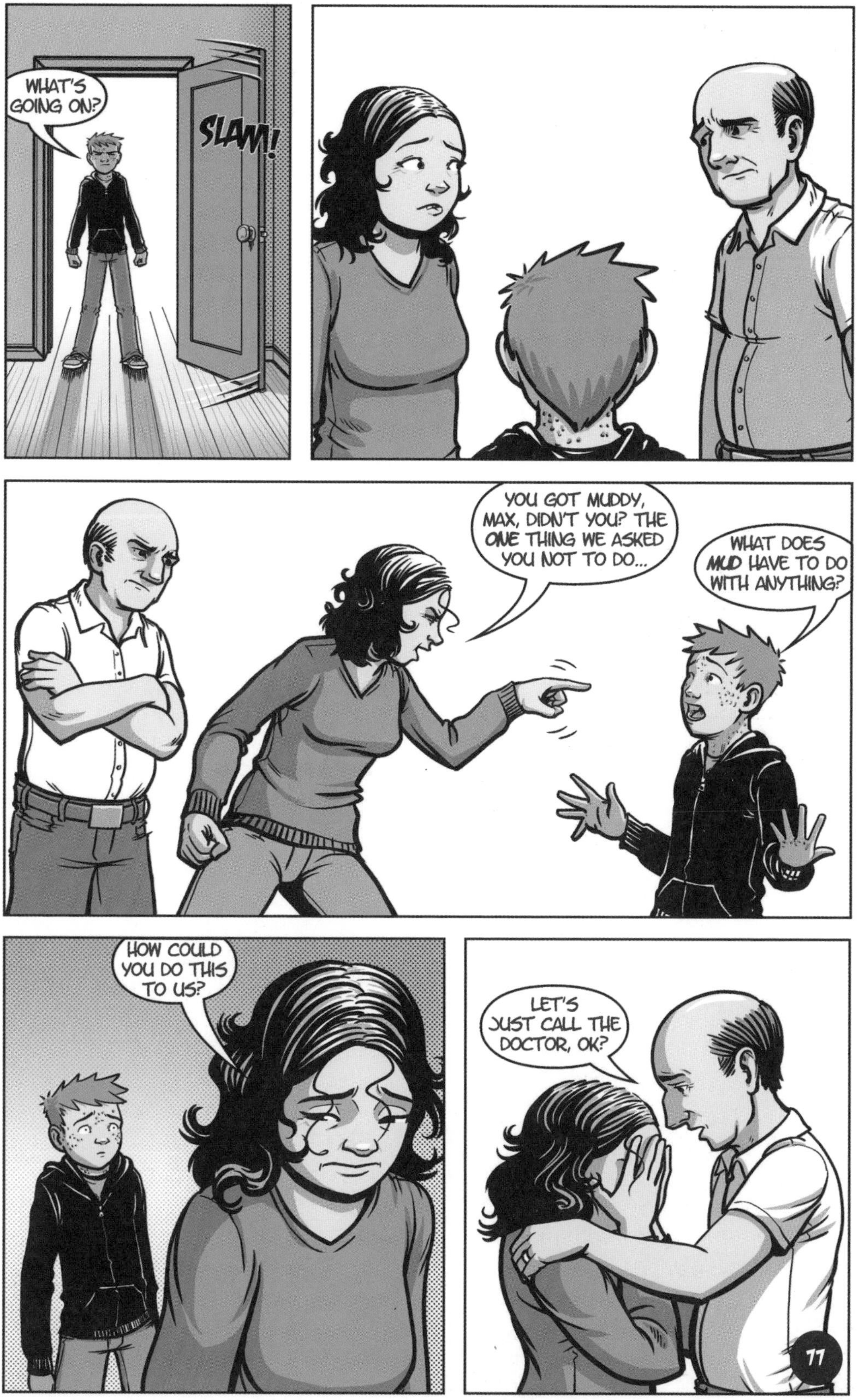
WHAT'S GOING ON?
SLAM!
YOU GOT MUDDY, MAX, DIDN'T YOU? THE ONE THING WE ASKED YOU NOT TO DO...
WHAT DOES MUD HAVE TO DO WITH ANYTHING?
HOW COULD YOU DO THIS TO US?
LET'S JUST CALL THE DOCTOR, OK?

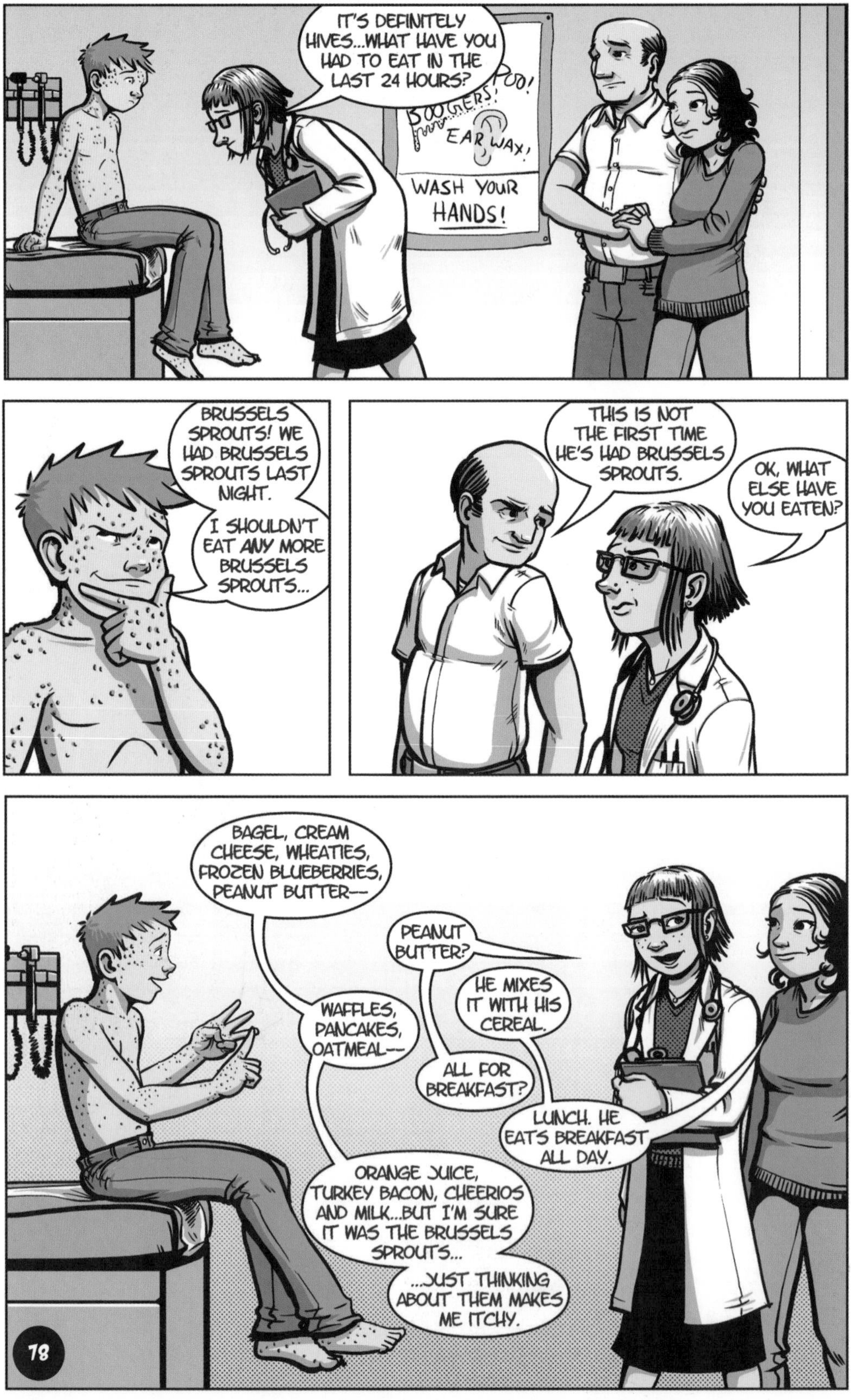

IT'S DEFINITELY HIVES...WHAT HAVE YOU HAD TO EAT IN THE LAST 24 HOURS?
BOOGERS! POO! EAR WAX!
WASH YOUR HANDS!
BRUSSELS SPROUTS! WE HAD BRUSSELS SPROUTS LAST NIGHT.
I SHOULDN'T EAT ANY MORE BRUSSELS SPROUTS...
THIS IS NOT THE FIRST TIME HE'S HAD BRUSSELS SPROUTS.
OK, WHAT ELSE HAVE YOU EATEN?
BAGEL, CREAM CHEESE, WHEATIES, FROZEN BLUEBERRIES, PEANUT BUTTER--
PEANUT BUTTER?
HE MIXES IT WITH HIS CEREAL.
WAFFLES, PANCAKES, OATMEAL--
ALL FOR BREAKFAST?
LUNCH. HE EATS BREAKFAST ALL DAY.
ORANGE JUICE, TURKEY BACON, CHEERIOS AND MILK...BUT I'M SURE IT WAS THE BRUSSELS SPROUTS...
...JUST THINKING ABOUT THEM MAKES ME ITCHY.

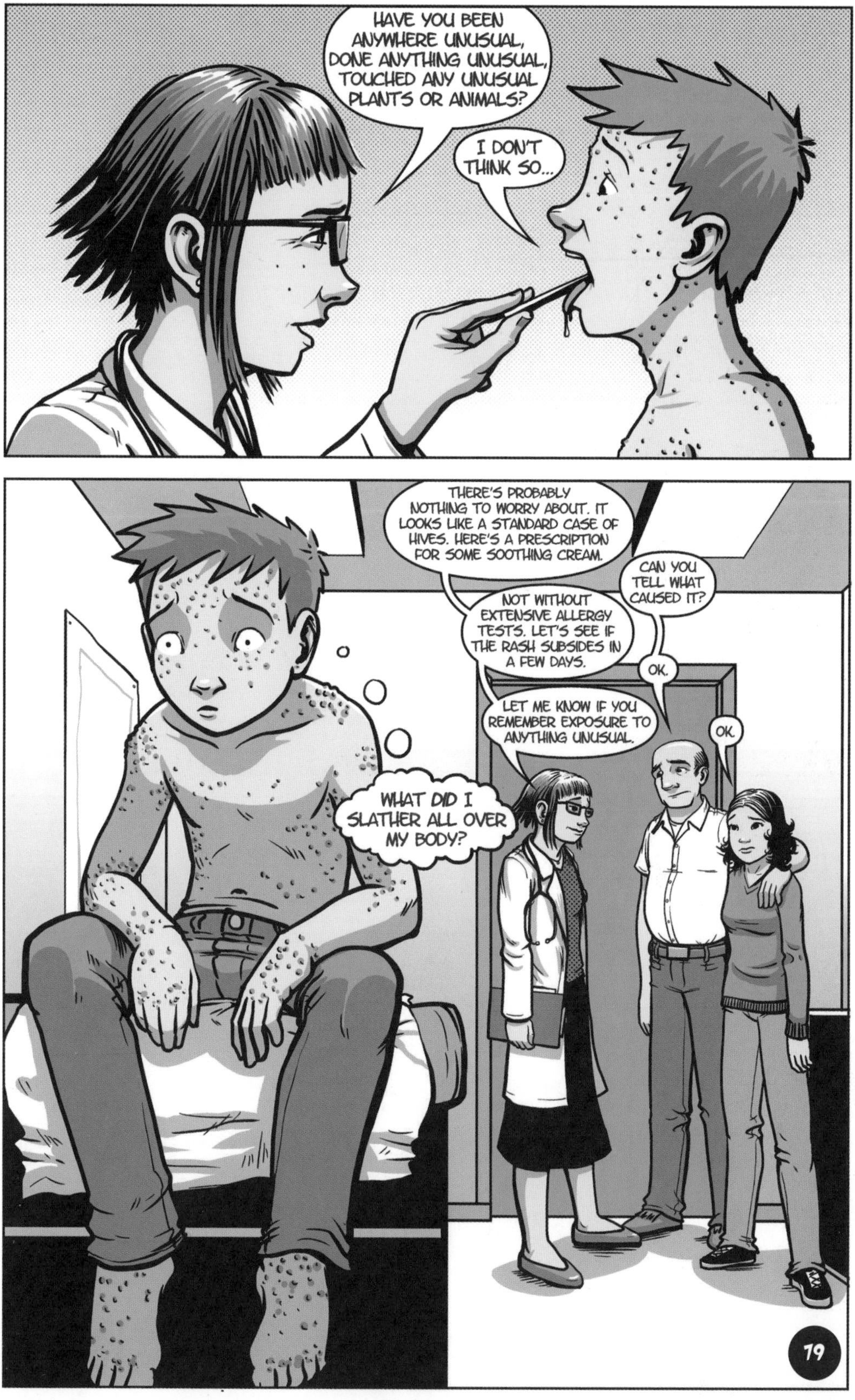
HAVE YOU BEEN ANYWHERE UNUSUAL, DONE ANYTHING UNUSUAL, TOUCHED ANY UNUSUAL PLANTS OR ANIMALS?
I DON'T THINK SO...
THERE'S PROBABLY NOTHING TO WORRY ABOUT. IT LOOKS LIKE A STANDARD CASE OF HIVES. HERE'S A PRESCRIPTION FOR SOME SOOTHING CREAM.
CAN YOU TELL WHAT CAUSED IT?
NOT WITHOUT EXTENSIVE ALLERGY TESTS. LET'S SEE IF THE RASH SUBSIDES IN A FEW DAYS.
OK.
LET ME KNOW IF YOU REMEMBER EXPOSURE TO ANYTHING UNUSUAL.
OK.
WHAT *DID* I SLATHER ALL OVER MY BODY?

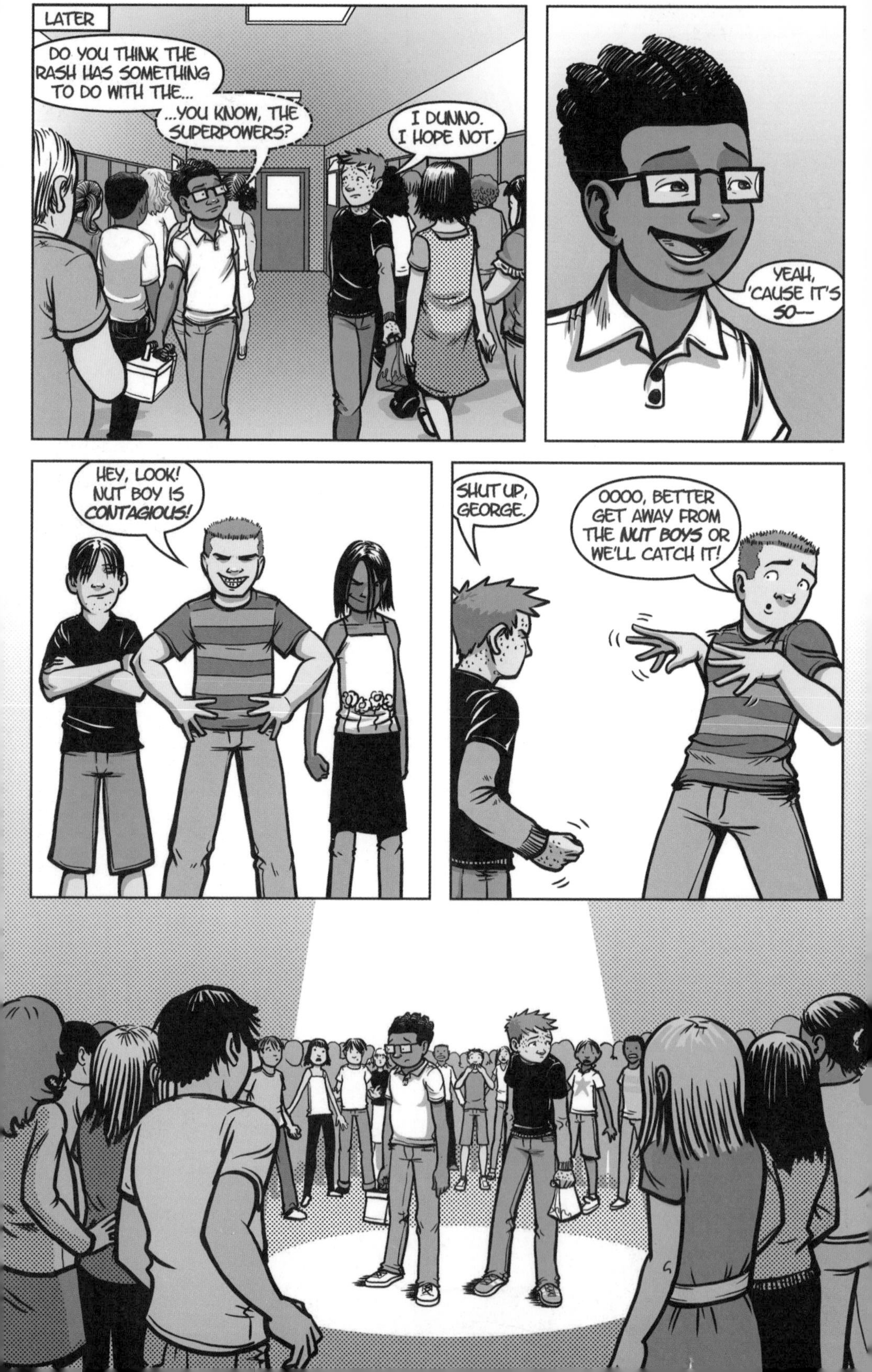
LATER
DO YOU THINK THE RASH HAS SOMETHING TO DO WITH THE...
...YOU KNOW, THE SUPERPOWERS?
I DUNNO. I HOPE NOT.
YEAH, 'CAUSE IT'S SO--
HEY, LOOK! NUT BOY IS CONTAGIOUS!
SHUT UP, GEORGE.
OOOO, BETTER GET AWAY FROM THE NUT BOYS OR WE'LL CATCH IT!

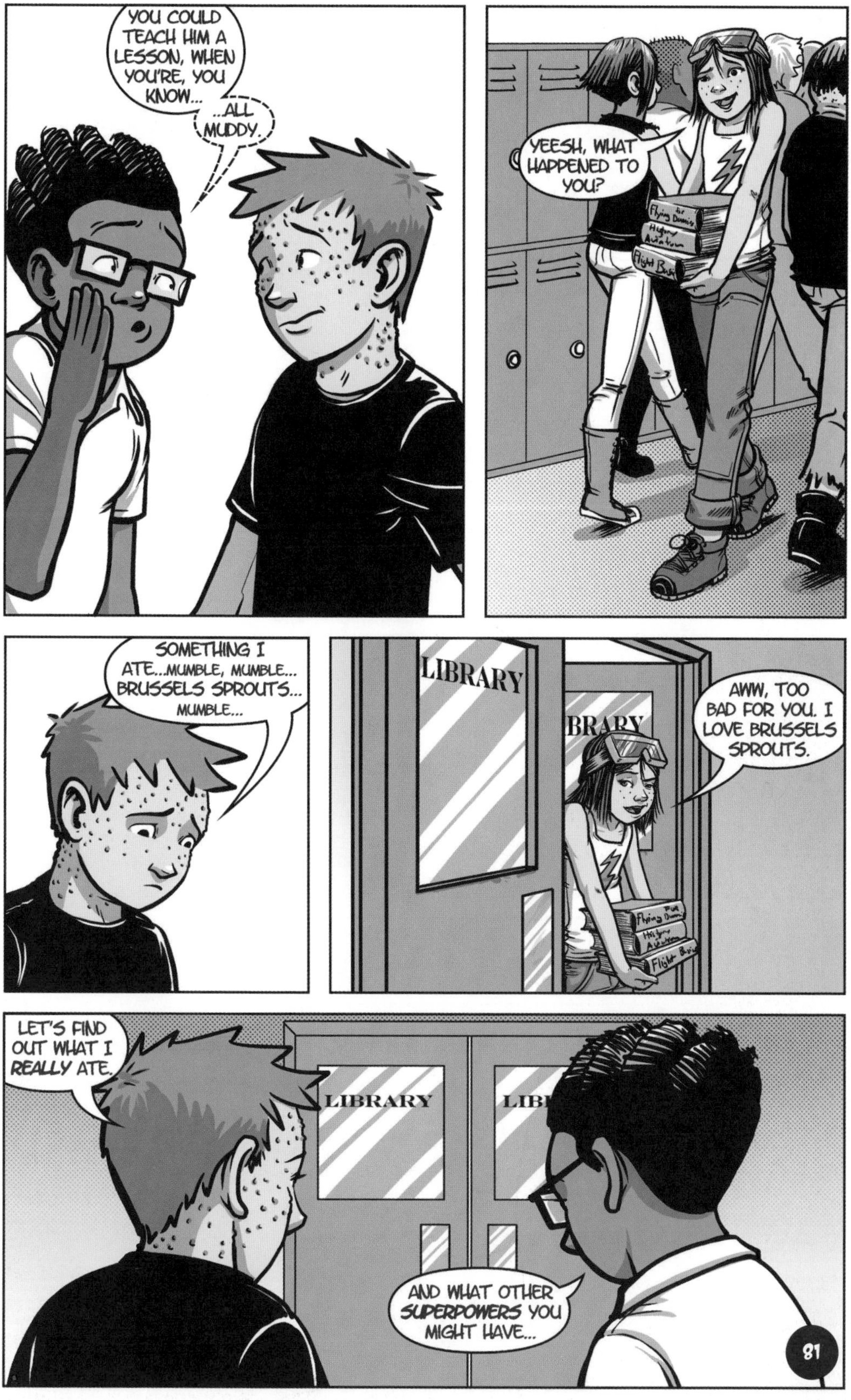
YOU COULD TEACH HIM A LESSON, WHEN YOU'RE, YOU KNOW...
...ALL MUDDY.
YEESH, WHAT HAPPENED TO YOU?
SOMETHING I ATE...MUMBLE, MUMBLE... BRUSSELS SPROUTS... MUMBLE...
LIBRARY
AWW, TOO BAD FOR YOU. I LOVE BRUSSELS SPROUTS.
LET'S FIND OUT WHAT I *REALLY* ATE.
LIBRARY
AND WHAT OTHER *SUPERPOWERS* YOU MIGHT HAVE...

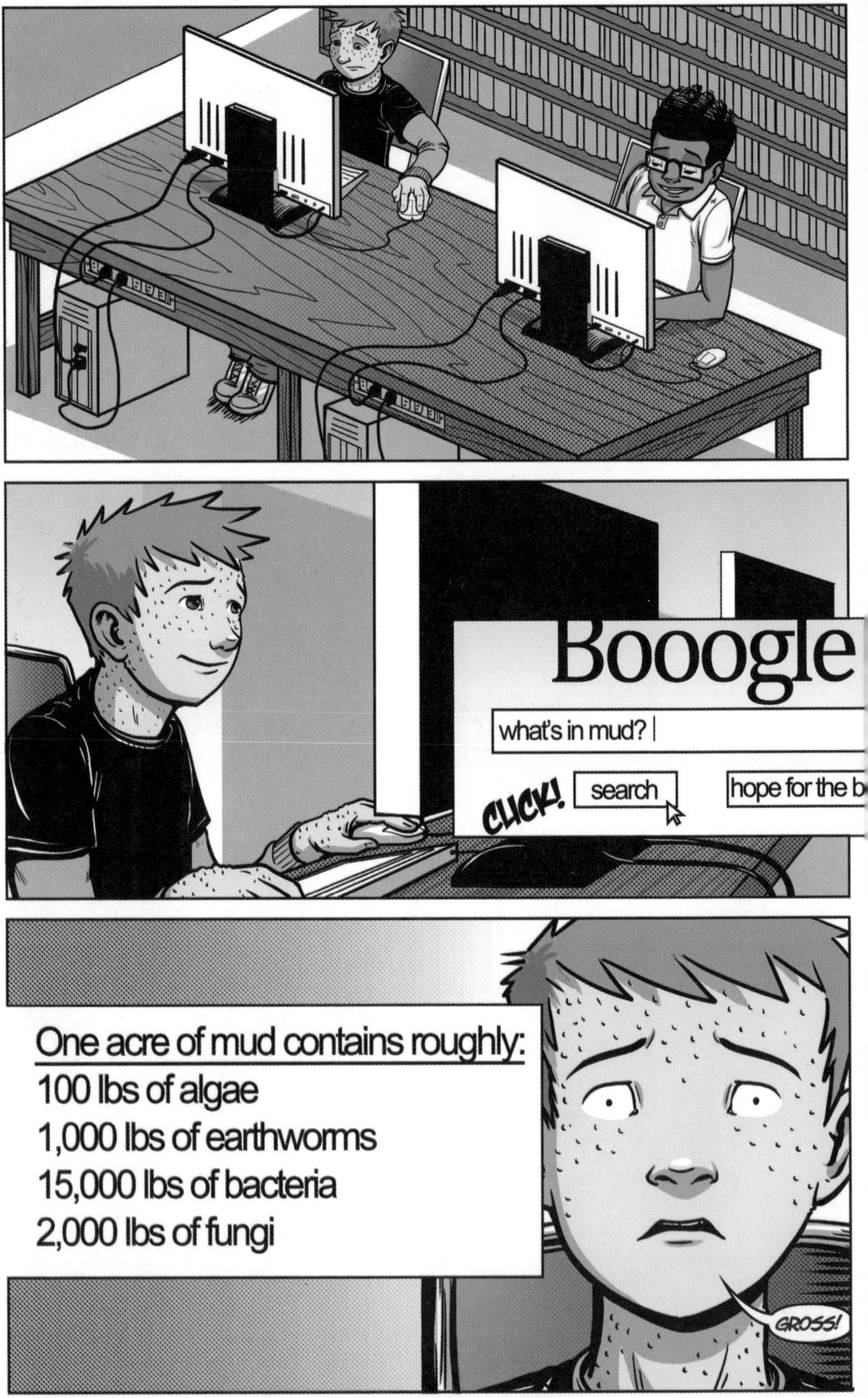

Booogle
what's in mud?
CLICK!
search
hope for the b
One acre of mud contains roughly:
100 lbs of algae
1,000 lbs of earthworms
15,000 lbs of bacteria
2,000 lbs of fungi
GROSS!

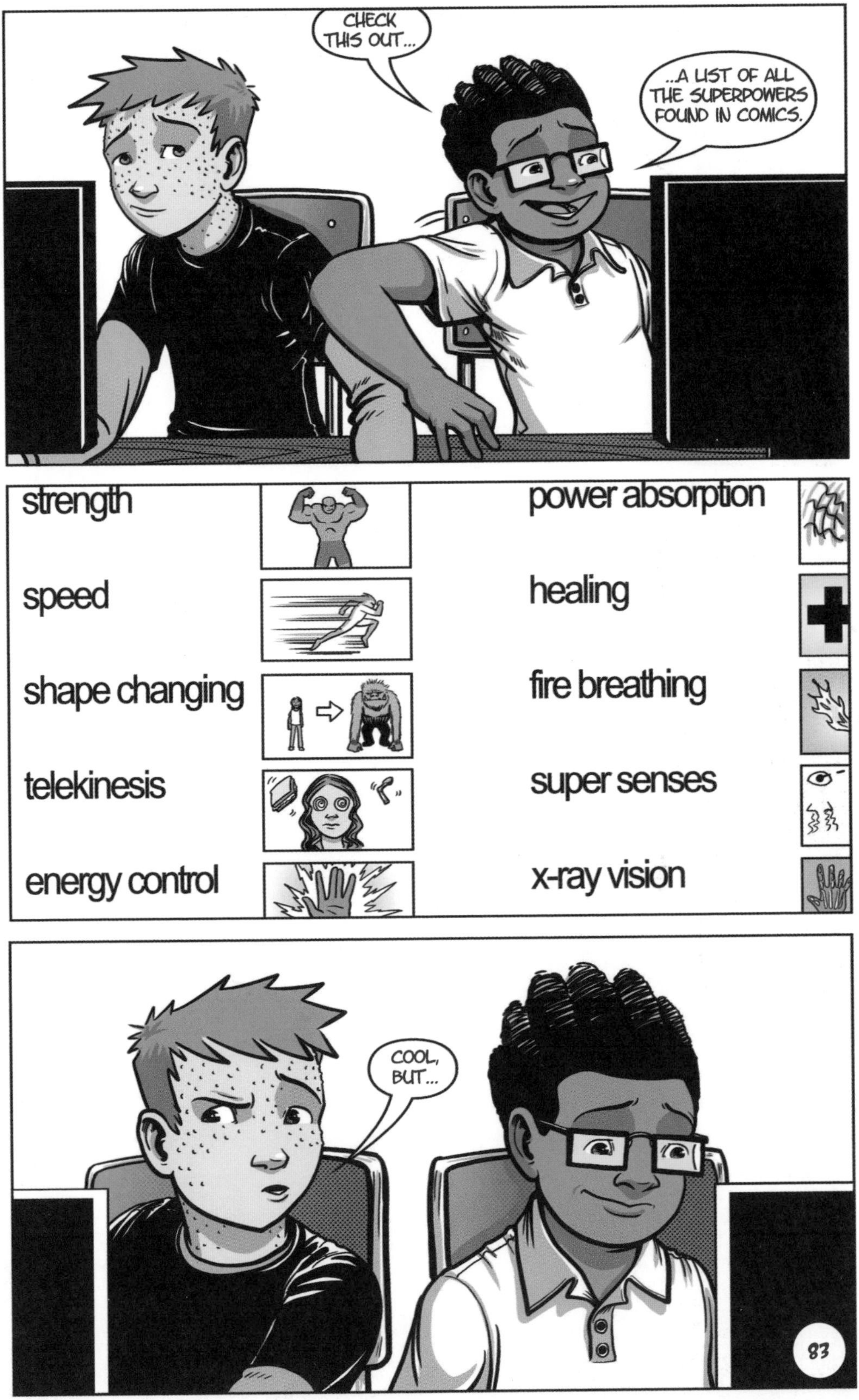
CHECK THIS OUT...
...A LIST OF ALL THE SUPERPOWERS FOUND IN COMICS.
strength
speed
shape changing
telekinesis
energy control
power absorption
healing
fire breathing
super senses
x-ray vision
COOL, BUT...

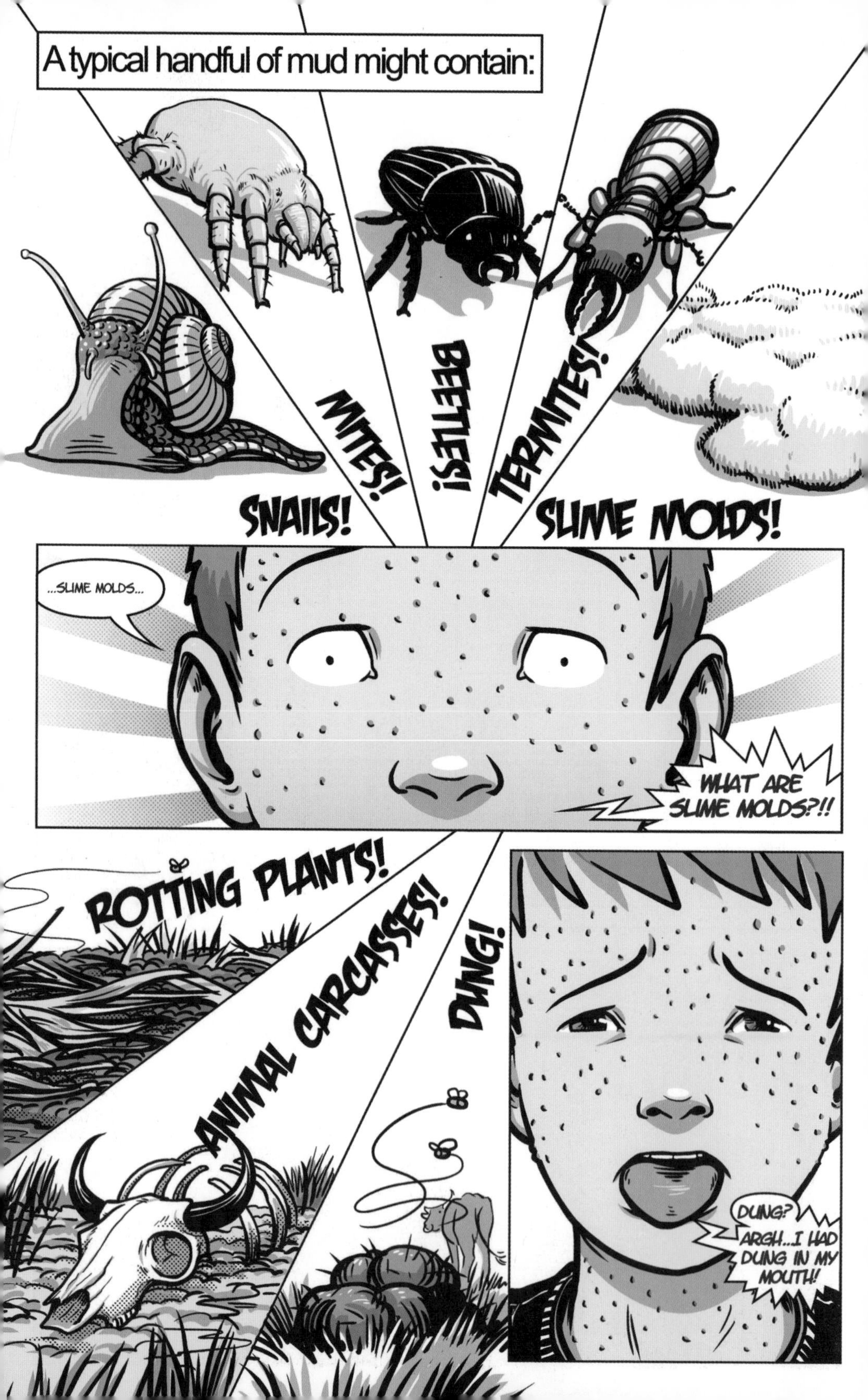
A typical handful of mud might contain:
SNAILS!
MITES!
BEETLES!
TERMITES!
SLIME MOLDS!
...SLIME MOLDS...
WHAT ARE SLIME MOLDS?!!
ROTTING PLANTS!
ANIMAL CARCASSES!
DUNG!
DUNG?
ARGH...I HAD DUNG IN MY MOUTH!

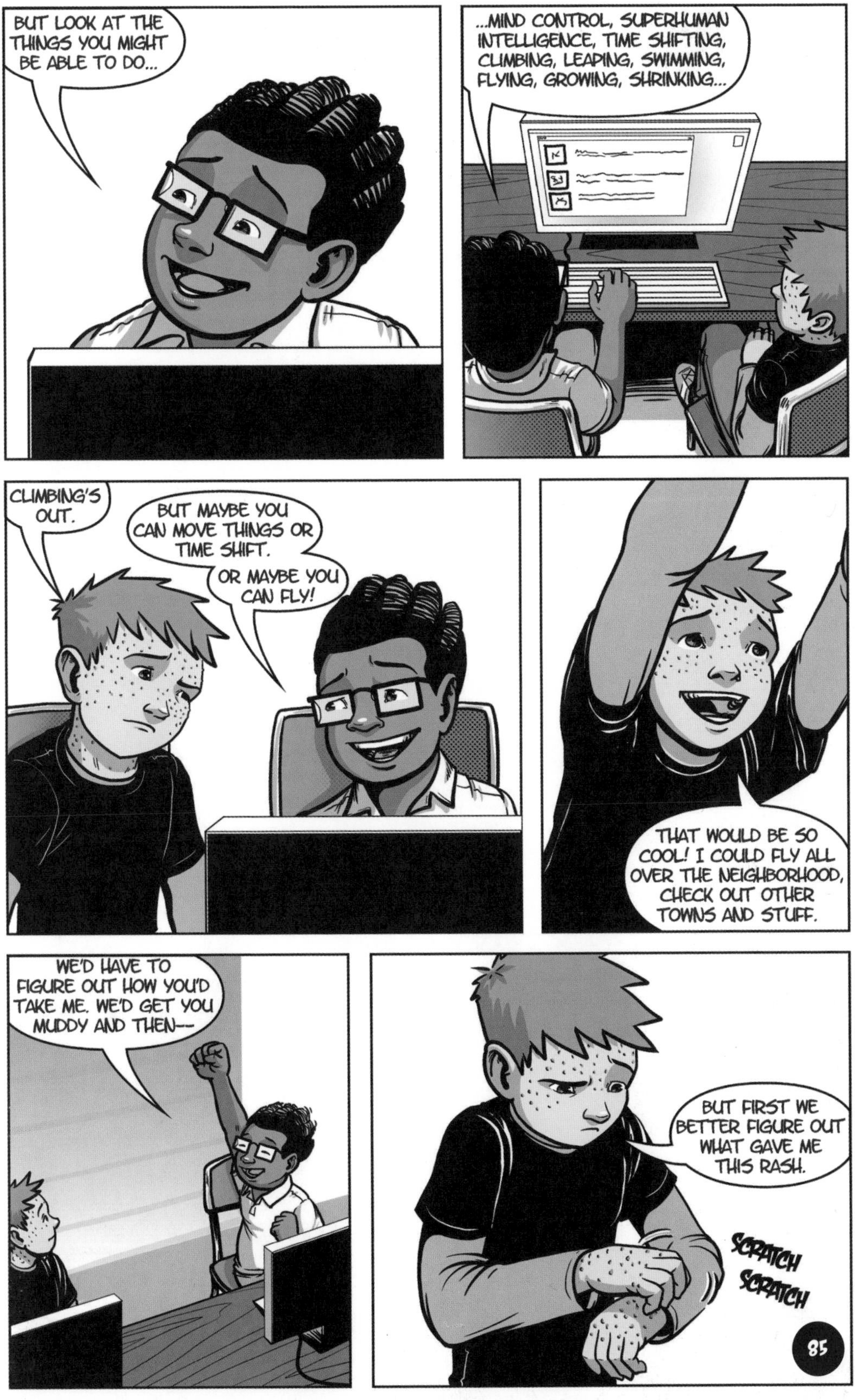
BUT LOOK AT THE THINGS YOU MIGHT BE ABLE TO DO...
...MIND CONTROL, SUPERHUMAN INTELLIGENCE, TIME SHIFTING, CLIMBING, LEAPING, SWIMMING, FLYING, GROWING, SHRINKING...
CLIMBING'S OUT.
BUT MAYBE YOU CAN MOVE THINGS OR TIME SHIFT.
OR MAYBE YOU CAN FLY!
THAT WOULD BE SO COOL! I COULD FLY ALL OVER THE NEIGHBORHOOD, CHECK OUT OTHER TOWNS AND STUFF.
WE'D HAVE TO FIGURE OUT HOW YOU'D TAKE ME. WE'D GET YOU MUDDY AND THEN--
BUT FIRST WE BETTER FIGURE OUT WHAT GAVE ME THIS RASH.
SCRATCH
SCRATCH

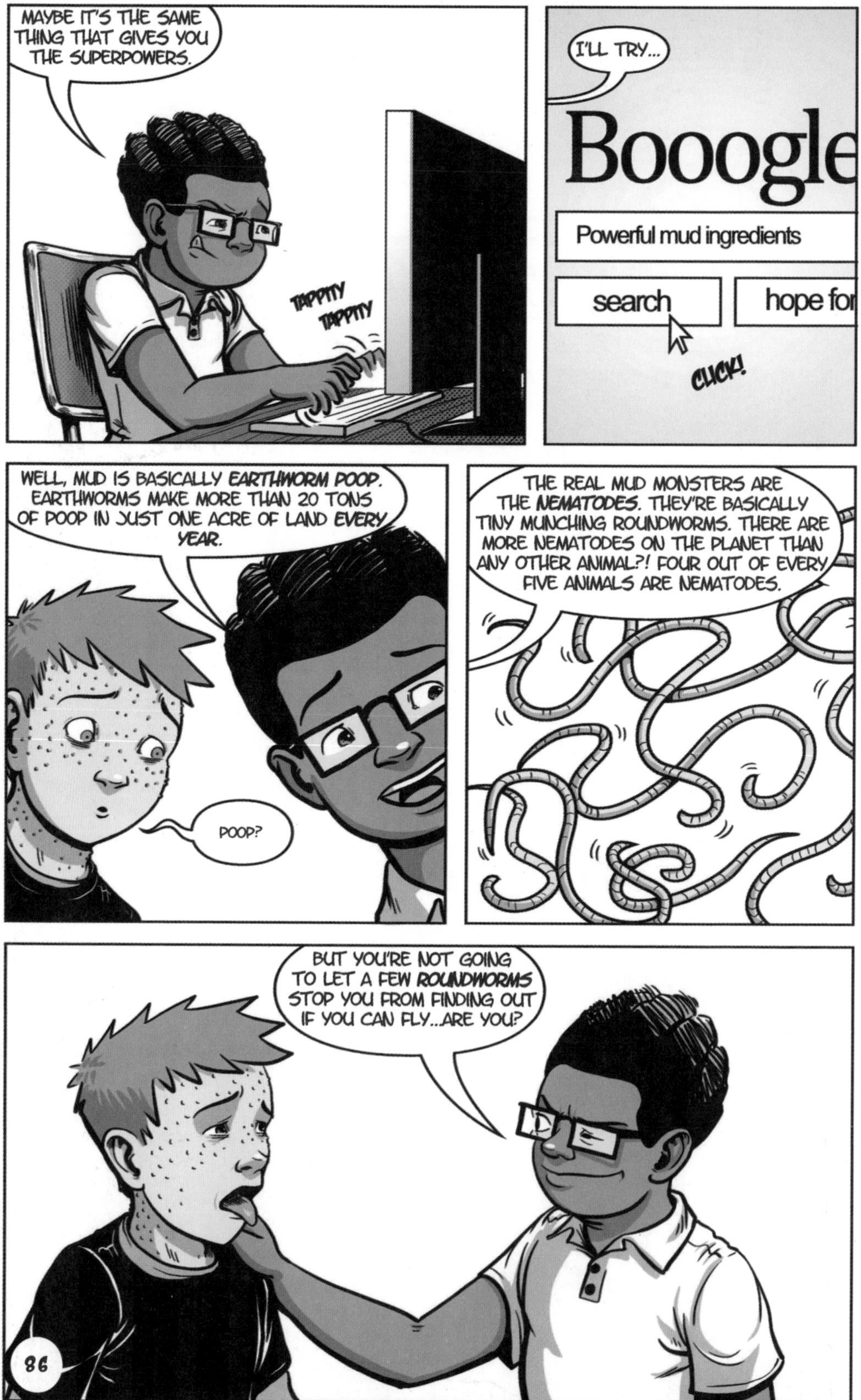
MAYBE IT'S THE SAME THING THAT GIVES YOU THE SUPERPOWERS.
TAPPITY TAPPITY
I'LL TRY...
Booogle
Powerful mud ingredients
search
hope for
CLICK!
WELL, MUD IS BASICALLY EARTHWORM POOP. EARTHWORMS MAKE MORE THAN 20 TONS OF POOP IN JUST ONE ACRE OF LAND EVERY YEAR.
POOP?
THE REAL MUD MONSTERS ARE THE NEMATODES. THEY'RE BASICALLY TINY MUNCHING ROUNDWORMS. THERE ARE MORE NEMATODES ON THE PLANET THAN ANY OTHER ANIMAL?! FOUR OUT OF EVERY FIVE ANIMALS ARE NEMATODES.
BUT YOU'RE NOT GOING TO LET A FEW ROUNDWORMS STOP YOU FROM FINDING OUT IF YOU CAN FLY...ARE YOU?

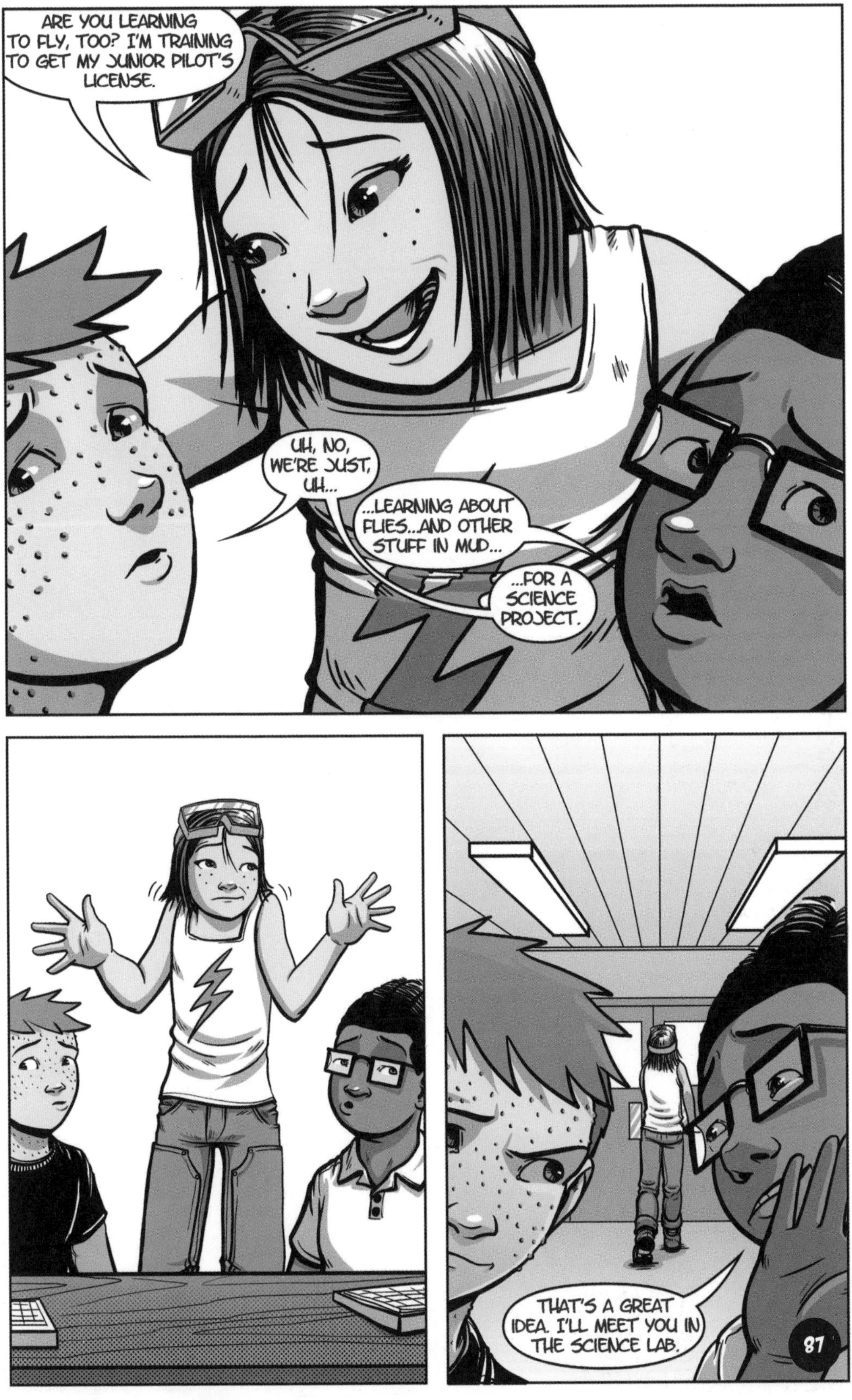
ARE YOU LEARNING TO FLY, TOO? I'M TRAINING TO GET MY JUNIOR PILOT'S LICENSE.
UH, NO, WE'RE JUST, UH...
...LEARNING ABOUT FLIES...AND OTHER STUFF IN MUD...
...FOR A SCIENCE PROJECT.
THAT'S A GREAT IDEA. I'LL MEET YOU IN THE SCIENCE LAB.

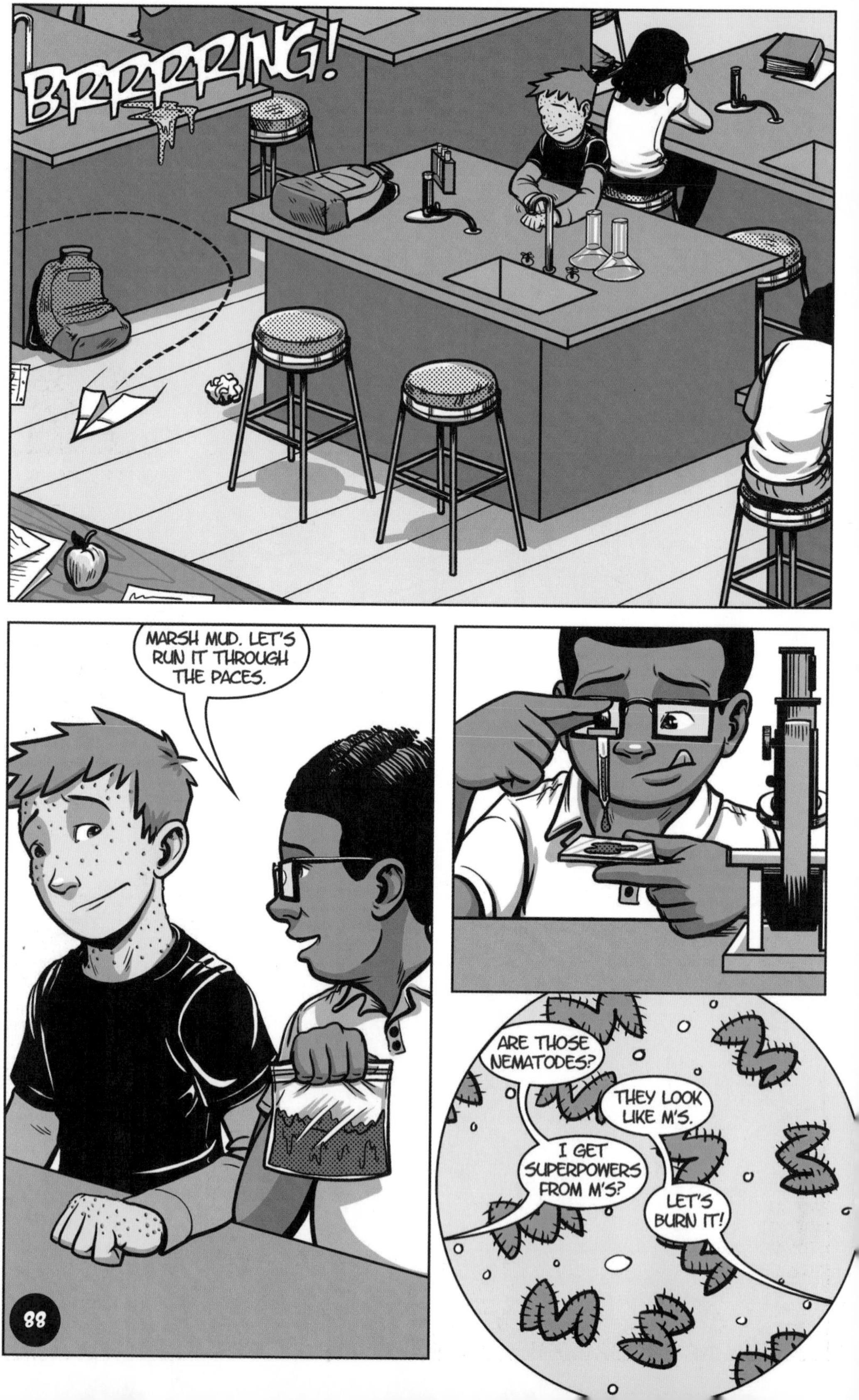
BRRRRING!
MARSH MUD. LET'S RUN IT THROUGH THE PACES.
ARE THOSE NEMATODES?
THEY LOOK LIKE M'S.
I GET SUPERPOWERS FROM M'S?
LET'S BURN IT!

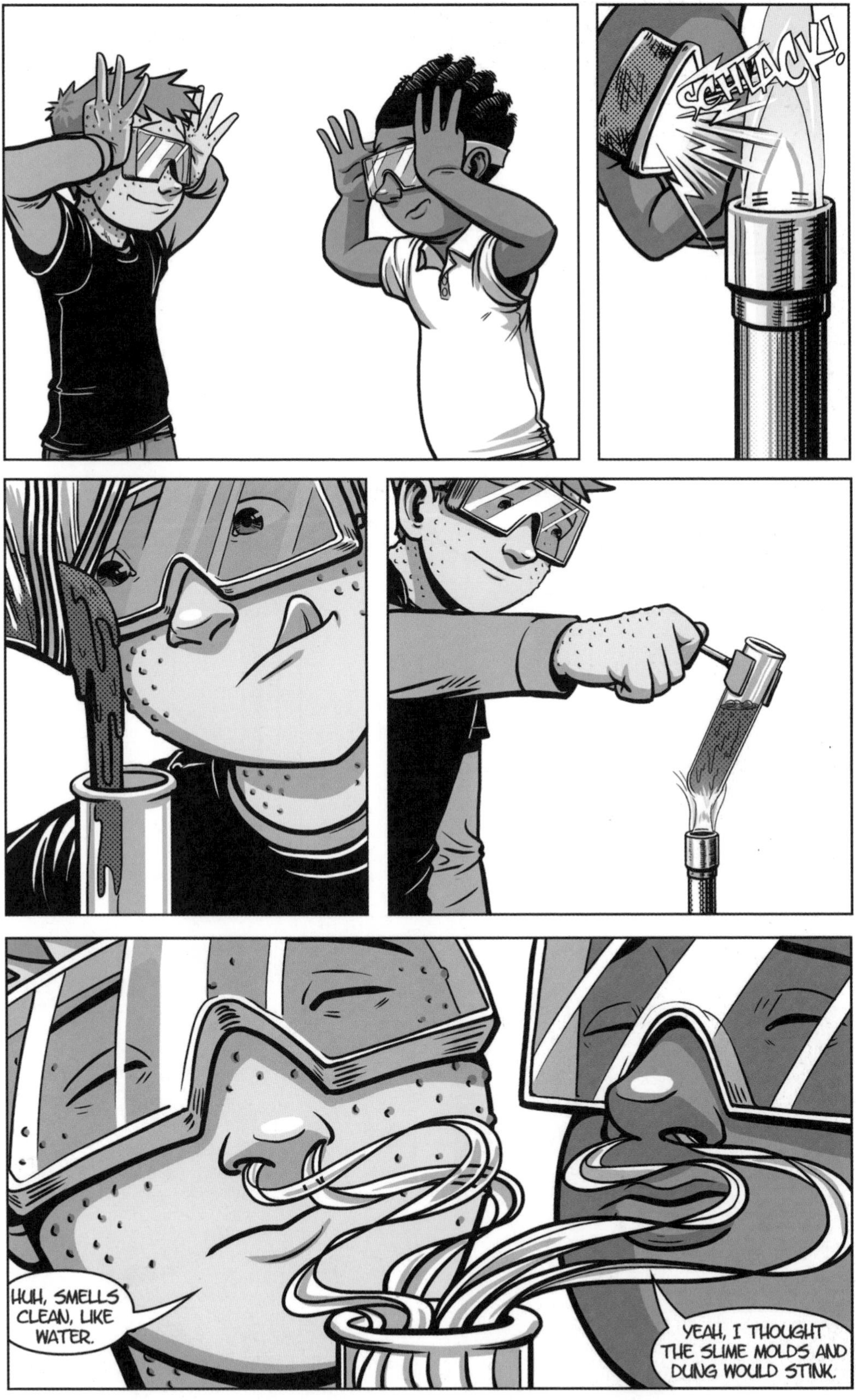
SCHLACK!
HUH, SMELLS CLEAN, LIKE WATER.
YEAH, I THOUGHT THE SLIME MOLDS AND DUNG WOULD STINK.

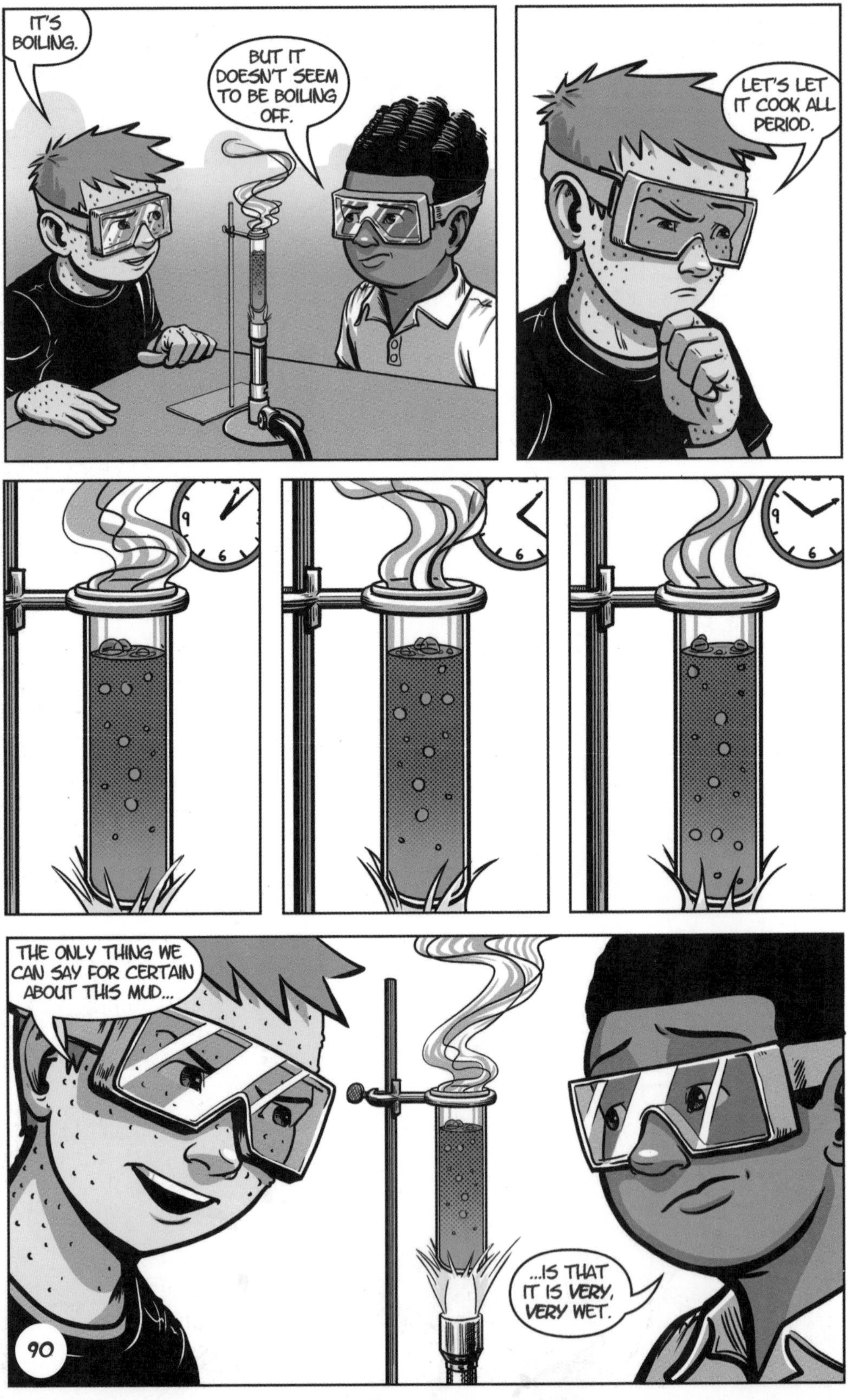
IT'S BOILING.
BUT IT DOESN'T SEEM TO BE BOILING OFF.
LET'S LET IT COOK ALL PERIOD.
THE ONLY THING WE CAN SAY FOR CERTAIN ABOUT THIS MUD...
...IS THAT IT IS VERY, VERY WET.

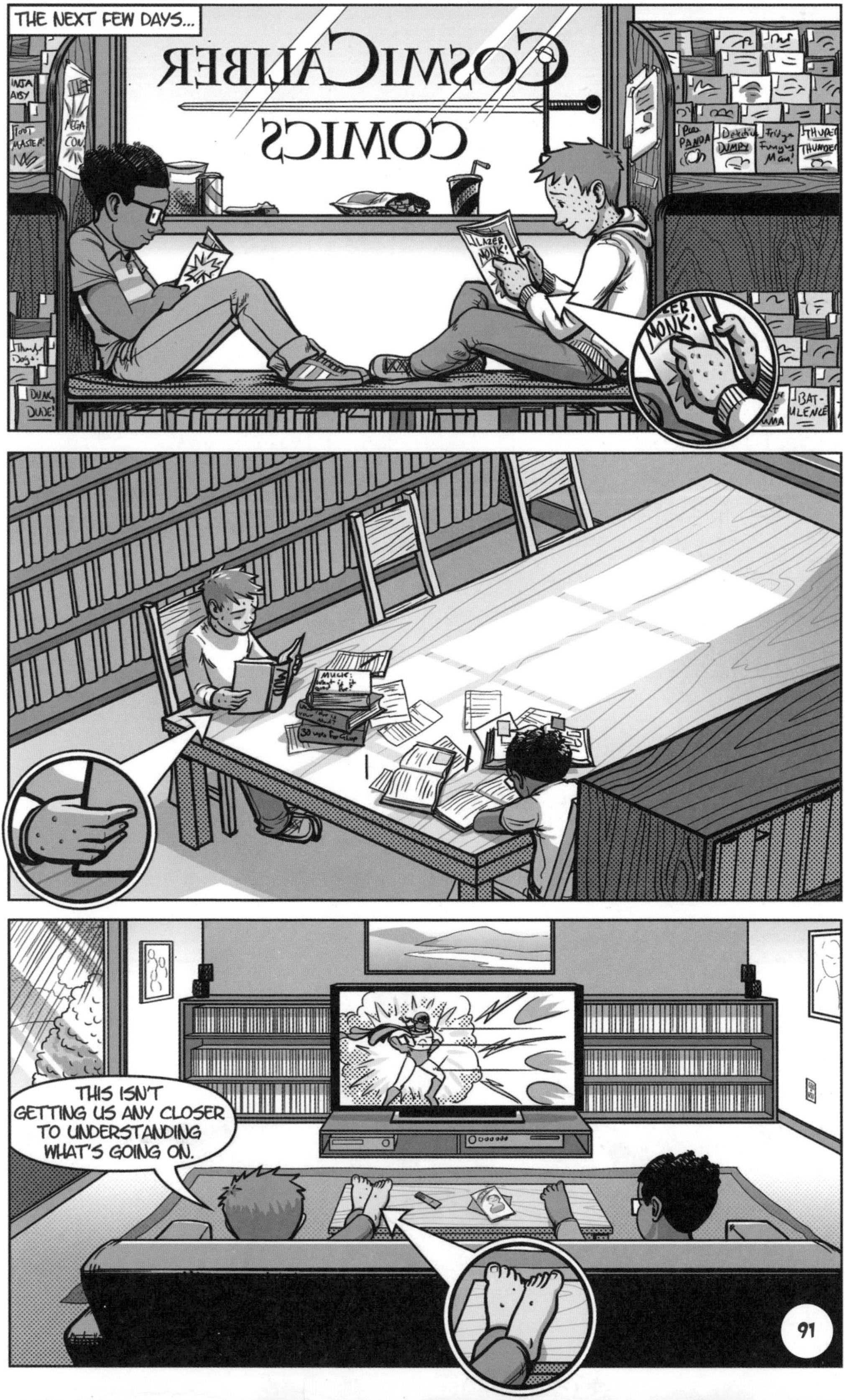
THE NEXT FEW DAYS...
COSMICALIBER COMICS
LAZER MONK!
THIS ISN'T GETTING US ANY CLOSER TO UNDERSTANDING WHAT'S GOING ON.

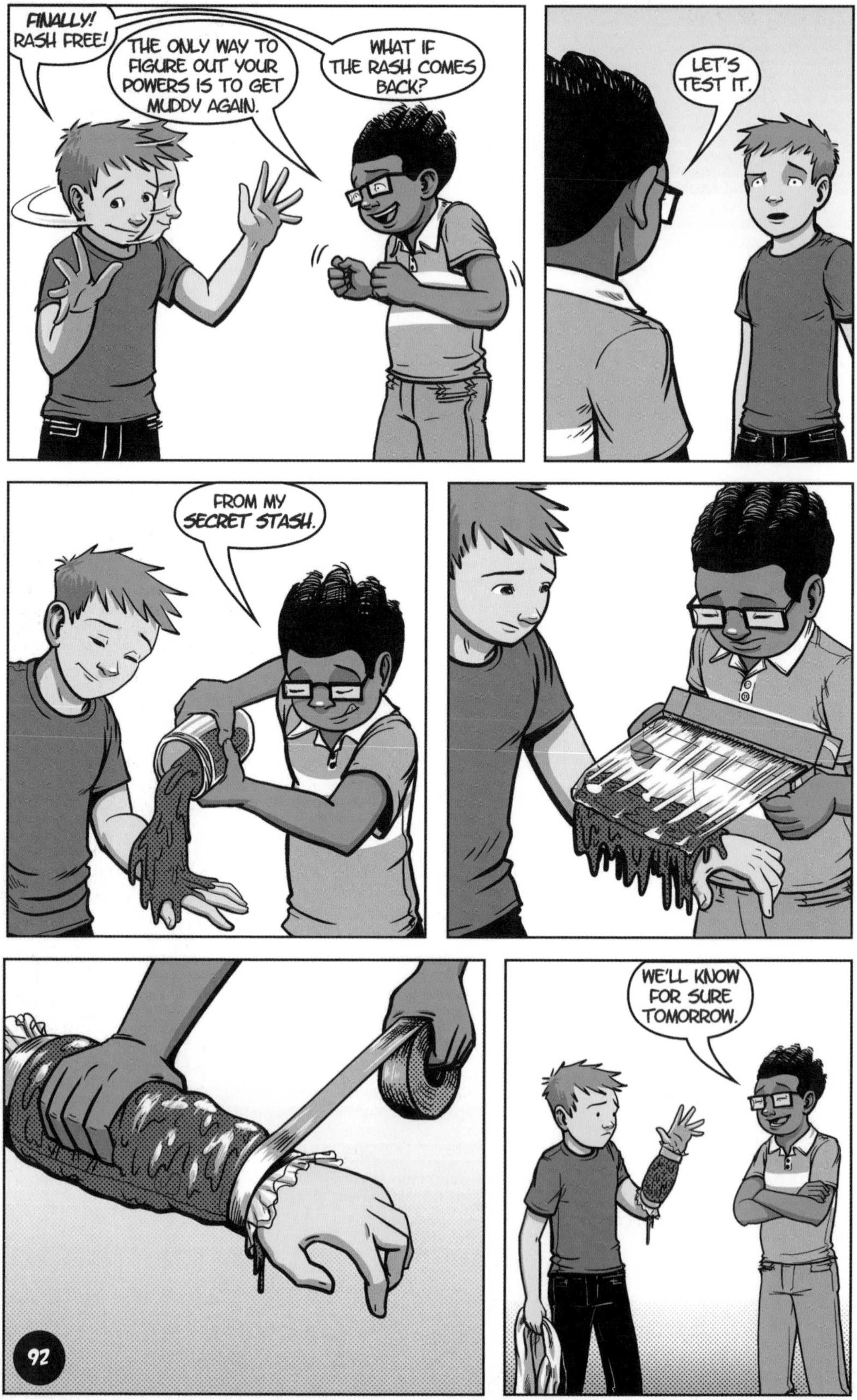
FINALLY! RASH FREE!
THE ONLY WAY TO FIGURE OUT YOUR POWERS IS TO GET MUDDY AGAIN.
WHAT IF THE RASH COMES BACK?
LET'S TEST IT.
FROM MY SECRET STASH.
WE'LL KNOW FOR SURE TOMORROW.

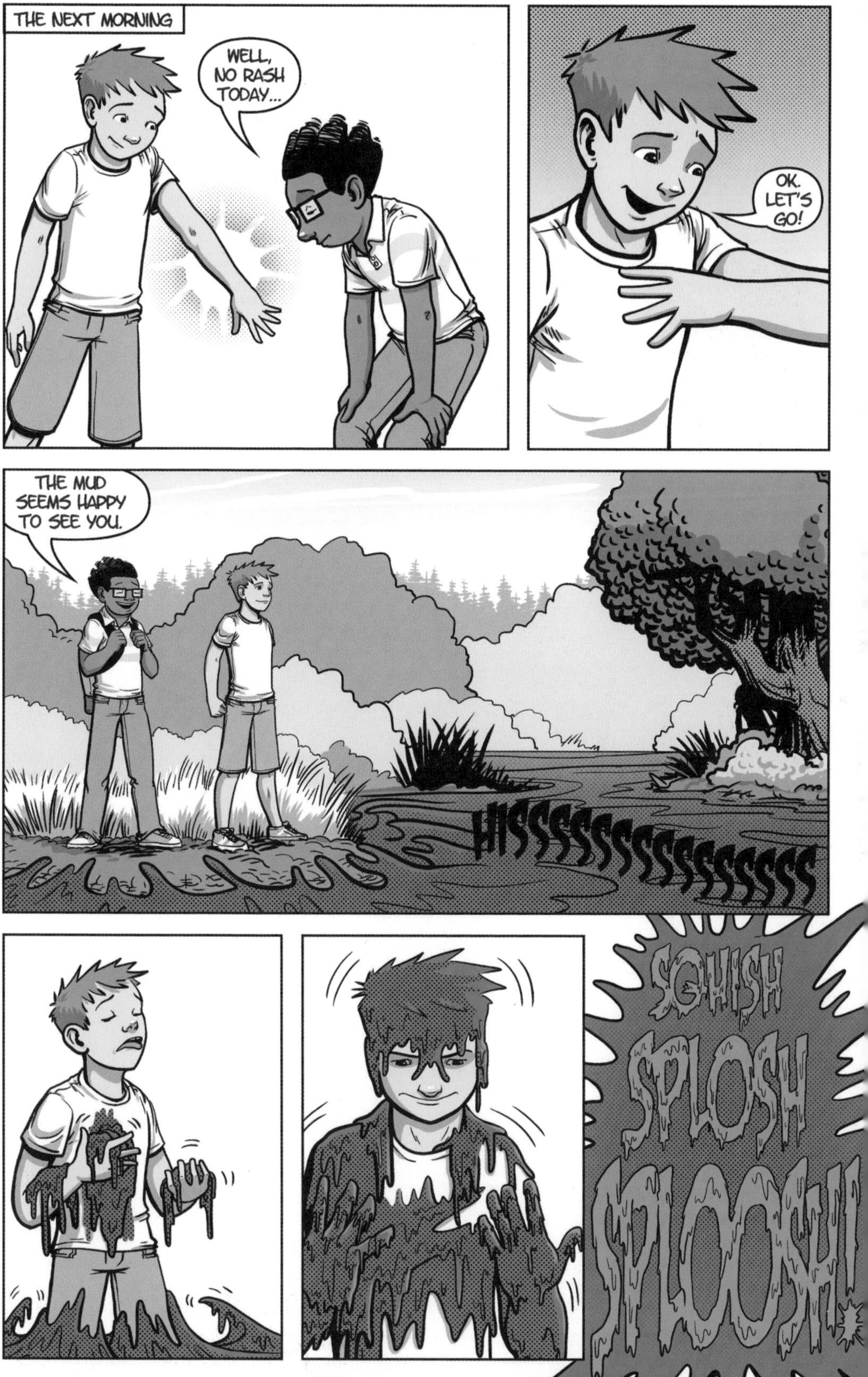
THE NEXT MORNING
WELL, NO RASH TODAY...
OK. LET'S GO!
THE MUD SEEMS HAPPY TO SEE YOU.
HISSSSSSSSSSSSSSSS
SQUISH
SPLOSH
SPLOOSH!

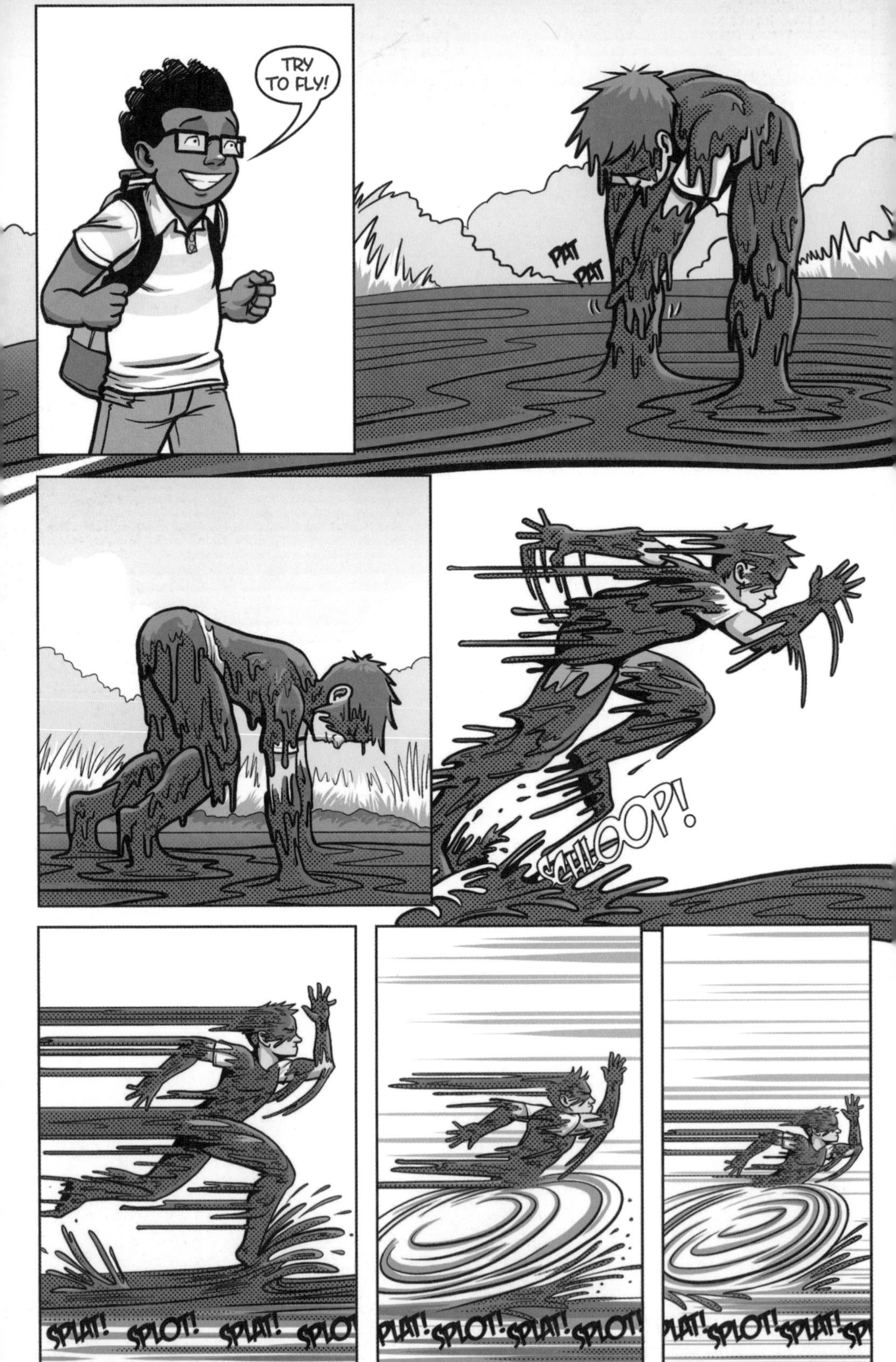
TRY TO FLY!
PAT
PAT
SHLOOP!
SPLAT! SPLOT! SPLAT! SPLOT
PLAT! SPLOT! SPLAT! SPLOT!
PLAT! SPLOT! SPLAT! SP

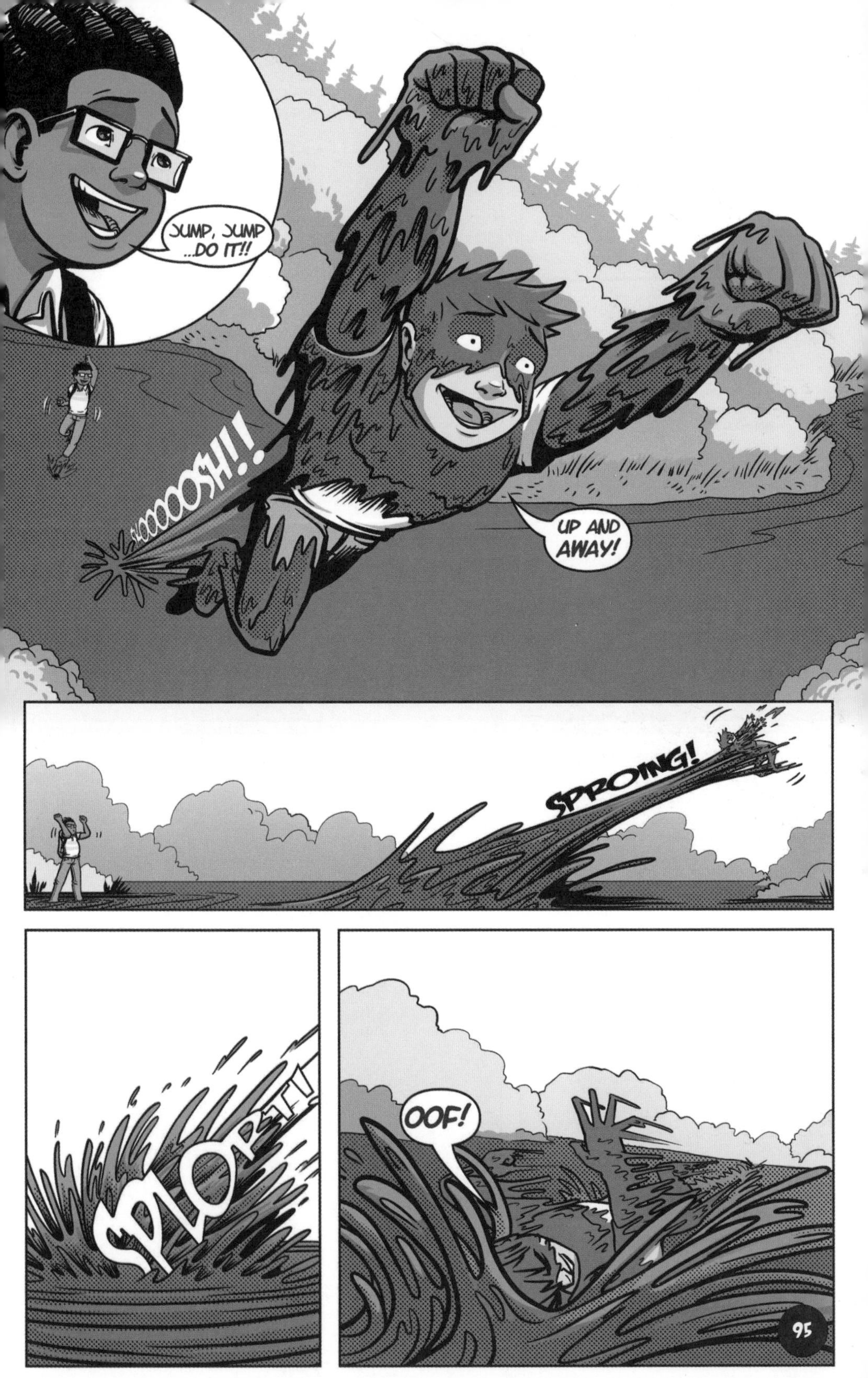
JUMP, JUMP ...DO IT!!
SHOOOOOOSH!!
UP AND AWAY!
SPROING!
OOF!

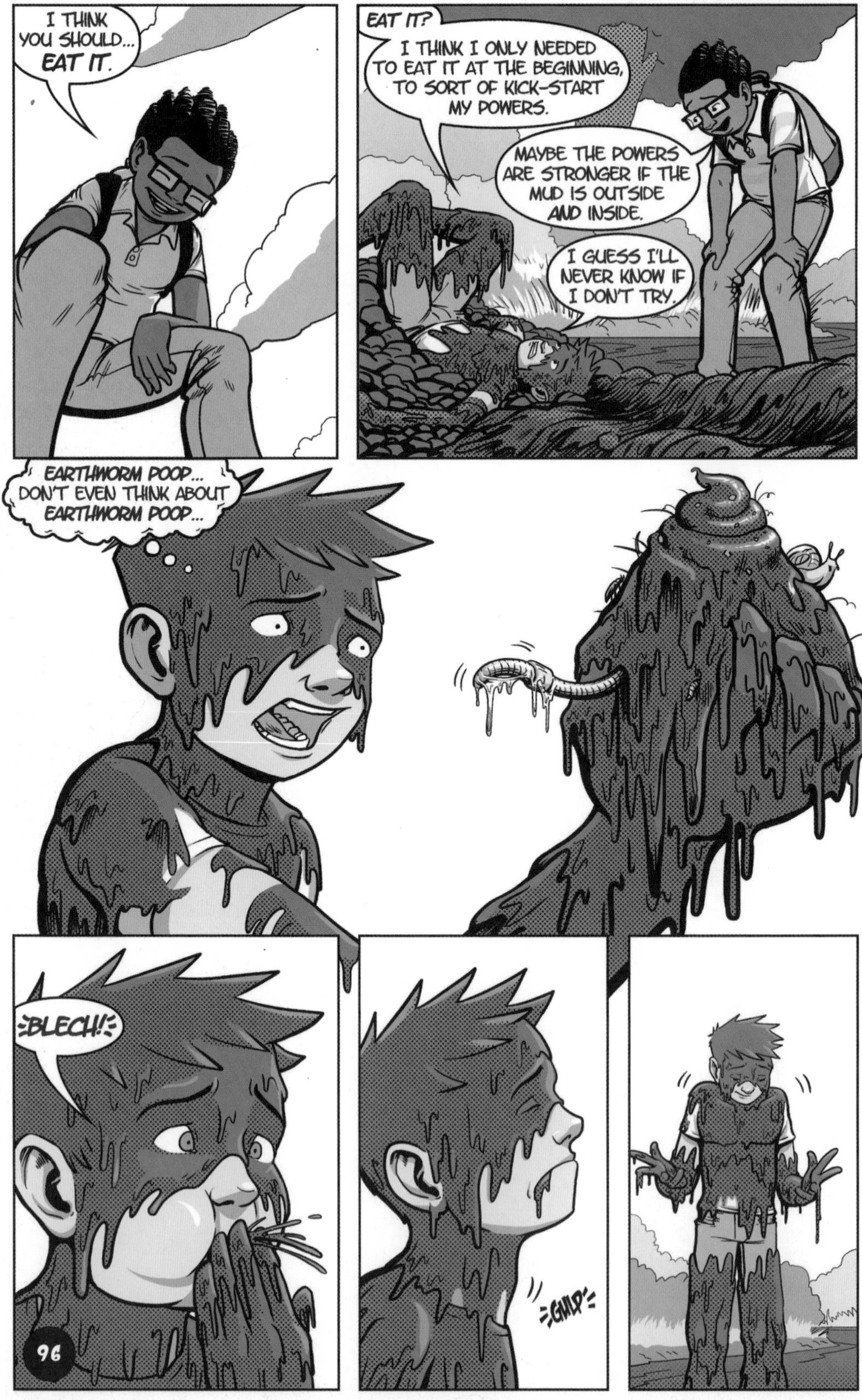
I THINK YOU SHOULD... EAT IT.
EAT IT?
I THINK I ONLY NEEDED TO EAT IT AT THE BEGINNING, TO SORT OF KICK-START MY POWERS.
MAYBE THE POWERS ARE STRONGER IF THE MUD IS OUTSIDE AND INSIDE.
I GUESS I'LL NEVER KNOW IF I DON'T TRY.
EARTHWORM POOP... DON'T EVEN THINK ABOUT EARTHWORM POOP...
BLECH!
GULP

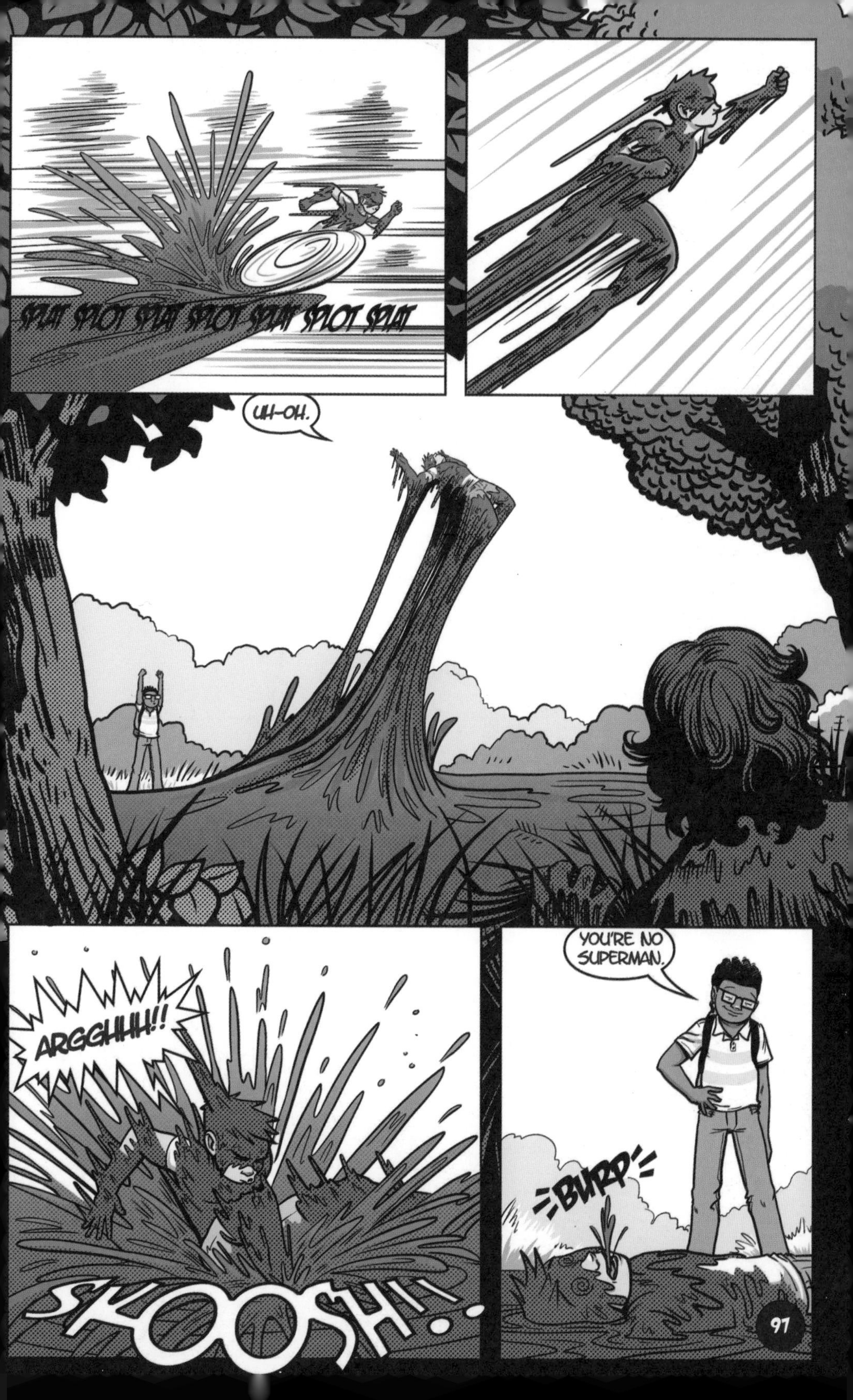
SPLAT SPLOT SPLAT SPLOT SPLAT SPLOT SPLAT
UH-OH.
ARGGHHH!!
SHOOSH!!
YOU'RE NO SUPERMAN.
BURP

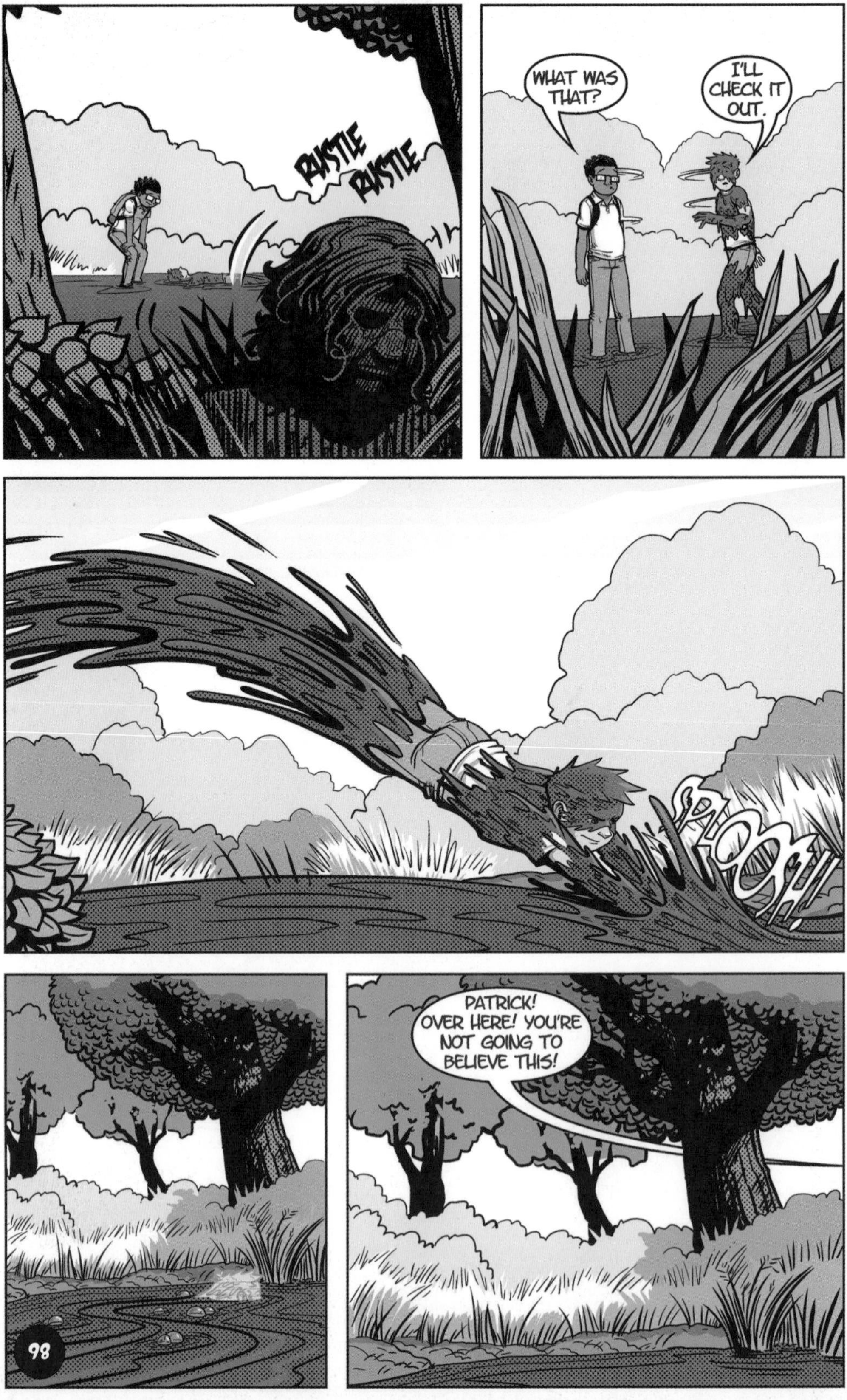
RUSTLE
RUSTLE
WHAT WAS THAT?
I'LL CHECK IT OUT.
SPLOOSH!
PATRICK! OVER HERE! YOU'RE NOT GOING TO BELIEVE THIS!

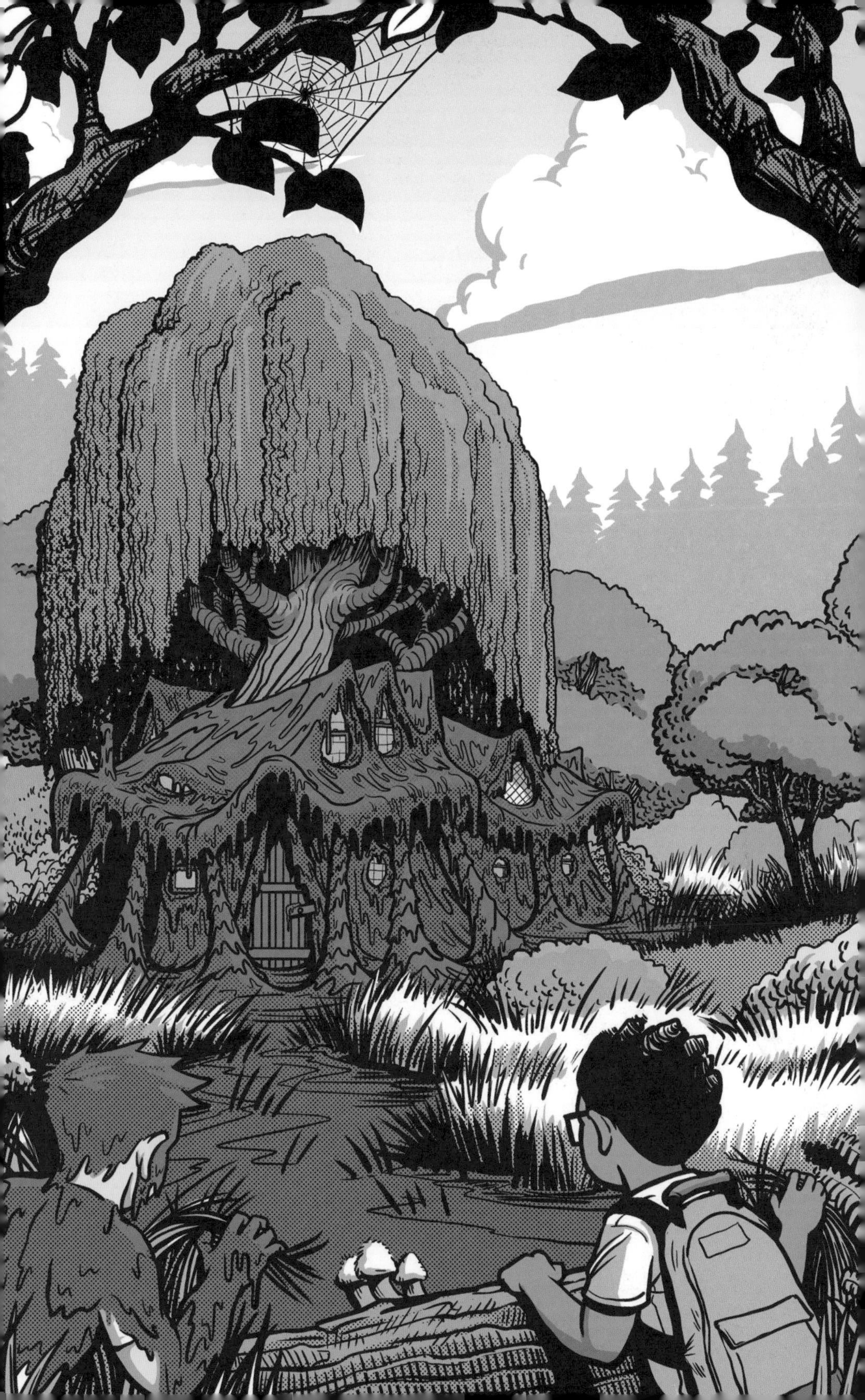

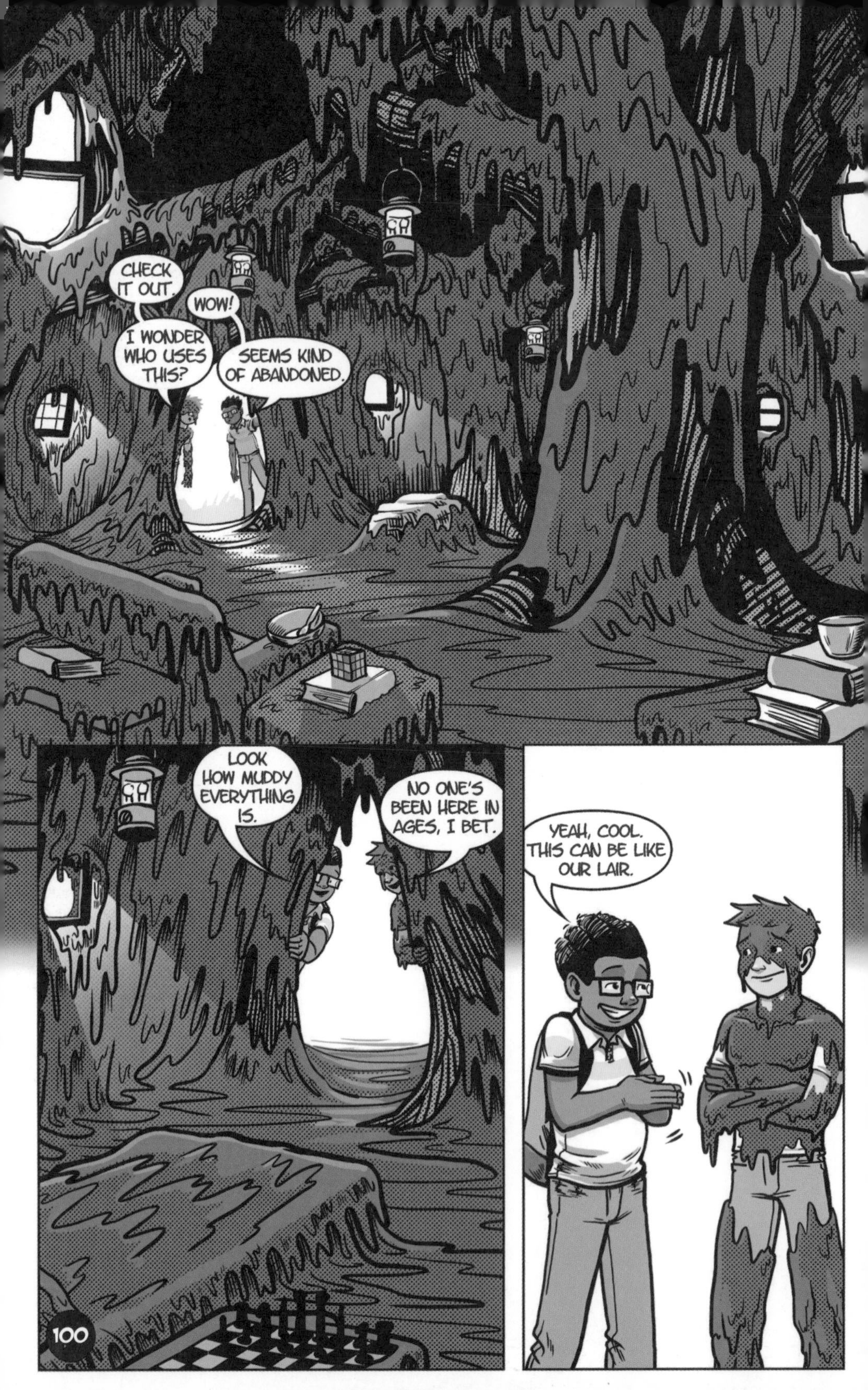
CHECK IT OUT.
WOW!
I WONDER WHO USES THIS?
SEEMS KIND OF ABANDONED.
LOOK HOW MUDDY EVERYTHING IS.
NO ONE'S BEEN HERE IN AGES, I BET.
YEAH, COOL. THIS CAN BE LIKE OUR LAIR.

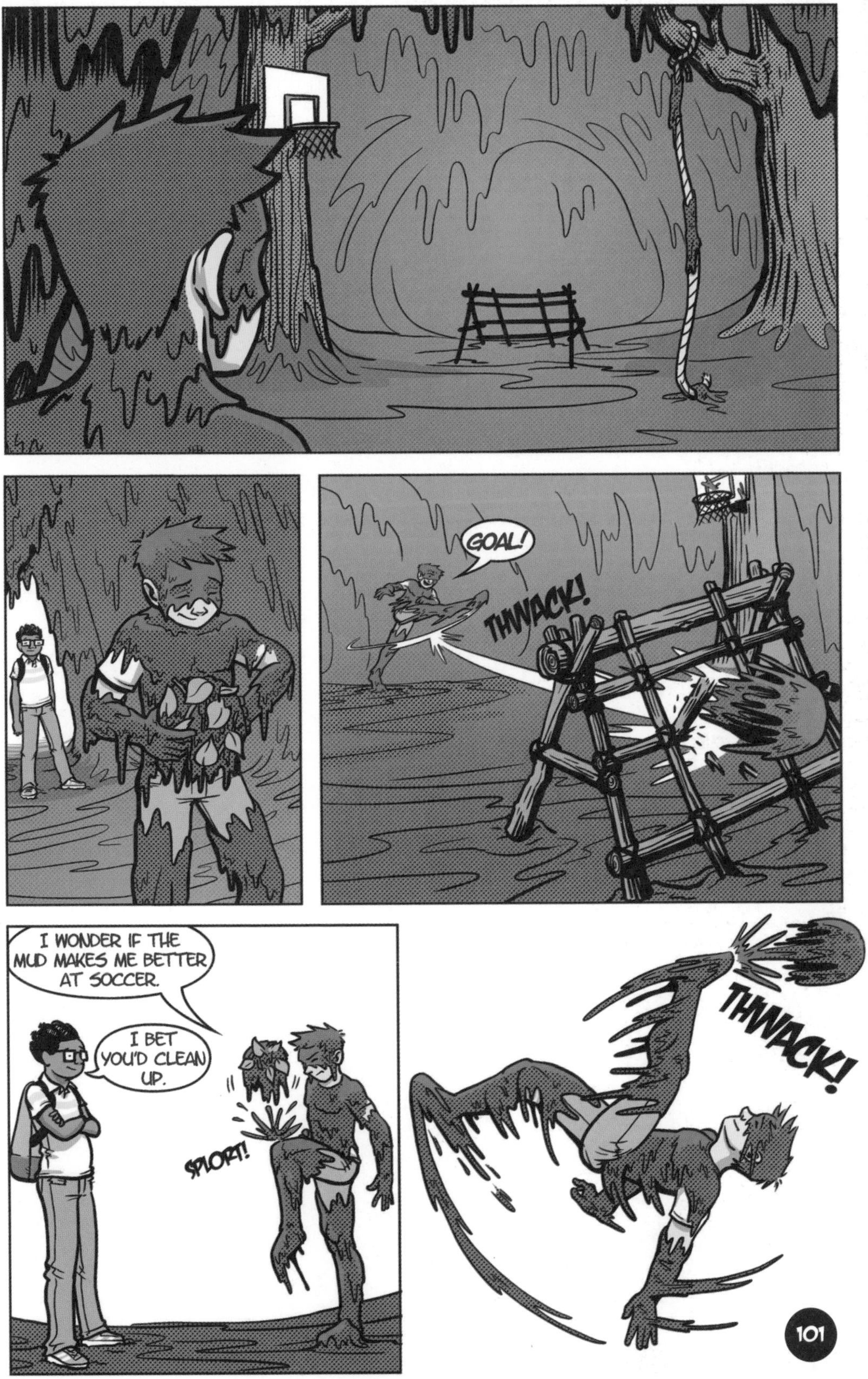
GOAL!
THWACK!
I WONDER IF THE MUD MAKES ME BETTER AT SOCCER.
I BET YOU'D CLEAN UP.
SPLORT!
THWACK!

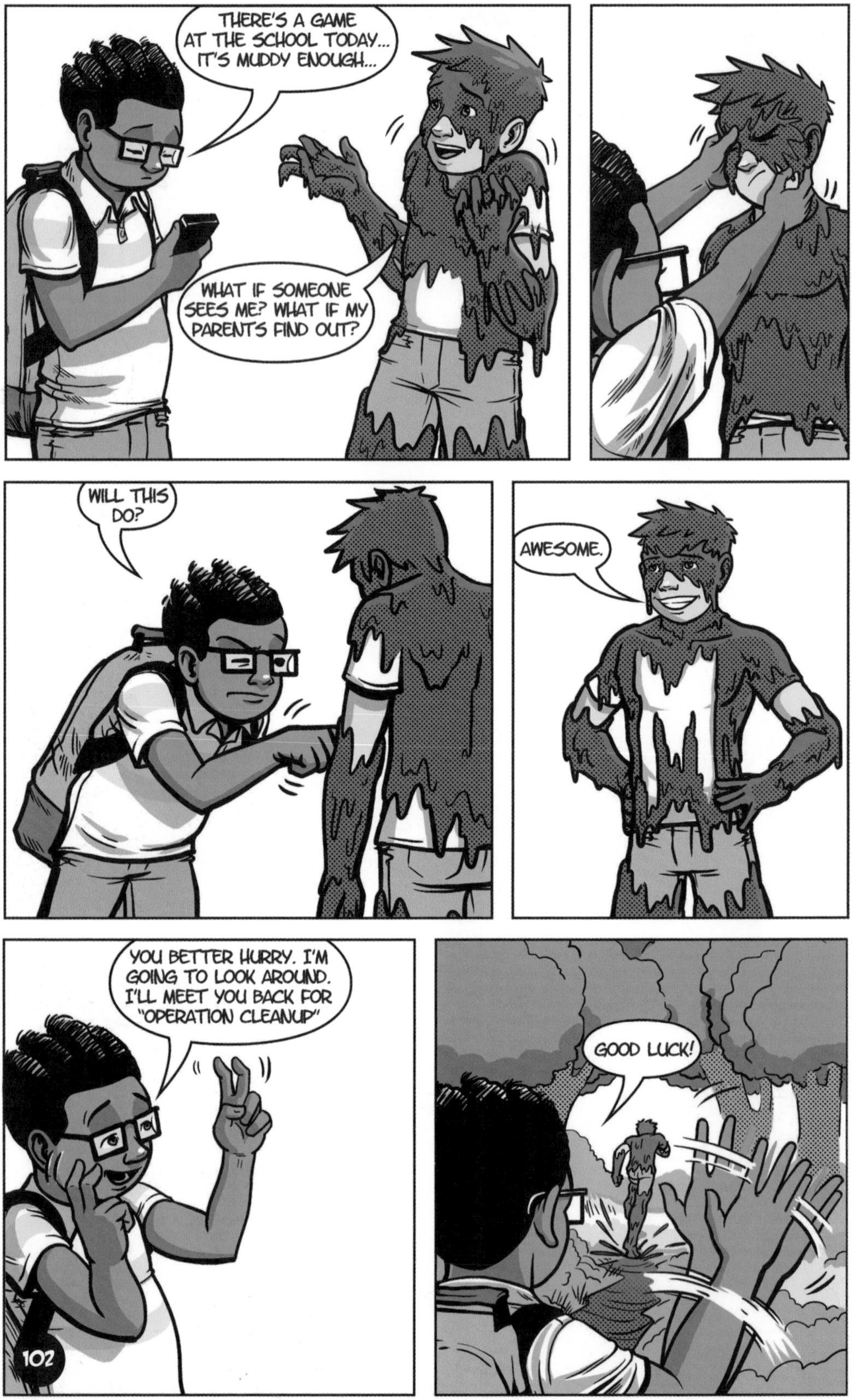
THERE'S A GAME AT THE SCHOOL TODAY... IT'S MUDDY ENOUGH...
WHAT IF SOMEONE SEES ME? WHAT IF MY PARENTS FIND OUT?
WILL THIS DO?
AWESOME.
YOU BETTER HURRY. I'M GOING TO LOOK AROUND. I'LL MEET YOU BACK FOR "OPERATION CLEANUP"
GOOD LUCK!

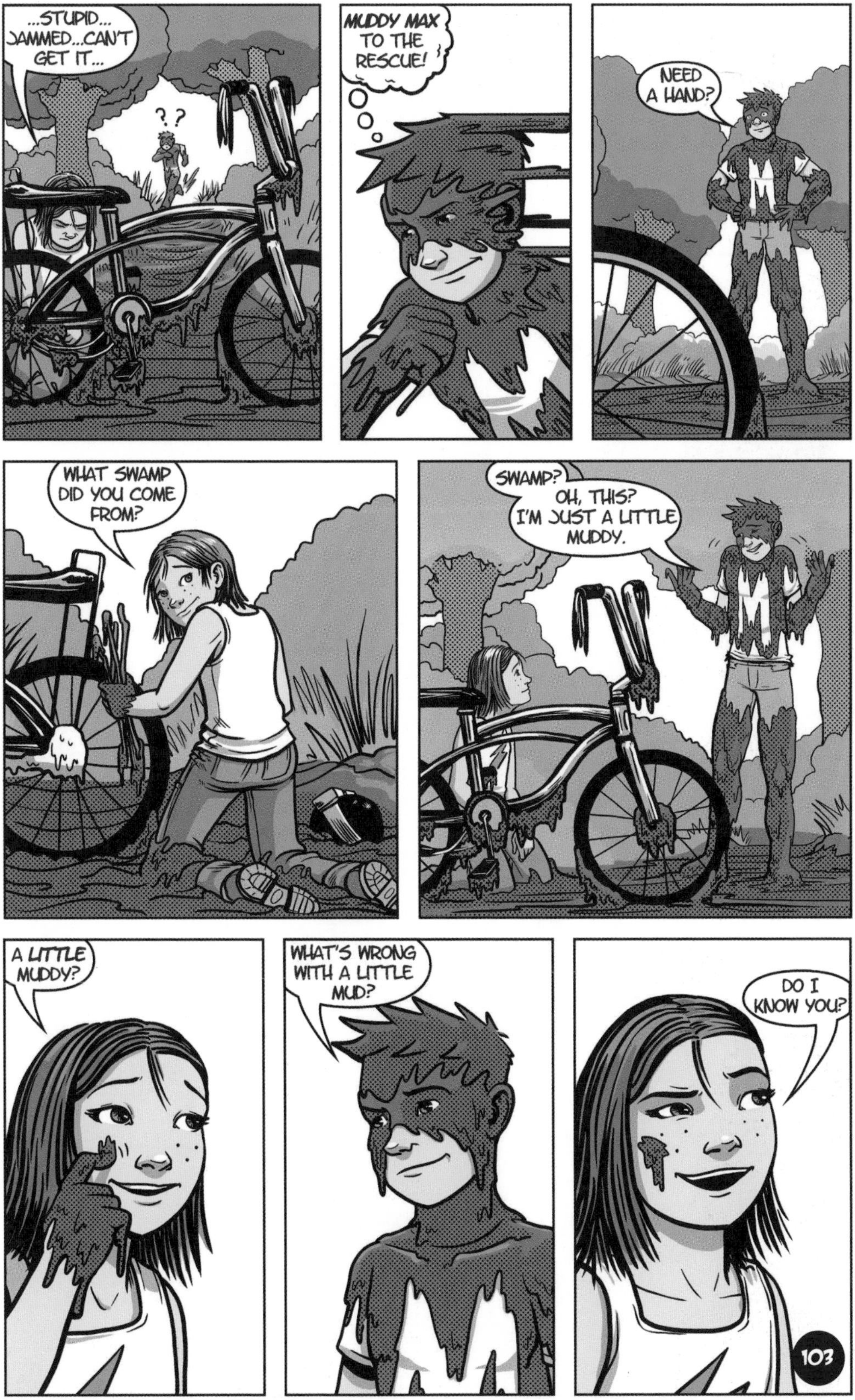

...STUPID... JAMMED...CAN'T GET IT...
? ?
MUDDY MAX TO THE RESCUE!
NEED A HAND?
WHAT SWAMP DID YOU COME FROM?
SWAMP?
OH, THIS? I'M JUST A LITTLE MUDDY.
A LITTLE MUDDY?
WHAT'S WRONG WITH A LITTLE MUD?
DO I KNOW YOU?

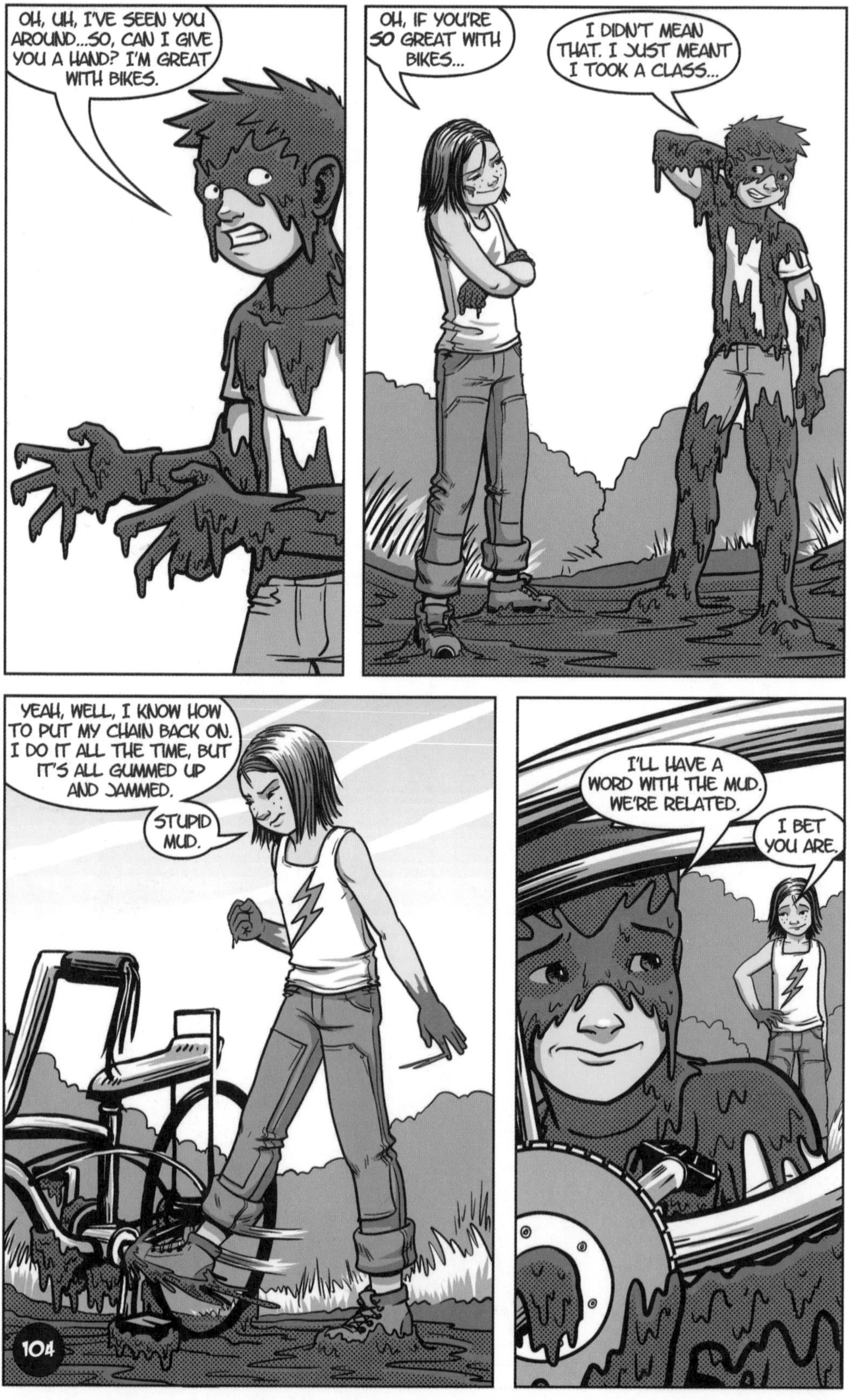
OH, UH, I'VE SEEN YOU AROUND...SO, CAN I GIVE YOU A HAND? I'M GREAT WITH BIKES.
OH, IF YOU'RE SO GREAT WITH BIKES...
I DIDN'T MEAN THAT. I JUST MEANT I TOOK A CLASS...
YEAH, WELL, I KNOW HOW TO PUT MY CHAIN BACK ON. I DO IT ALL THE TIME, BUT IT'S ALL GUMMED UP AND JAMMED.
STUPID MUD.
I'LL HAVE A WORD WITH THE MUD. WE'RE RELATED.
I BET YOU ARE.

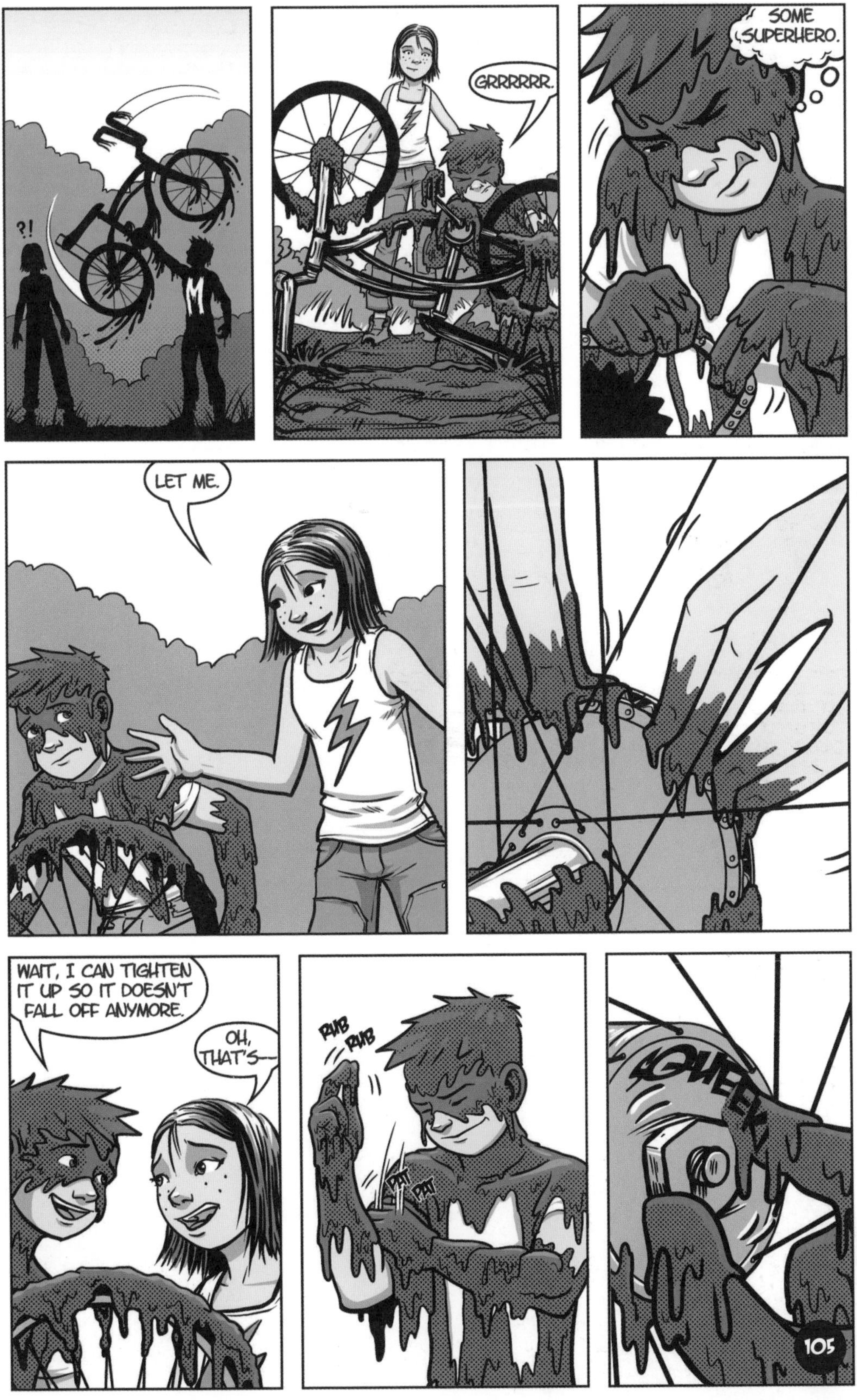
?!
GRRRRRR.
SOME SUPERHERO.
LET ME.
WAIT, I CAN TIGHTEN IT UP SO IT DOESN'T FALL OFF ANYMORE.
OH, THAT'S--
RUB RUB
PAT PAT
SQUEEK

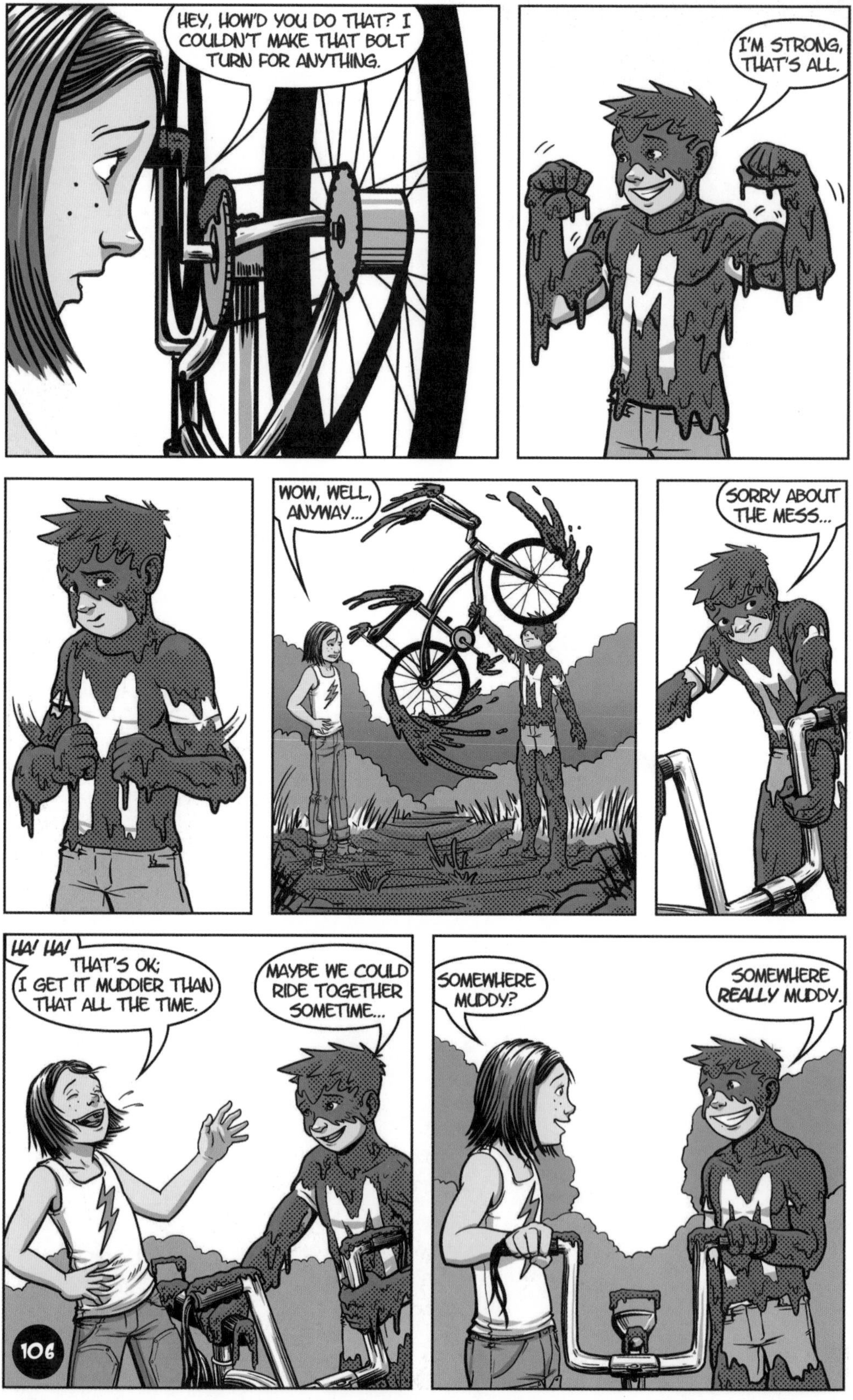
HEY, HOW'D YOU DO THAT? I COULDN'T MAKE THAT BOLT TURN FOR ANYTHING.
I'M STRONG, THAT'S ALL.
WOW, WELL, ANYWAY...
SORRY ABOUT THE MESS...
HA! HA! THAT'S OK; I GET IT MUDDIER THAN THAT ALL THE TIME.
MAYBE WE COULD RIDE TOGETHER SOMETIME...
SOMEWHERE MUDDY?
SOMEWHERE *REALLY* MUDDY.

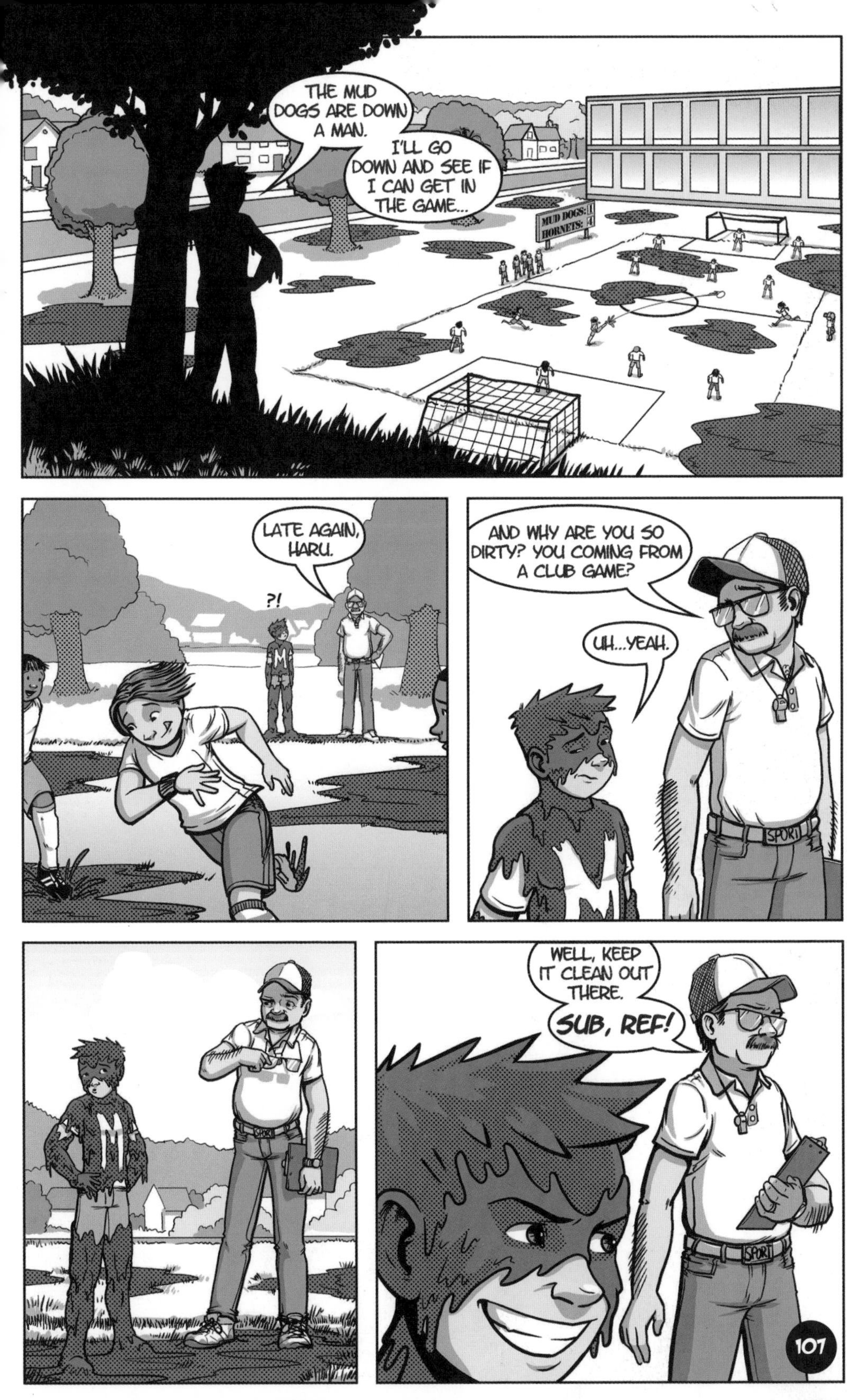
THE MUD DOGS ARE DOWN A MAN.
I'LL GO DOWN AND SEE IF I CAN GET IN THE GAME...
MUD DOGS: 1
HORNETS: 4
LATE AGAIN, HARU.
?!
AND WHY ARE YOU SO DIRTY? YOU COMING FROM A CLUB GAME?
UH...YEAH.
SPORT
WELL, KEEP IT CLEAN OUT THERE.
SUB, REF!

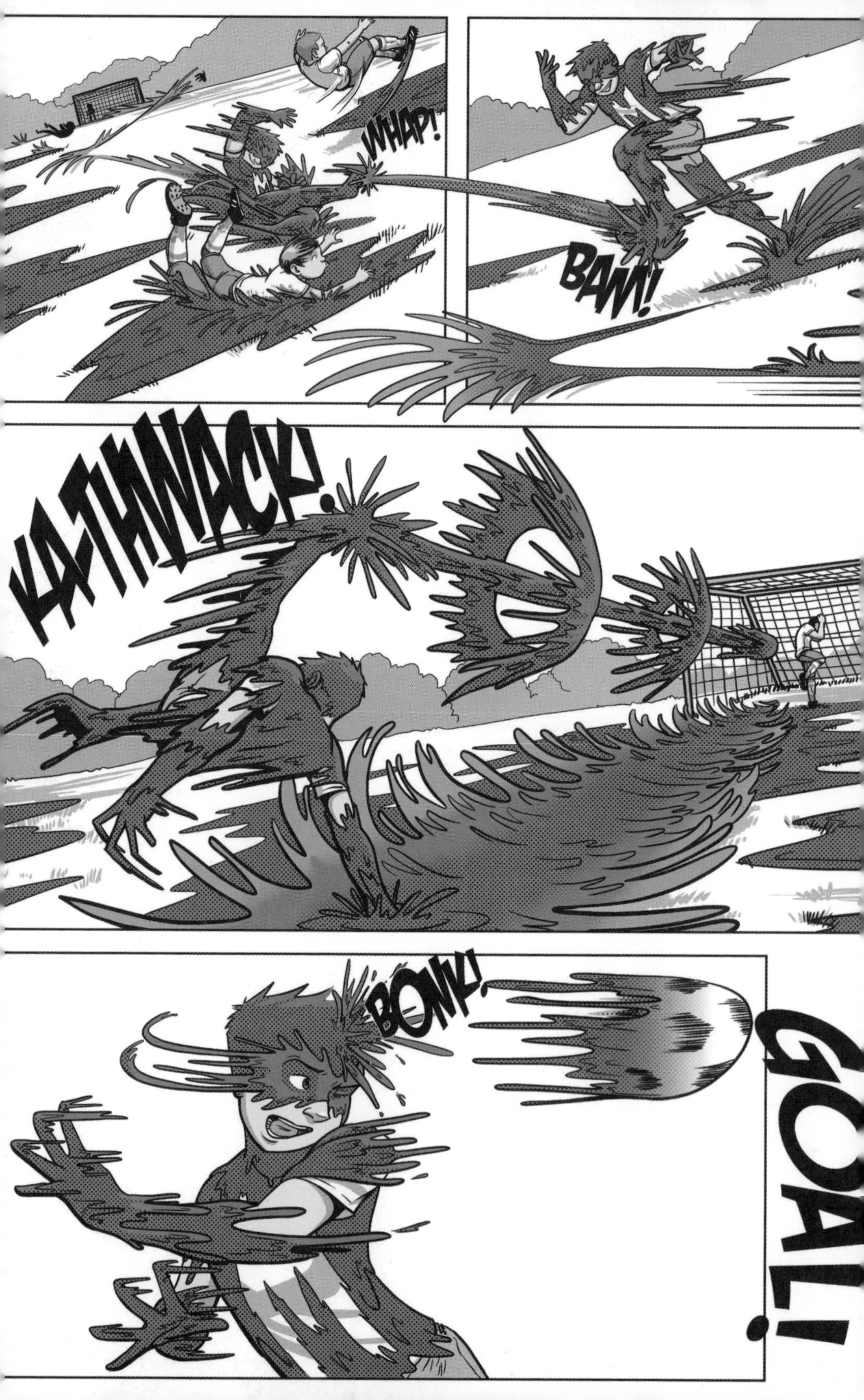

WHAP!
BAM!
KA-THWACK!
BONK!
GOAL!

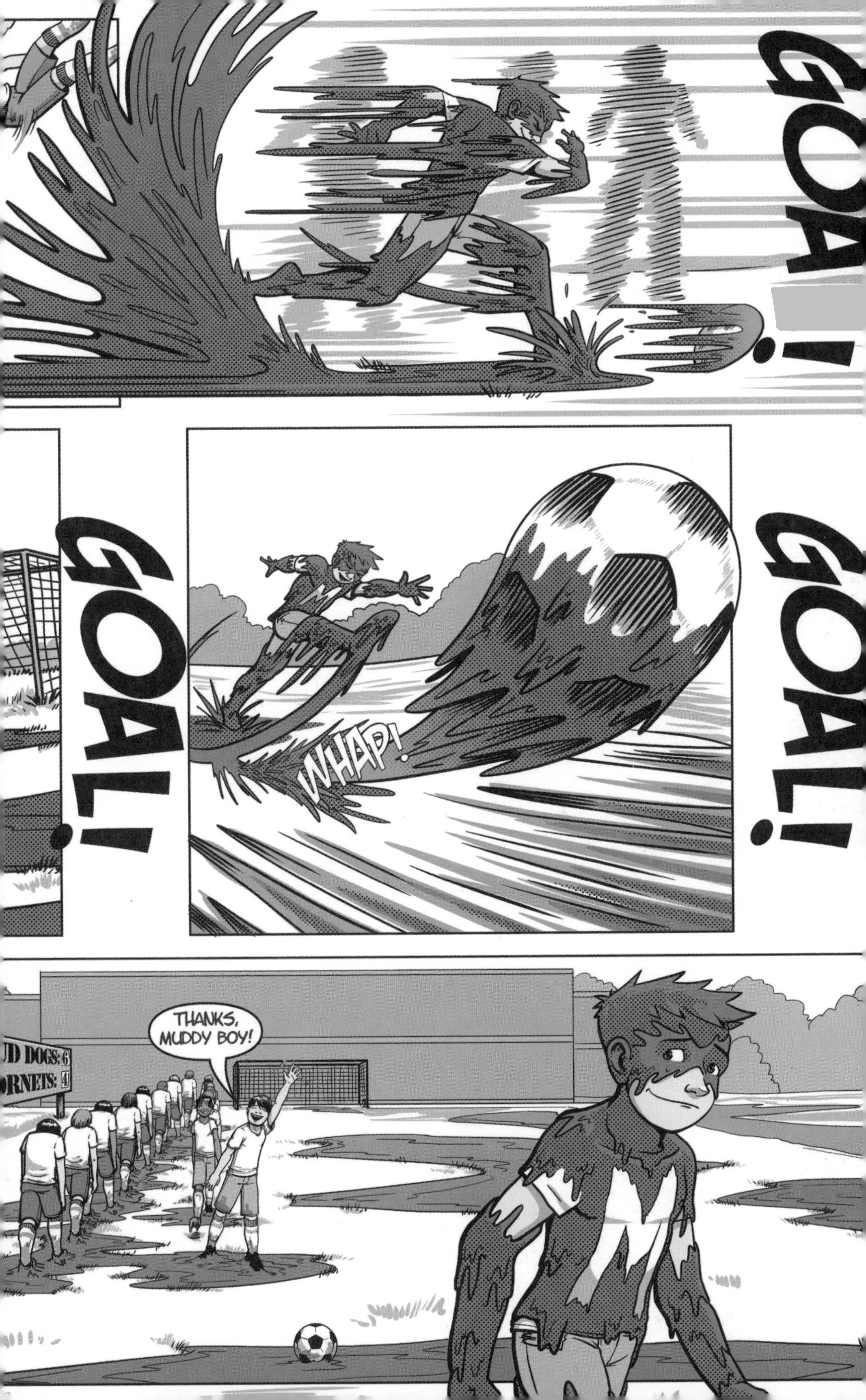

GOAL!
WHAP!
GOAL!
THANKS, MUDDY BOY!

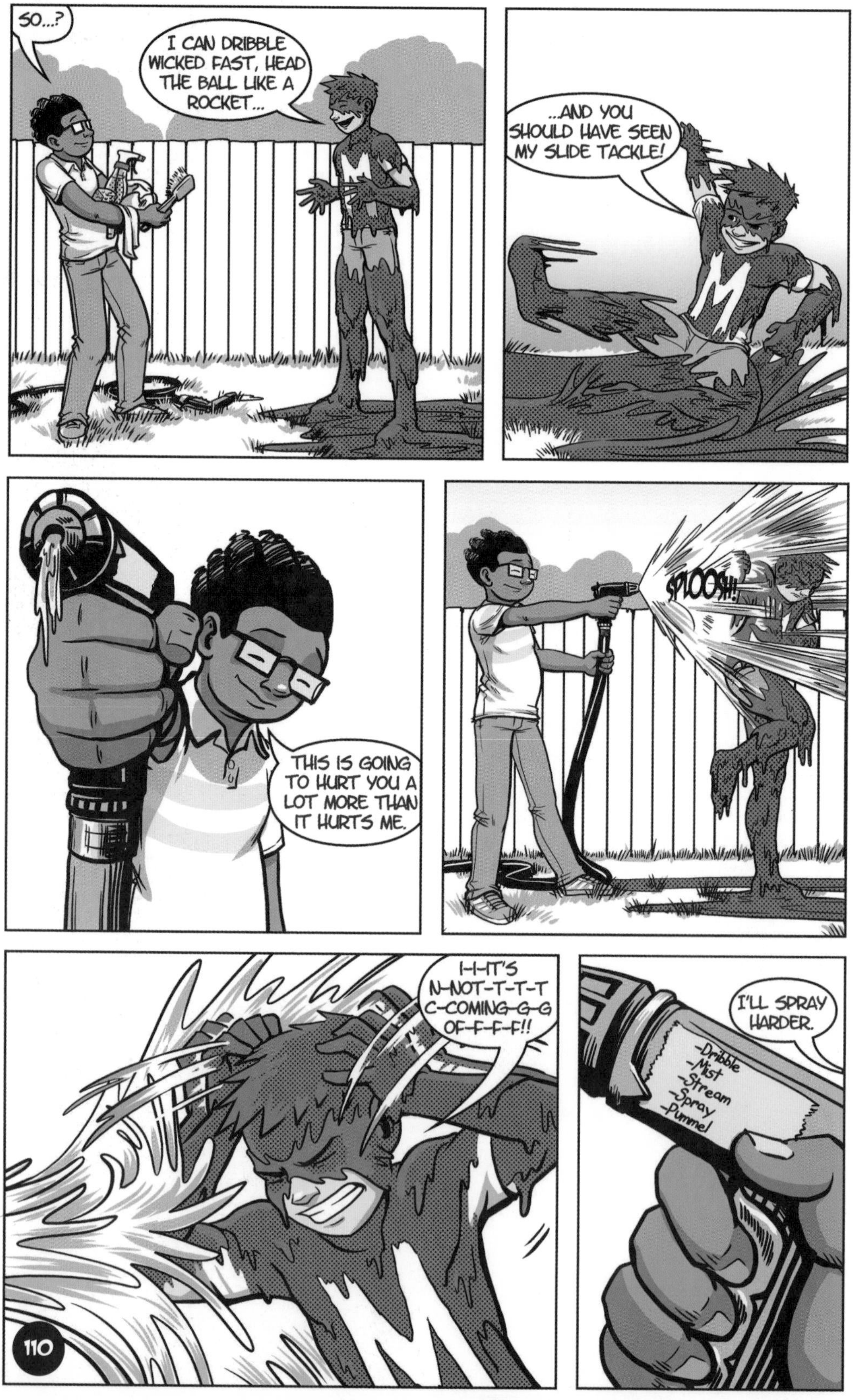
SO...?
I CAN DRIBBLE WICKED FAST, HEAD THE BALL LIKE A ROCKET...
...AND YOU SHOULD HAVE SEEN MY SLIDE TACKLE!
THIS IS GOING TO HURT YOU A LOT MORE THAN IT HURTS ME.
SPLOOSH!
I-I-IT'S N-NOT-T-T-T C-COMING-G-G OF-F-F-F!!
I'LL SPRAY HARDER.
-Dribble
-Mist
-Stream
-Spray
-Pummel

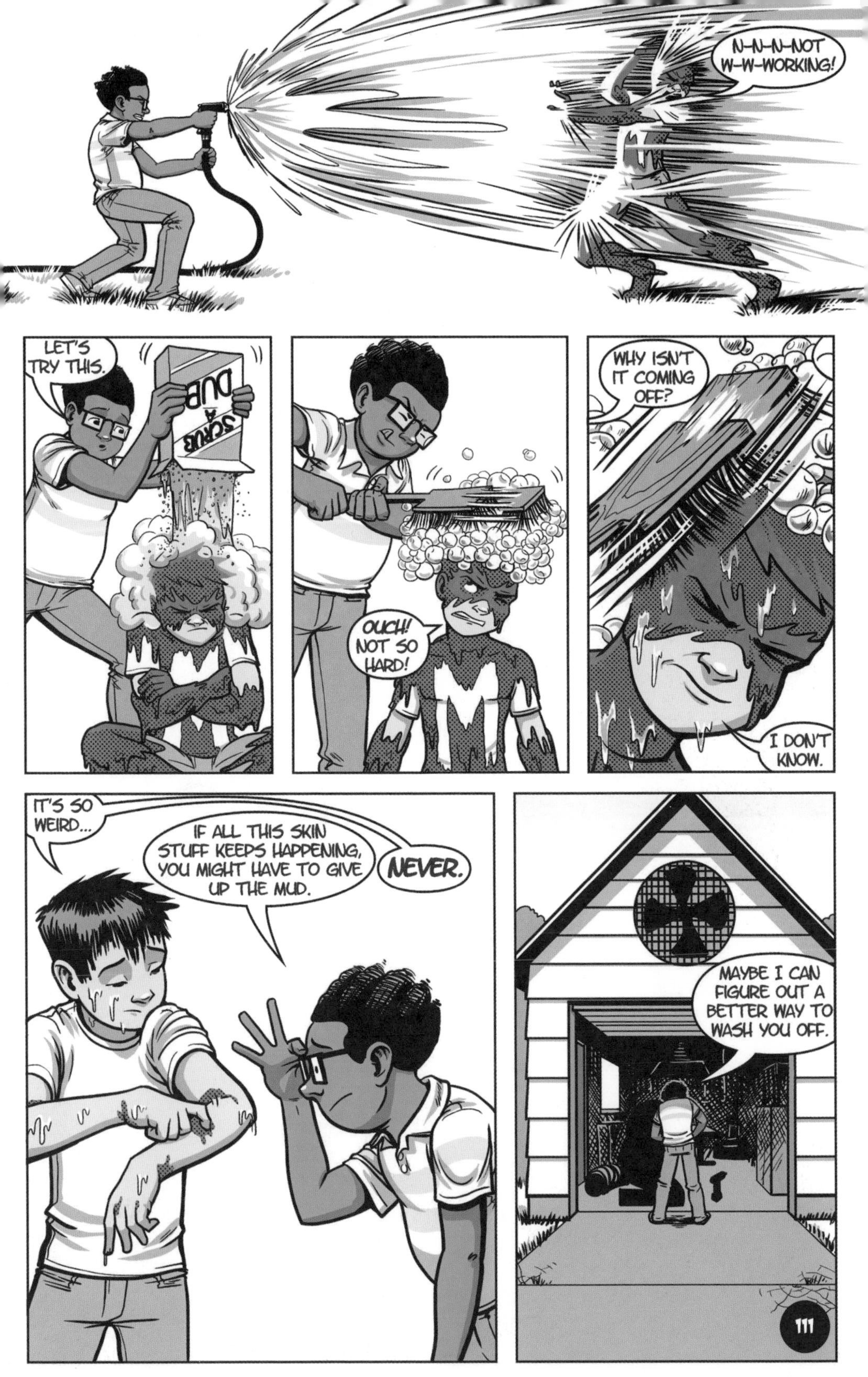
N-N-N-NOT W-W-WORKING!
LET'S TRY THIS.
SCRUB A DUB
OUCH! NOT SO HARD!
WHY ISN'T IT COMING OFF?
I DON'T KNOW.
IT'S SO WEIRD...
IF ALL THIS SKIN STUFF KEEPS HAPPENING, YOU MIGHT HAVE TO GIVE UP THE MUD.
NEVER.
MAYBE I CAN FIGURE OUT A BETTER WAY TO WASH YOU OFF.

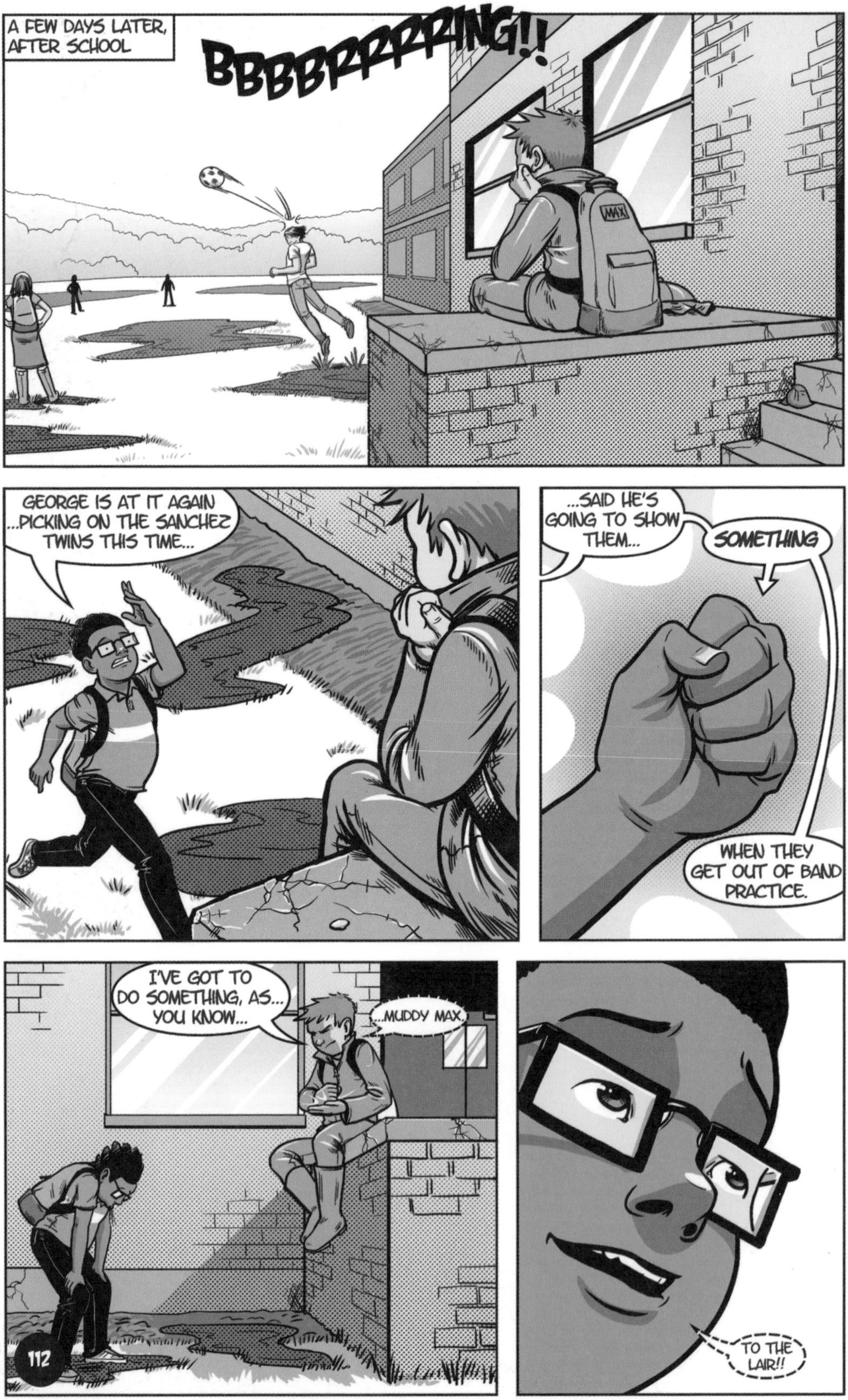
A FEW DAYS LATER, AFTER SCHOOL
BBBBRRRRRING!!
MAX
GEORGE IS AT IT AGAIN ...PICKING ON THE SANCHEZ TWINS THIS TIME...
...SAID HE'S GOING TO SHOW THEM...
SOMETHING
WHEN THEY GET OUT OF BAND PRACTICE.
I'VE GOT TO DO SOMETHING, AS... YOU KNOW...
...MUDDY MAX.
TO THE LAIR!!

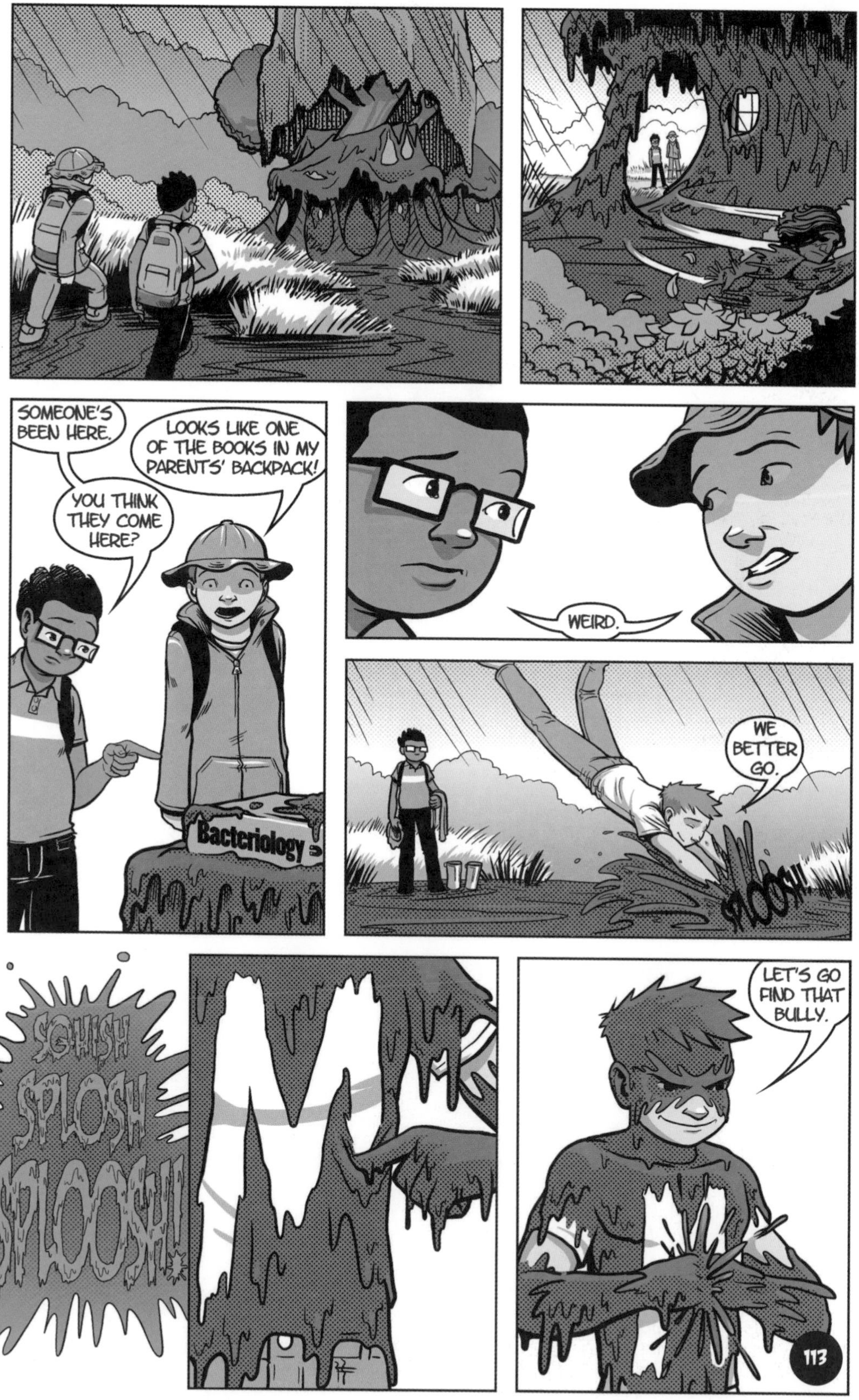
SOMEONE'S BEEN HERE.
LOOKS LIKE ONE OF THE BOOKS IN MY PARENTS' BACKPACK!
YOU THINK THEY COME HERE?
Bacteriology
WEIRD.
WE BETTER GO.
SPLOOSH!
SQUISH
SPLOSH
SPLOOSH!
LET'S GO FIND THAT BULLY.

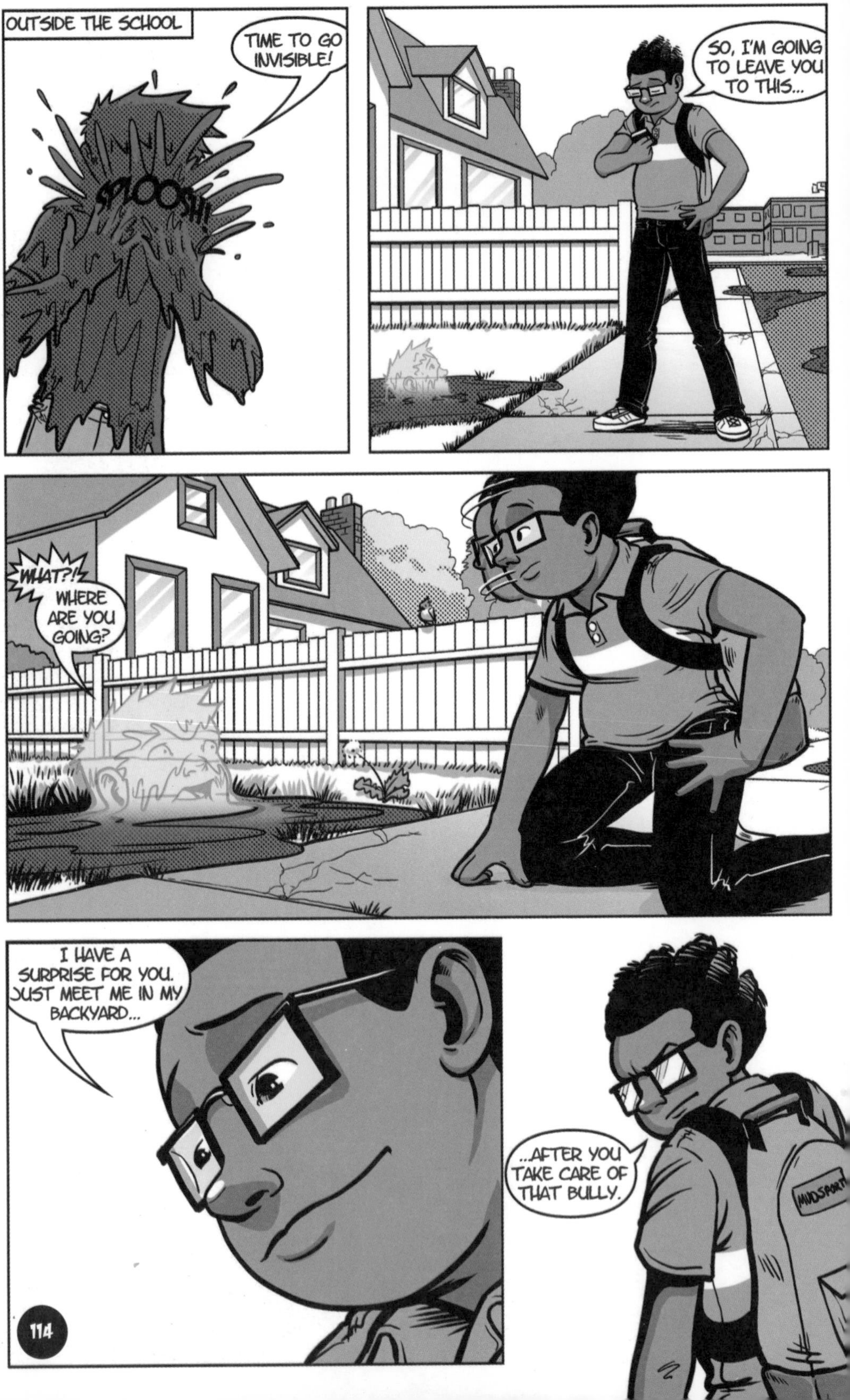
OUTSIDE THE SCHOOL
TIME TO GO INVISIBLE!
SPLOOSH!
SO, I'M GOING TO LEAVE YOU TO THIS...
WHAT?!
WHERE ARE YOU GOING?
I HAVE A SURPRISE FOR YOU. JUST MEET ME IN MY BACKYARD...
...AFTER YOU TAKE CARE OF THAT BULLY.
MUDSPORT

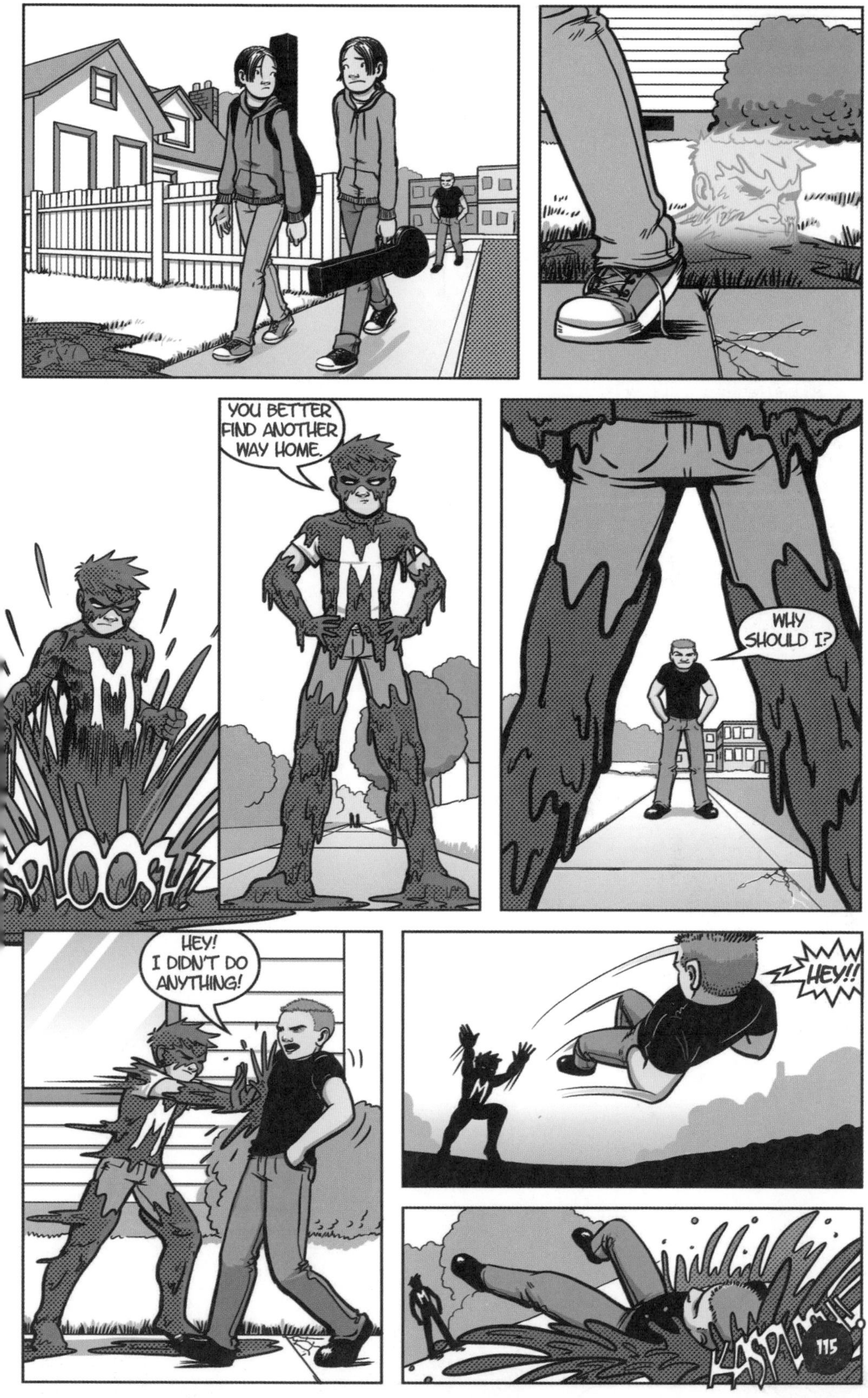

YOU BETTER FIND ANOTHER WAY HOME.
SPLOOSH!
WHY SHOULD I?
HEY! I DIDN'T DO ANYTHING!
HEY!!

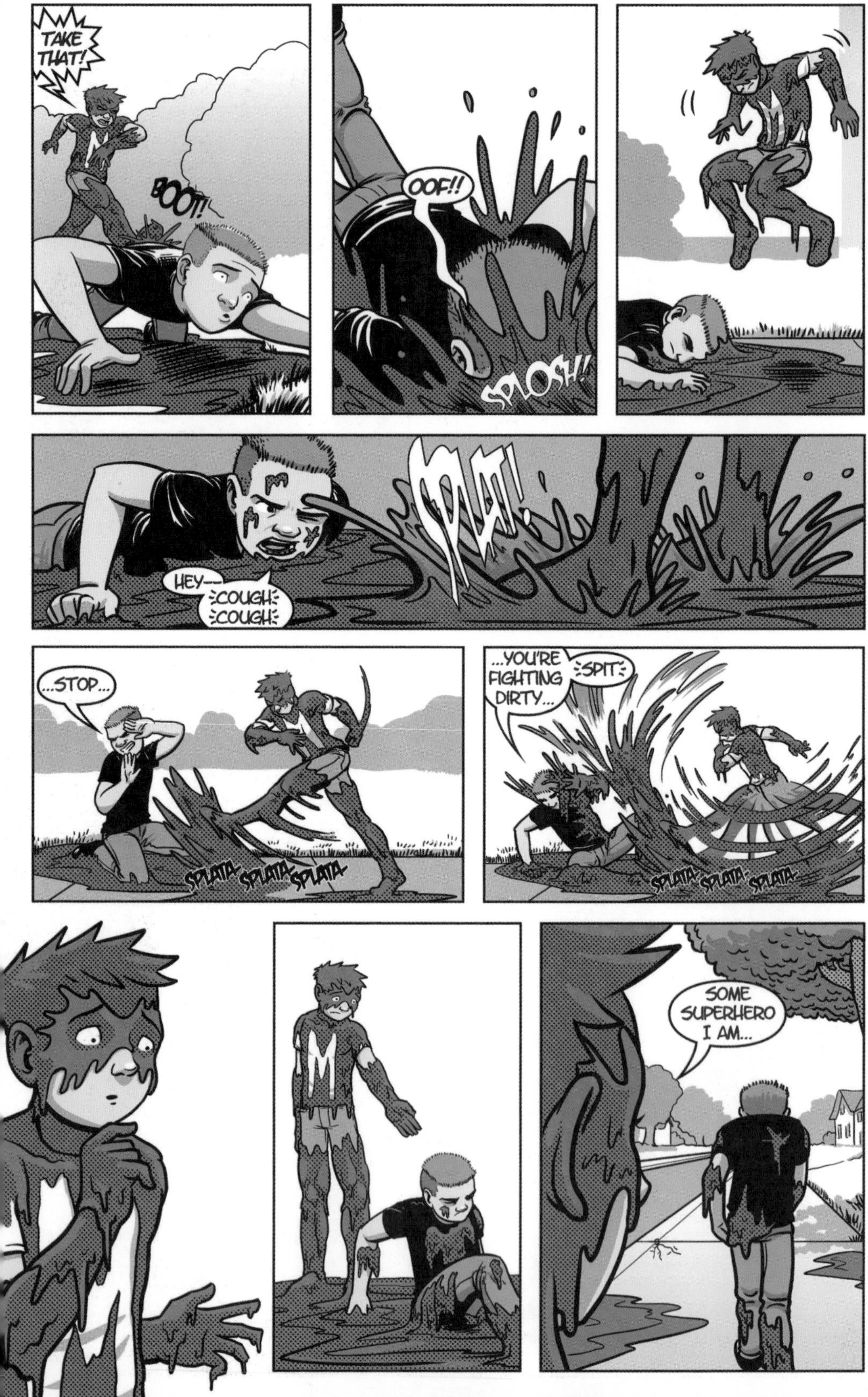
TAKE THAT!
BOOT!
OOF!!
SPLOSH!!
SPLAT!
HEY—
COUGH
COUGH
...STOP...
SPLATA SPLATA SPLATA
...YOU'RE FIGHTING DIRTY...
SPIT
SPLATA SPLATA SPLATA
SOME SUPERHERO I AM...

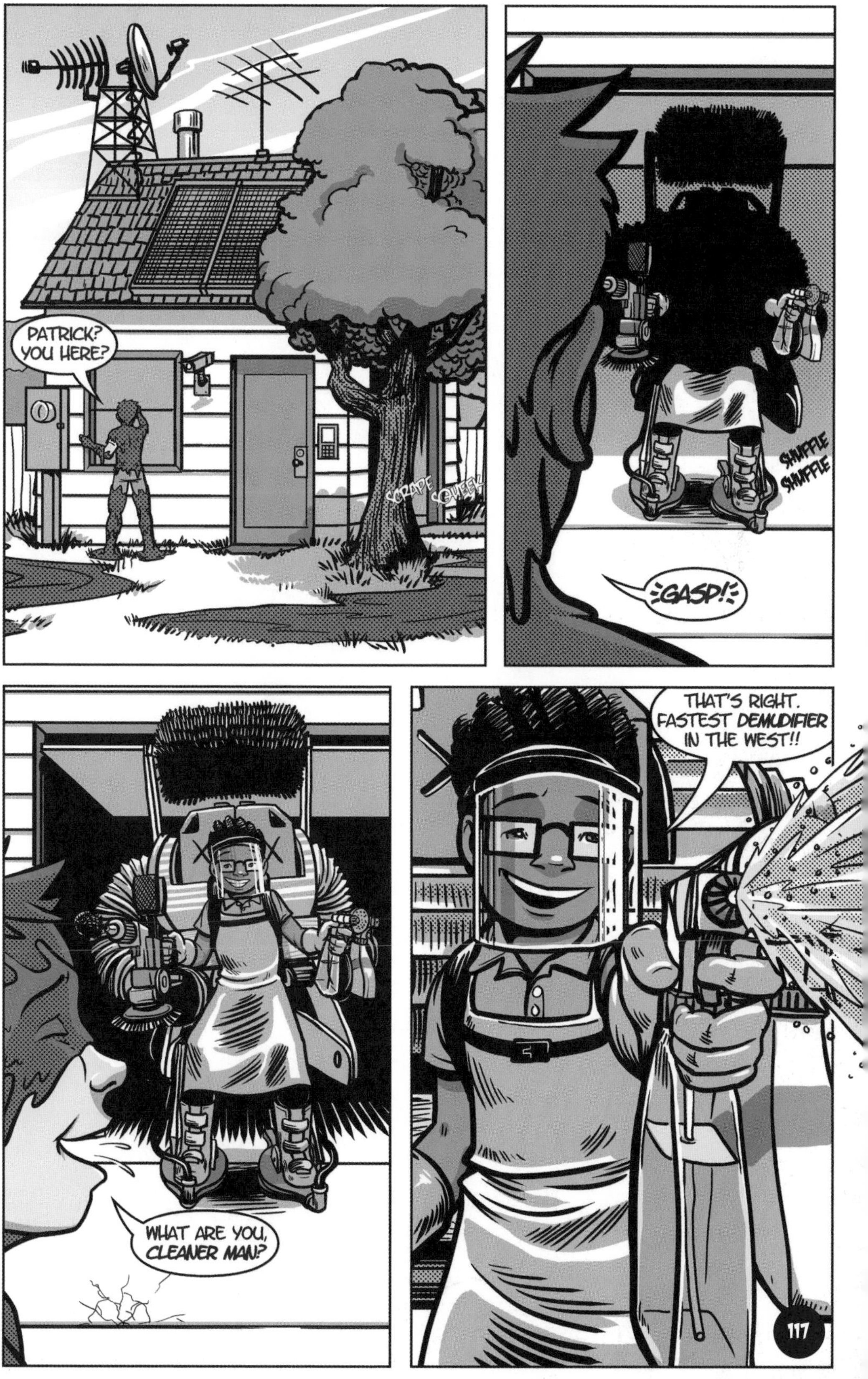
PATRICK? YOU HERE?
SCRAPE
SQUEEK
SHUFFLE SHUFFLE
GASP!
WHAT ARE YOU, CLEANER MAN?
THAT'S RIGHT. FASTEST DEMUDIFIER IN THE WEST!!

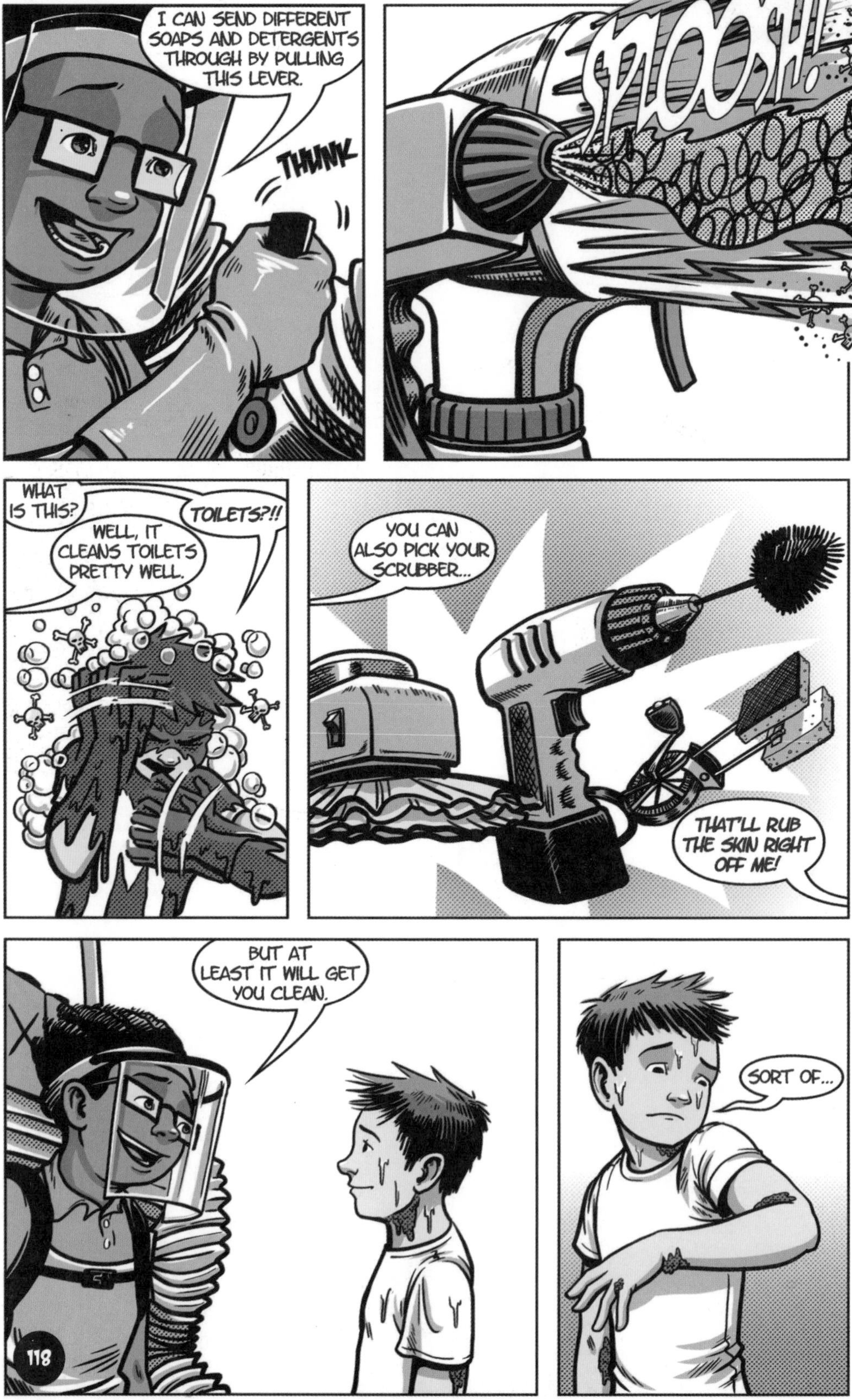

I CAN SEND DIFFERENT SOAPS AND DETERGENTS THROUGH BY PULLING THIS LEVER.
THUNK
SPLOOSH!!
WHAT IS THIS?
TOILETS?!!
WELL, IT CLEANS TOILETS PRETTY WELL.
YOU CAN ALSO PICK YOUR SCRUBBER...
THAT'LL RUB THE SKIN RIGHT OFF ME!
BUT AT LEAST IT WILL GET YOU CLEAN.
SORT OF...

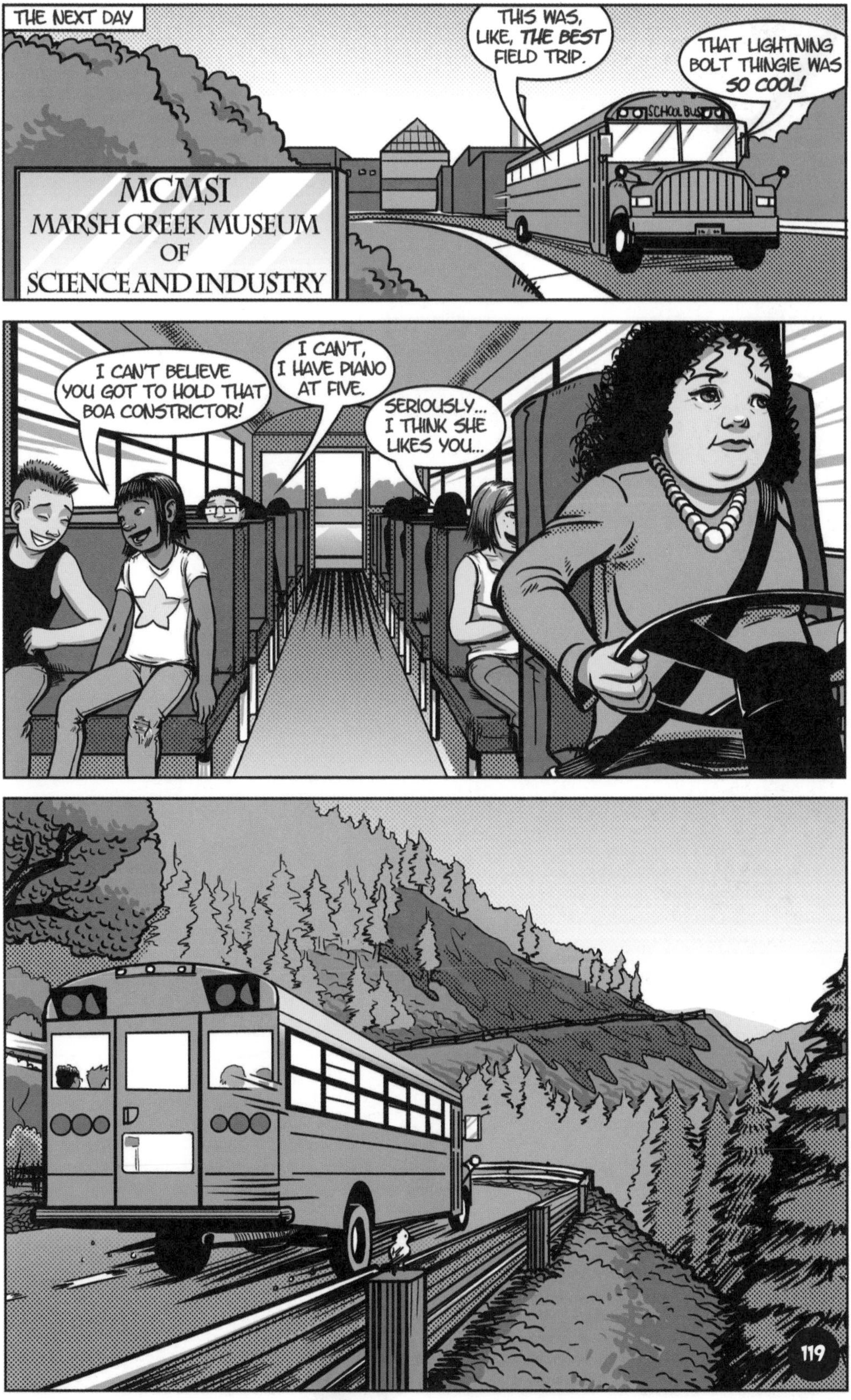
THE NEXT DAY
THIS WAS, LIKE, THE BEST FIELD TRIP.
THAT LIGHTNING BOLT THINGIE WAS SO COOL!
SCHOOL BUS
MCMSI
MARSH CREEK MUSEUM OF SCIENCE AND INDUSTRY
I CAN'T BELIEVE YOU GOT TO HOLD THAT BOA CONSTRICTOR!
I CAN'T, I HAVE PIANO AT FIVE.
SERIOUSLY... I THINK SHE LIKES YOU...

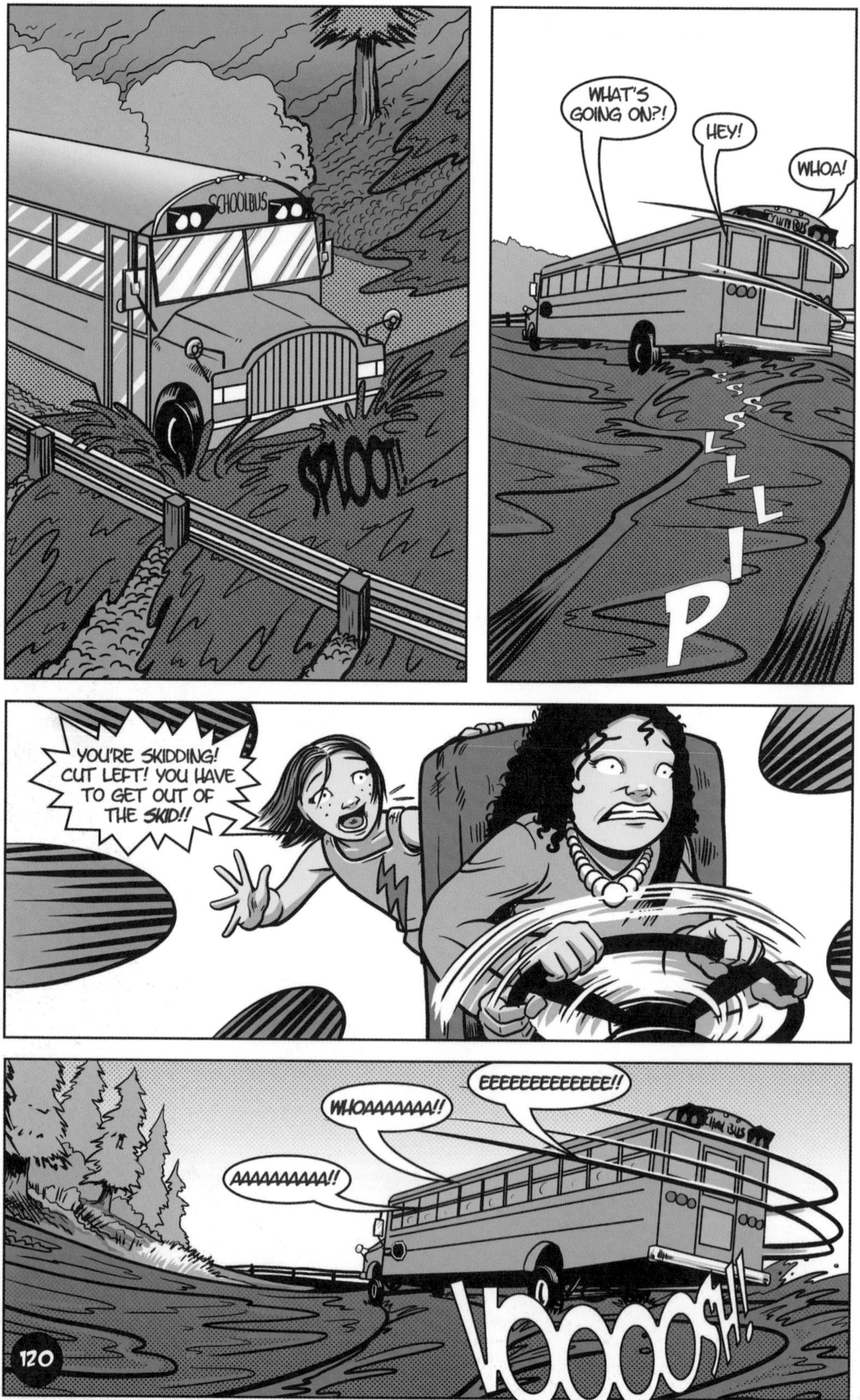
SCHOOLBUS
SPLOOT!
WHAT'S GOING ON?!
HEY!
WHOA!
SSSLLLIP
YOU'RE SKIDDING! CUT LEFT! YOU HAVE TO GET OUT OF THE SKID!!
EEEEEEEEEEEEE!!
WHOAAAAAAA!!
AAAAAAAAAA!!
VOOOOSH!!

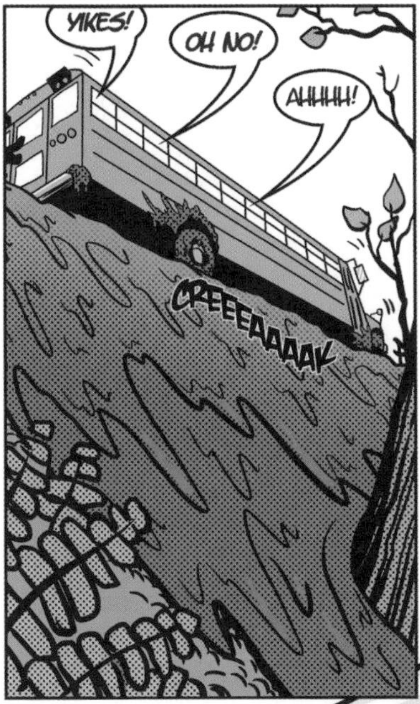
YIKES!
OH NO!
AHHHH!
CREEEAAAAK

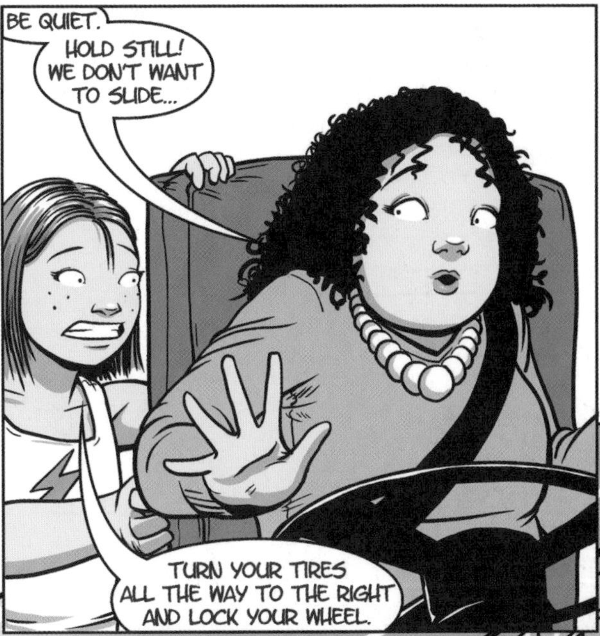
BE QUIET.
HOLD STILL! WE DON'T WANT TO SLIDE...
TURN YOUR TIRES ALL THE WAY TO THE RIGHT AND LOCK YOUR WHEEL.

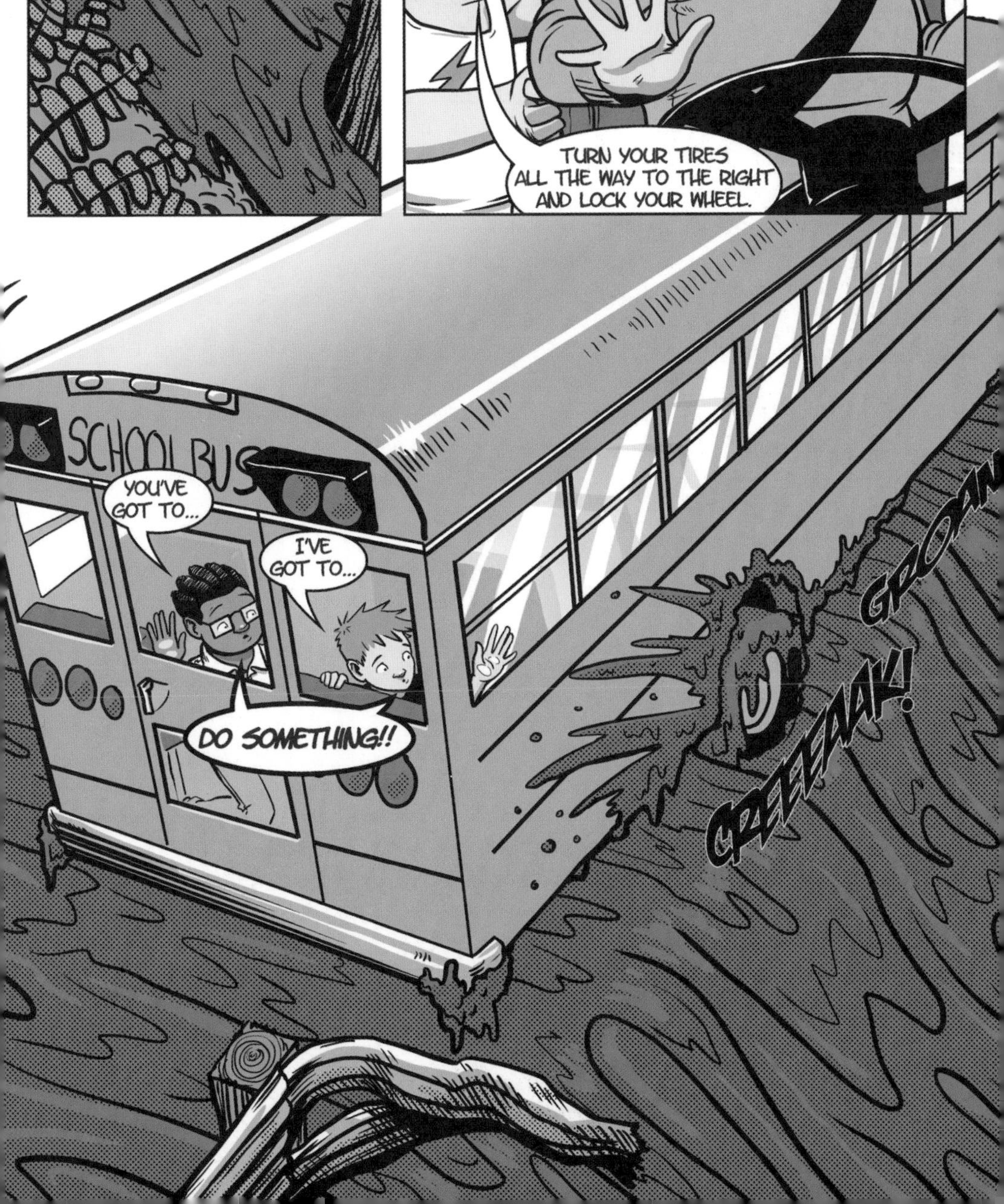
SCHOOL BUS
YOU'VE GOT TO...
I'VE GOT TO...
DO SOMETHING!!
CREEEAAK!
GROAN

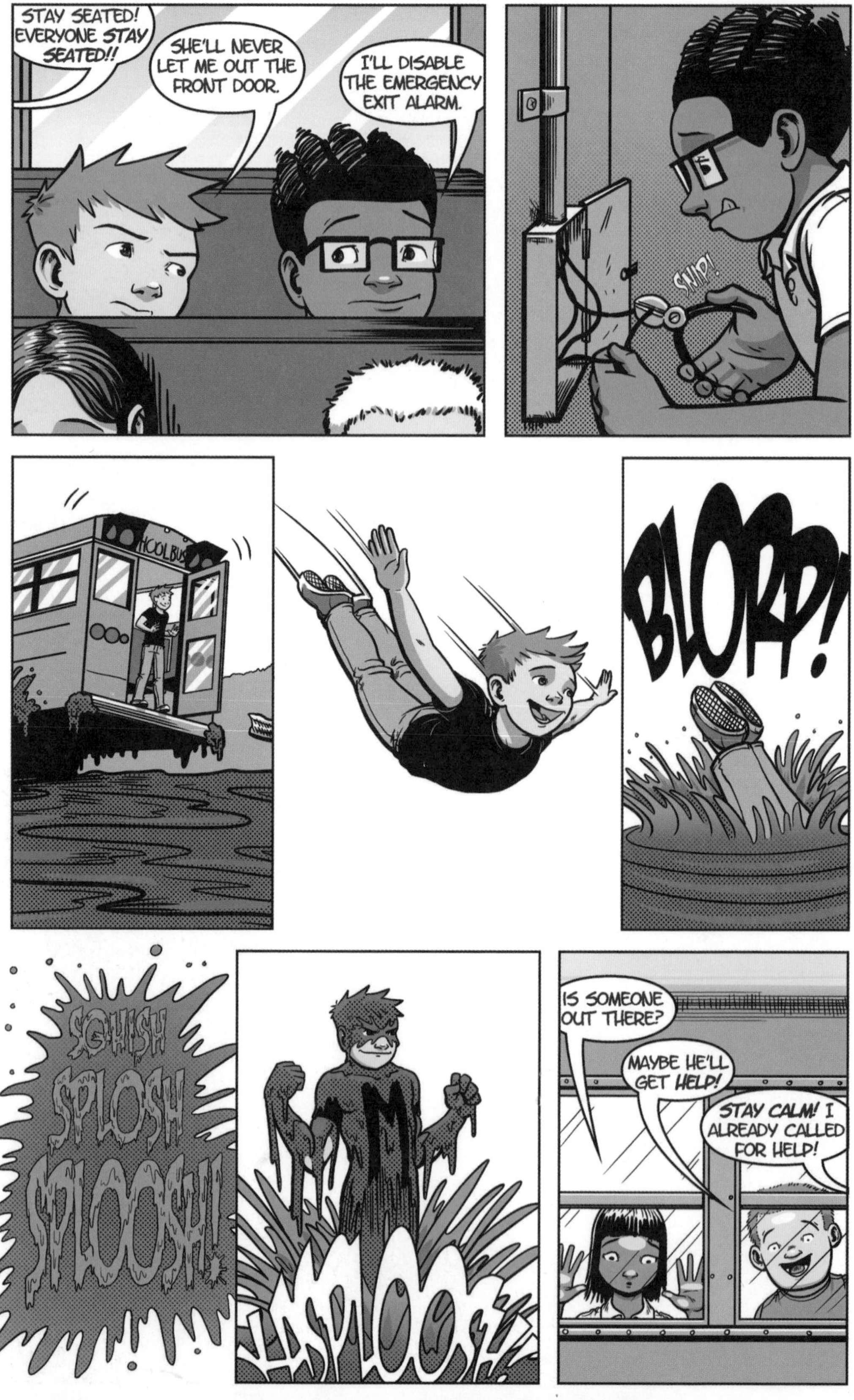
STAY SEATED! EVERYONE STAY SEATED!!
SHE'LL NEVER LET ME OUT THE FRONT DOOR.
I'LL DISABLE THE EMERGENCY EXIT ALARM.
SNIP!
BLORP!
SQUISH
SPLOSH
SPLOOSH!
SPLOOSH!
IS SOMEONE OUT THERE?
MAYBE HE'LL GET HELP!
STAY CALM! I ALREADY CALLED FOR HELP!

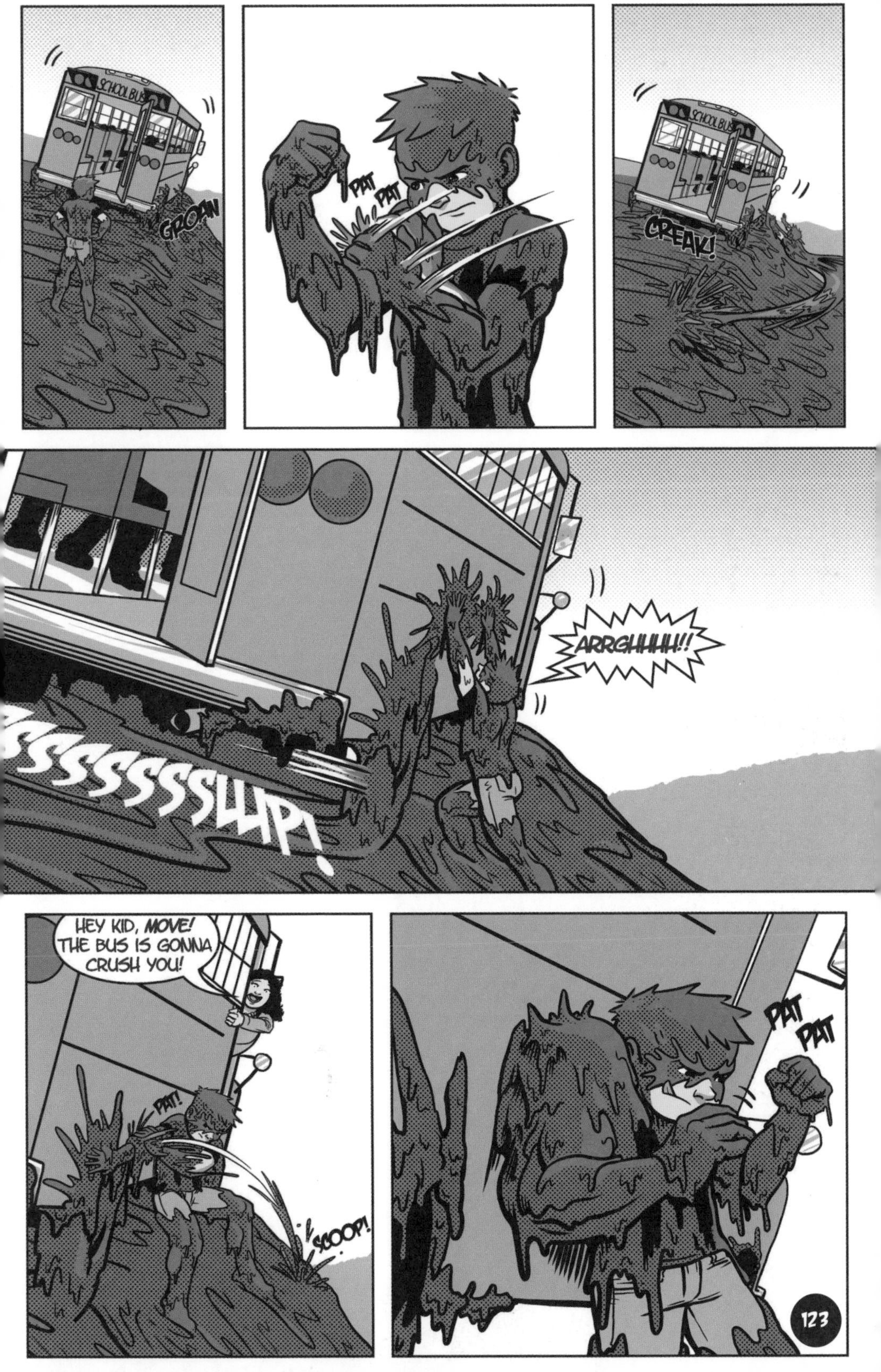
GROAN
PAT PAT
CREAK!
SSSSSSSSLUP!
ARRGHHHH!!
HEY KID, MOVE! THE BUS IS GONNA CRUSH YOU!
PAT!
SCOOP!
PAT PAT

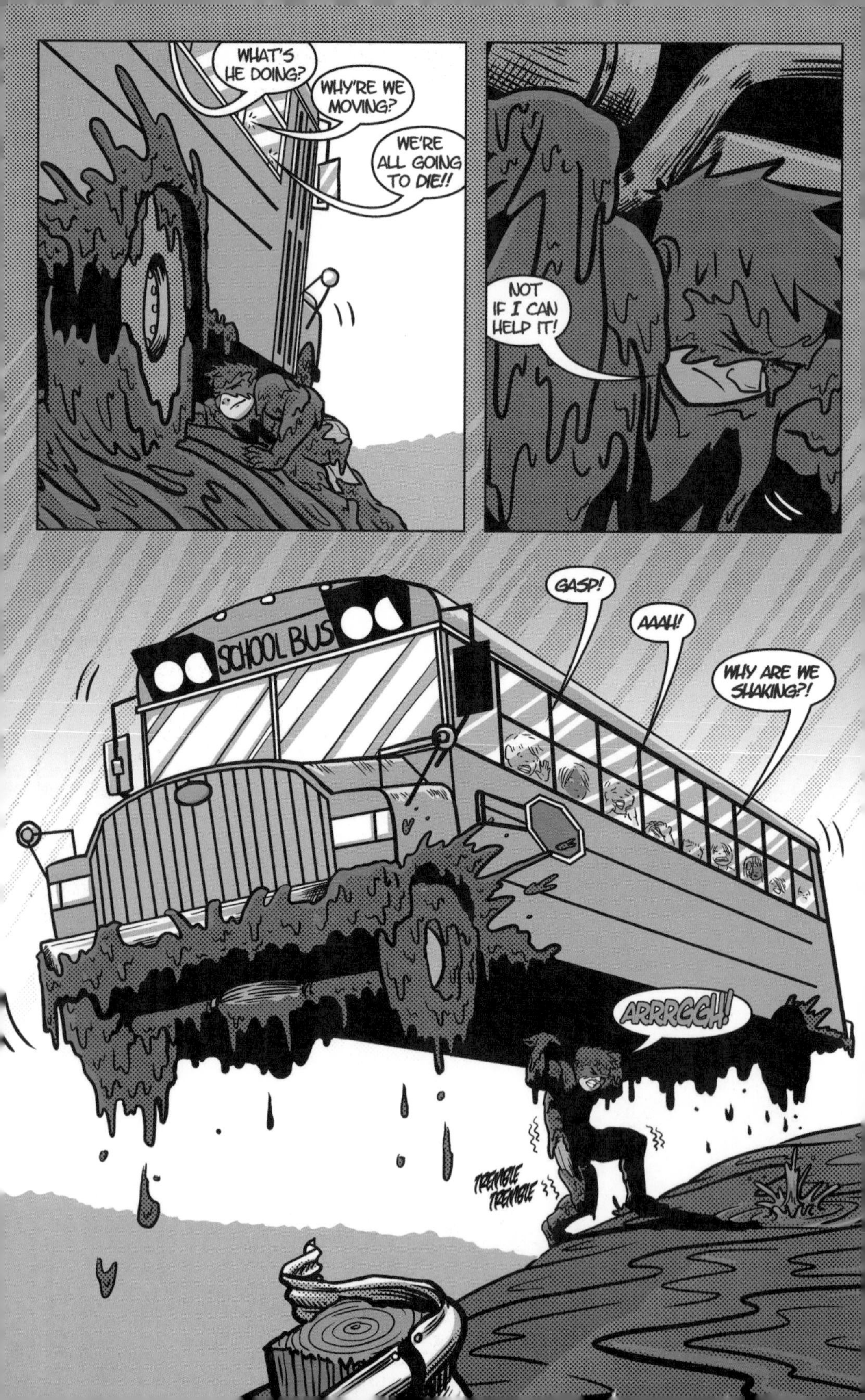
WHAT'S HE DOING?
WHY'RE WE MOVING?
WE'RE ALL GOING TO DIE!!
NOT IF I CAN HELP IT!
SCHOOL BUS
GASP!
AAAH!
WHY ARE WE SHAKING?!
ARRRGGH!
TREMBLE TREMBLE

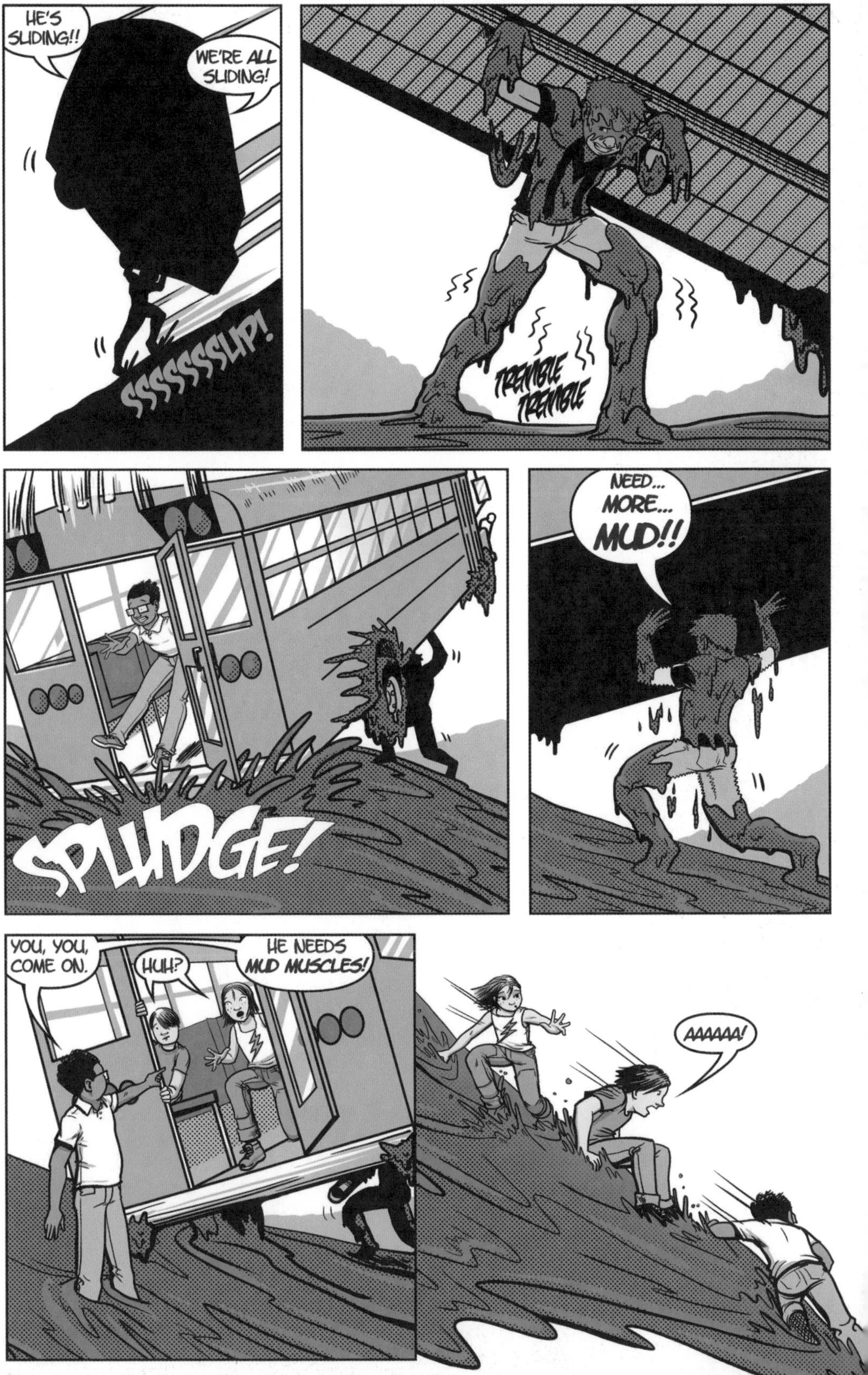
HE'S SLIDING!!
WE'RE ALL SLIDING!
SSSSSSSLIP!
TREMBLE TREMBLE
SPLUDGE!
NEED... MORE... MUD!!
YOU, YOU, COME ON.
HUH?
HE NEEDS MUD MUSCLES!
AAAAAA!

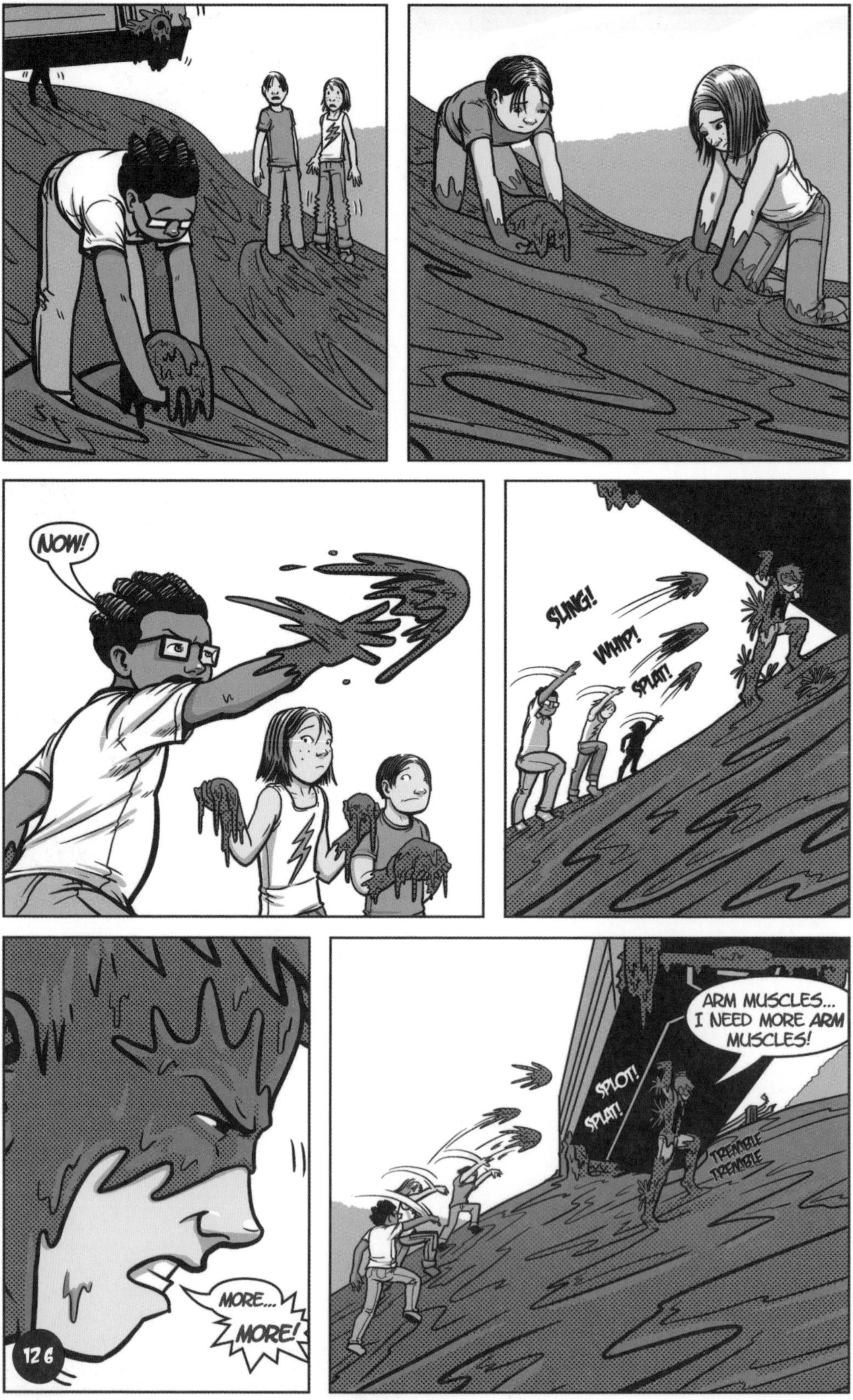
NOW!
SLING!
WHIP!
SPLAT!
MORE...
MORE!
ARM MUSCLES... I NEED MORE ARM MUSCLES!
SPLOT!
SPLAT!
TREMBLE
TREMBLE

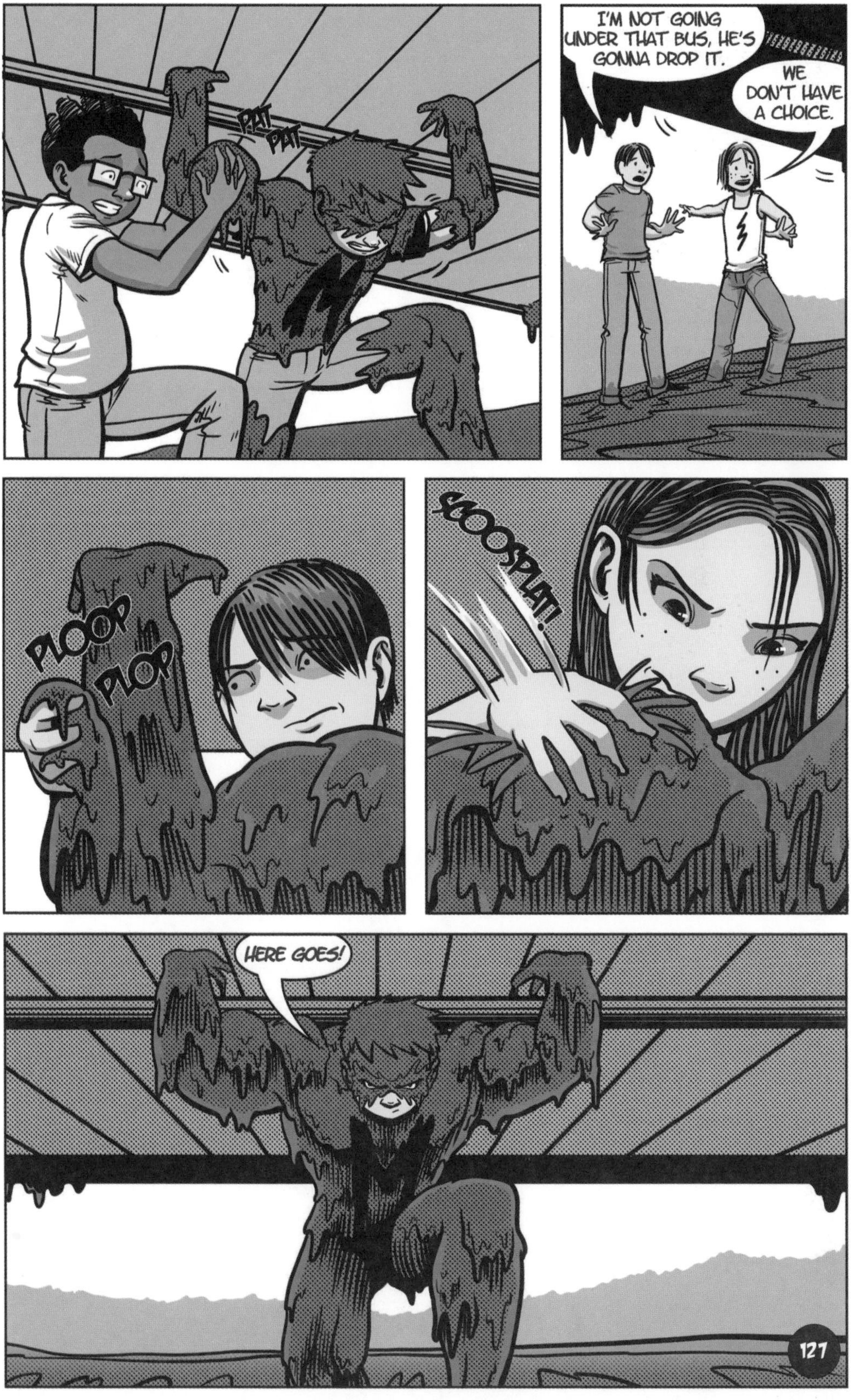
PAT PAT
I'M NOT GOING UNDER THAT BUS, HE'S GONNA DROP IT.
WE DON'T HAVE A CHOICE.
PLOOP PLOP
SCOOSPLAT!
HERE GOES!

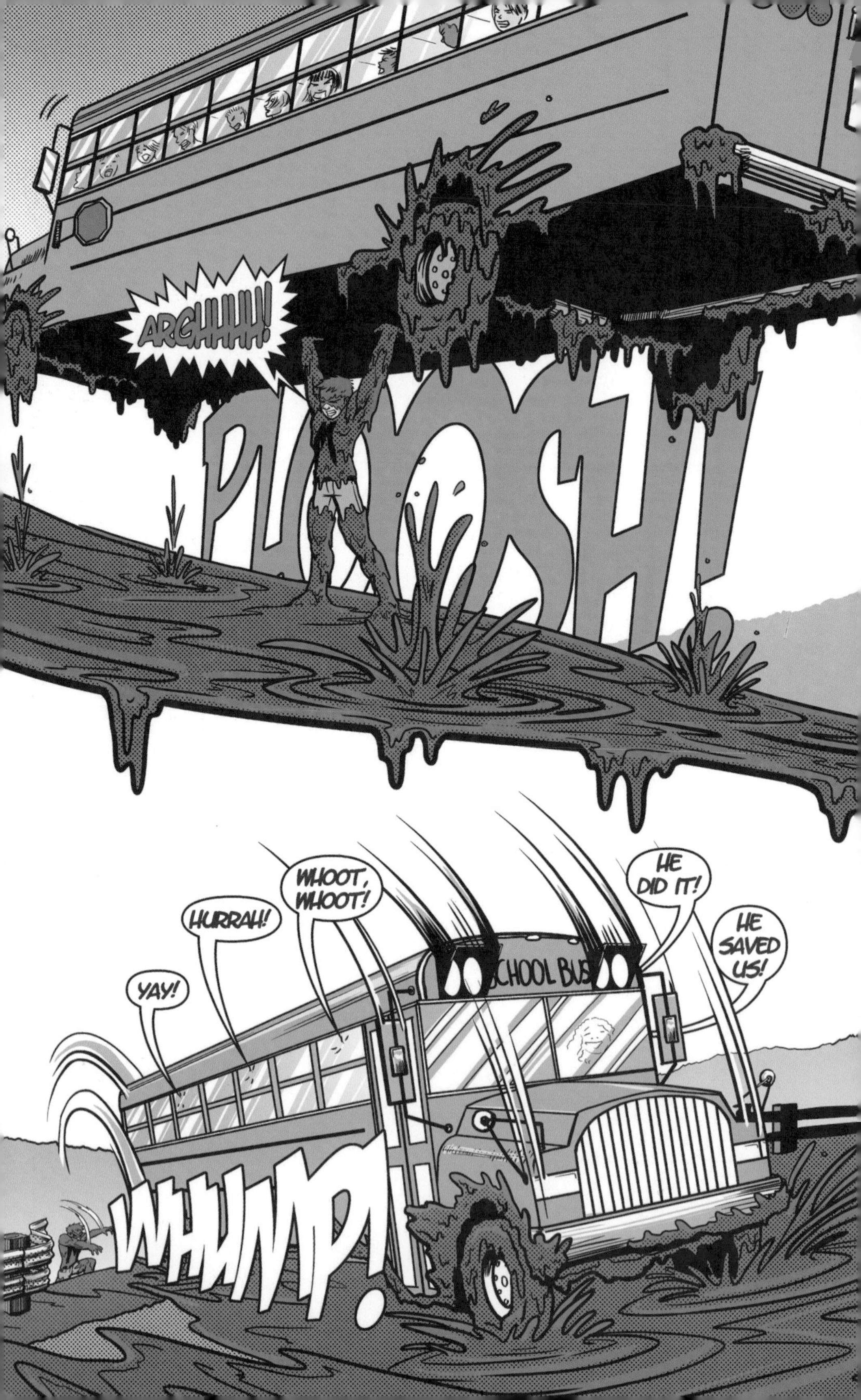

ARGHHHH!
YAY!
HURRAH!
WHOOT, WHOOT!
HE DID IT!
HE SAVED US!
WHUMP!

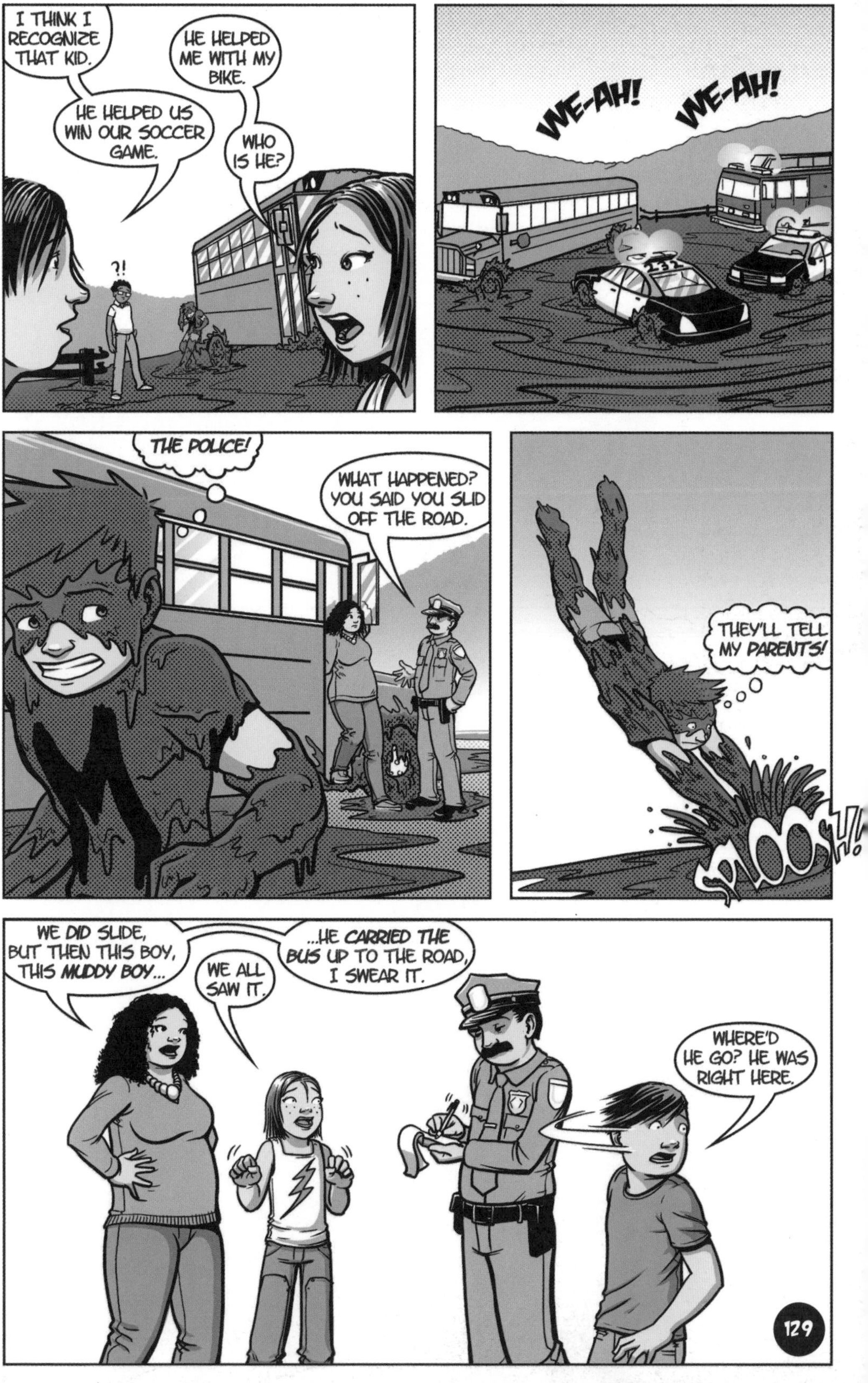
I THINK I RECOGNIZE THAT KID.
HE HELPED US WIN OUR SOCCER GAME.
HE HELPED ME WITH MY BIKE.
WHO IS HE?
?!
WE-AH! WE-AH!
232
THE POLICE!
WHAT HAPPENED? YOU SAID YOU SLID OFF THE ROAD.
THEY'LL TELL MY PARENTS!
SPLOOSH!
WE DID SLIDE, BUT THEN THIS BOY, THIS MUDDY BOY...
WE ALL SAW IT.
...HE CARRIED THE BUS UP TO THE ROAD, I SWEAR IT.
WHERE'D HE GO? HE WAS RIGHT HERE.

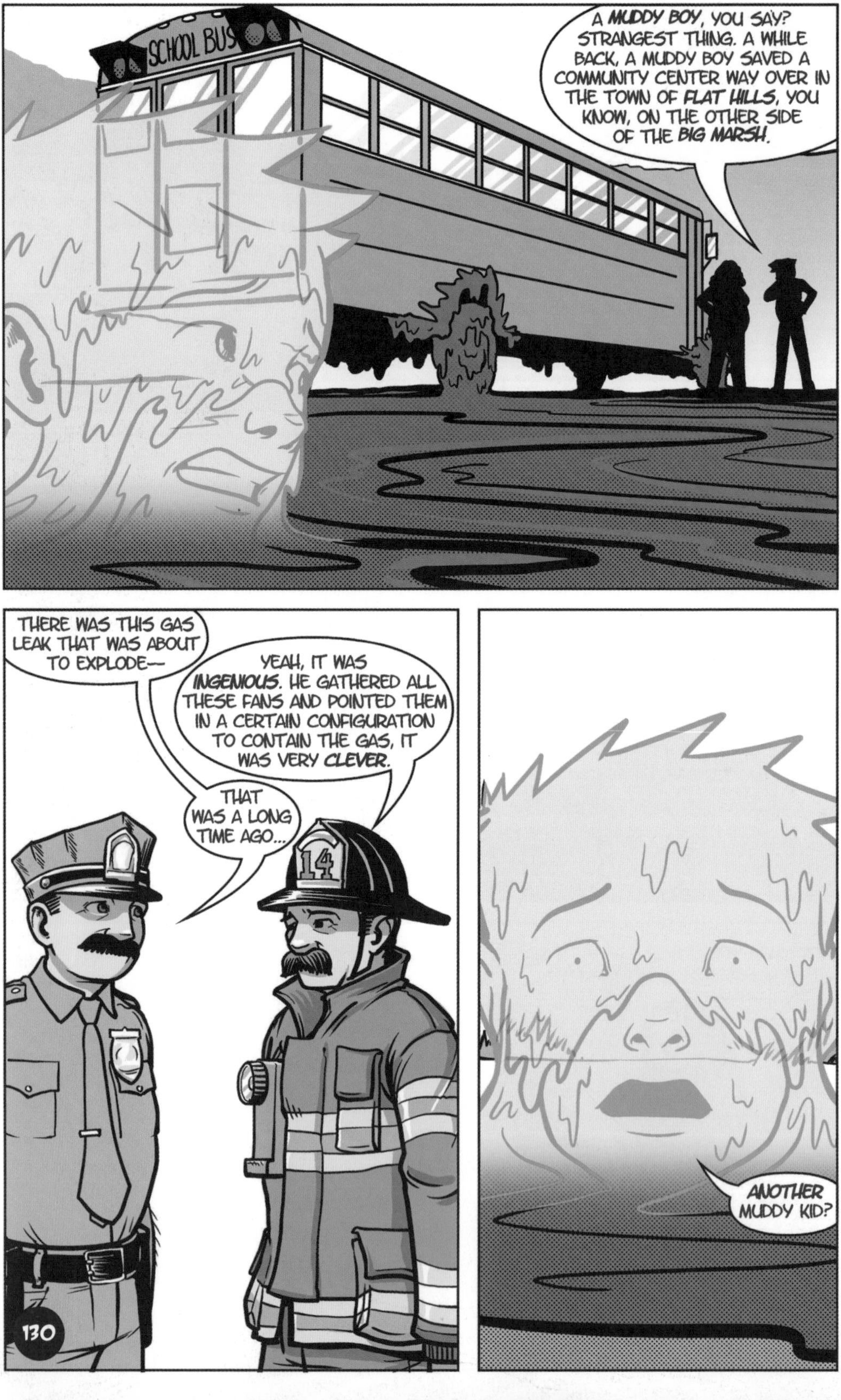
SCHOOL BUS
A MUDDY BOY, YOU SAY? STRANGEST THING. A WHILE BACK, A MUDDY BOY SAVED A COMMUNITY CENTER WAY OVER IN THE TOWN OF FLAT HILLS, YOU KNOW, ON THE OTHER SIDE OF THE BIG MARSH.
THERE WAS THIS GAS LEAK THAT WAS ABOUT TO EXPLODE--
YEAH, IT WAS INGENIOUS. HE GATHERED ALL THESE FANS AND POINTED THEM IN A CERTAIN CONFIGURATION TO CONTAIN THE GAS, IT WAS VERY CLEVER.
THAT WAS A LONG TIME AGO...
14
ANOTHER MUDDY KID?

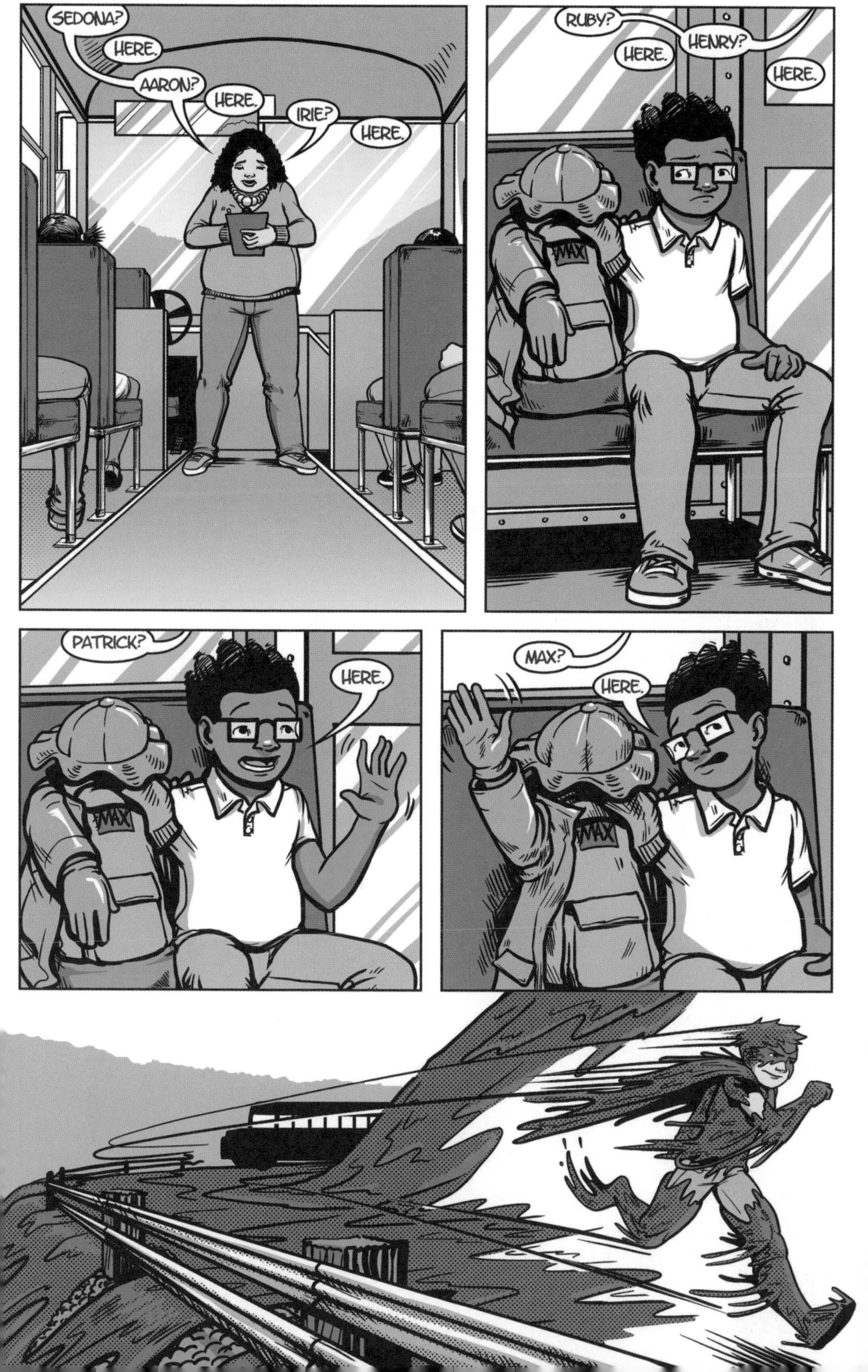
SEDONA?
HERE.
AARON?
HERE.
IRIE?
HERE.
RUBY?
HERE.
HENRY?
HERE.
PATRICK?
HERE.
MAX?
HERE.
MAX
MAX
MAX

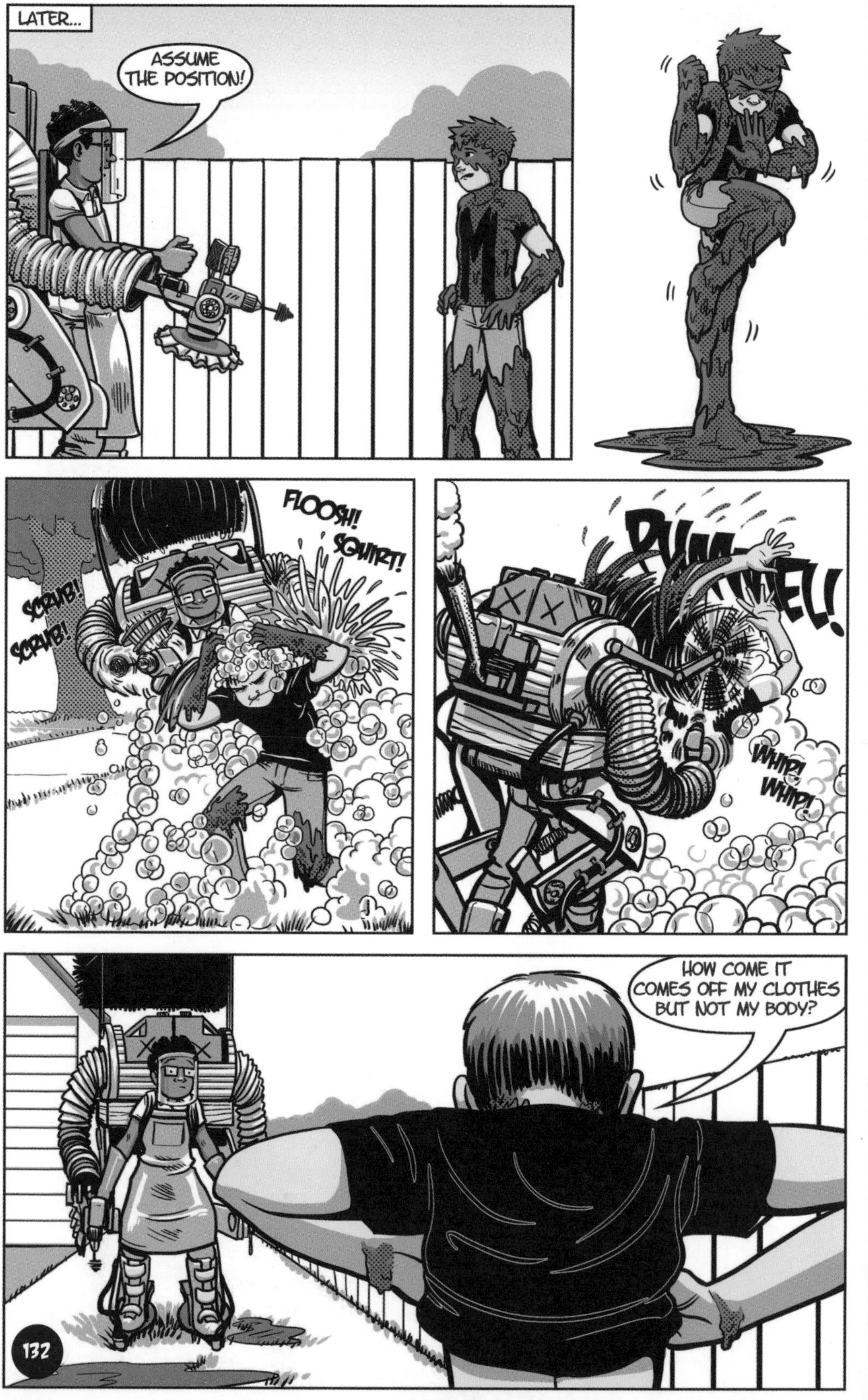
LATER...
ASSUME THE POSITION!
FLOOSH!
SQUIRT!
SCRUB!
SCRUB!
WHIP!
WHIP!
HOW COME IT COMES OFF MY CLOTHES BUT NOT MY BODY?

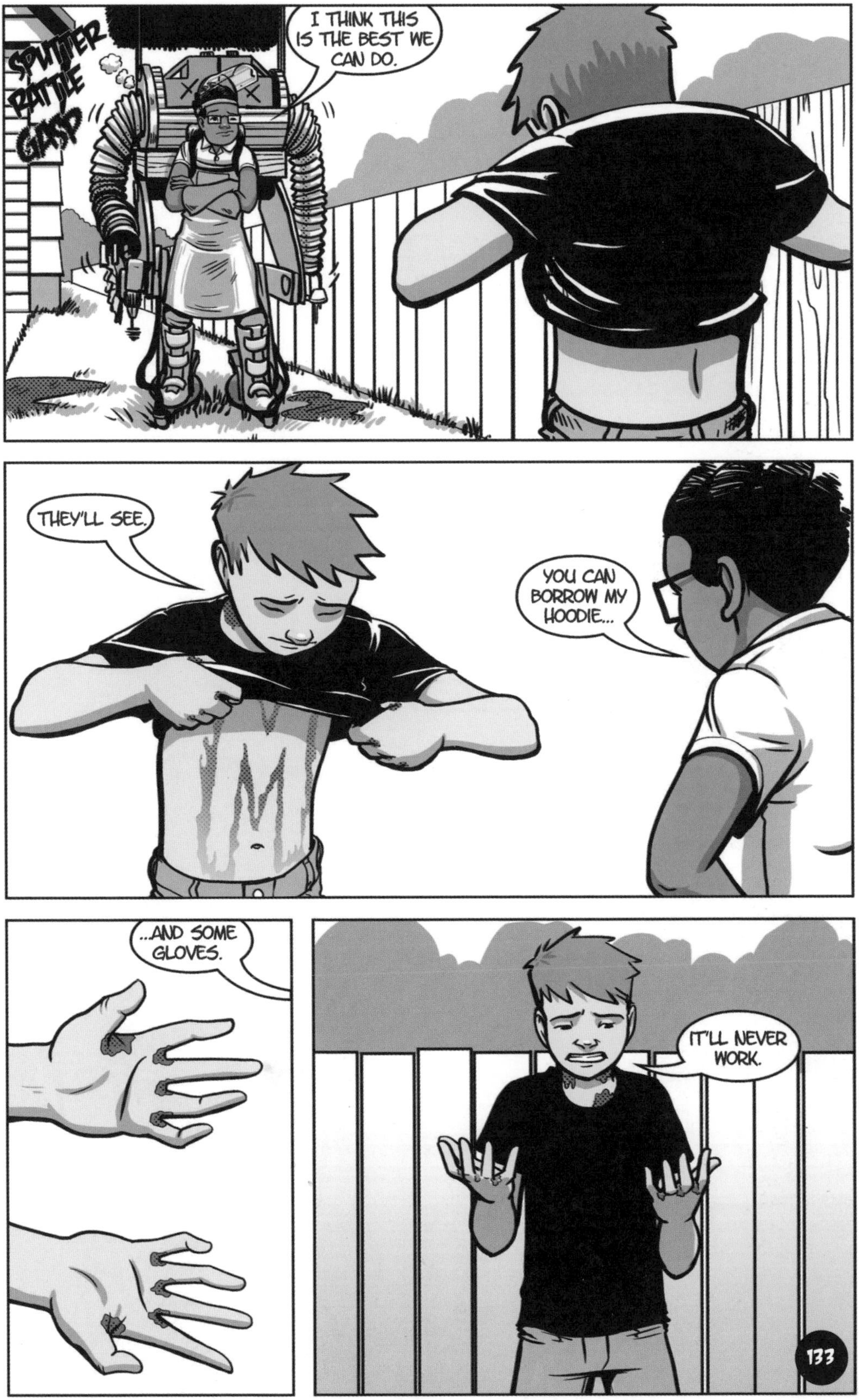
SPUTTER
RATTLE
GASP
I THINK THIS IS THE BEST WE CAN DO.
THEY'LL SEE.
YOU CAN BORROW MY HOODIE...
...AND SOME GLOVES.
IT'LL NEVER WORK.

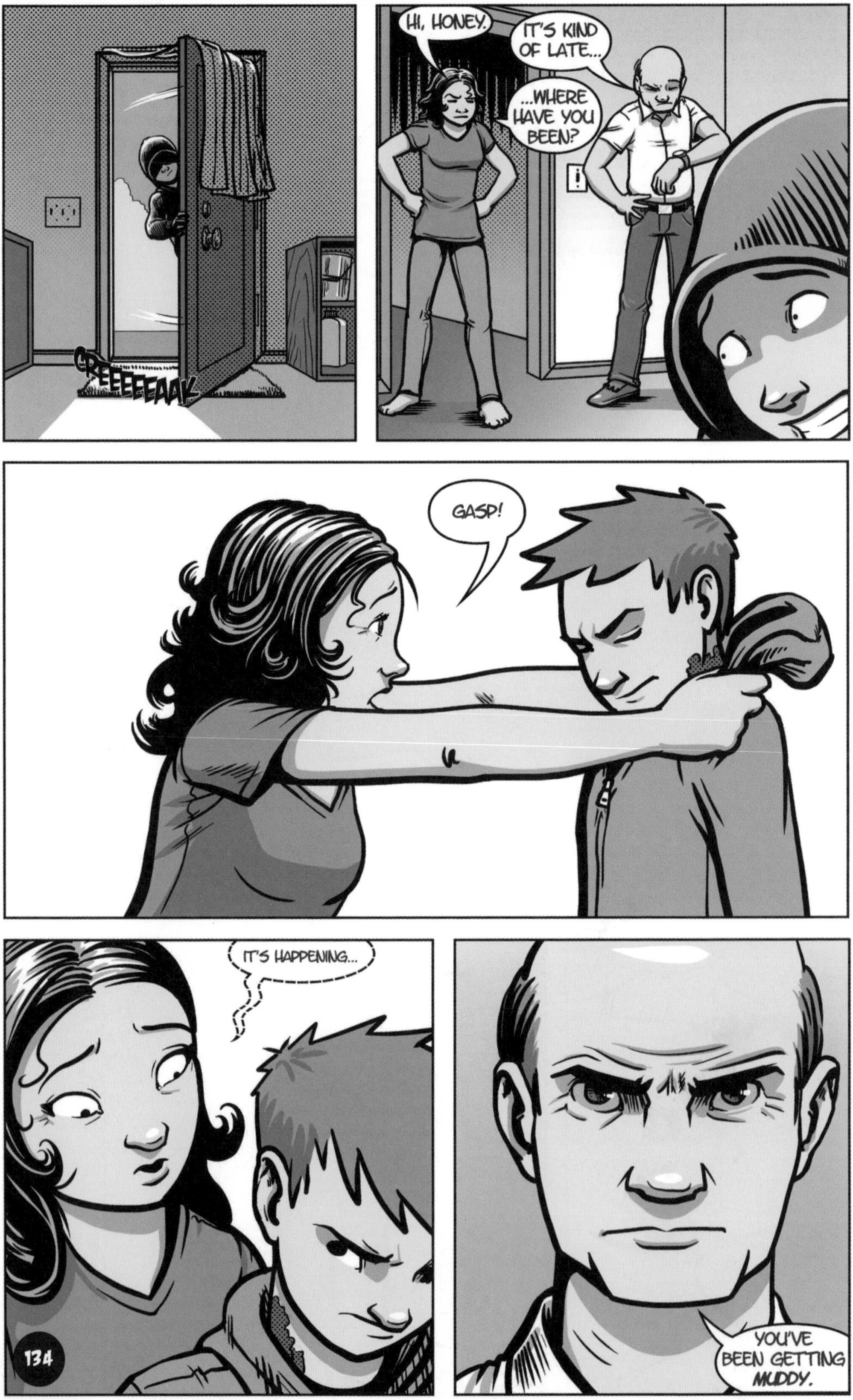
CREEEEEAAK
HI, HONEY.
IT'S KIND OF LATE...
...WHERE HAVE YOU BEEN?
GASP!
IT'S HAPPENING...
YOU'VE BEEN GETTING *MUDDY.*

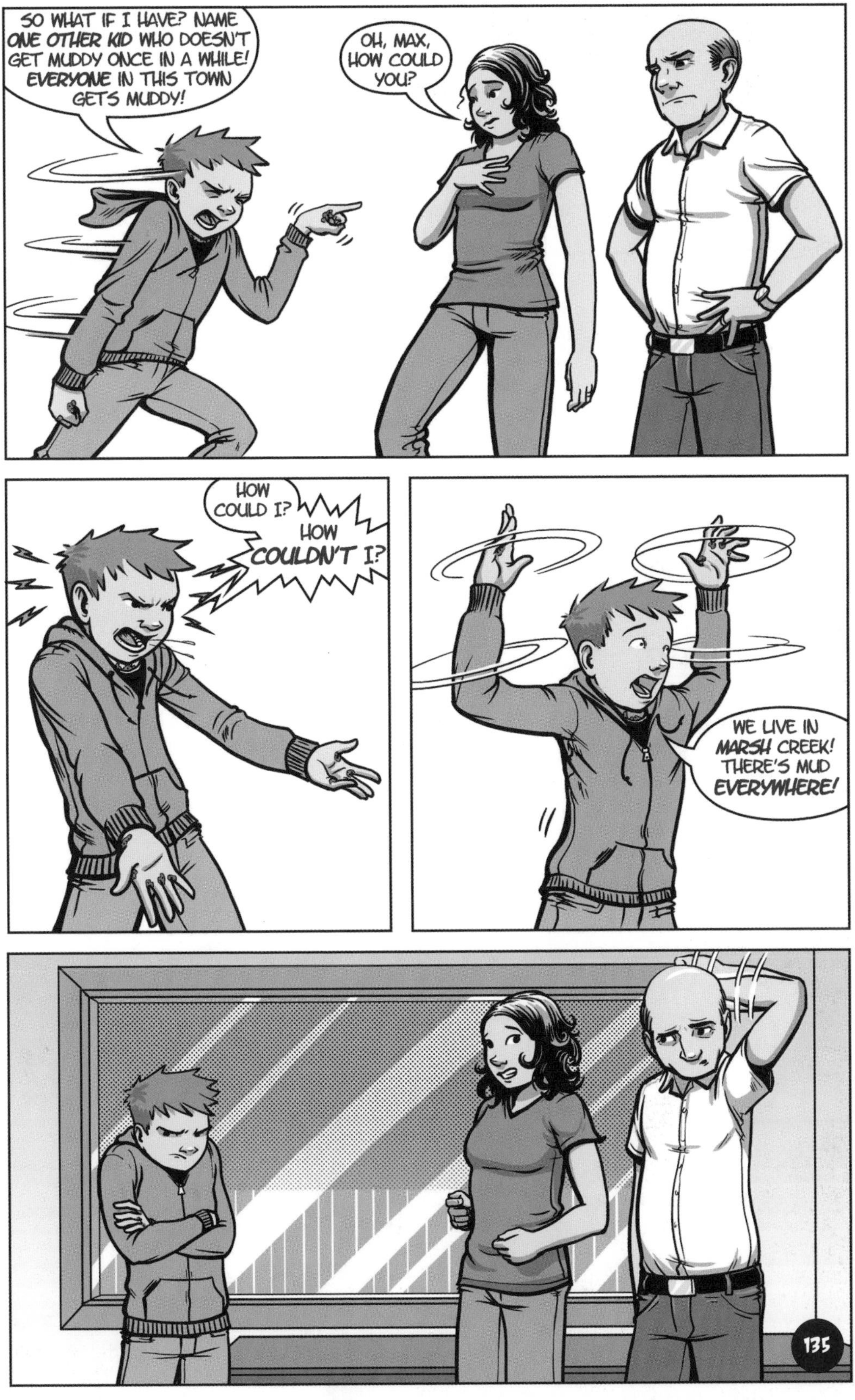
SO WHAT IF I HAVE? NAME ONE OTHER KID WHO DOESN'T GET MUDDY ONCE IN A WHILE! EVERYONE IN THIS TOWN GETS MUDDY!
OH, MAX, HOW COULD YOU?
HOW COULD I?
HOW COULDN'T I?
WE LIVE IN MARSH CREEK! THERE'S MUD EVERYWHERE!

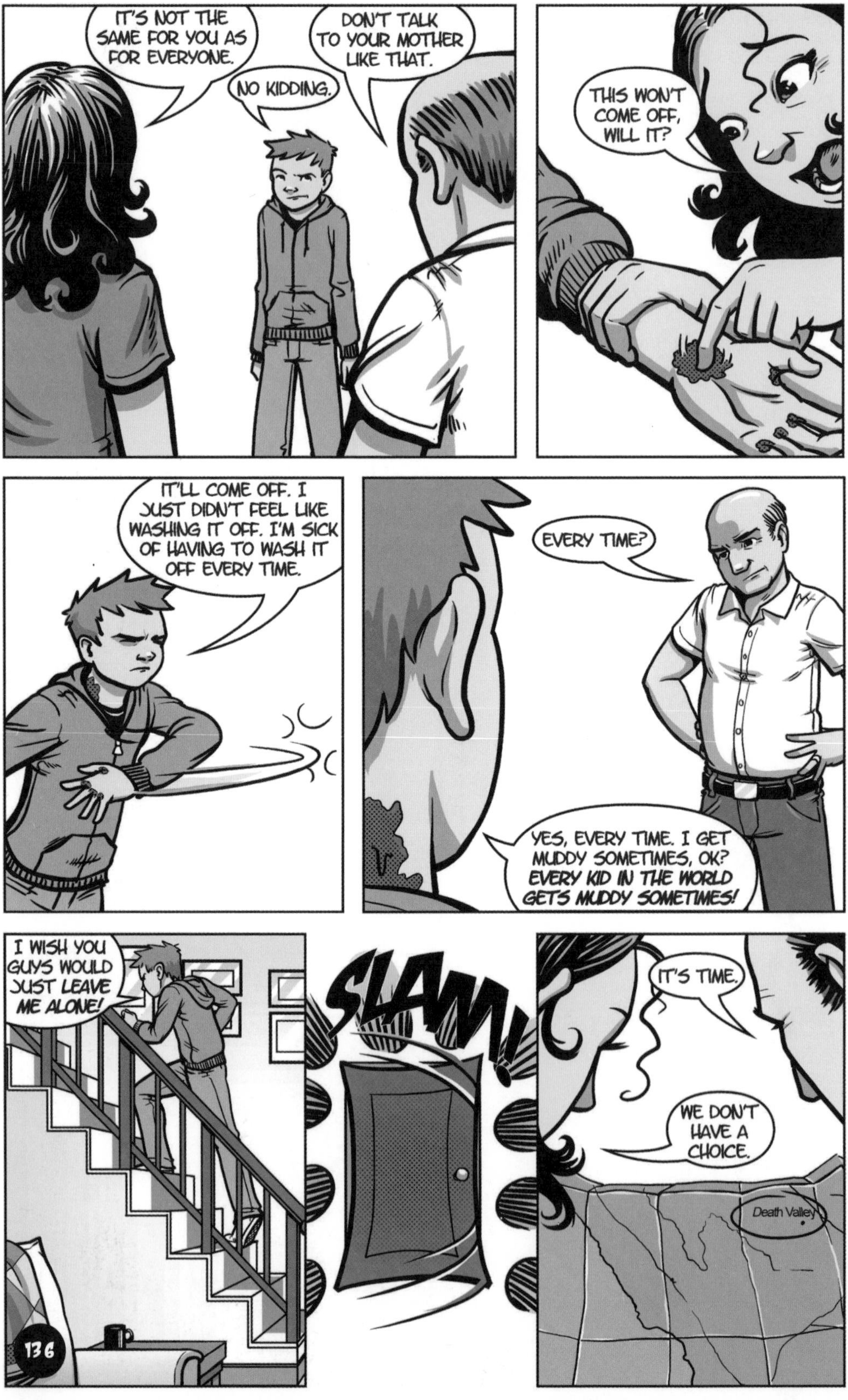

IT'S NOT THE SAME FOR YOU AS FOR EVERYONE.
NO KIDDING.
DON'T TALK TO YOUR MOTHER LIKE THAT.
THIS WON'T COME OFF, WILL IT?
IT'LL COME OFF. I JUST DIDN'T FEEL LIKE WASHING IT OFF. I'M SICK OF HAVING TO WASH IT OFF EVERY TIME.
EVERY TIME?
YES, EVERY TIME. I GET MUDDY SOMETIMES, OK? EVERY KID IN THE WORLD GETS MUDDY SOMETIMES!
I WISH YOU GUYS WOULD JUST LEAVE ME ALONE!
SLAM!!
IT'S TIME.
WE DON'T HAVE A CHOICE.
Death Valley

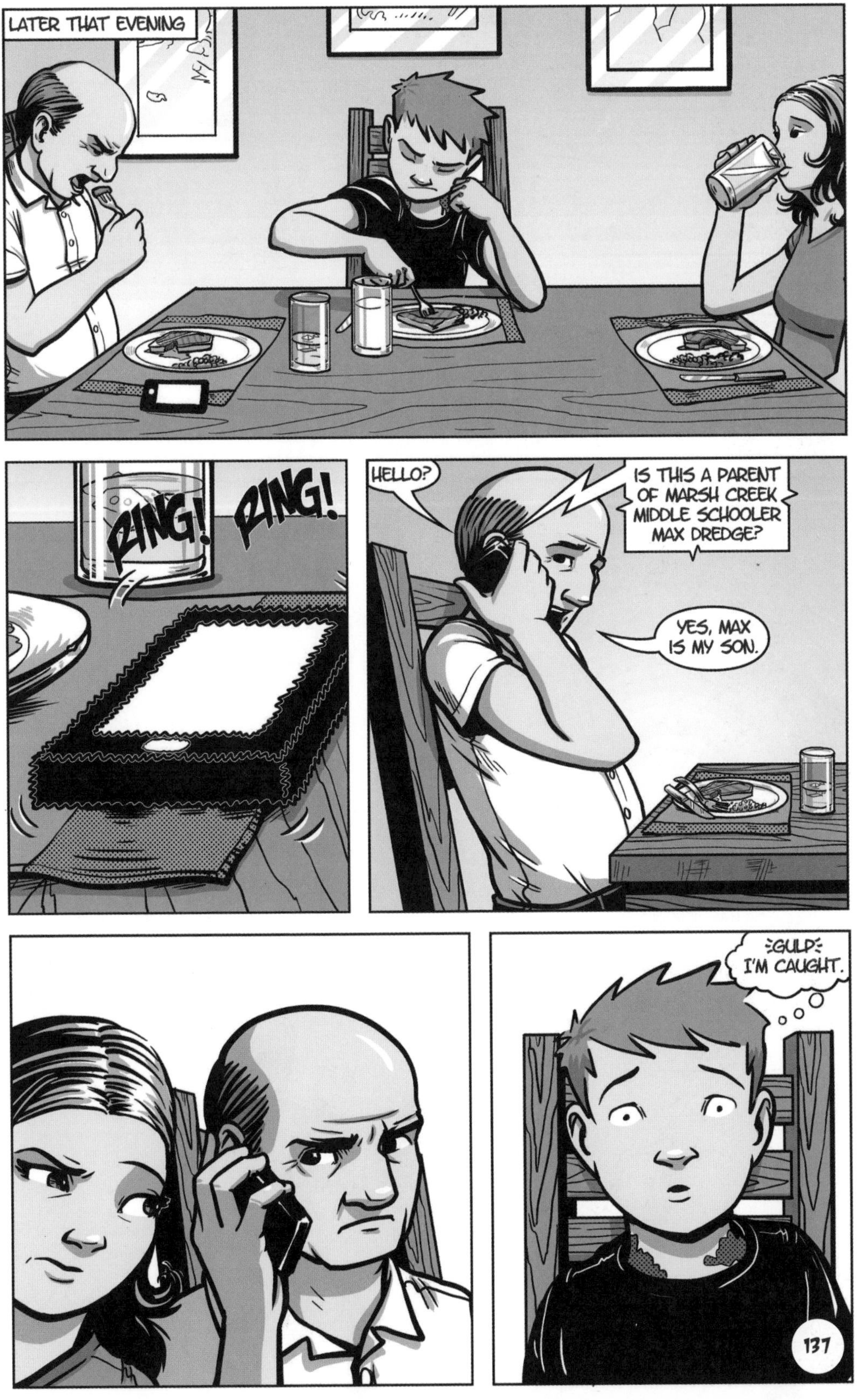
LATER THAT EVENING
RING! RING!
HELLO?
IS THIS A PARENT OF MARSH CREEK MIDDLE SCHOOLER MAX DREDGE?
YES, MAX IS MY SON.
GULP
I'M CAUGHT.

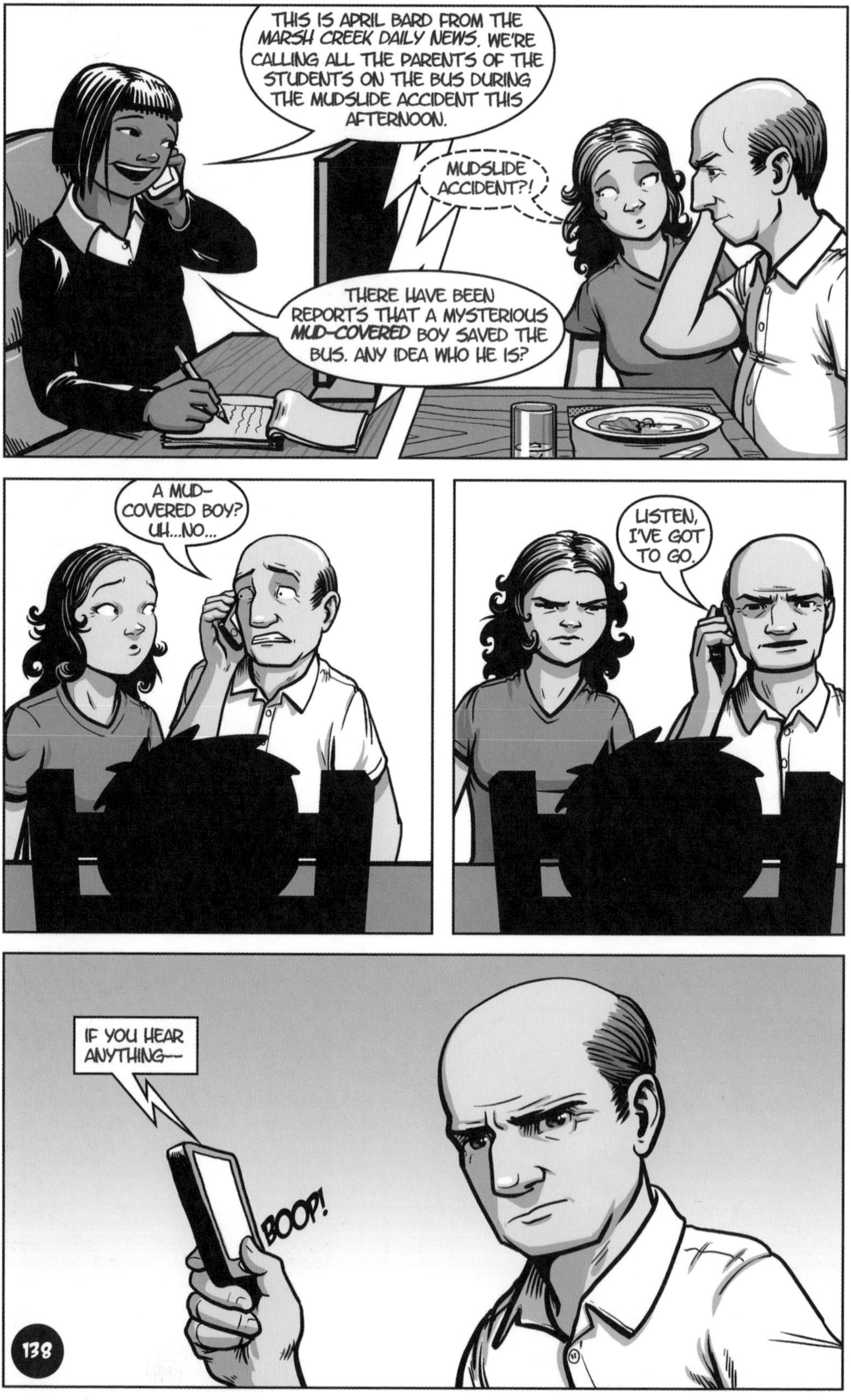
THIS IS APRIL BARD FROM THE MARSH CREEK DAILY NEWS. WE'RE CALLING ALL THE PARENTS OF THE STUDENTS ON THE BUS DURING THE MUDSLIDE ACCIDENT THIS AFTERNOON.
MUDSLIDE ACCIDENT?!
THERE HAVE BEEN REPORTS THAT A MYSTERIOUS MUD-COVERED BOY SAVED THE BUS. ANY IDEA WHO HE IS?
A MUD-COVERED BOY? UH...NO...
LISTEN, I'VE GOT TO GO.
IF YOU HEAR ANYTHING--
BOOP!

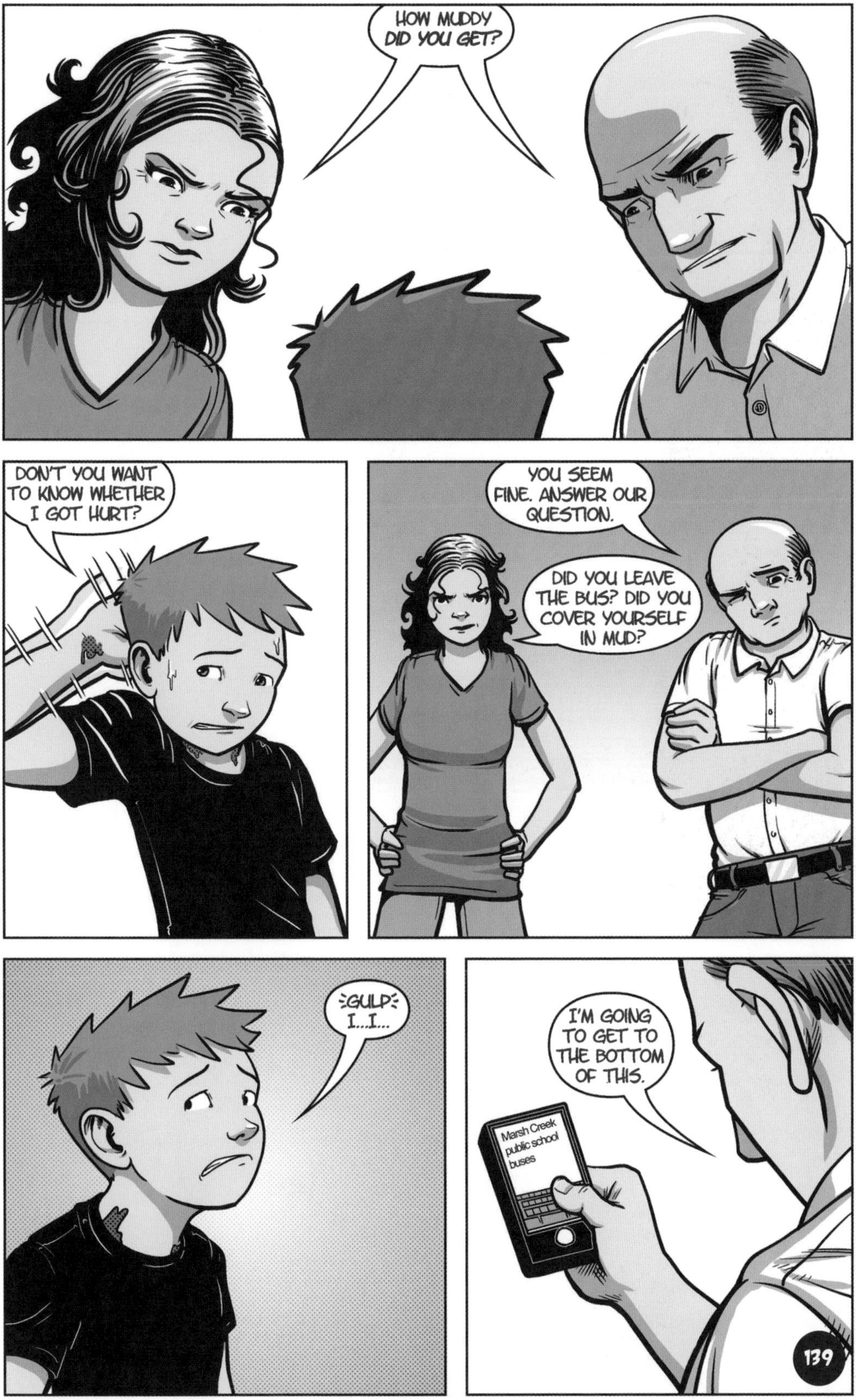
HOW MUDDY DID YOU GET?
DON'T YOU WANT TO KNOW WHETHER I GOT HURT?
YOU SEEM FINE. ANSWER OUR QUESTION.
DID YOU LEAVE THE BUS? DID YOU COVER YOURSELF IN MUD?
GULP
I...I...
I'M GOING TO GET TO THE BOTTOM OF THIS.
Marsh Creek public school buses

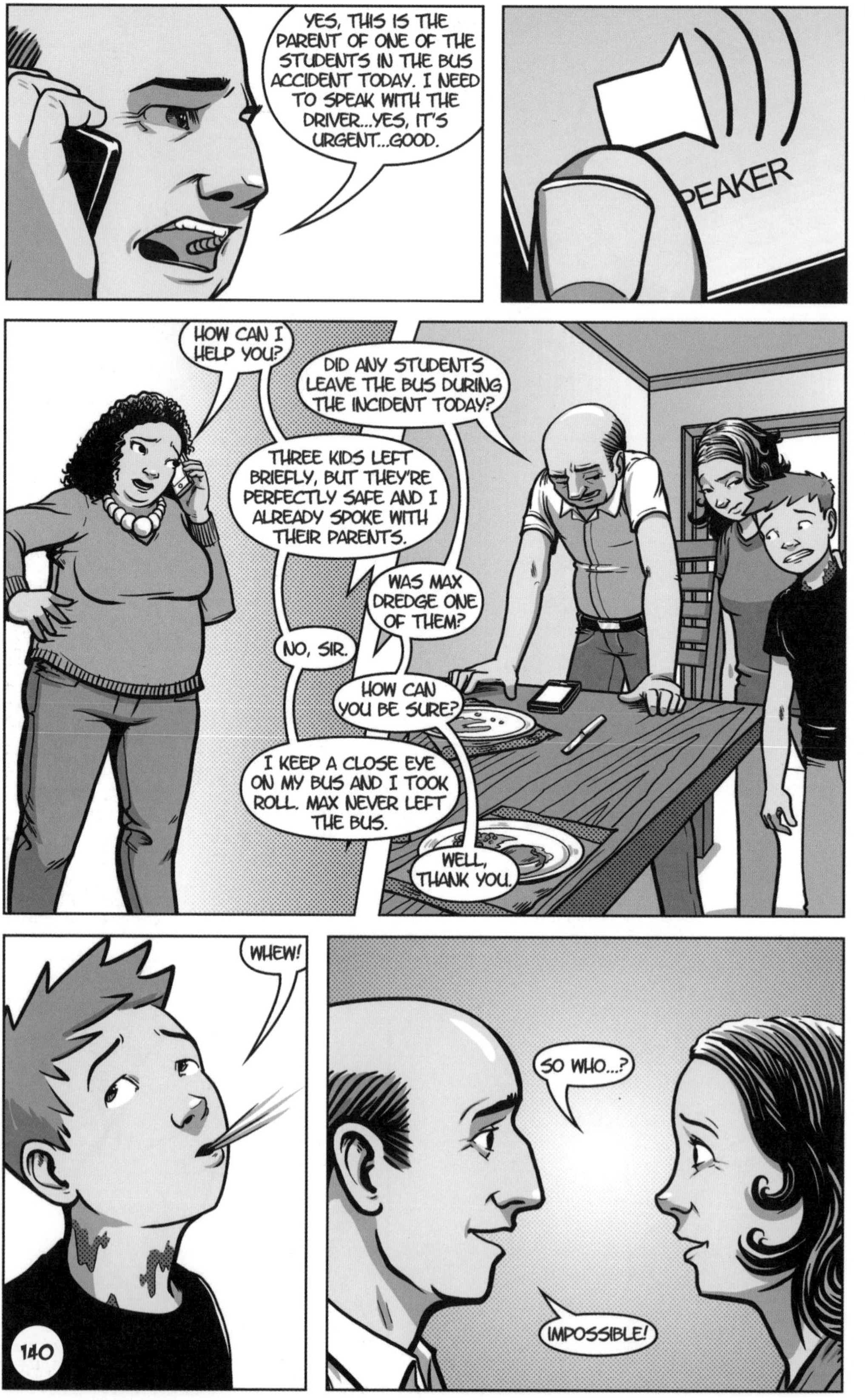

YES, THIS IS THE PARENT OF ONE OF THE STUDENTS IN THE BUS ACCIDENT TODAY. I NEED TO SPEAK WITH THE DRIVER...YES, IT'S URGENT...GOOD.
PEAKER
HOW CAN I HELP YOU?
DID ANY STUDENTS LEAVE THE BUS DURING THE INCIDENT TODAY?
THREE KIDS LEFT BRIEFLY, BUT THEY'RE PERFECTLY SAFE AND I ALREADY SPOKE WITH THEIR PARENTS.
WAS MAX DREDGE ONE OF THEM?
NO, SIR.
HOW CAN YOU BE SURE?
I KEEP A CLOSE EYE ON MY BUS AND I TOOK ROLL. MAX NEVER LEFT THE BUS.
WELL, THANK YOU.
WHEW!
SO WHO...?
IMPOSSIBLE!

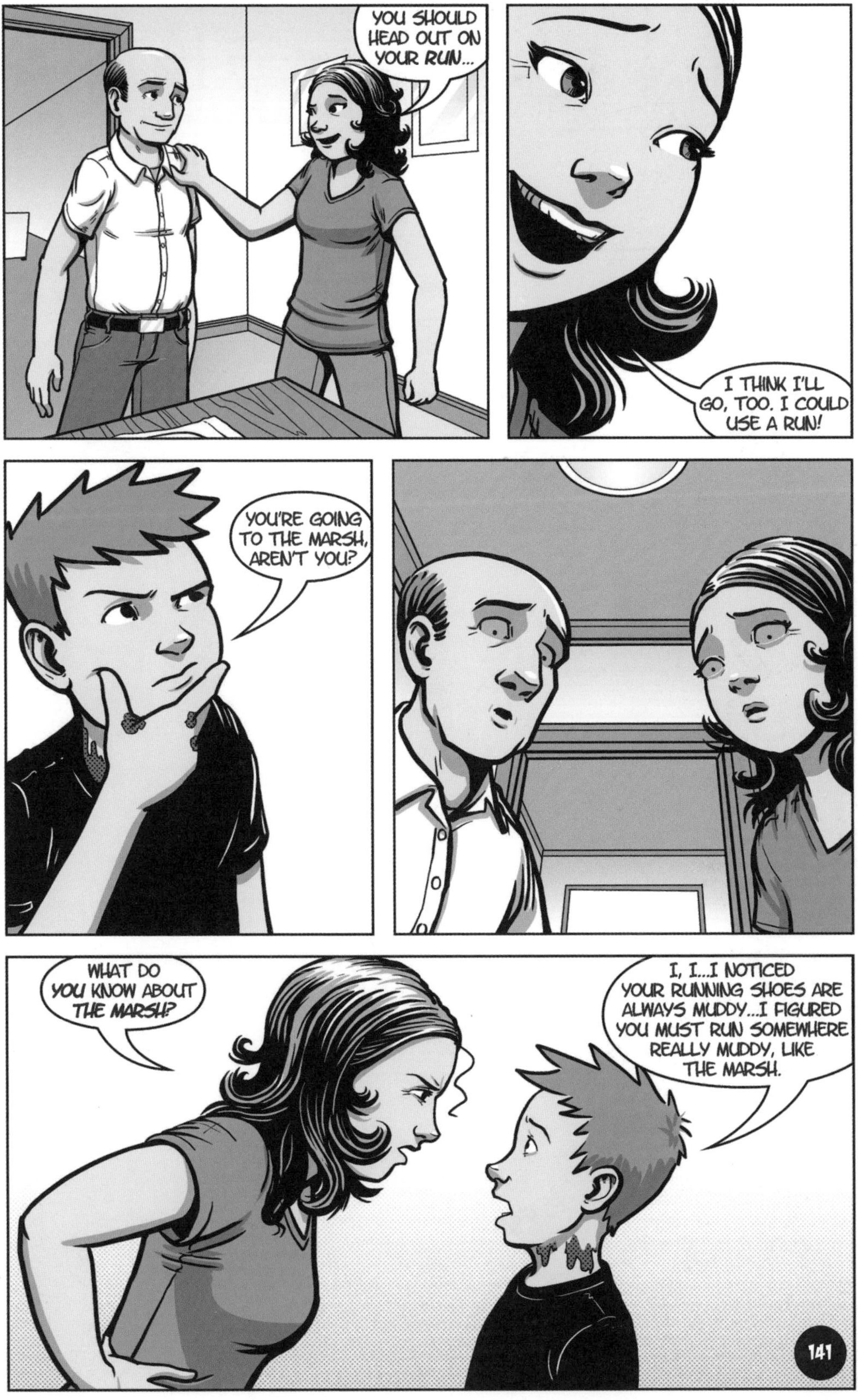
YOU SHOULD HEAD OUT ON YOUR *RUN*...
I THINK I'LL GO, TOO. I COULD USE A RUN!
YOU'RE GOING TO THE MARSH, AREN'T YOU?
WHAT DO YOU KNOW ABOUT *THE MARSH?*
I, I...I NOTICED YOUR RUNNING SHOES ARE ALWAYS MUDDY...I FIGURED YOU MUST RUN SOMEWHERE REALLY MUDDY, LIKE THE MARSH.

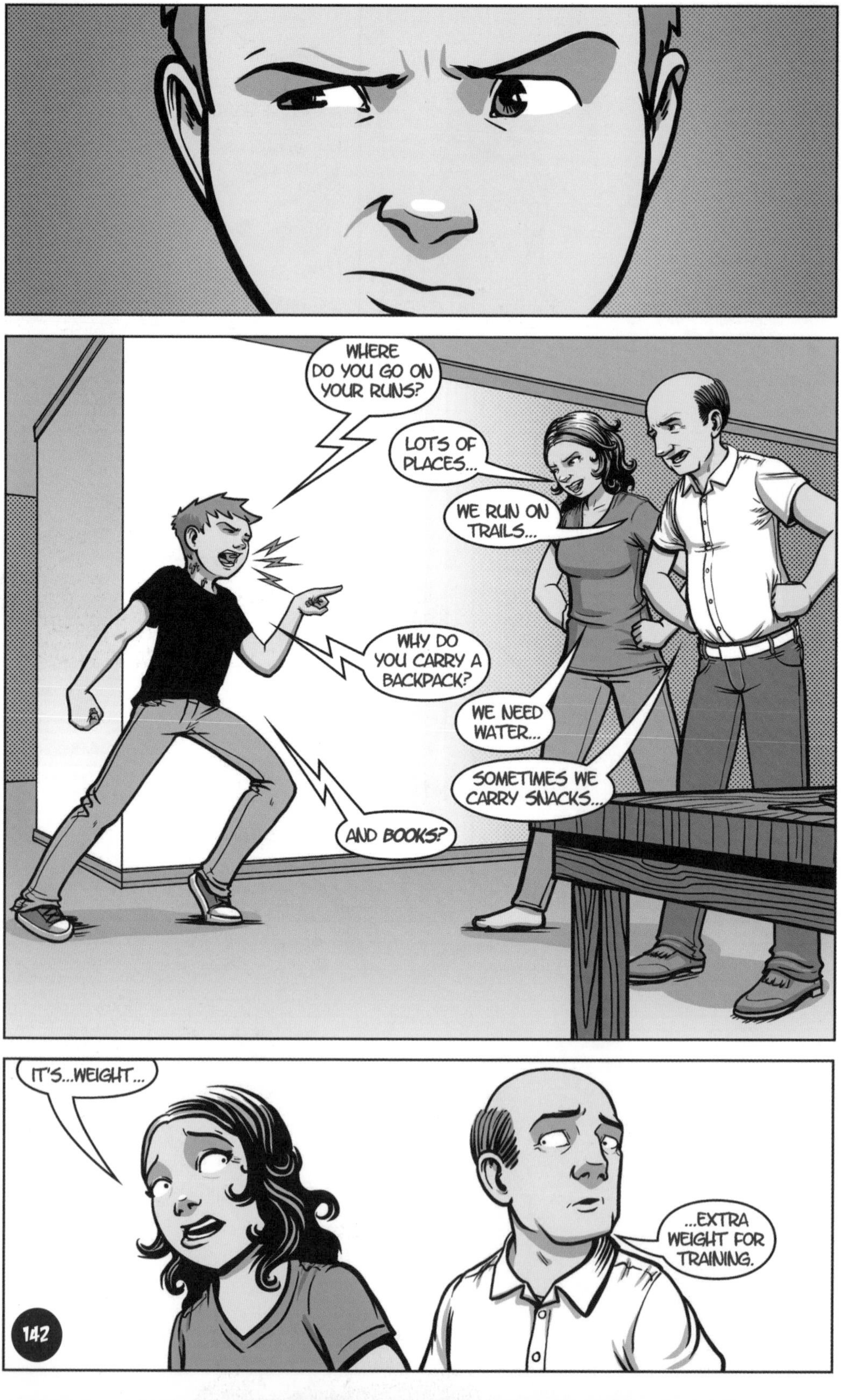
WHERE DO YOU GO ON YOUR RUNS?
LOTS OF PLACES...
WE RUN ON TRAILS...
WHY DO YOU CARRY A BACKPACK?
WE NEED WATER...
SOMETIMES WE CARRY SNACKS...
AND *BOOKS?*
IT'S...WEIGHT...
...EXTRA WEIGHT FOR TRAINING.

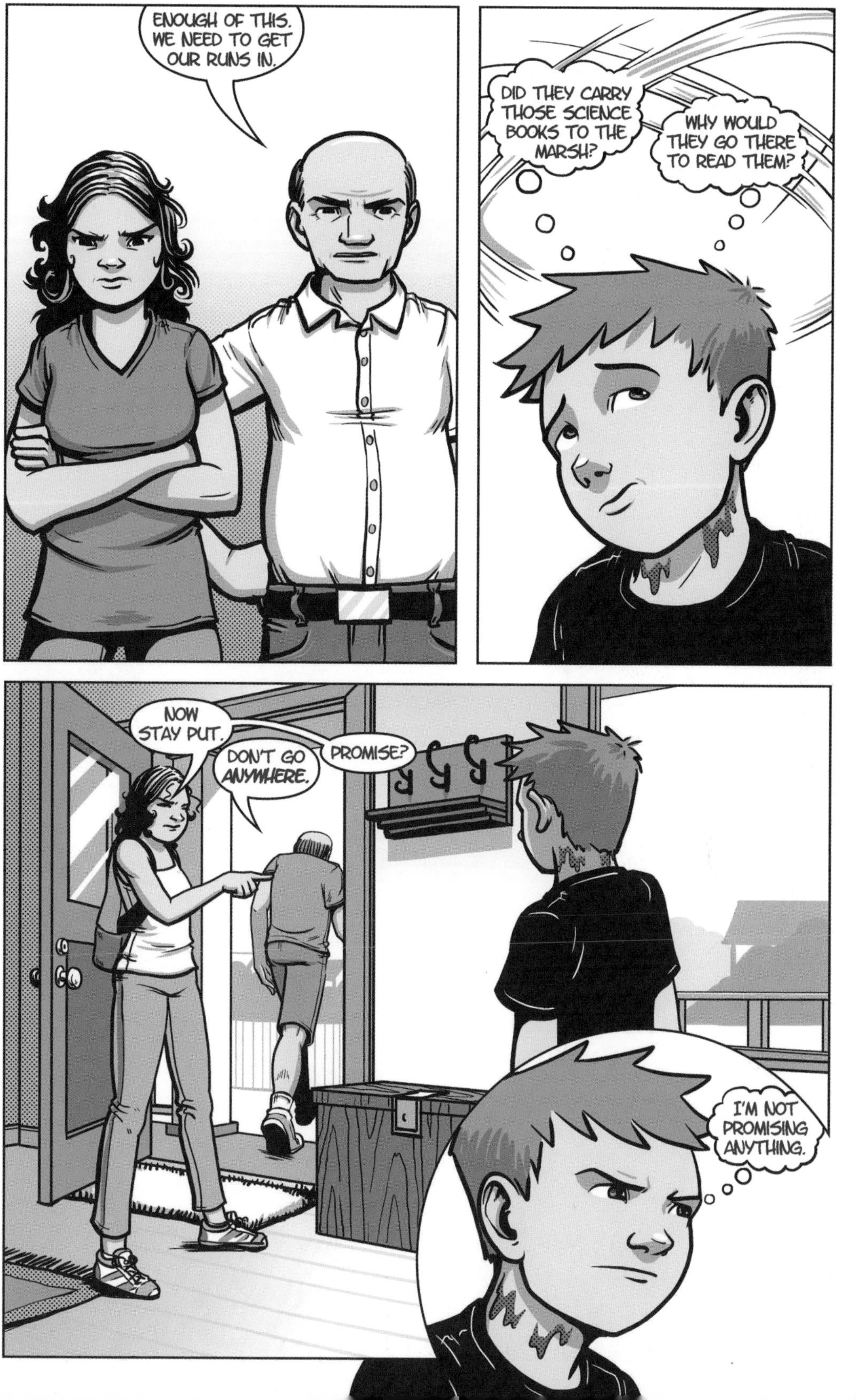
ENOUGH OF THIS. WE NEED TO GET OUR RUNS IN.
DID THEY CARRY THOSE SCIENCE BOOKS TO THE MARSH?
WHY WOULD THEY GO THERE TO READ THEM?
NOW STAY PUT.
DON'T GO ANYWHERE.
PROMISE?
I'M NOT PROMISING ANYTHING.

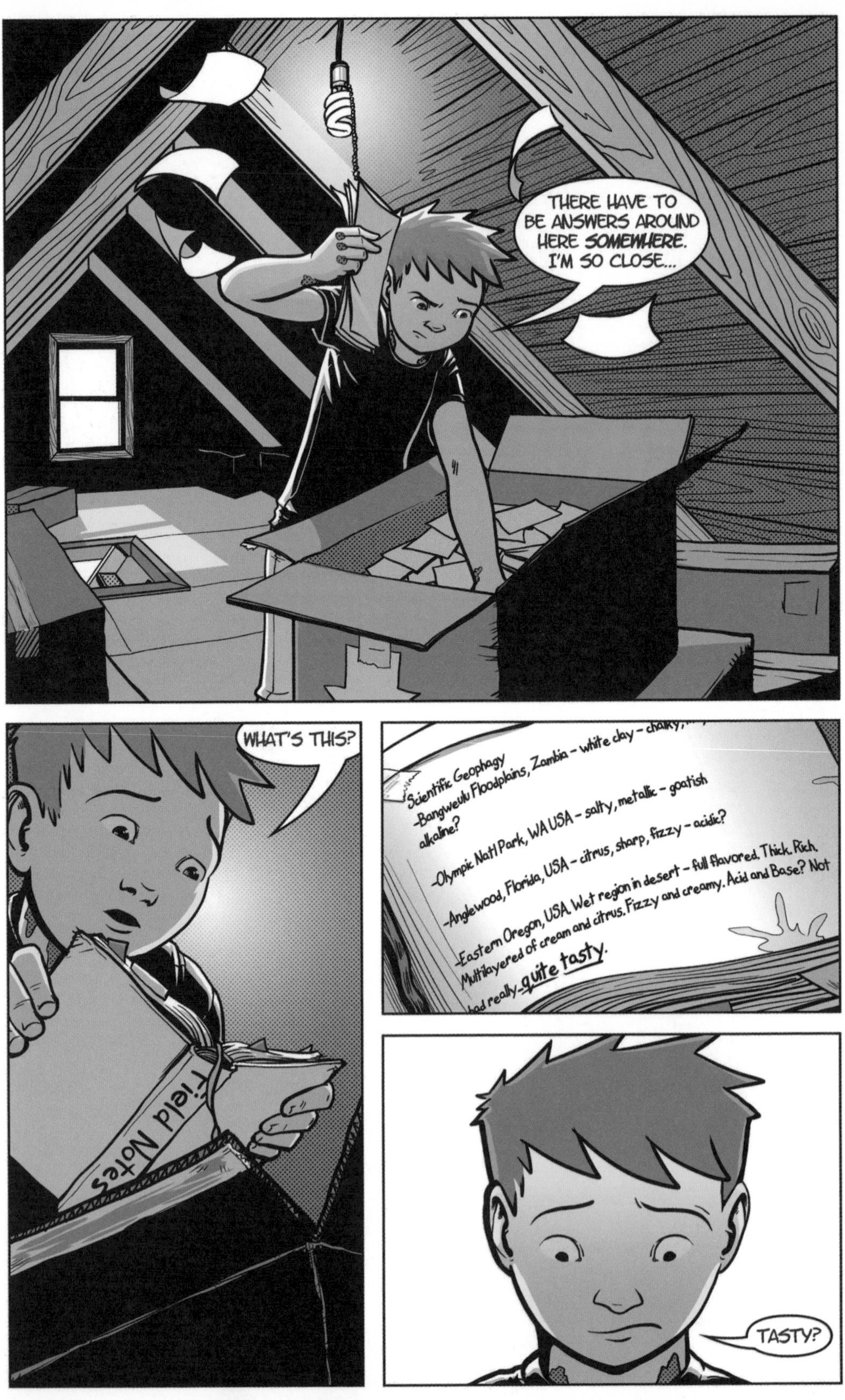
THERE HAVE TO BE ANSWERS AROUND HERE SOMEWHERE. I'M SO CLOSE...
WHAT'S THIS?
Field Notes
Scientific Geophagy
-Bangweulu Floodplains, Zambia - white clay - chalky,
alkaline?
-Olympic Natl Park, WA USA - salty, metallic - goatish
-Anglewood, Florida, USA - citrus, sharp, fizzy - acidic?
-Eastern Oregon, USA. Wet region in desert - full flavored. Thick. Rich. Multilayered of cream and citrus. Fizzy and creamy. Acid and Base? Not bad really- quite tasty.
TASTY?

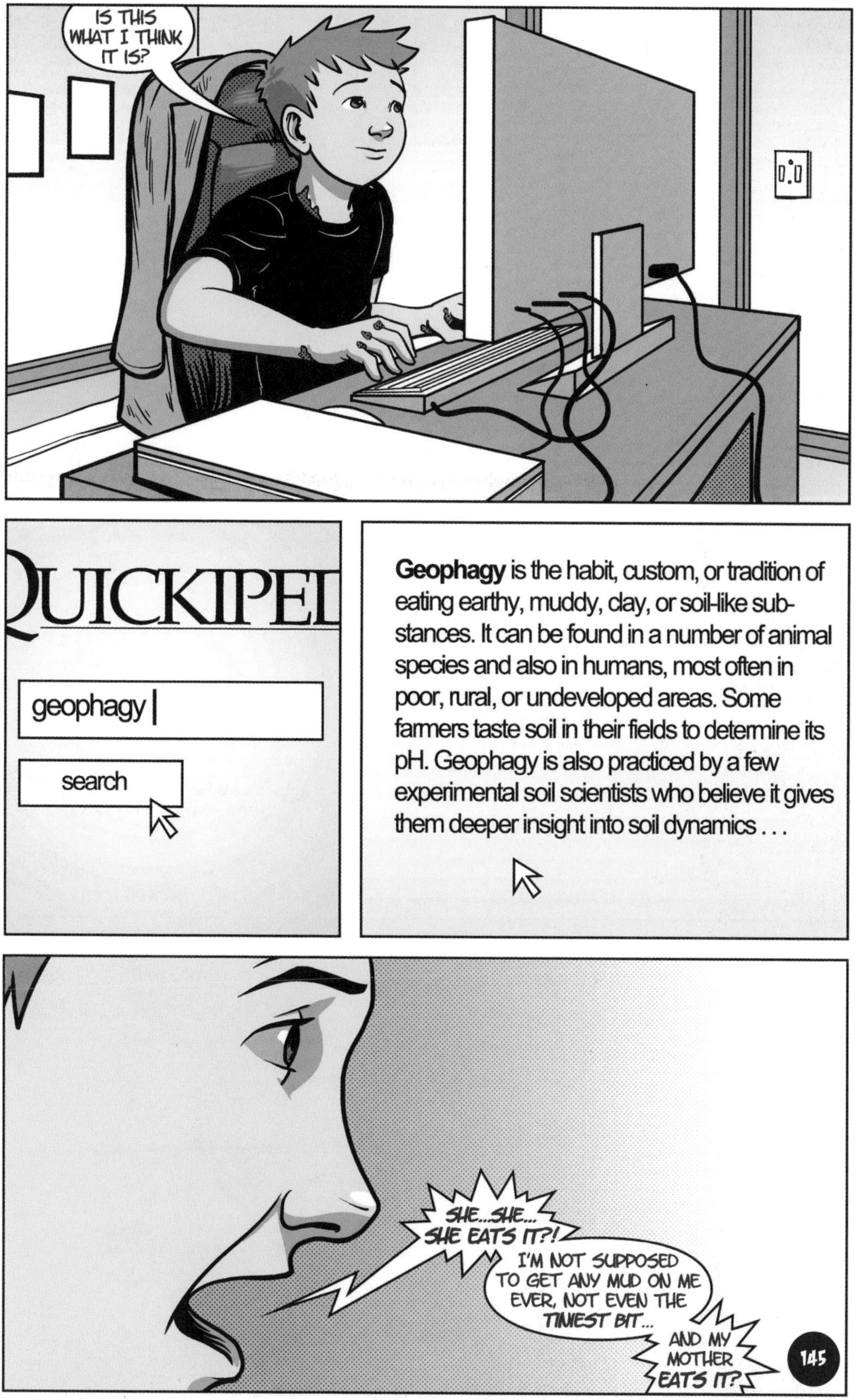
IS THIS WHAT I THINK IT IS?
QUICKIPED
geophagy
search
Geophagy is the habit, custom, or tradition of eating earthy, muddy, clay, or soil-like substances. It can be found in a number of animal species and also in humans, most often in poor, rural, or undeveloped areas. Some farmers taste soil in their fields to determine its pH. Geophagy is also practiced by a few experimental soil scientists who believe it gives them deeper insight into soil dynamics . . .
SHE...SHE... SHE EATS IT?!
I'M NOT SUPPOSED TO GET ANY MUD ON ME EVER, NOT EVEN THE TINIEST BIT...
AND MY MOTHER EATS IT?

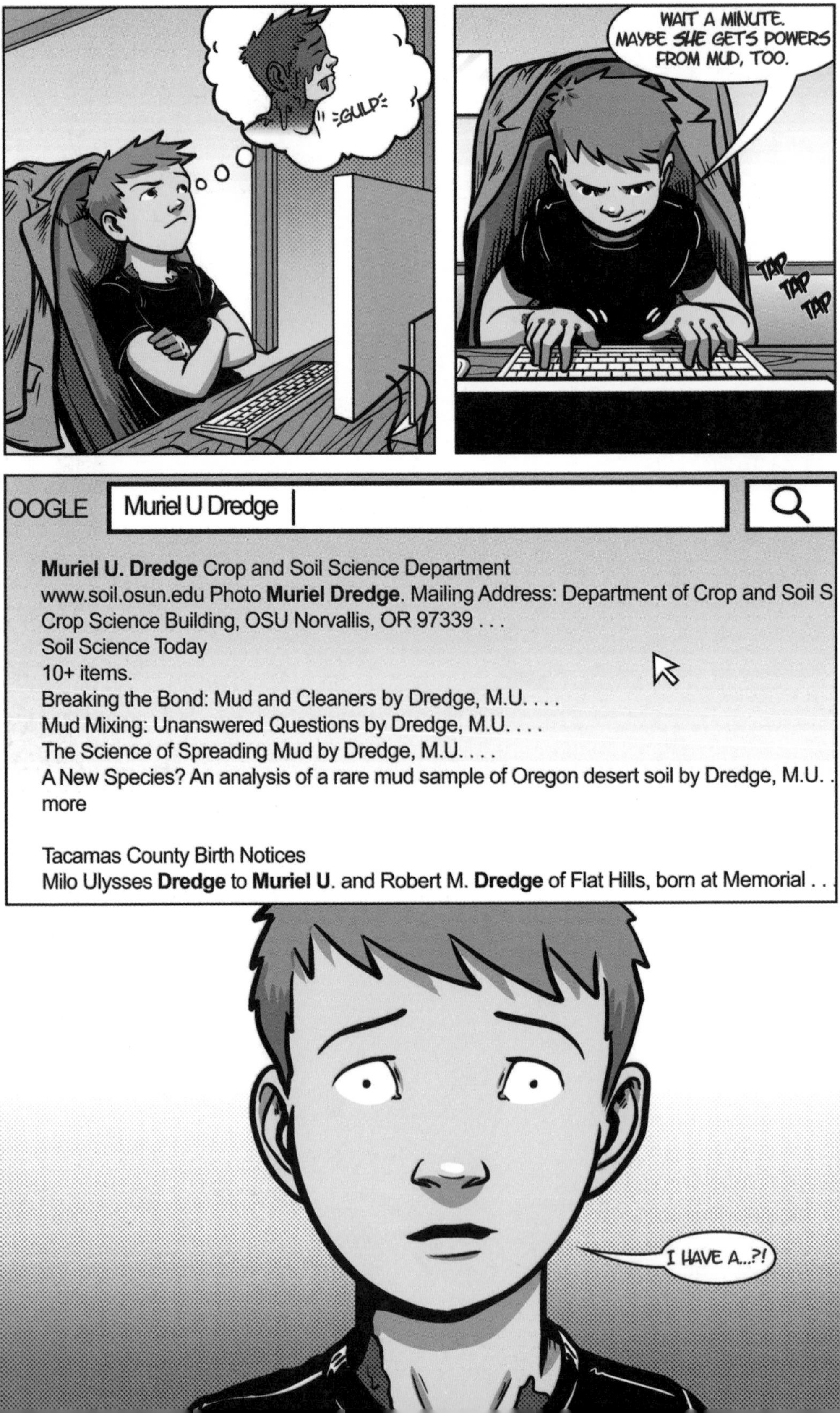
GULP
WAIT A MINUTE. MAYBE SHE GETS POWERS FROM MUD, TOO.
TAP TAP TAP
OOGLE
Muriel U Dredge
Muriel U. Dredge Crop and Soil Science Department
www.soil.osun.edu Photo Muriel Dredge. Mailing Address: Department of Crop and Soil S
Crop Science Building, OSU Norvallis, OR 97339 . . .
Soil Science Today
10+ items.
Breaking the Bond: Mud and Cleaners by Dredge, M.U. . . .
Mud Mixing: Unanswered Questions by Dredge, M.U. . . .
The Science of Spreading Mud by Dredge, M.U. . . .
A New Species? An analysis of a rare mud sample of Oregon desert soil by Dredge, M.U. .
more
Tacamas County Birth Notices
Milo Ulysses Dredge to Muriel U. and Robert M. Dredge of Flat Hills, born at Memorial . . .
I HAVE A...?!

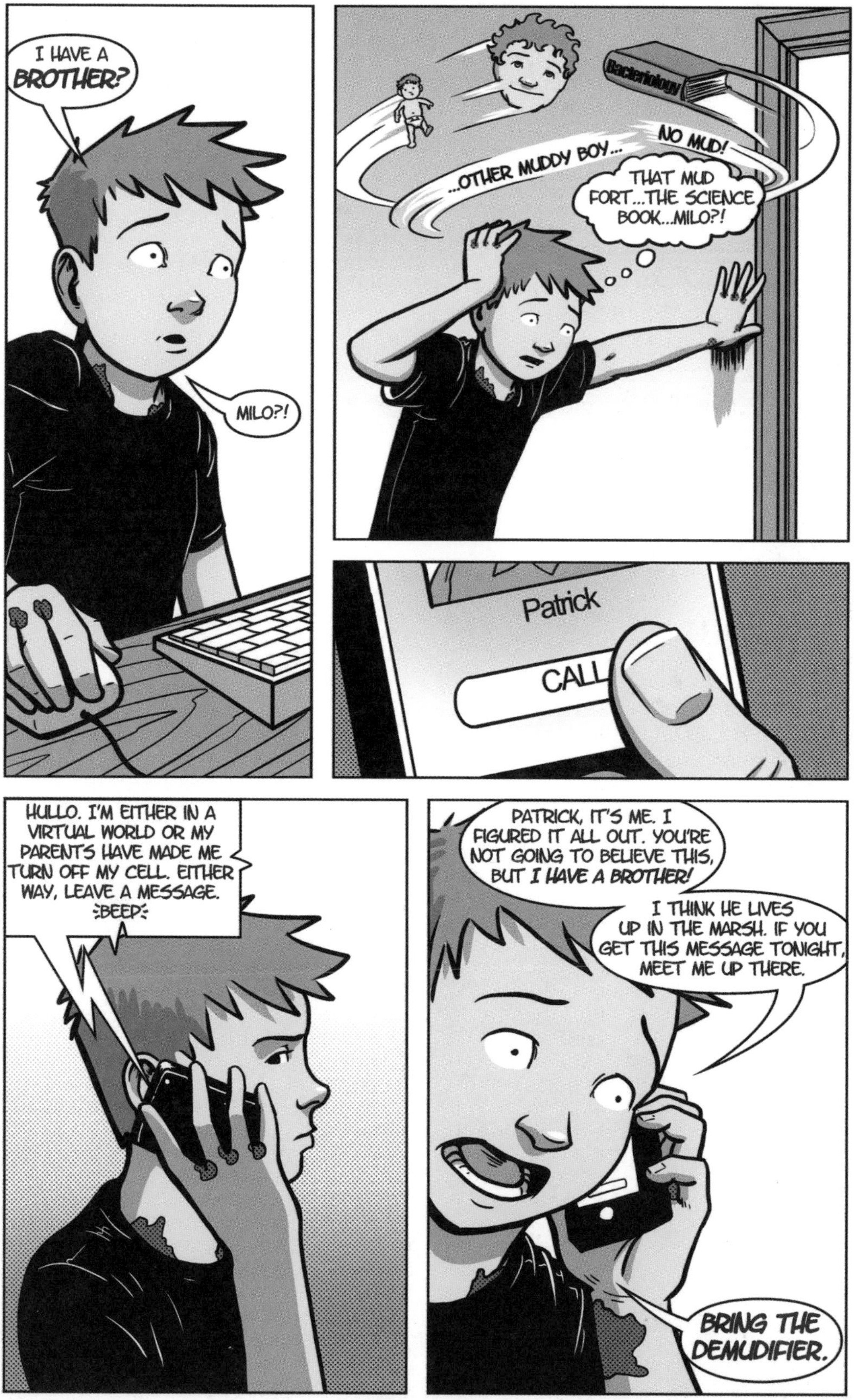
I HAVE A BROTHER?
MILO?!
Bacteriology
...OTHER MUDDY BOY...
NO MUD!
THAT MUD FORT...THE SCIENCE BOOK...MILO?!
Patrick
CALL
HULLO. I'M EITHER IN A VIRTUAL WORLD OR MY PARENT'S HAVE MADE ME TURN OFF MY CELL. EITHER WAY, LEAVE A MESSAGE.
BEEP
PATRICK, IT'S ME. I FIGURED IT ALL OUT. YOU'RE NOT GOING TO BELIEVE THIS, BUT I HAVE A BROTHER!
I THINK HE LIVES UP IN THE MARSH. IF YOU GET THIS MESSAGE TONIGHT, MEET ME UP THERE.
BRING THE DEMUDIFIER.

PART 3

STUCK IN THE MUD

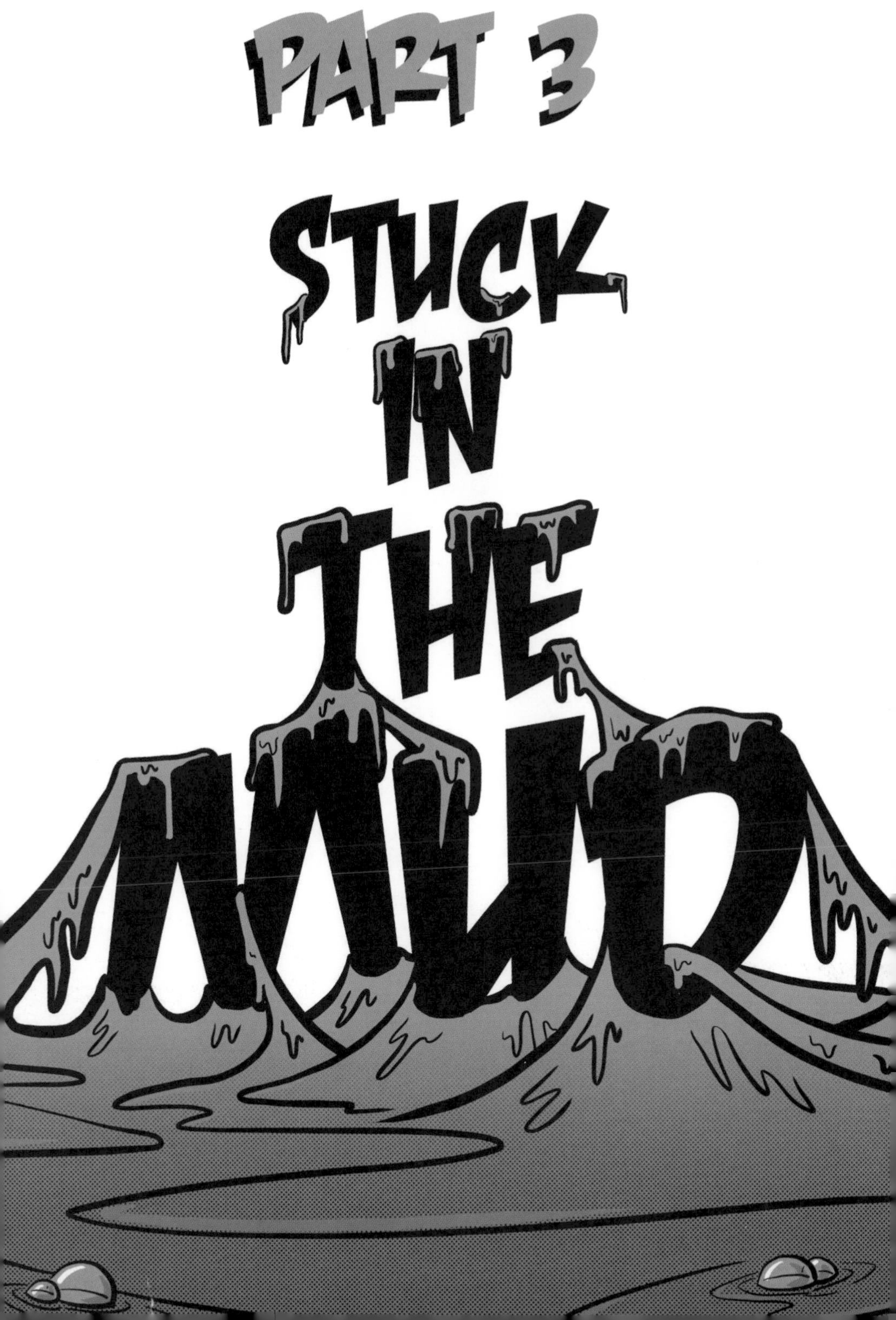

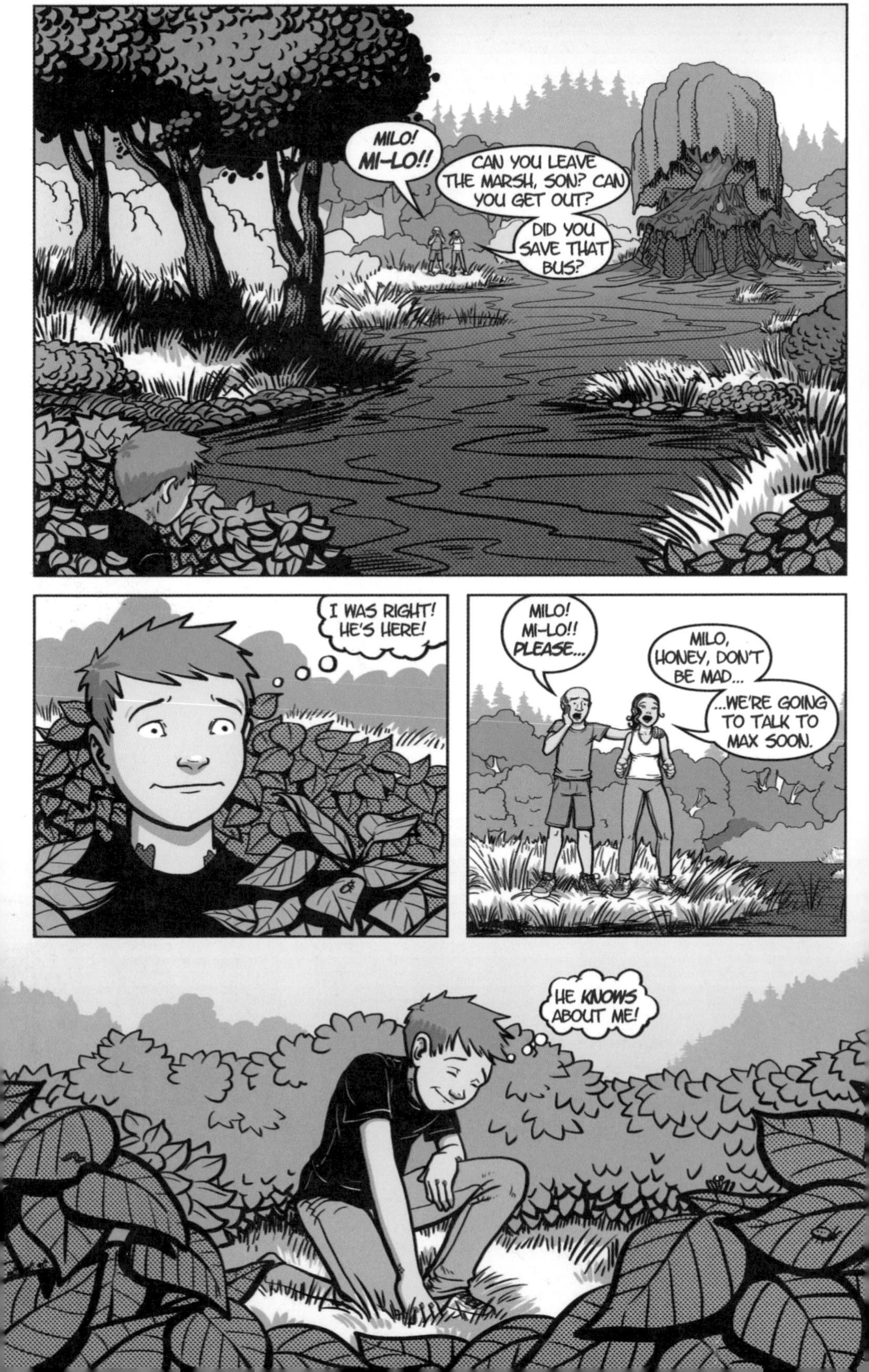
MILO! MI-LO!!
CAN YOU LEAVE THE MARSH, SON? CAN YOU GET OUT?
DID YOU SAVE THAT BUS?
I WAS RIGHT! HE'S HERE!
MILO! MI-LO!! PLEASE...
MILO, HONEY, DON'T BE MAD...
...WE'RE GOING TO TALK TO MAX SOON.
HE KNOWS ABOUT ME!

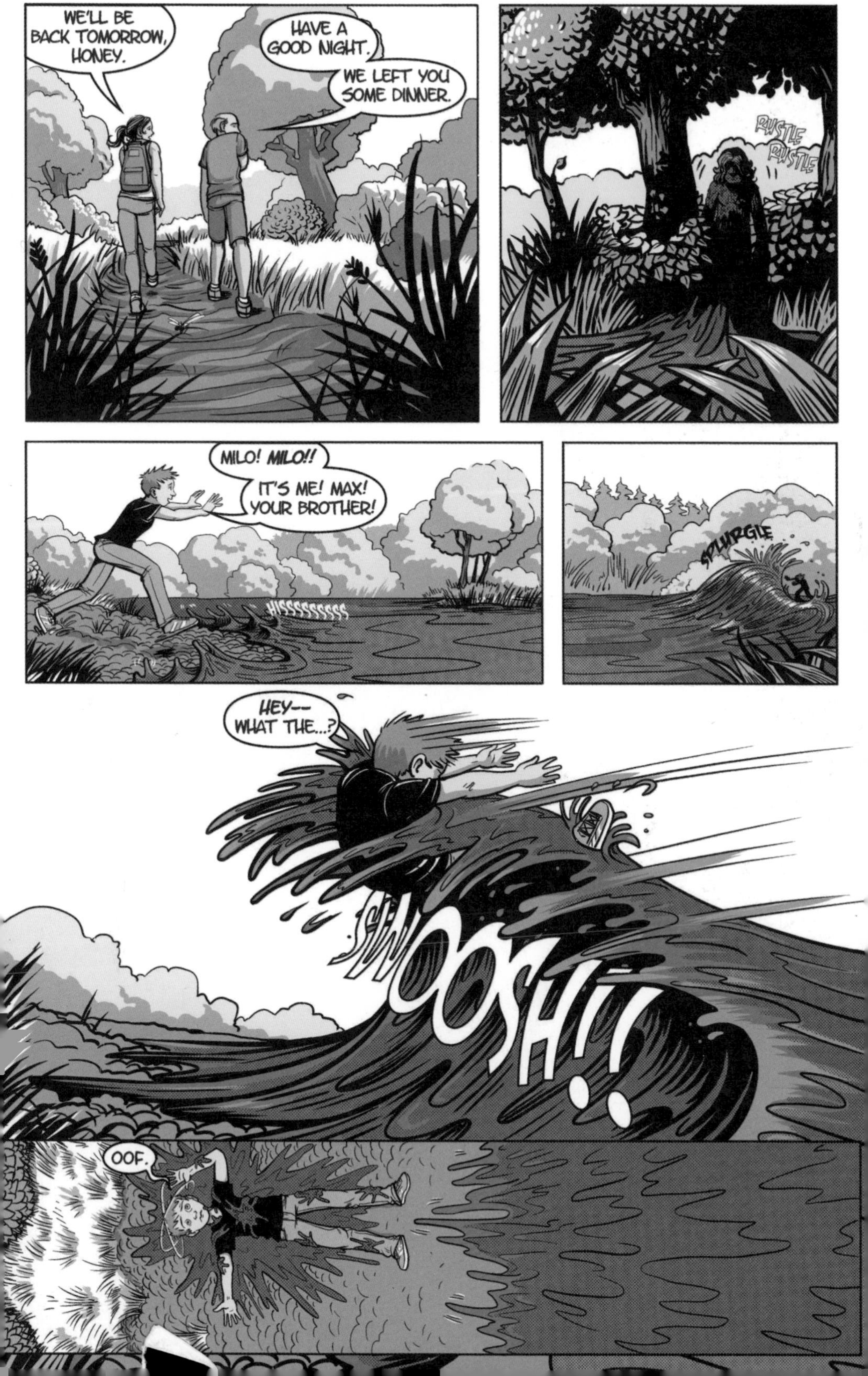
WE'LL BE BACK TOMORROW, HONEY.
HAVE A GOOD NIGHT.
WE LEFT YOU SOME DINNER.
RUSTLE
RUSTLE
MILO! MILO!!
IT'S ME! MAX! YOUR BROTHER!
HISSSSSSSSS
SPLURGLE
HEY-- WHAT THE...?
SHOOSH!!
OOF.

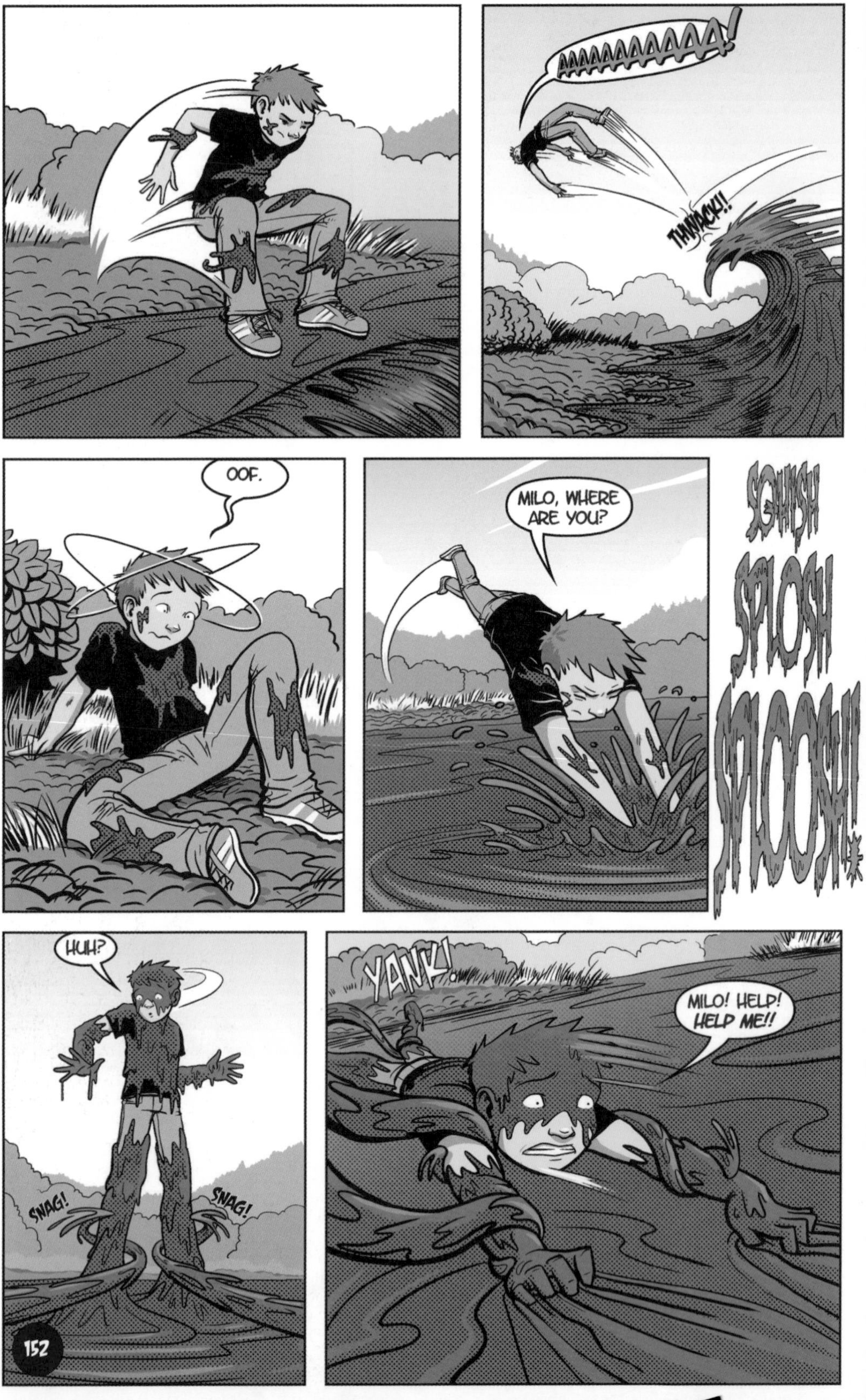
AAAAAAAAAAA!
THWACK!!
OOF.
MILO, WHERE ARE YOU?
SQUISH
SPLOSH
SPLOOSH!
HUH?
SNAG!
SNAG!
YANK!
MILO! HELP! HELP ME!!

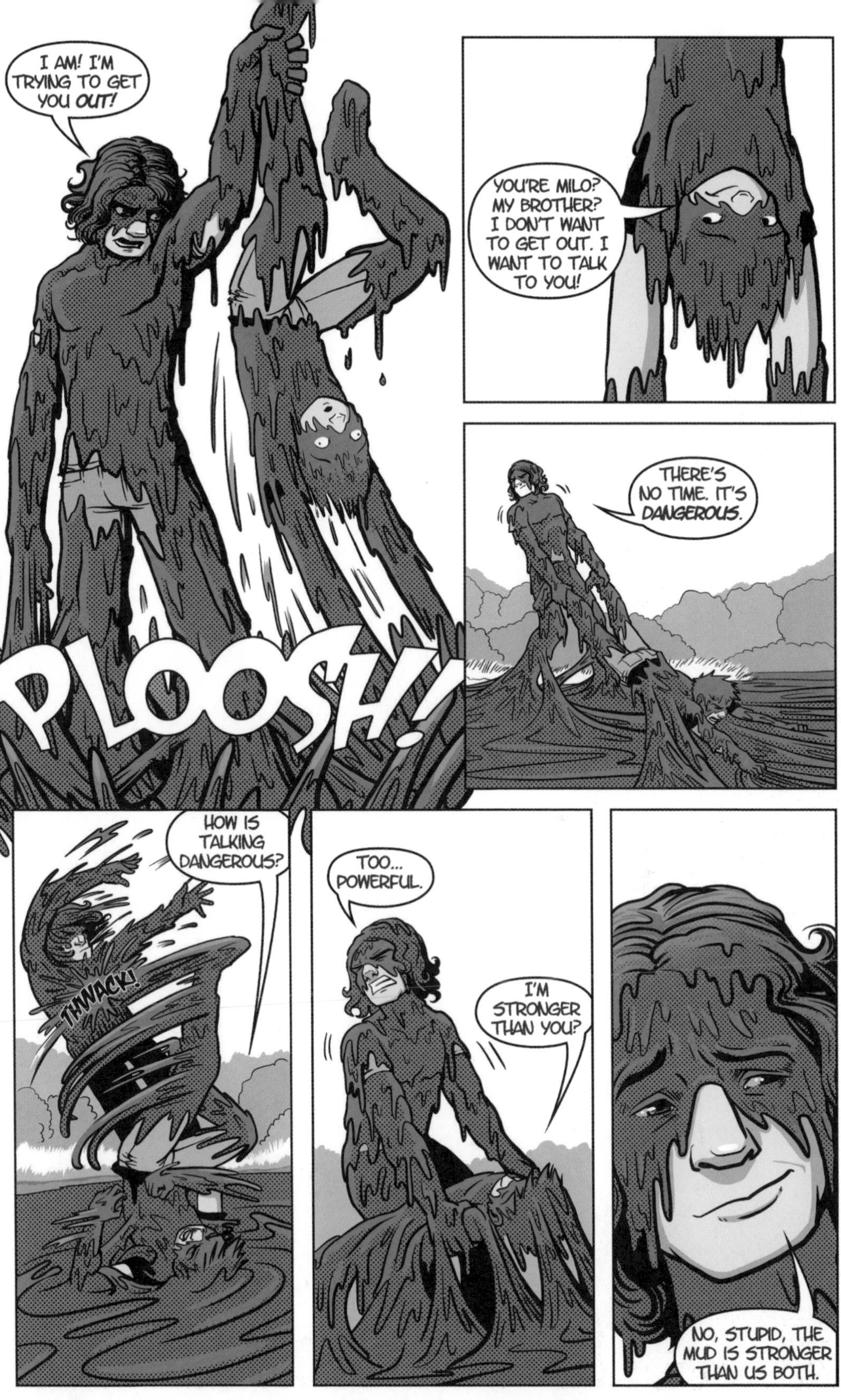
I AM! I'M TRYING TO GET YOU OUT!
PLOOSH!
YOU'RE MILO? MY BROTHER? I DON'T WANT TO GET OUT. I WANT TO TALK TO YOU!
THERE'S NO TIME. IT'S DANGEROUS.
HOW IS TALKING DANGEROUS?
THWACK!
TOO... POWERFUL.
I'M STRONGER THAN YOU?
NO, STUPID, THE MUD IS STRONGER THAN US BOTH.

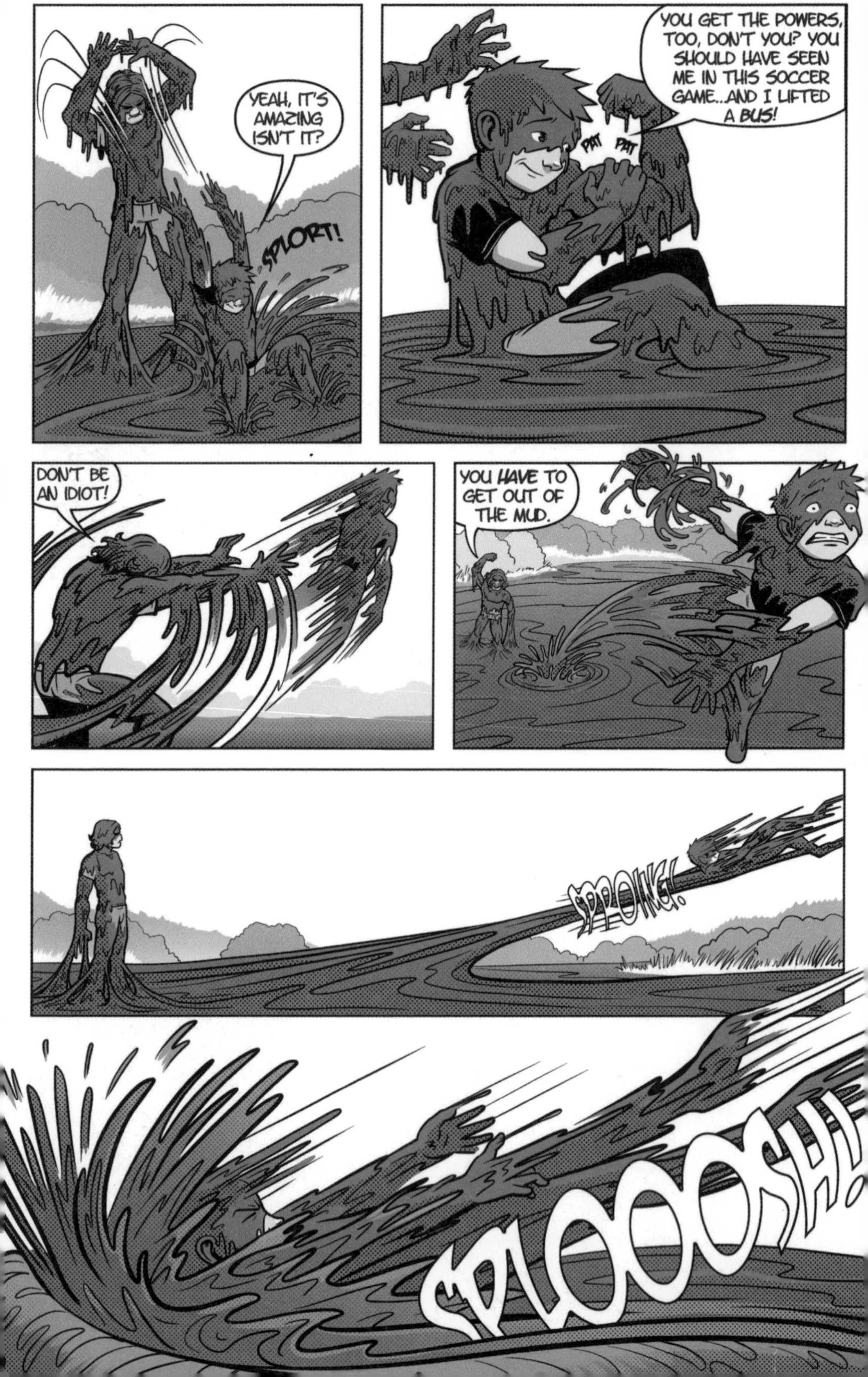

YEAH, IT'S AMAZING ISN'T IT?
SPLORT!
YOU GET THE POWERS, TOO, DON'T YOU? YOU SHOULD HAVE SEEN ME IN THIS SOCCER GAME...AND I LIFTED A BUS!
PAT PAT
DON'T BE AN IDIOT!
YOU HAVE TO GET OUT OF THE MUD.
SPROING!
SPLOOOSH!

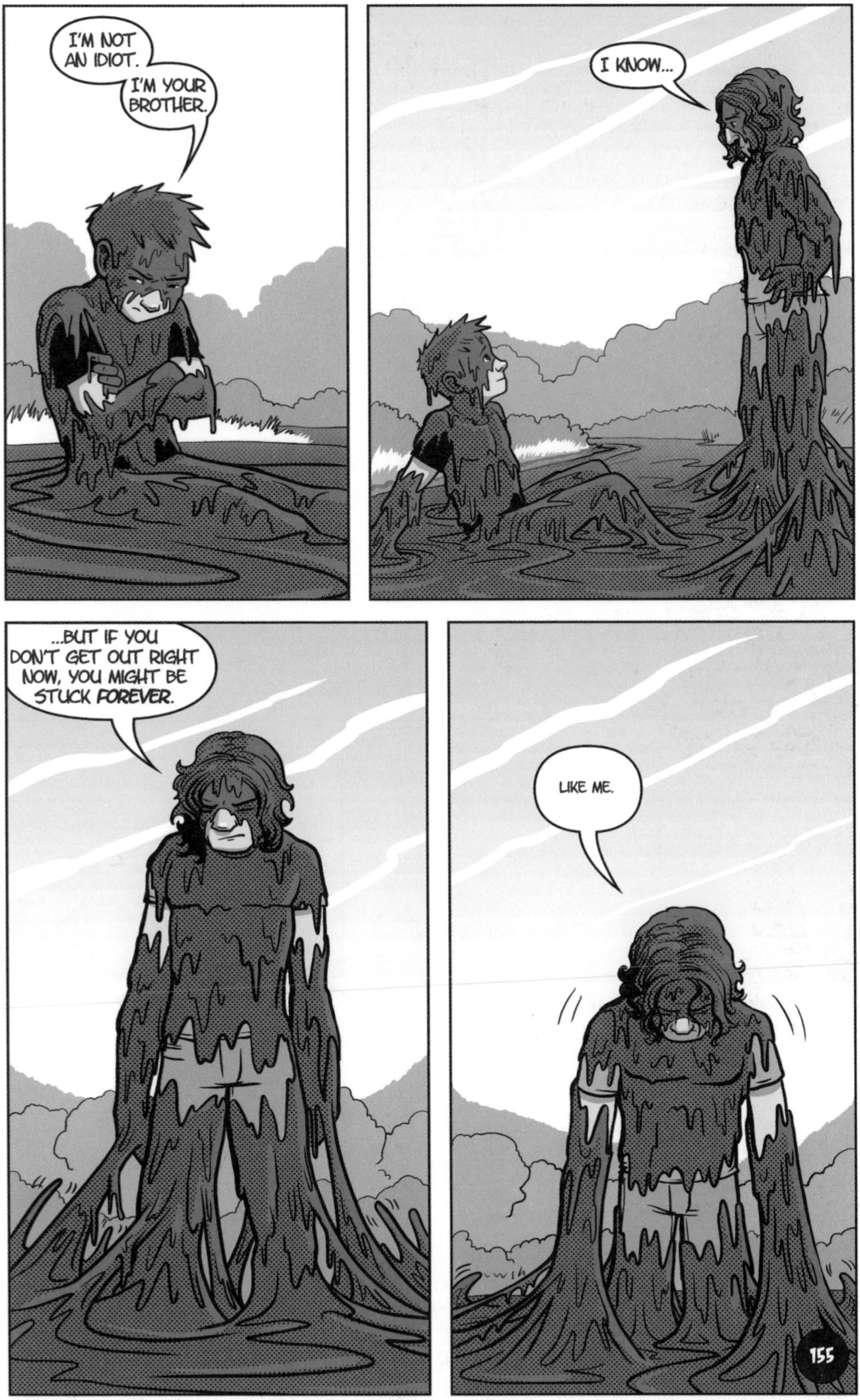
I'M NOT AN IDIOT.
I'M YOUR BROTHER.
I KNOW...
...BUT IF YOU DON'T GET OUT RIGHT NOW, YOU MIGHT BE STUCK *FOREVER.*
LIKE ME.

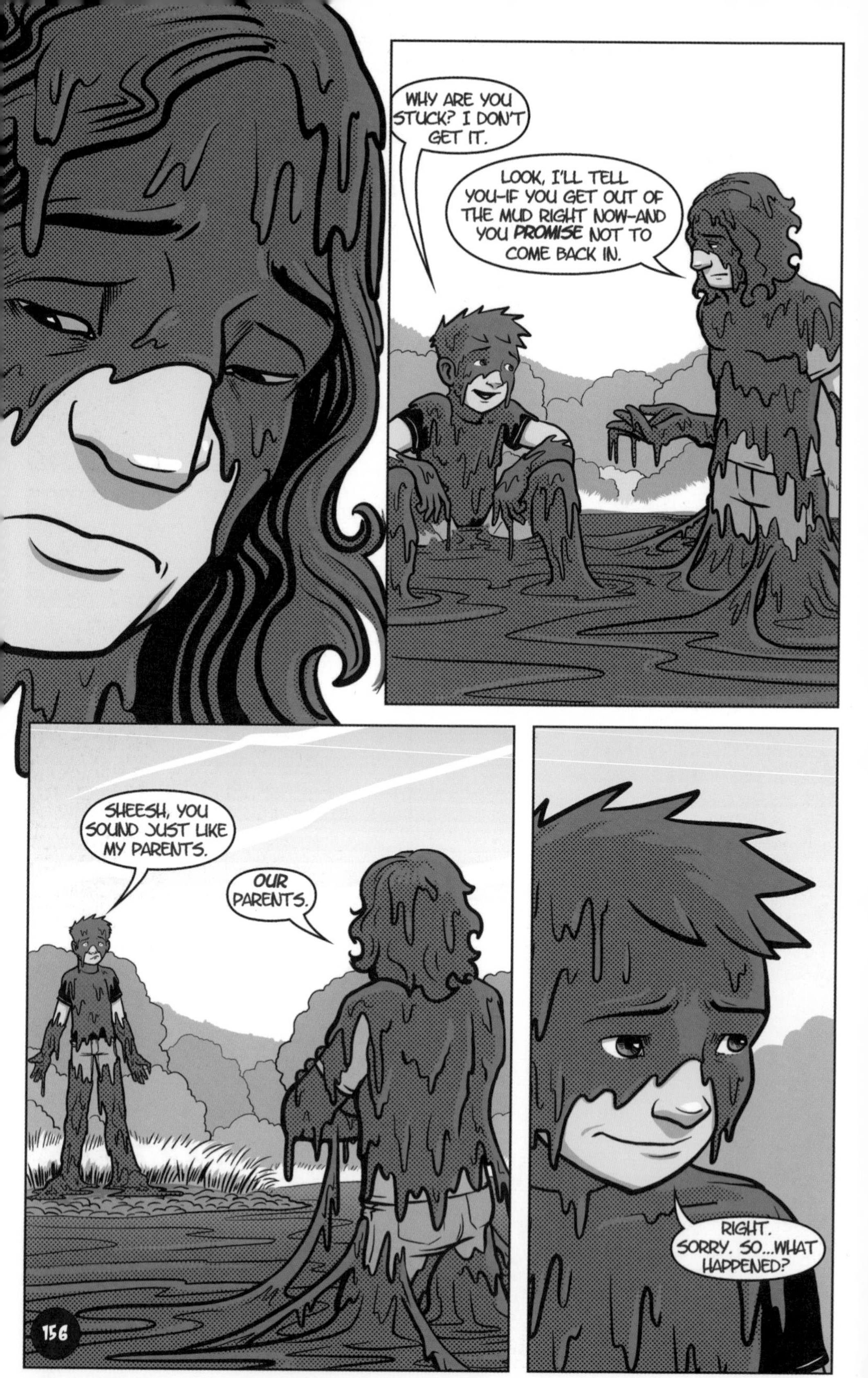
WHY ARE YOU STUCK? I DON'T GET IT.
LOOK, I'LL TELL YOU—IF YOU GET OUT OF THE MUD RIGHT NOW—AND YOU **PROMISE** NOT TO COME BACK IN.
SHEESH, YOU SOUND JUST LIKE MY PARENTS.
OUR PARENTS.
RIGHT. SORRY. SO...WHAT HAPPENED?

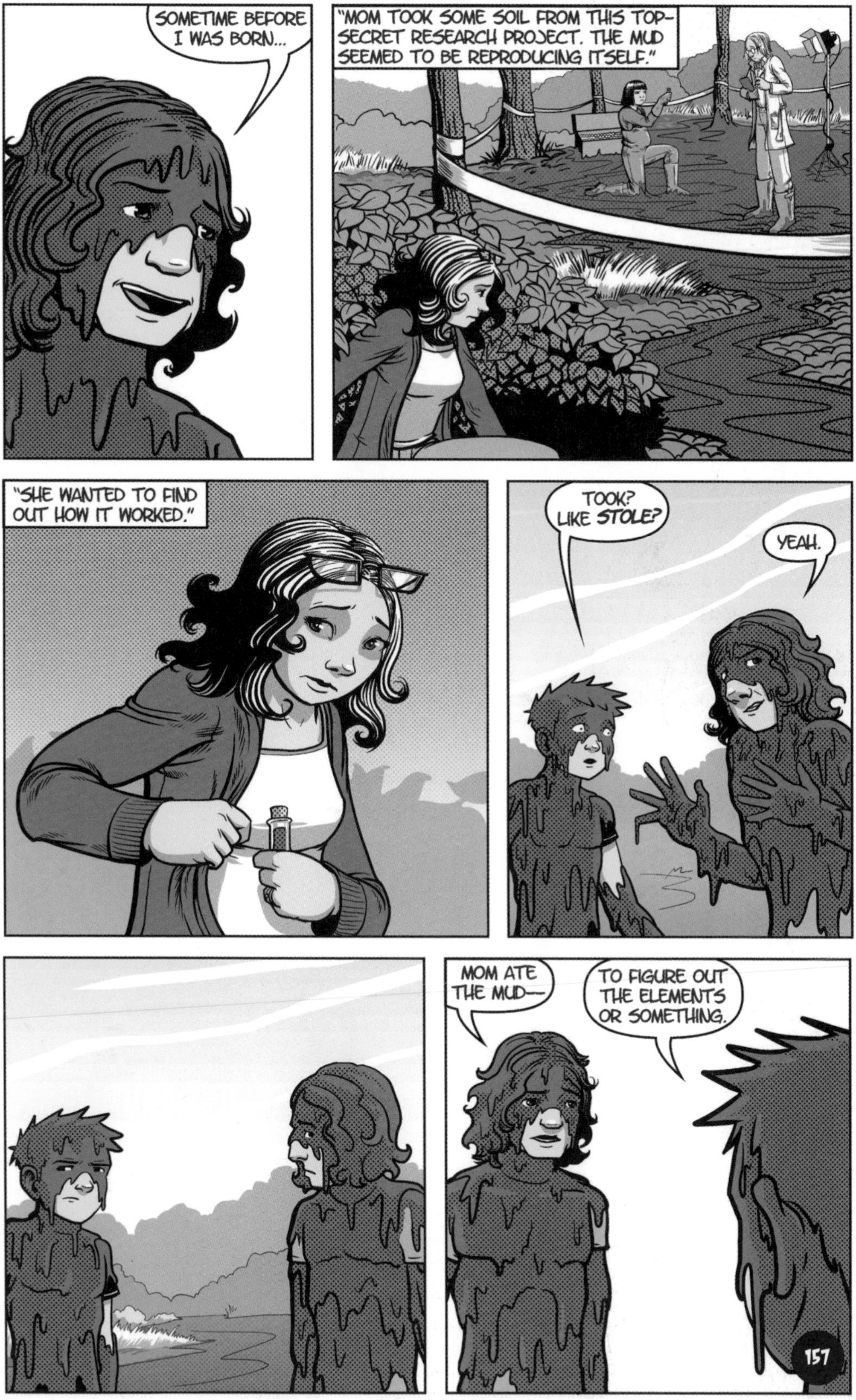
SOMETIME BEFORE I WAS BORN...
"MOM TOOK SOME SOIL FROM THIS TOP-SECRET RESEARCH PROJECT. THE MUD SEEMED TO BE REPRODUCING ITSELF."
"SHE WANTED TO FIND OUT HOW IT WORKED."
TOOK? LIKE STOLE?
YEAH.
MOM ATE THE MUD—
TO FIGURE OUT THE ELEMENTS OR SOMETHING.

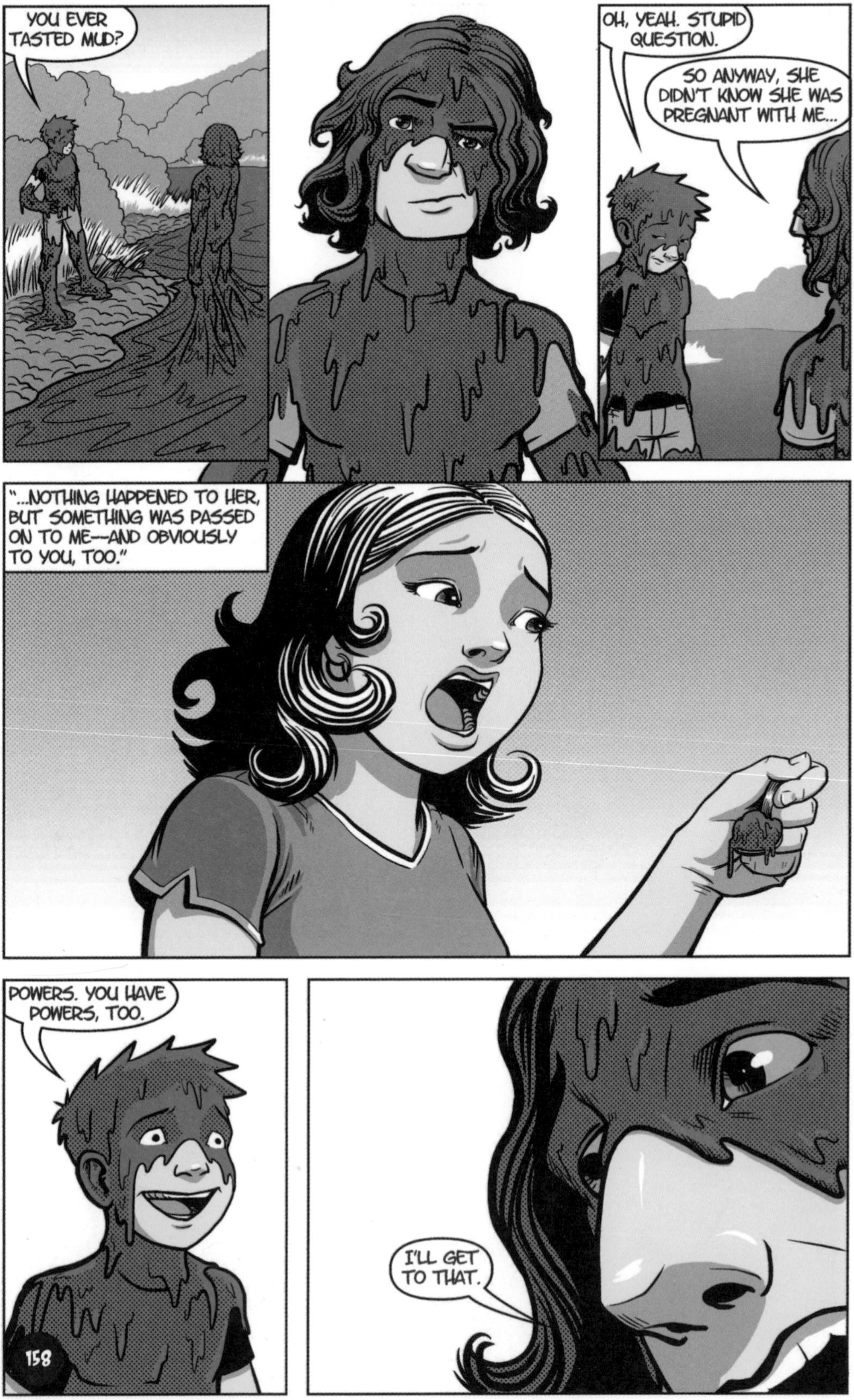
YOU EVER TASTED MUD?
OH, YEAH. STUPID QUESTION.
SO ANYWAY, SHE DIDN'T KNOW SHE WAS PREGNANT WITH ME...
"...NOTHING HAPPENED TO HER, BUT SOMETHING WAS PASSED ON TO ME--AND OBVIOUSLY TO YOU, TOO."
POWERS. YOU HAVE POWERS, TOO.
I'LL GET TO THAT.

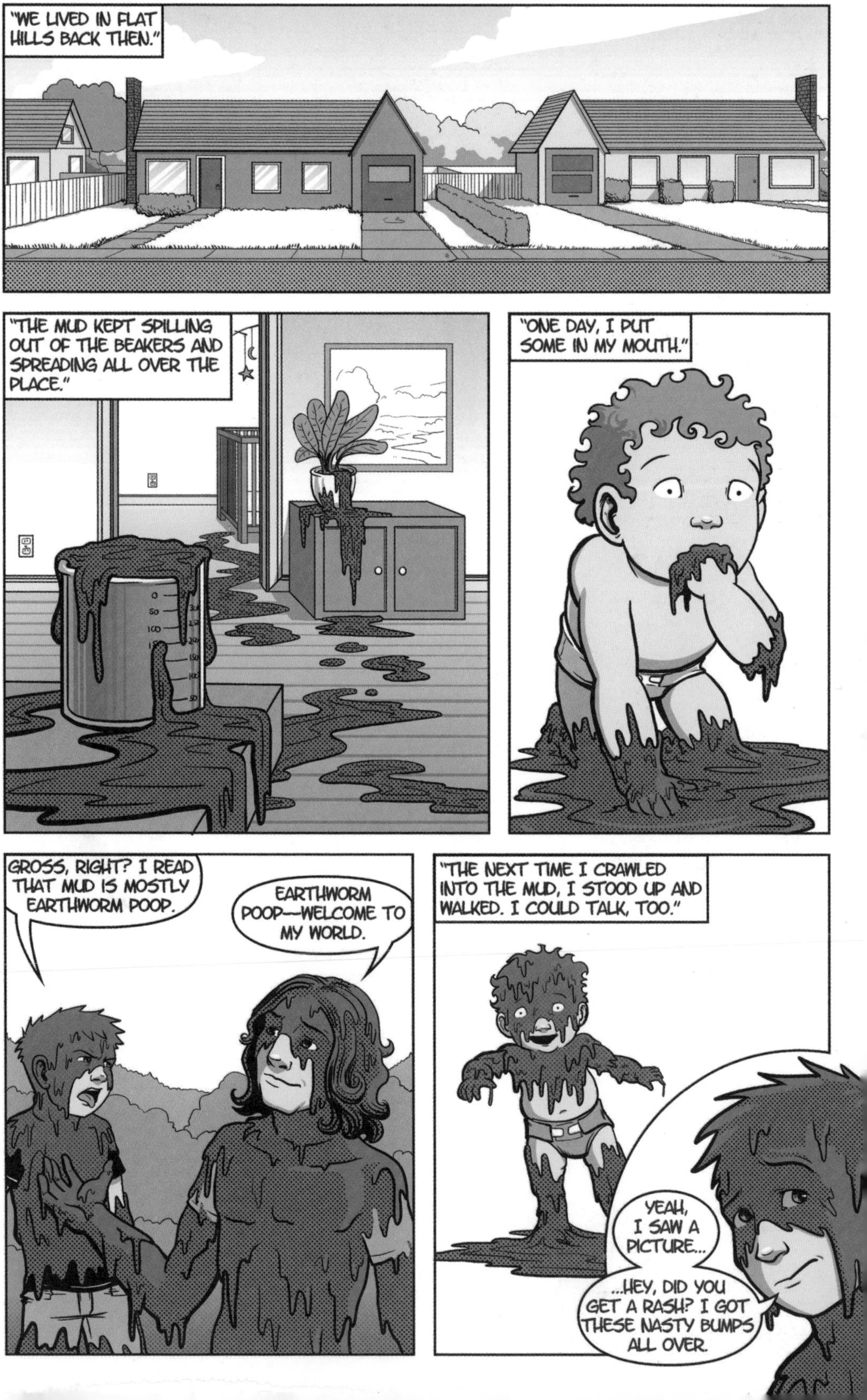
"WE LIVED IN FLAT HILLS BACK THEN."
"THE MUD KEPT SPILLING OUT OF THE BEAKERS AND SPREADING ALL OVER THE PLACE."
"ONE DAY, I PUT SOME IN MY MOUTH."
GROSS, RIGHT? I READ THAT MUD IS MOSTLY EARTHWORM POOP.
EARTHWORM POOP--WELCOME TO MY WORLD.
"THE NEXT TIME I CRAWLED INTO THE MUD, I STOOD UP AND WALKED. I COULD TALK, TOO."
YEAH, I SAW A PICTURE...
...HEY, DID YOU GET A RASH? I GOT THESE NASTY BUMPS ALL OVER.

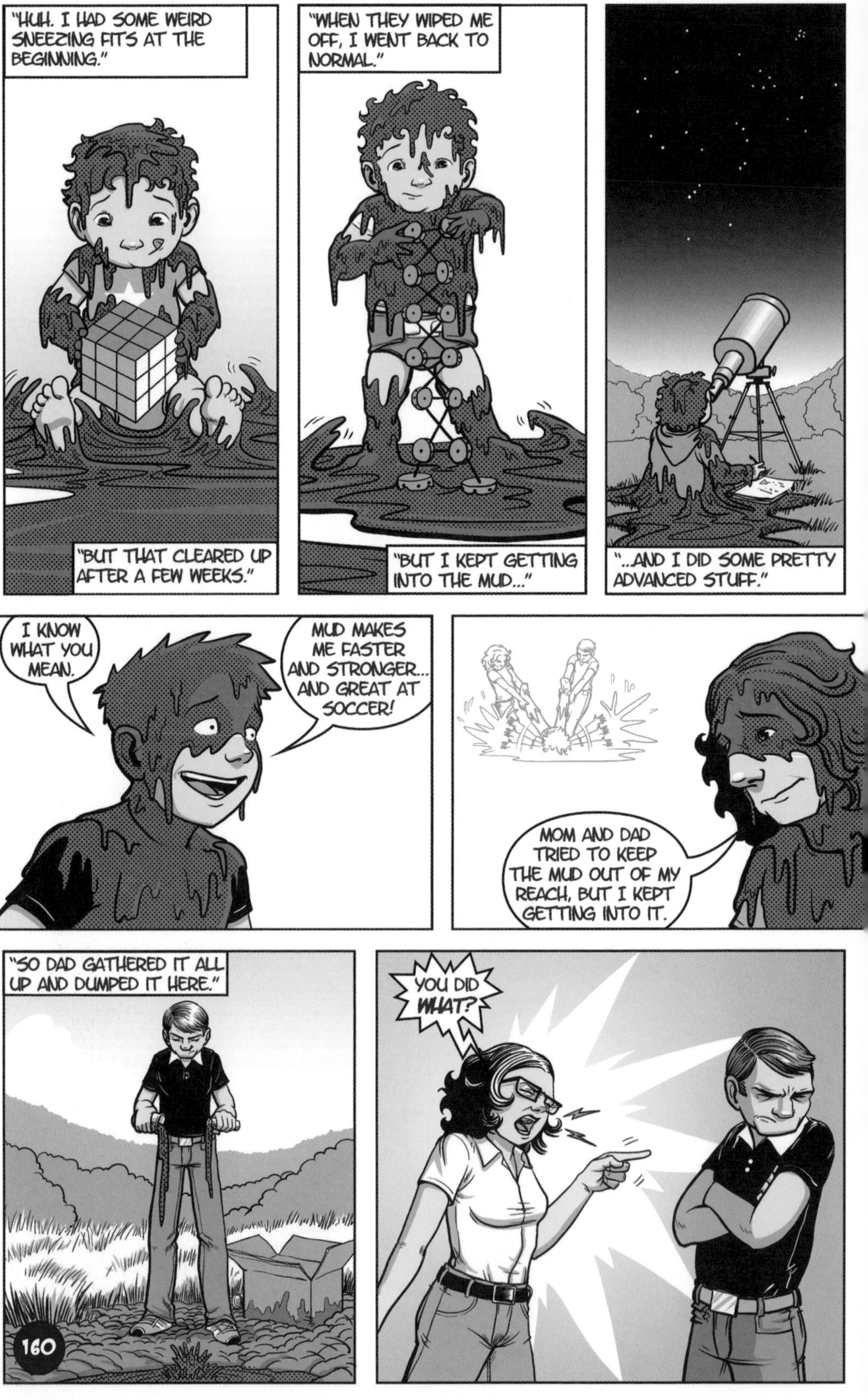

"HUH. I HAD SOME WEIRD SNEEZING FITS AT THE BEGINNING."
"BUT THAT CLEARED UP AFTER A FEW WEEKS."
"WHEN THEY WIPED ME OFF, I WENT BACK TO NORMAL."
"BUT I KEPT GETTING INTO THE MUD..."
"...AND I DID SOME PRETTY ADVANCED STUFF."
I KNOW WHAT YOU MEAN.
MUD MAKES ME FASTER AND STRONGER... AND GREAT AT SOCCER!
MOM AND DAD TRIED TO KEEP THE MUD OUT OF MY REACH, BUT I KEPT GETTING INTO IT.
"SO DAD GATHERED IT ALL UP AND DUMPED IT HERE."
YOU DID *WHAT?*

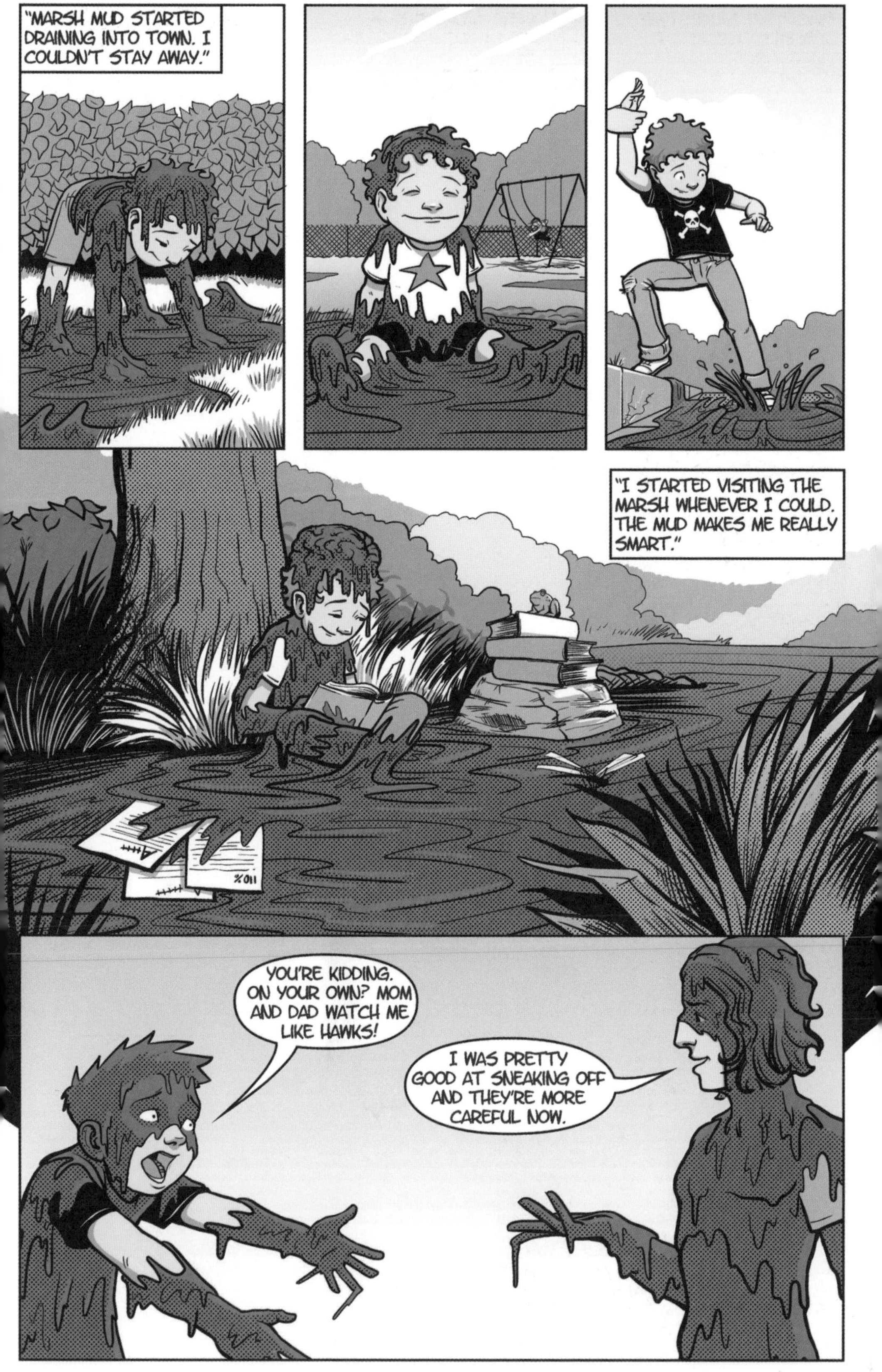
"MARSH MUD STARTED DRAINING INTO TOWN. I COULDN'T STAY AWAY."
"I STARTED VISITING THE MARSH WHENEVER I COULD. THE MUD MAKES ME REALLY SMART."
YOU'RE KIDDING. ON YOUR OWN? MOM AND DAD WATCH ME LIKE HAWKS!
I WAS PRETTY GOOD AT SNEAKING OFF AND THEY'RE MORE CAREFUL NOW.

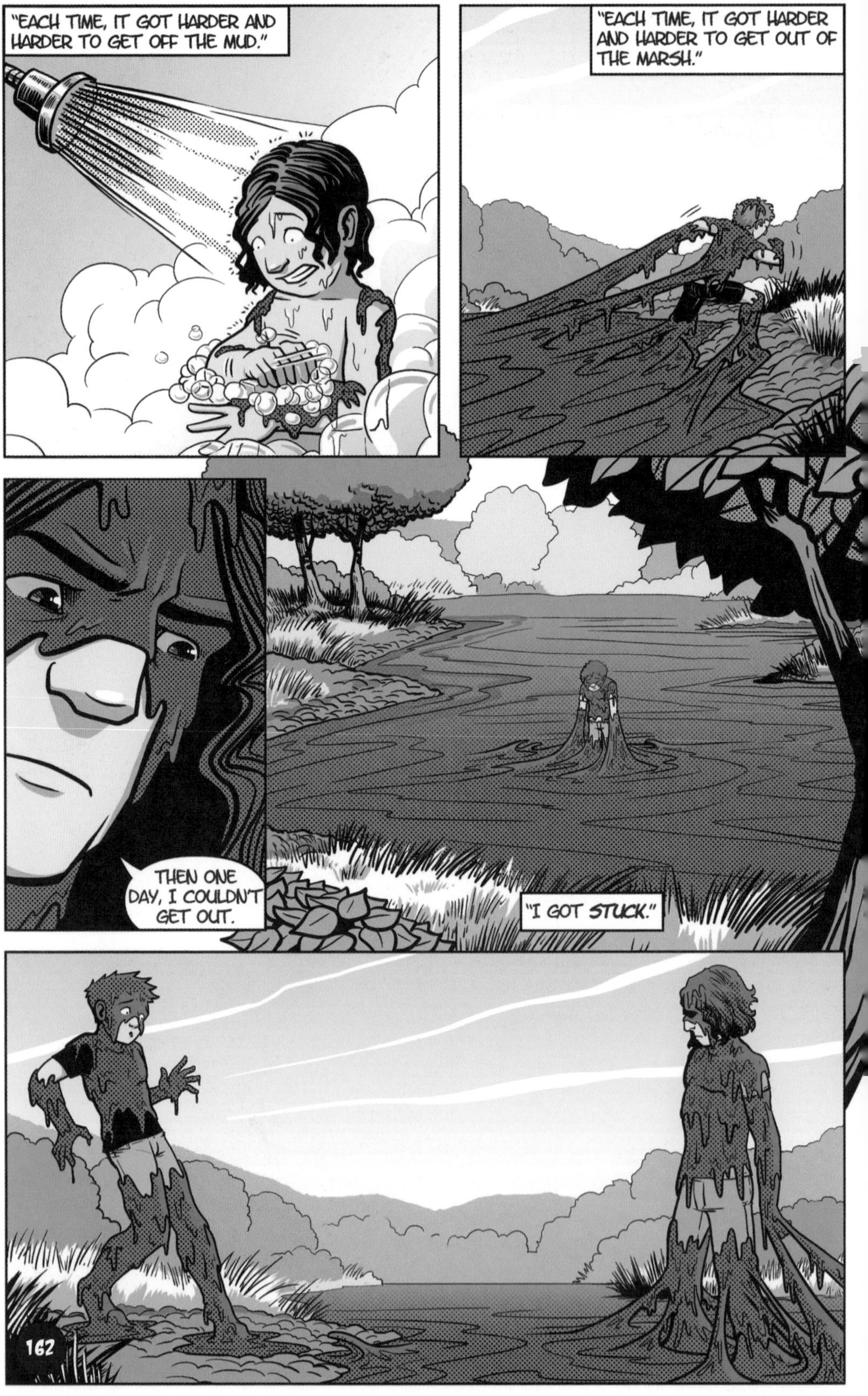
"EACH TIME, IT GOT HARDER AND HARDER TO GET OFF THE MUD."
"EACH TIME, IT GOT HARDER AND HARDER TO GET OUT OF THE MARSH."
THEN ONE DAY, I COULDN'T GET OUT.
"I GOT STUCK."

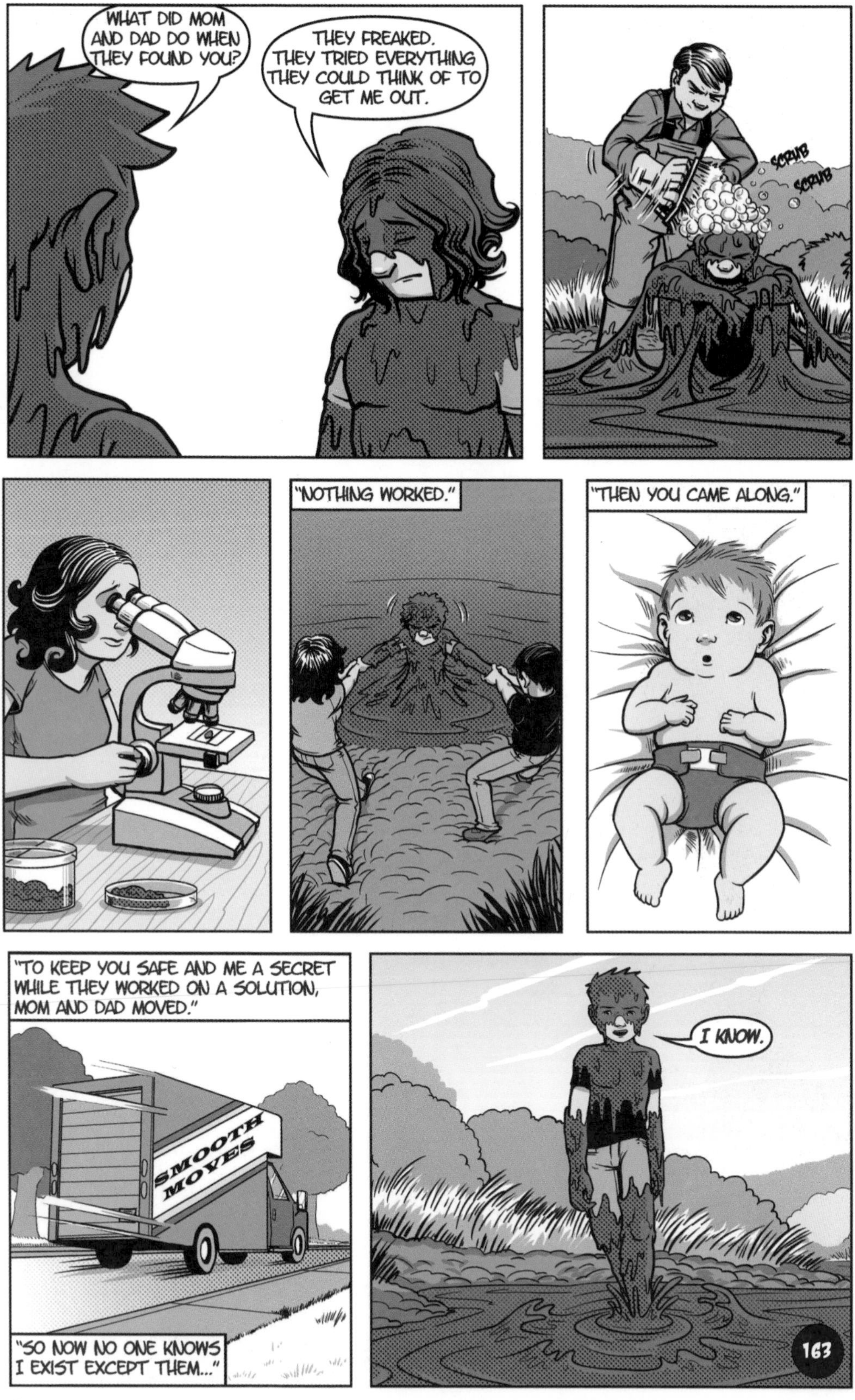
WHAT DID MOM AND DAD DO WHEN THEY FOUND YOU?
THEY FREAKED. THEY TRIED EVERYTHING THEY COULD THINK OF TO GET ME OUT.
SCRUB
SCRUB
"NOTHING WORKED."
"THEN YOU CAME ALONG."
"TO KEEP YOU SAFE AND ME A SECRET WHILE THEY WORKED ON A SOLUTION, MOM AND DAD MOVED."
SMOOTH MOVES
"SO NOW NO ONE KNOWS I EXIST EXCEPT THEM..."
I KNOW.

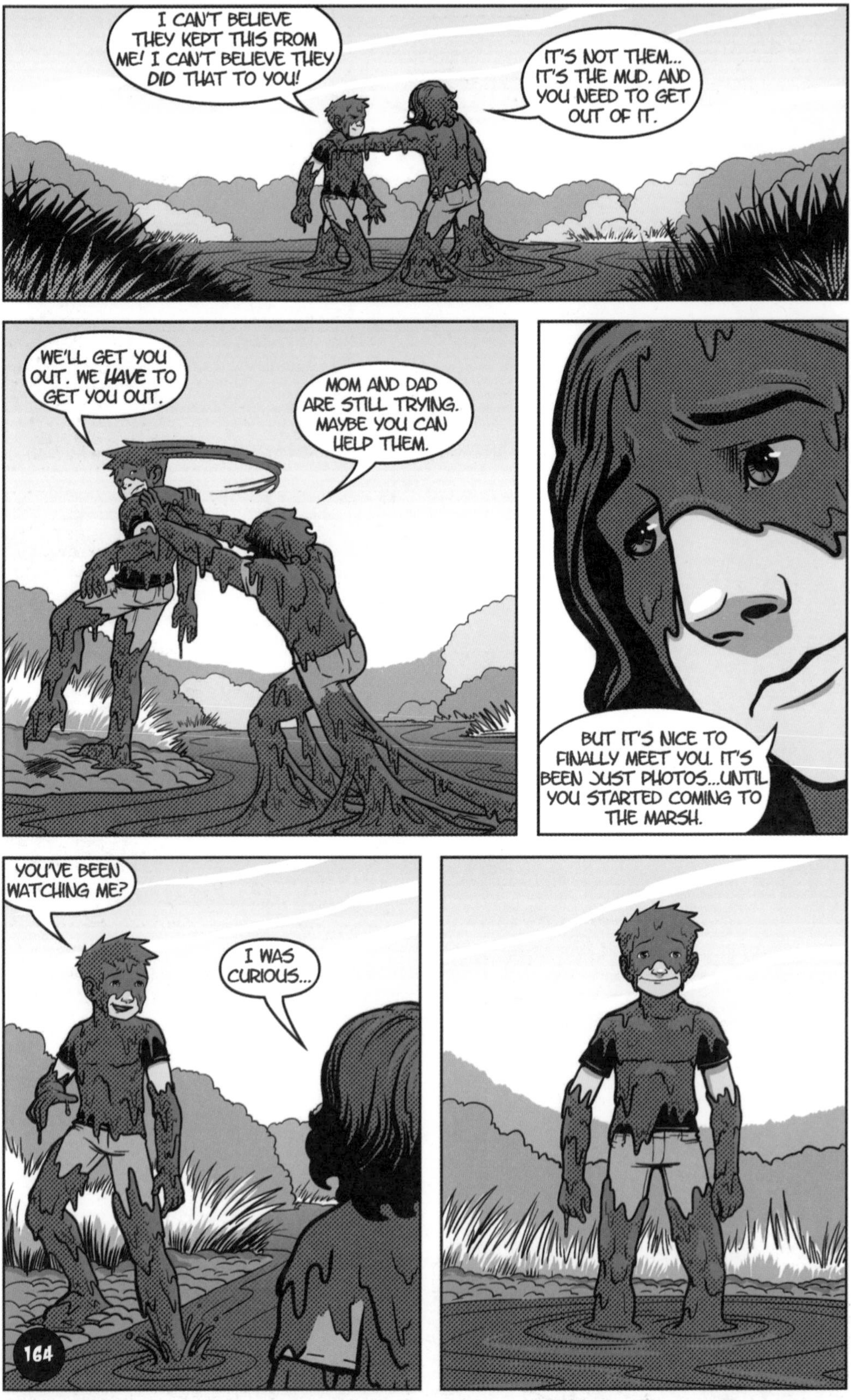
I CAN'T BELIEVE THEY KEPT THIS FROM ME! I CAN'T BELIEVE THEY DID THAT TO YOU!
IT'S NOT THEM... IT'S THE MUD. AND YOU NEED TO GET OUT OF IT.
WE'LL GET YOU OUT. WE HAVE TO GET YOU OUT.
MOM AND DAD ARE STILL TRYING. MAYBE YOU CAN HELP THEM.
BUT IT'S NICE TO FINALLY MEET YOU. IT'S BEEN JUST PHOTOS...UNTIL YOU STARTED COMING TO THE MARSH.
YOU'VE BEEN WATCHING ME?
I WAS CURIOUS...

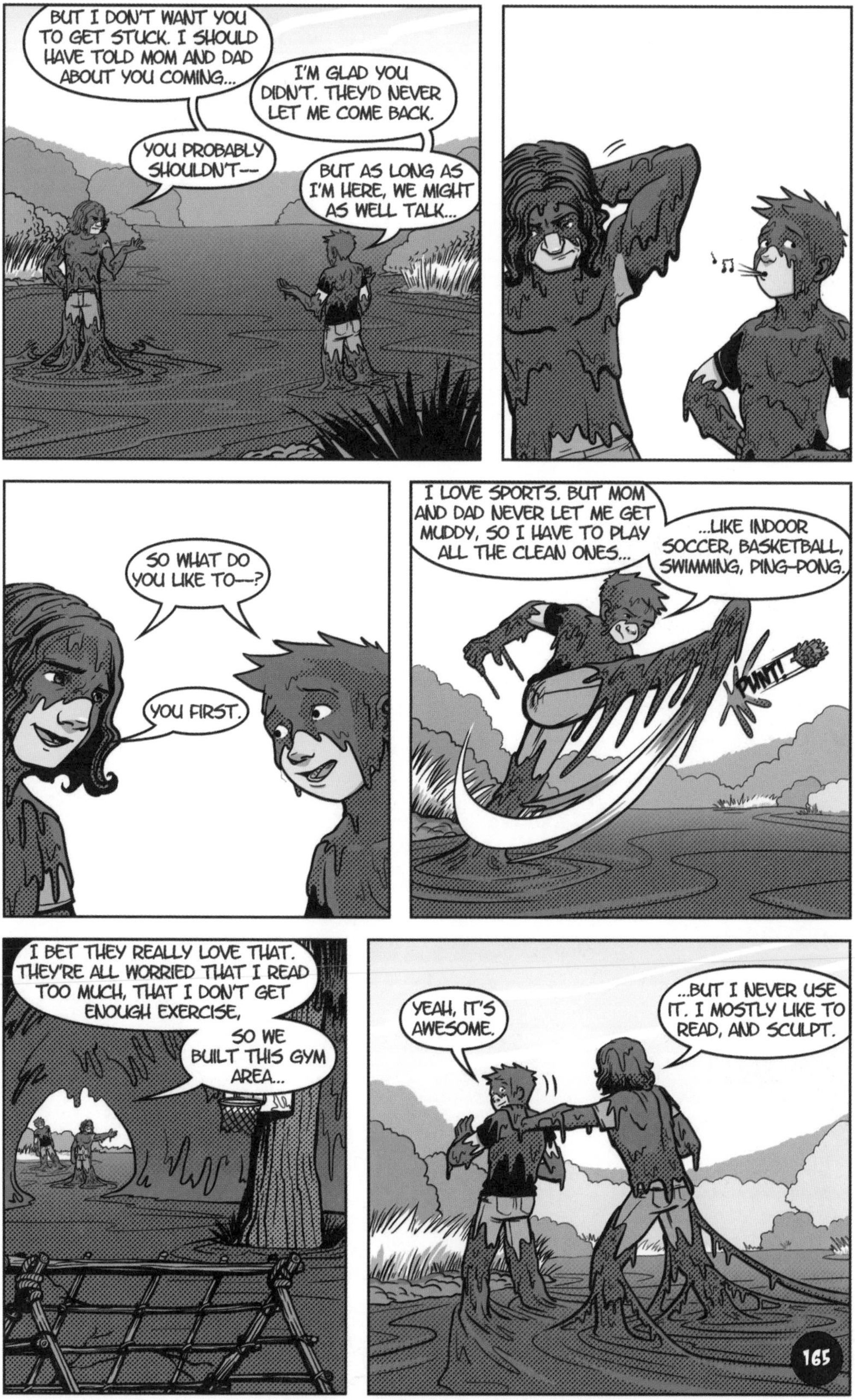
BUT I DON'T WANT YOU TO GET STUCK. I SHOULD HAVE TOLD MOM AND DAD ABOUT YOU COMING...
I'M GLAD YOU DIDN'T. THEY'D NEVER LET ME COME BACK.
YOU PROBABLY SHOULDN'T--
BUT AS LONG AS I'M HERE, WE MIGHT AS WELL TALK...
SO WHAT DO YOU LIKE TO--?
YOU FIRST.
I LOVE SPORTS. BUT MOM AND DAD NEVER LET ME GET MUDDY, SO I HAVE TO PLAY ALL THE CLEAN ONES...
...LIKE INDOOR SOCCER, BASKETBALL, SWIMMING, PING-PONG.
PUNT!
I BET THEY REALLY LOVE THAT. THEY'RE ALL WORRIED THAT I READ TOO MUCH, THAT I DON'T GET ENOUGH EXERCISE,
SO WE BUILT THIS GYM AREA...
YEAH, IT'S AWESOME.
...BUT I NEVER USE IT. I MOSTLY LIKE TO READ, AND SCULPT.

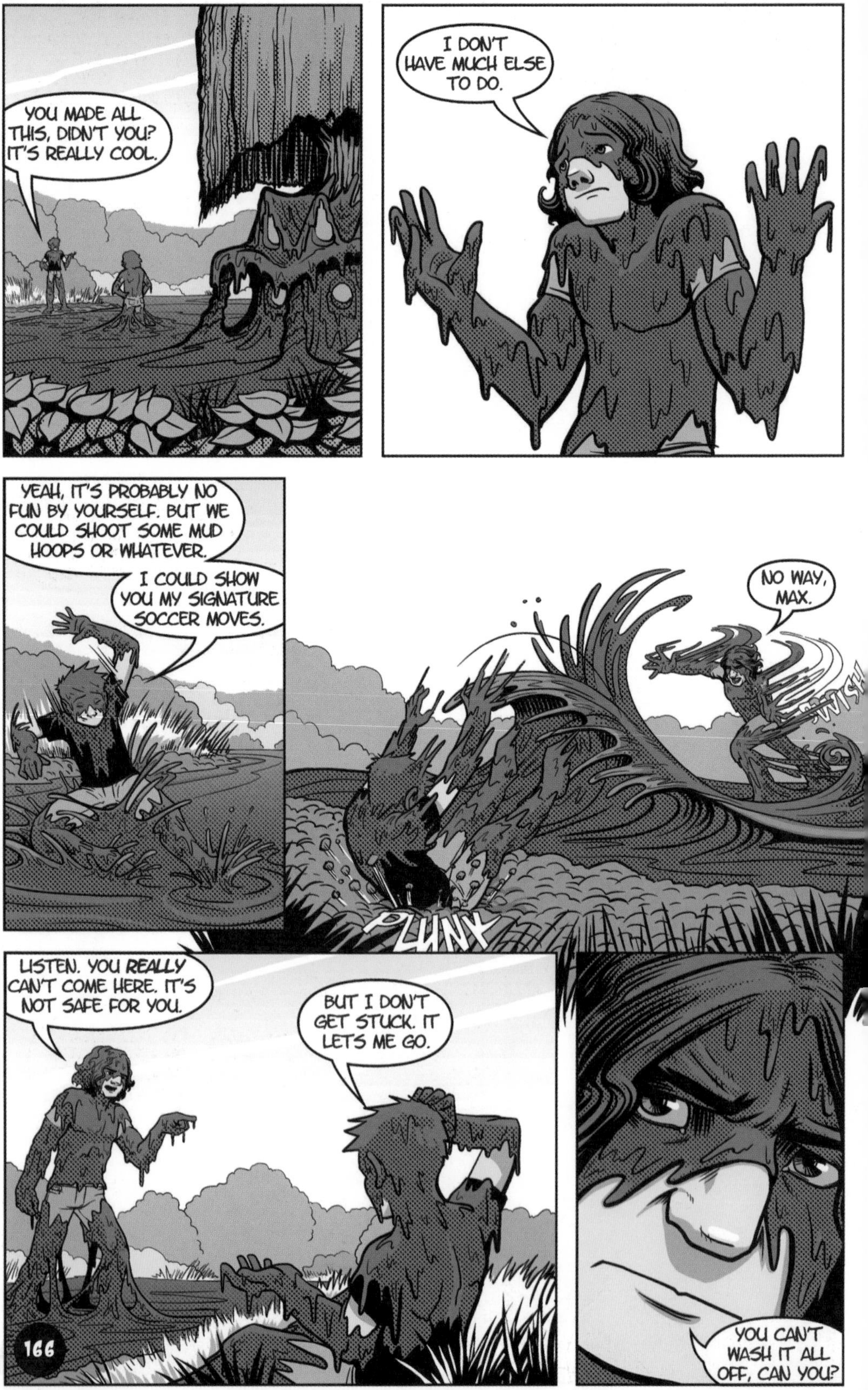
YOU MADE ALL THIS, DIDN'T YOU? IT'S REALLY COOL.
I DON'T HAVE MUCH ELSE TO DO.
YEAH, IT'S PROBABLY NO FUN BY YOURSELF. BUT WE COULD SHOOT SOME MUD HOOPS OR WHATEVER.
I COULD SHOW YOU MY SIGNATURE SOCCER MOVES.
NO WAY, MAX.
SWISH
PLUNK
LISTEN. YOU REALLY CAN'T COME HERE. IT'S NOT SAFE FOR YOU.
BUT I DON'T GET STUCK. IT LETS ME GO.
YOU CAN'T WASH IT ALL OFF, CAN YOU?

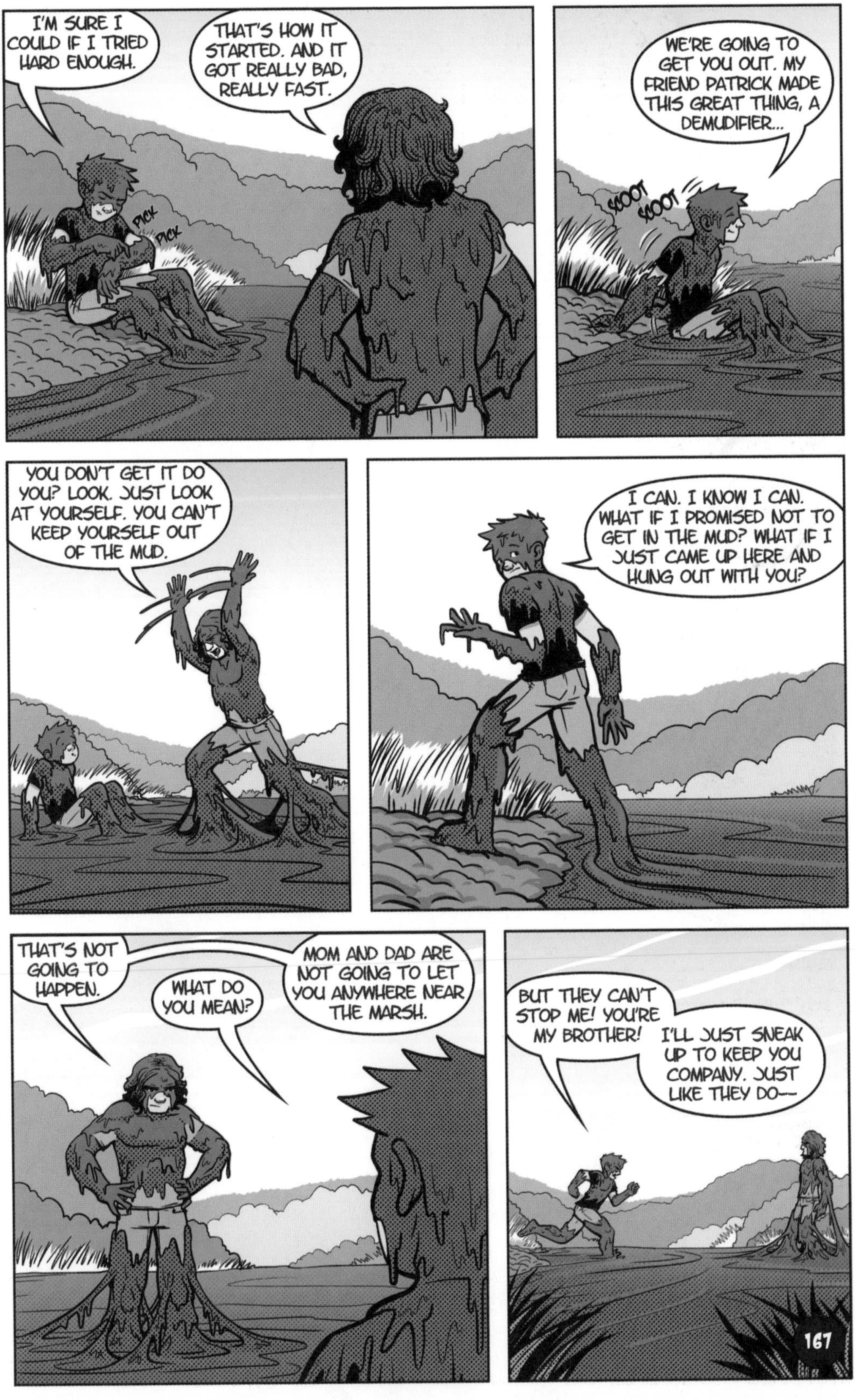
I'M SURE I COULD IF I TRIED HARD ENOUGH.
PICK PICK
THAT'S HOW IT STARTED. AND IT GOT REALLY BAD, REALLY FAST.
WE'RE GOING TO GET YOU OUT. MY FRIEND PATRICK MADE THIS GREAT THING, A DEMUDIFIER...
SCOOT SCOOT
YOU DON'T GET IT DO YOU? LOOK. JUST LOOK AT YOURSELF. YOU CAN'T KEEP YOURSELF OUT OF THE MUD.
I CAN. I KNOW I CAN. WHAT IF I PROMISED NOT TO GET IN THE MUD? WHAT IF I JUST CAME UP HERE AND HUNG OUT WITH YOU?
THAT'S NOT GOING TO HAPPEN.
WHAT DO YOU MEAN?
MOM AND DAD ARE NOT GOING TO LET YOU ANYWHERE NEAR THE MARSH.
BUT THEY CAN'T STOP ME! YOU'RE MY BROTHER!
I'LL JUST SNEAK UP TO KEEP YOU COMPANY. JUST LIKE THEY DO—

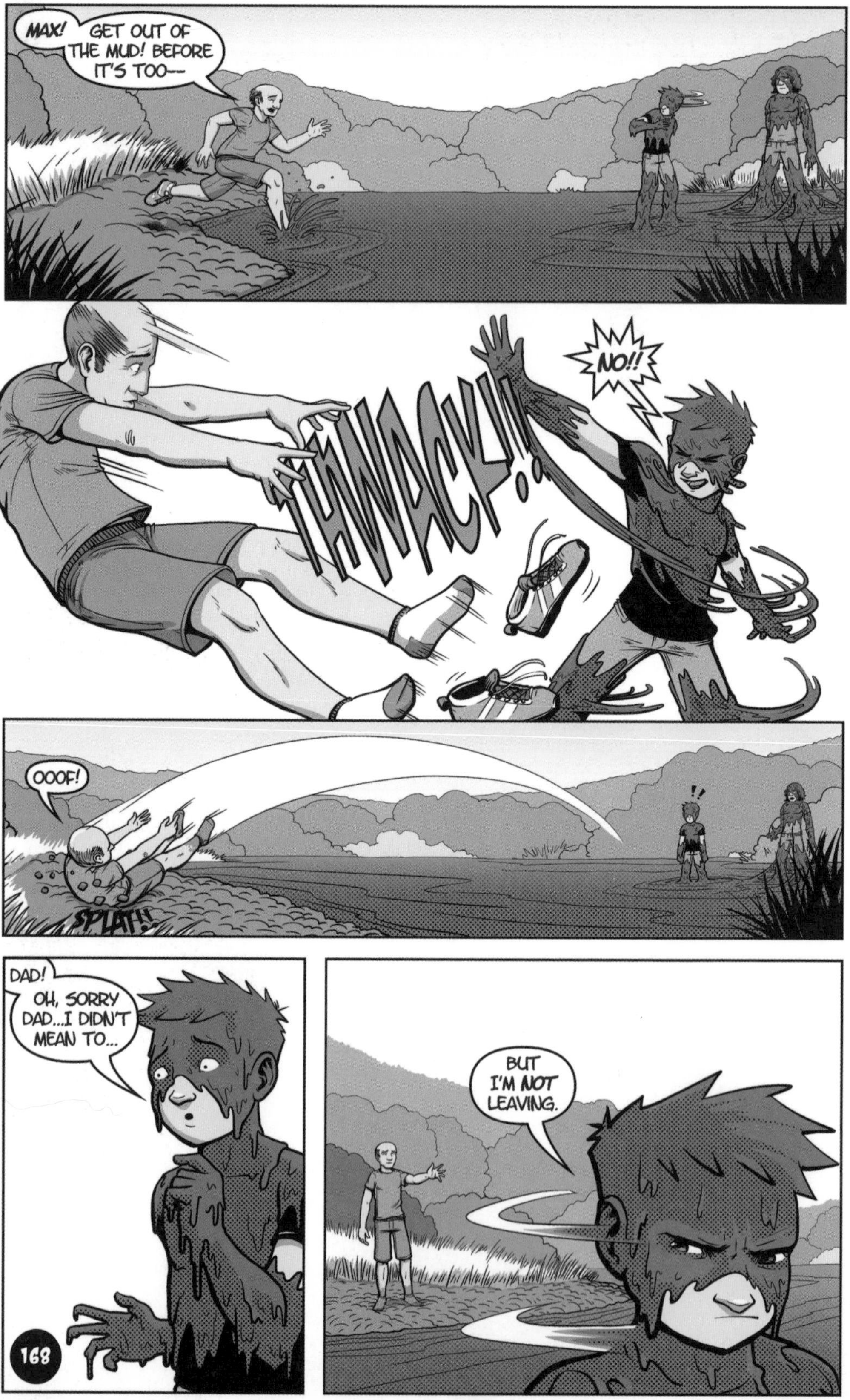
MAX!
GET OUT OF THE MUD! BEFORE IT'S TOO--
THWACK!!
NO!!
OOOF!
!!
SPLAT!!
DAD!
OH, SORRY DAD...I DIDN'T MEAN TO...
BUT I'M NOT LEAVING.

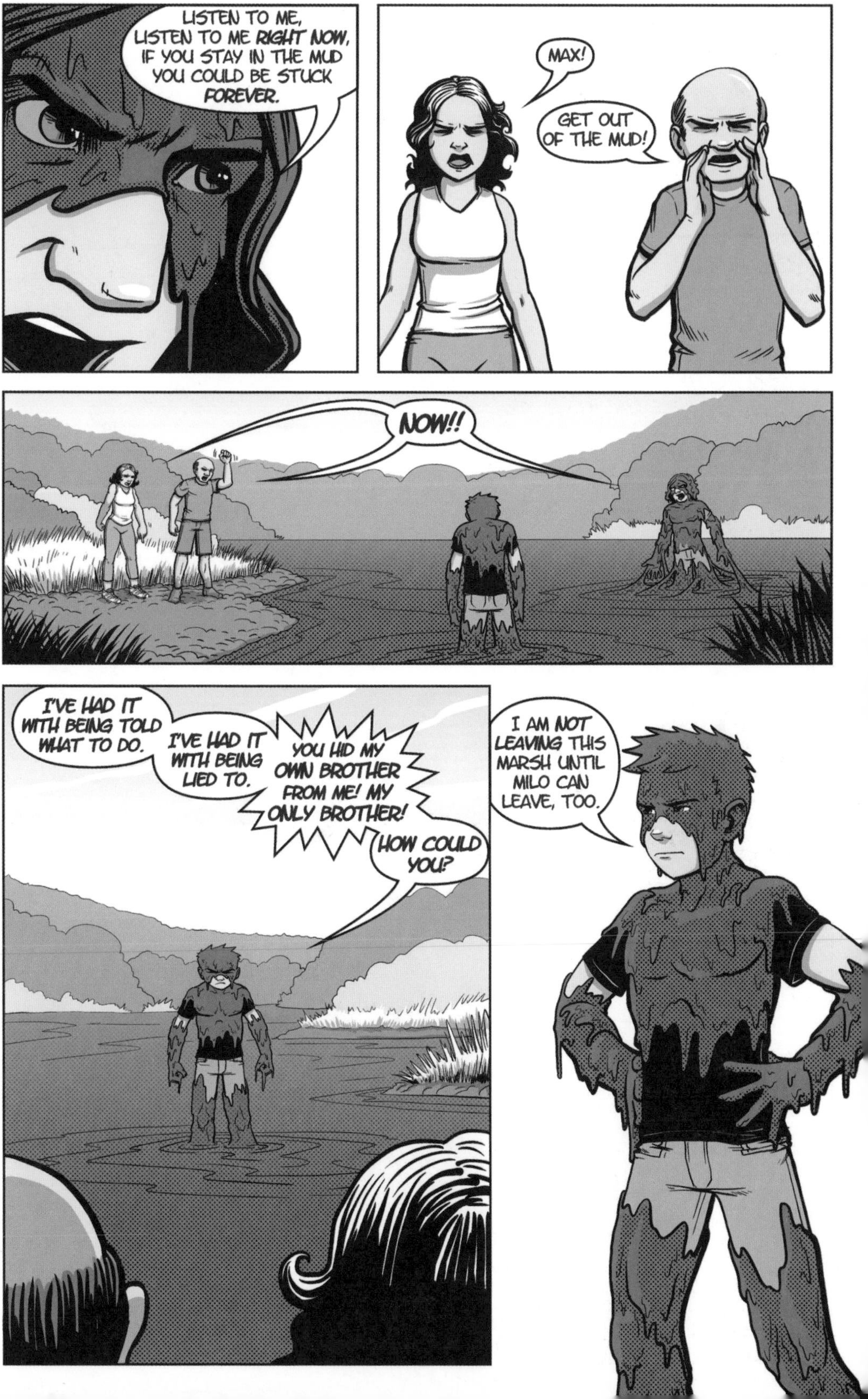
LISTEN TO ME, LISTEN TO ME RIGHT NOW, IF YOU STAY IN THE MUD YOU COULD BE STUCK FOREVER.
MAX!
GET OUT OF THE MUD!
NOW!!
I'VE HAD IT WITH BEING TOLD WHAT TO DO.
I'VE HAD IT WITH BEING LIED TO.
YOU HID MY OWN BROTHER FROM ME! MY ONLY BROTHER!
HOW COULD YOU?
I AM NOT LEAVING THIS MARSH UNTIL MILO CAN LEAVE, TOO.

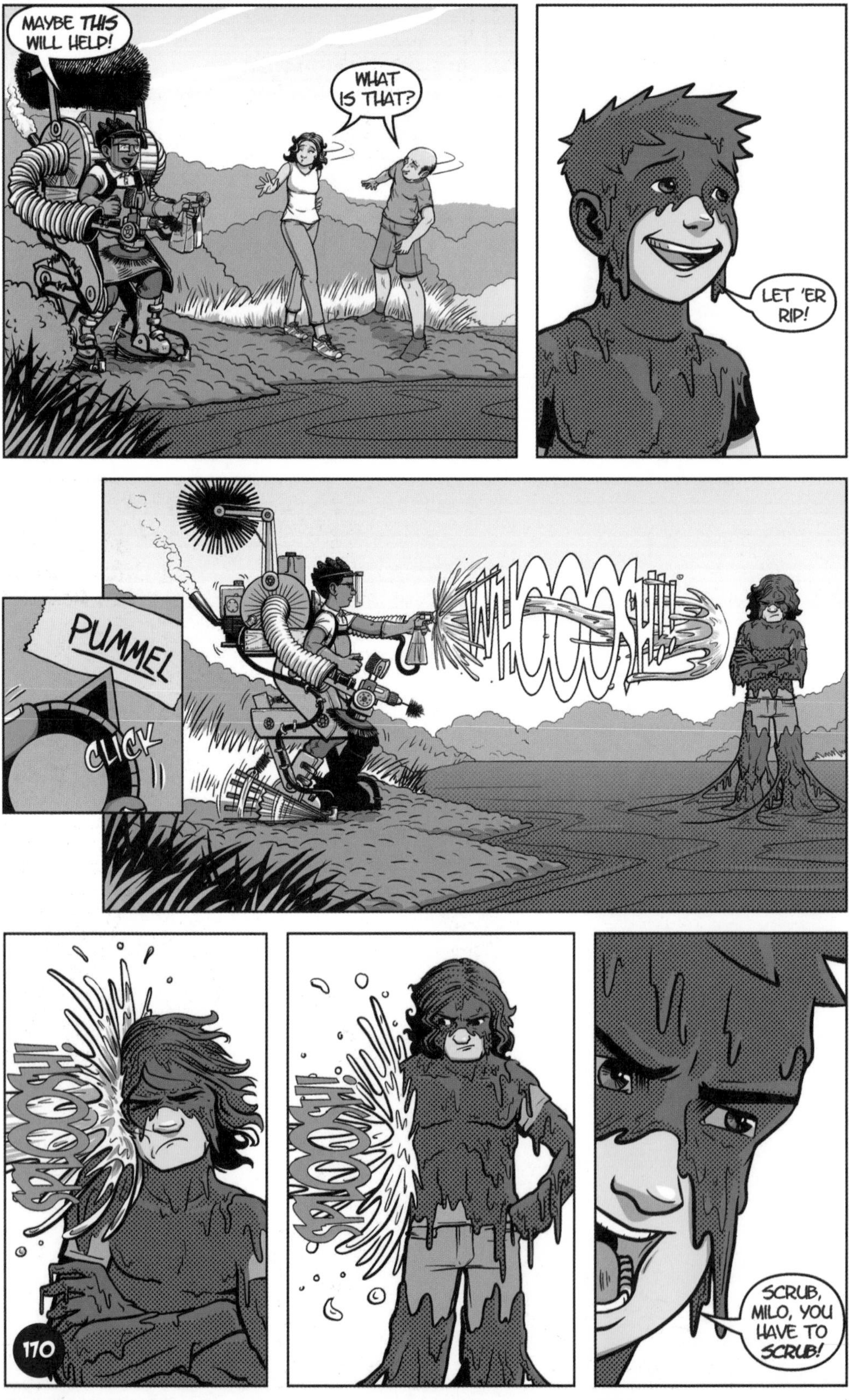
MAYBE THIS WILL HELP!
WHAT IS THAT?
LET 'ER RIP!
PUMMEL
CLICK
SCRUB, MILO, YOU HAVE TO SCRUB!

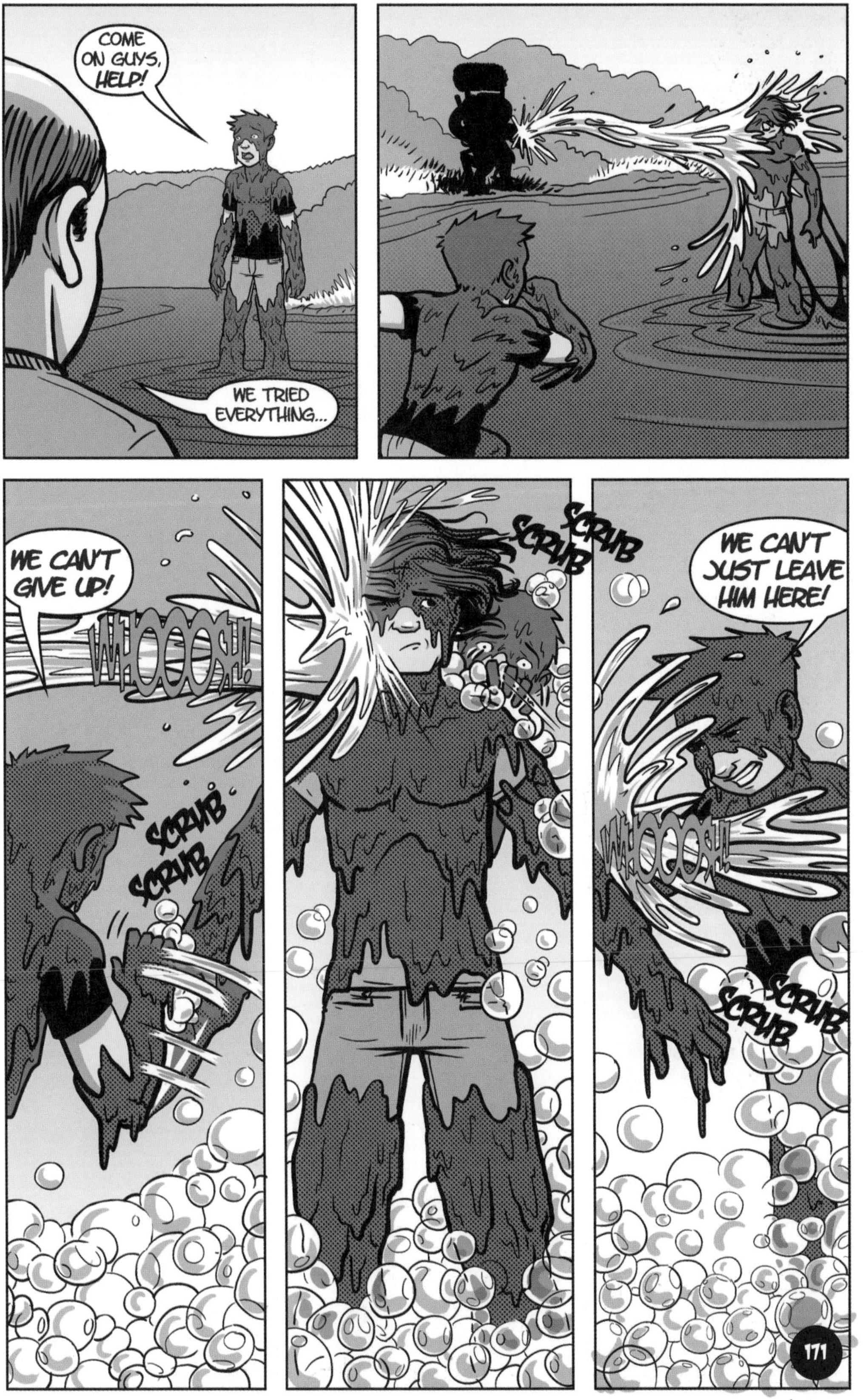
COME ON GUYS, HELP!
WE TRIED EVERYTHING...
WE CAN'T GIVE UP!
WHOOOSH!
SCRUB SCRUB
SCRUB SCRUB
WE CAN'T JUST LEAVE HIM HERE!
WHOOOSH!
SCRUB SCRUB

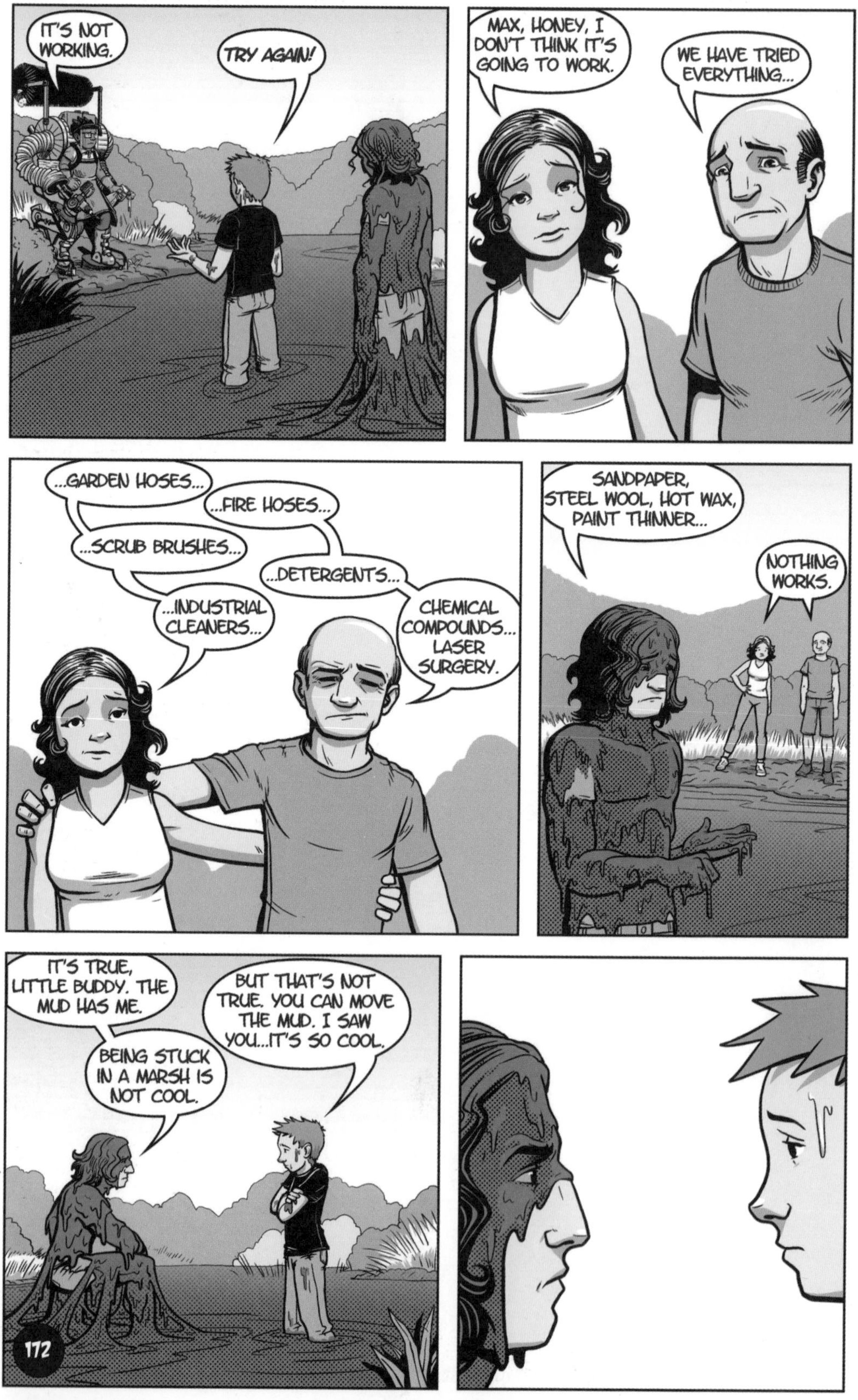
IT'S NOT WORKING.
TRY AGAIN!
MAX, HONEY, I DON'T THINK IT'S GOING TO WORK.
WE HAVE TRIED EVERYTHING...
...GARDEN HOSES...
...FIRE HOSES...
...SCRUB BRUSHES...
...DETERGENTS...
...INDUSTRIAL CLEANERS...
CHEMICAL COMPOUNDS... LASER SURGERY.
SANDPAPER, STEEL WOOL, HOT WAX, PAINT THINNER...
NOTHING WORKS.
IT'S TRUE, LITTLE BUDDY. THE MUD HAS ME.
BEING STUCK IN A MARSH IS NOT COOL.
BUT THAT'S NOT TRUE. YOU CAN MOVE THE MUD. I SAW YOU...IT'S SO COOL.

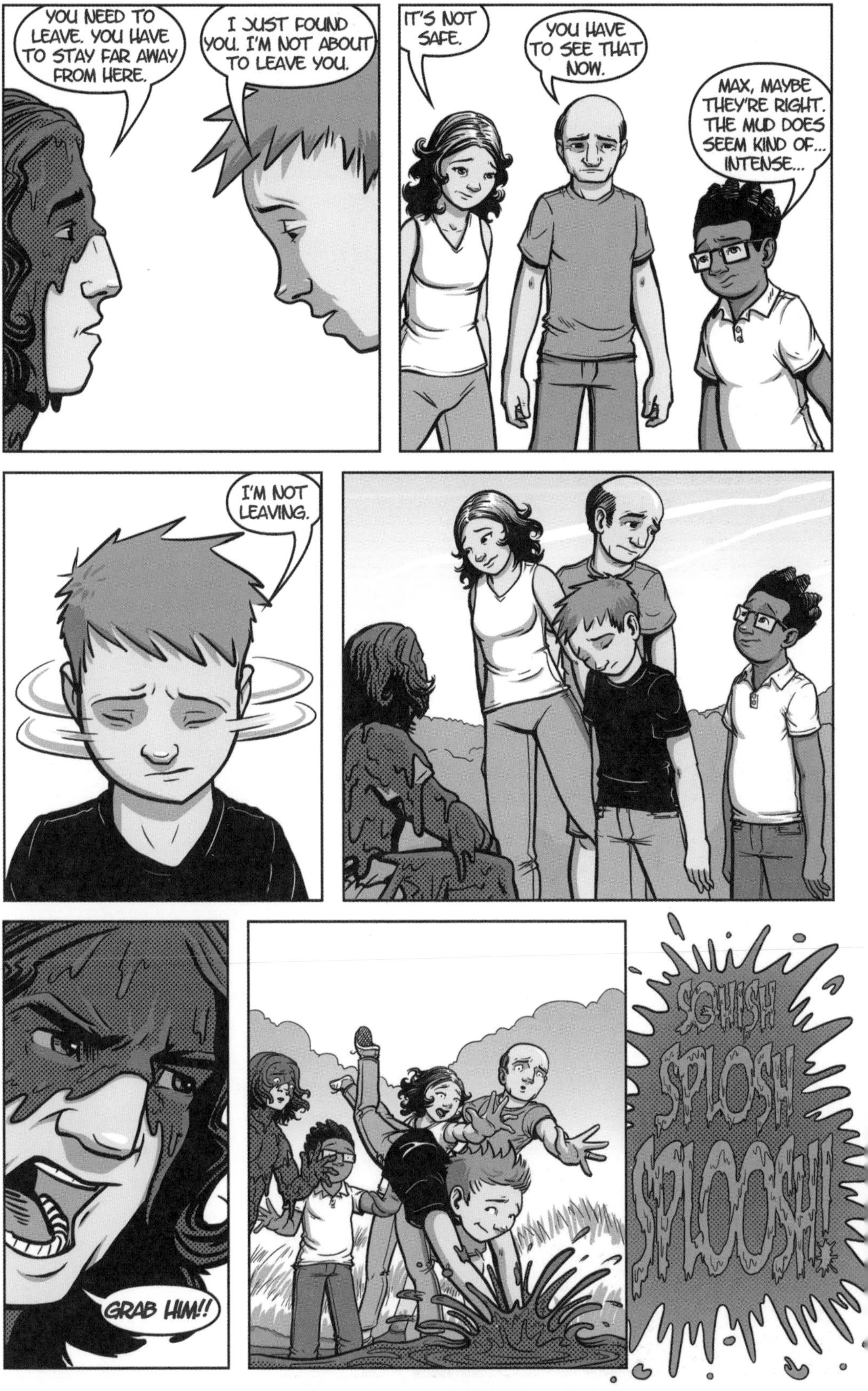
YOU NEED TO LEAVE. YOU HAVE TO STAY FAR AWAY FROM HERE.
I JUST FOUND YOU. I'M NOT ABOUT TO LEAVE YOU.
IT'S NOT SAFE.
YOU HAVE TO SEE THAT NOW.
MAX, MAYBE THEY'RE RIGHT. THE MUD DOES SEEM KIND OF... INTENSE...
I'M NOT LEAVING.
GRAB HIM!!
SQUISH
SPLOSH
SPLOOSH!

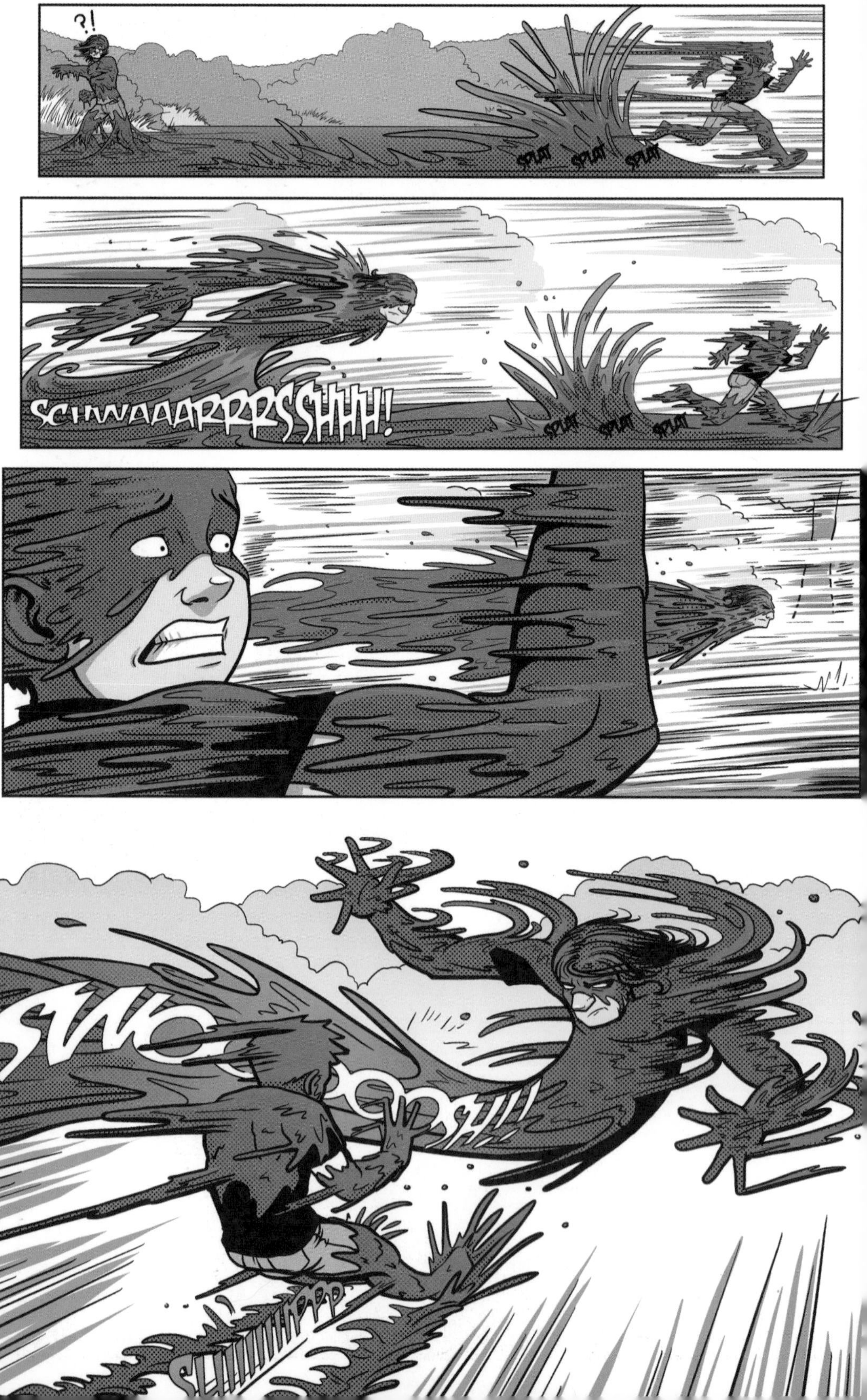
?!
SPLAT SPLAT SPLAT
SCHWAAAARRRRSSHHHH!
SPLAT SPLAT SPLAT
SWOOOOOSH!!
SHHHHHHPPP

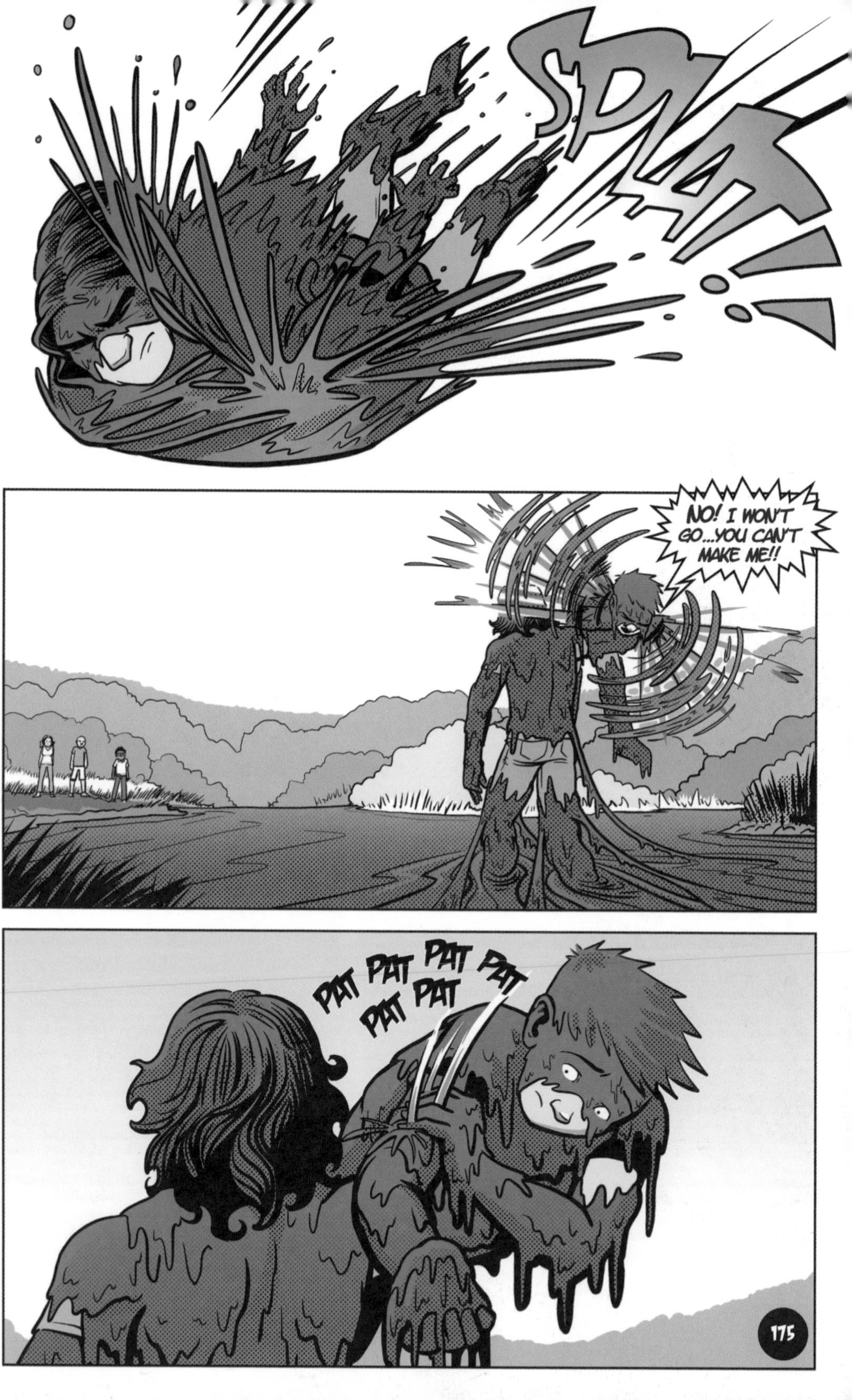
SPLAT!
NO! I WON'T GO...YOU CAN'T MAKE ME!!
PAT PAT PAT PAT PAT PAT

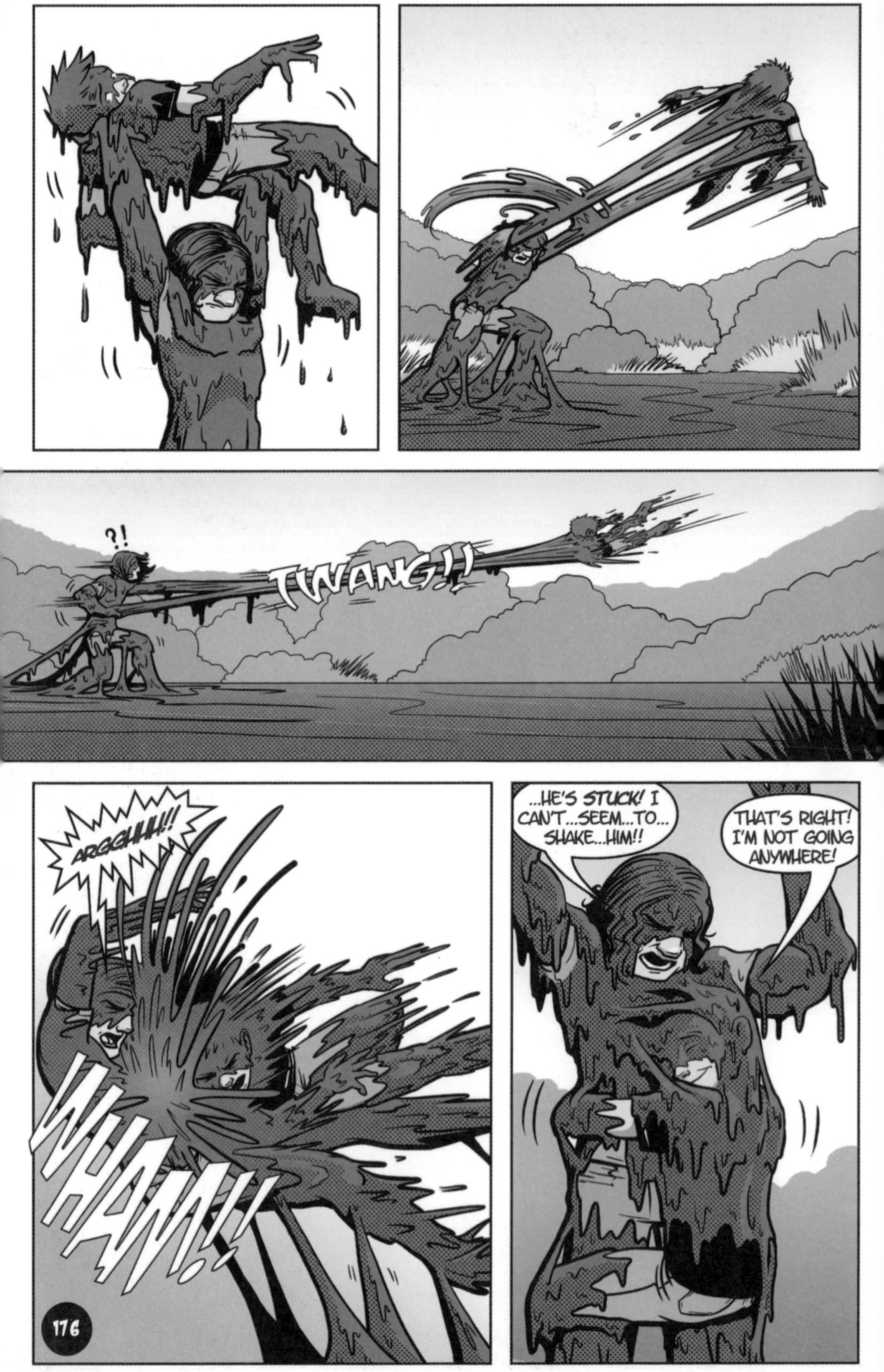
?!
TWANG!!
ARGGHHH!!
WHAM!!
...HE'S STUCK! I CAN'T...SEEM...TO... SHAKE...HIM!!
THAT'S RIGHT! I'M NOT GOING ANYWHERE!

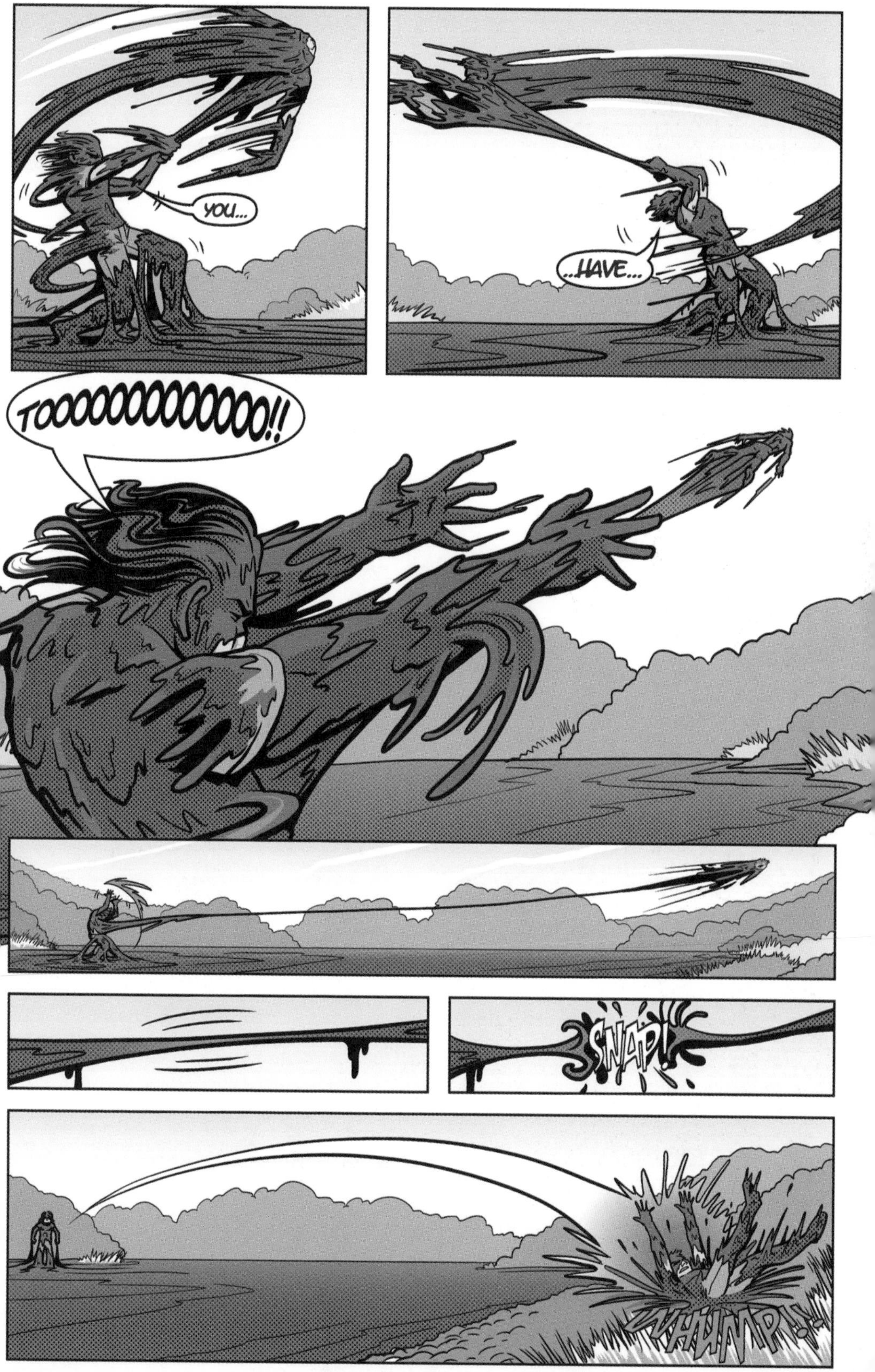

YOU...
..HAVE...
TOOOOOOOOOOOOO!!
SNAP!
WHUMP!!

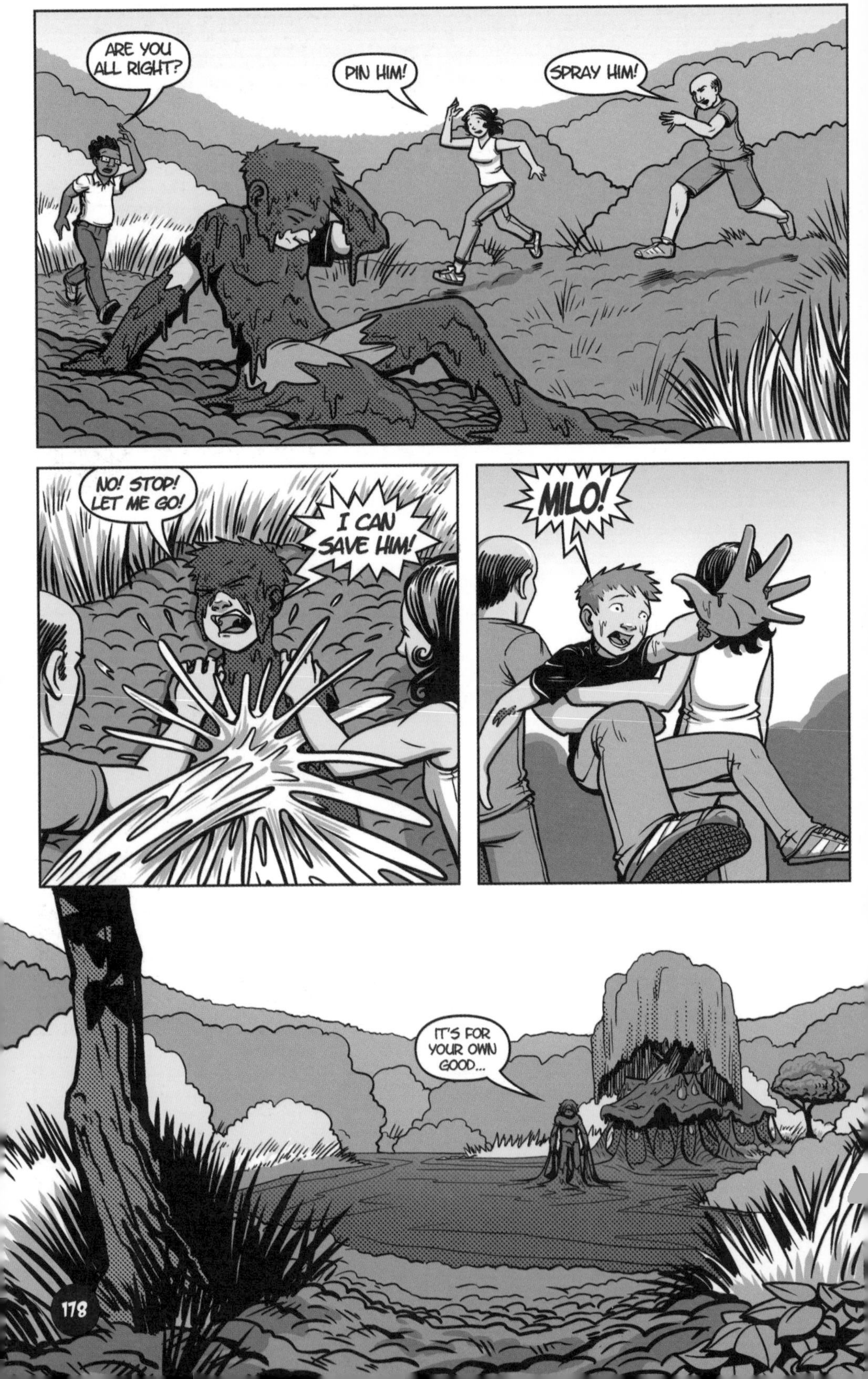
ARE YOU ALL RIGHT?
PIN HIM!
SPRAY HIM!
NO! STOP! LET ME GO!
I CAN SAVE HIM!
MILO!
IT'S FOR YOUR OWN GOOD...

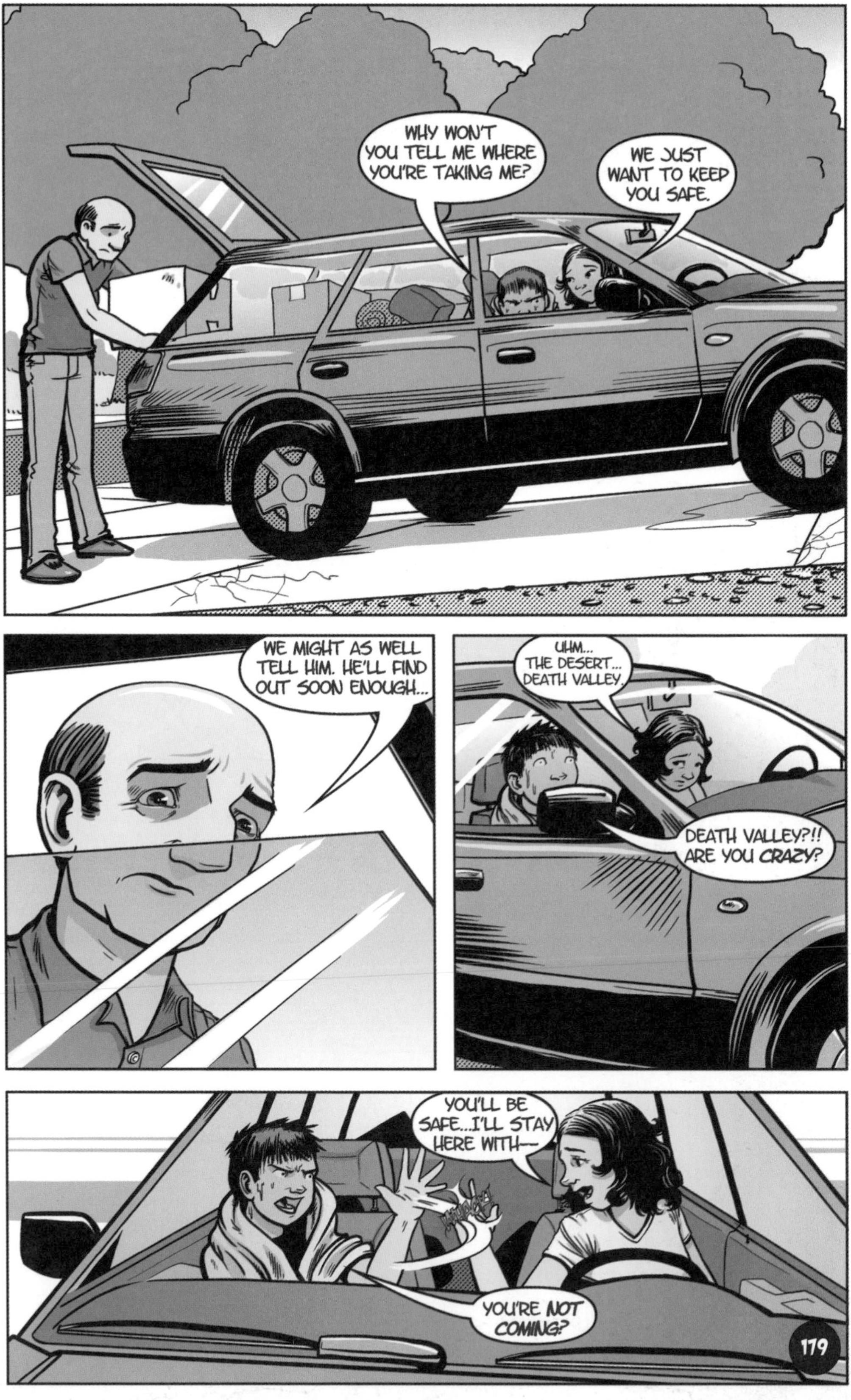
WHY WON'T YOU TELL ME WHERE YOU'RE TAKING ME?
WE JUST WANT TO KEEP YOU SAFE.
WE MIGHT AS WELL TELL HIM. HE'LL FIND OUT SOON ENOUGH...
UHM... THE DESERT... DEATH VALLEY.
DEATH VALLEY?!! ARE YOU CRAZY?
YOU'LL BE SAFE...I'LL STAY HERE WITH—
YOU'RE NOT COMING?

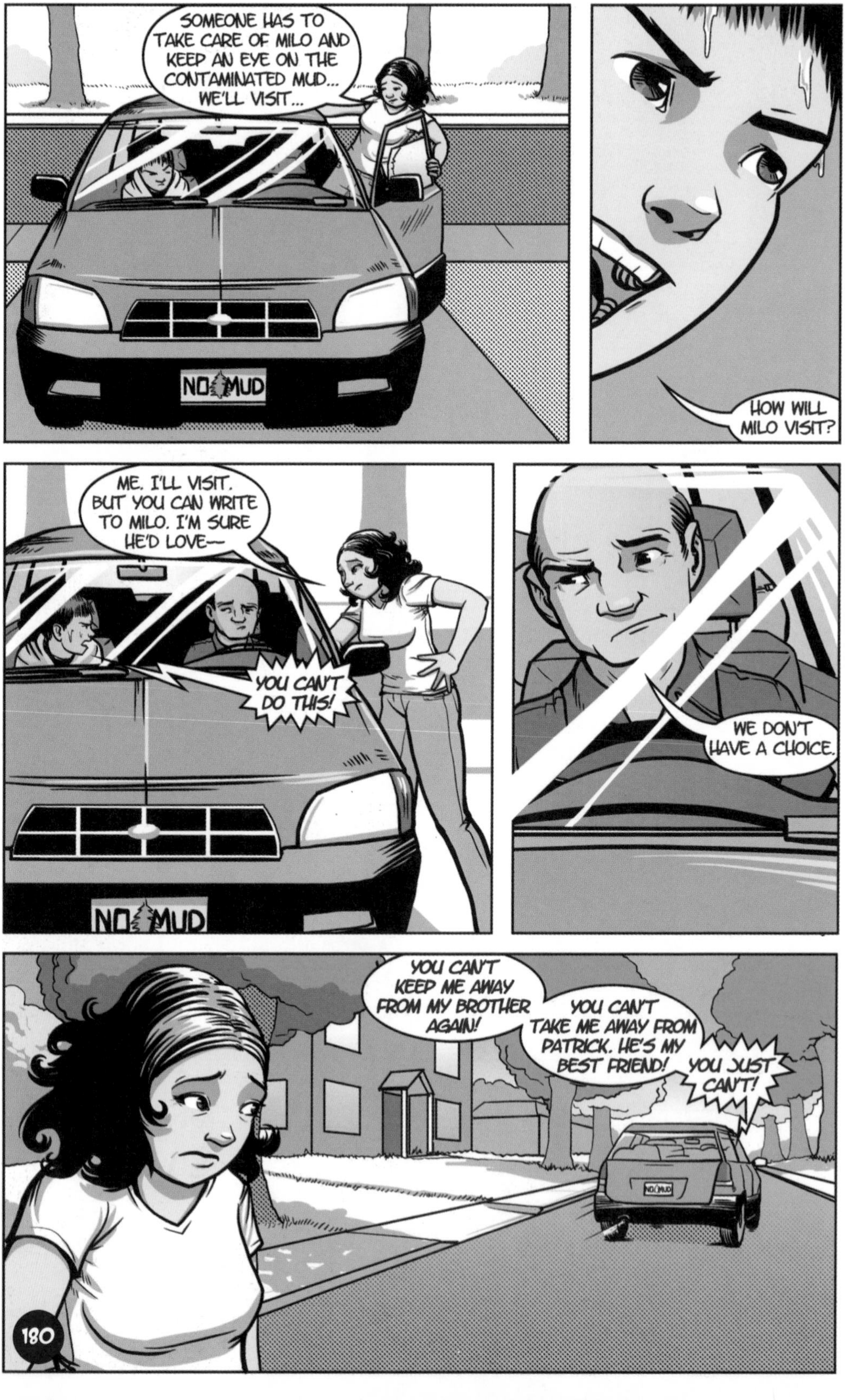
SOMEONE HAS TO TAKE CARE OF MILO AND KEEP AN EYE ON THE CONTAMINATED MUD... WE'LL VISIT...
NO MUD
HOW WILL MILO VISIT?
ME. I'LL VISIT. BUT YOU CAN WRITE TO MILO. I'M SURE HE'D LOVE--
YOU CAN'T DO THIS!
NO MUD
WE DON'T HAVE A CHOICE.
YOU CAN'T KEEP ME AWAY FROM MY BROTHER AGAIN!
YOU CAN'T TAKE ME AWAY FROM PATRICK. HE'S MY BEST FRIEND!
YOU JUST CAN'T!
NO MUD

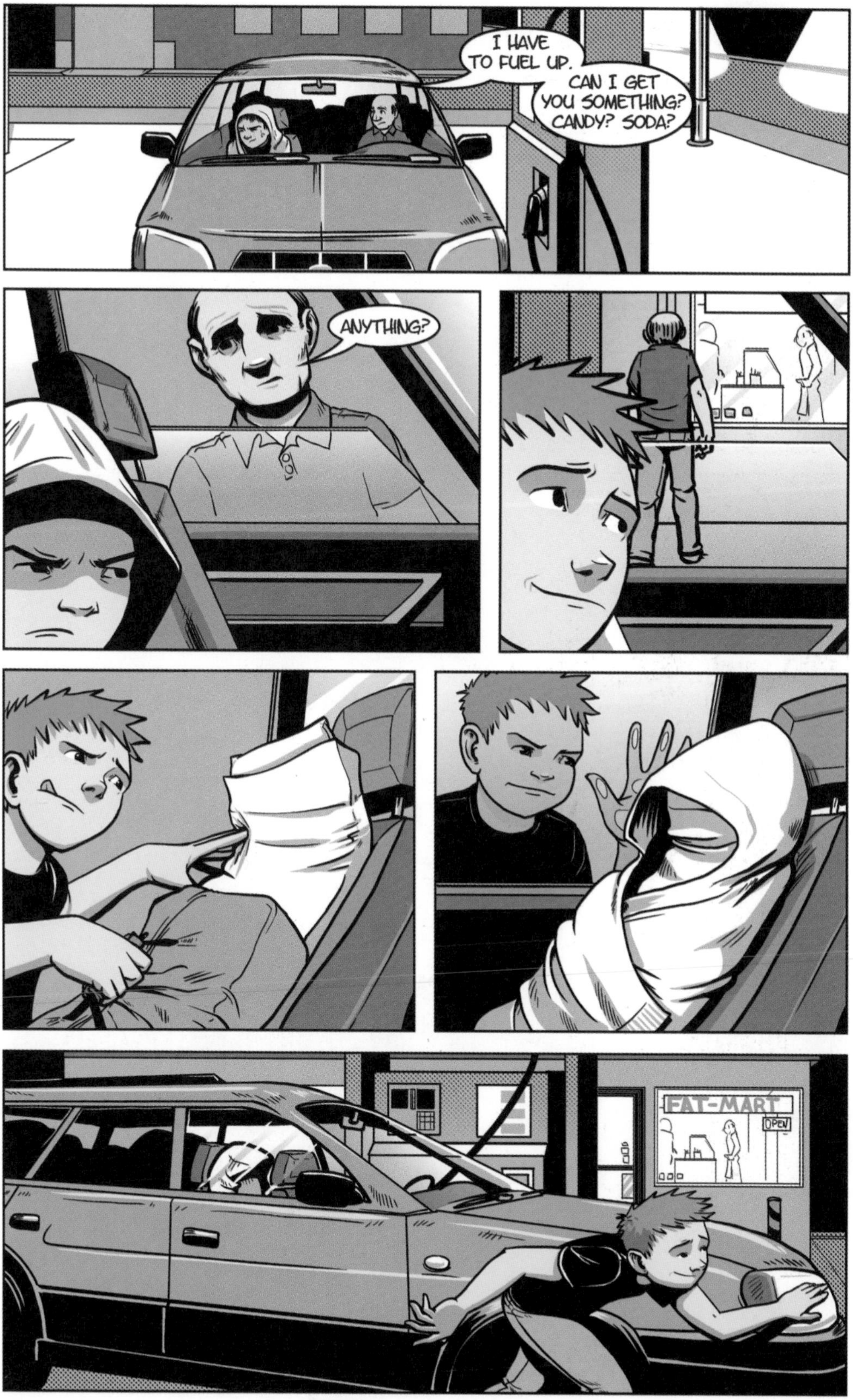
I HAVE TO FUEL UP.
CAN I GET YOU SOMETHING? CANDY? SODA?
ANYTHING?
FAT-MART
OPEN

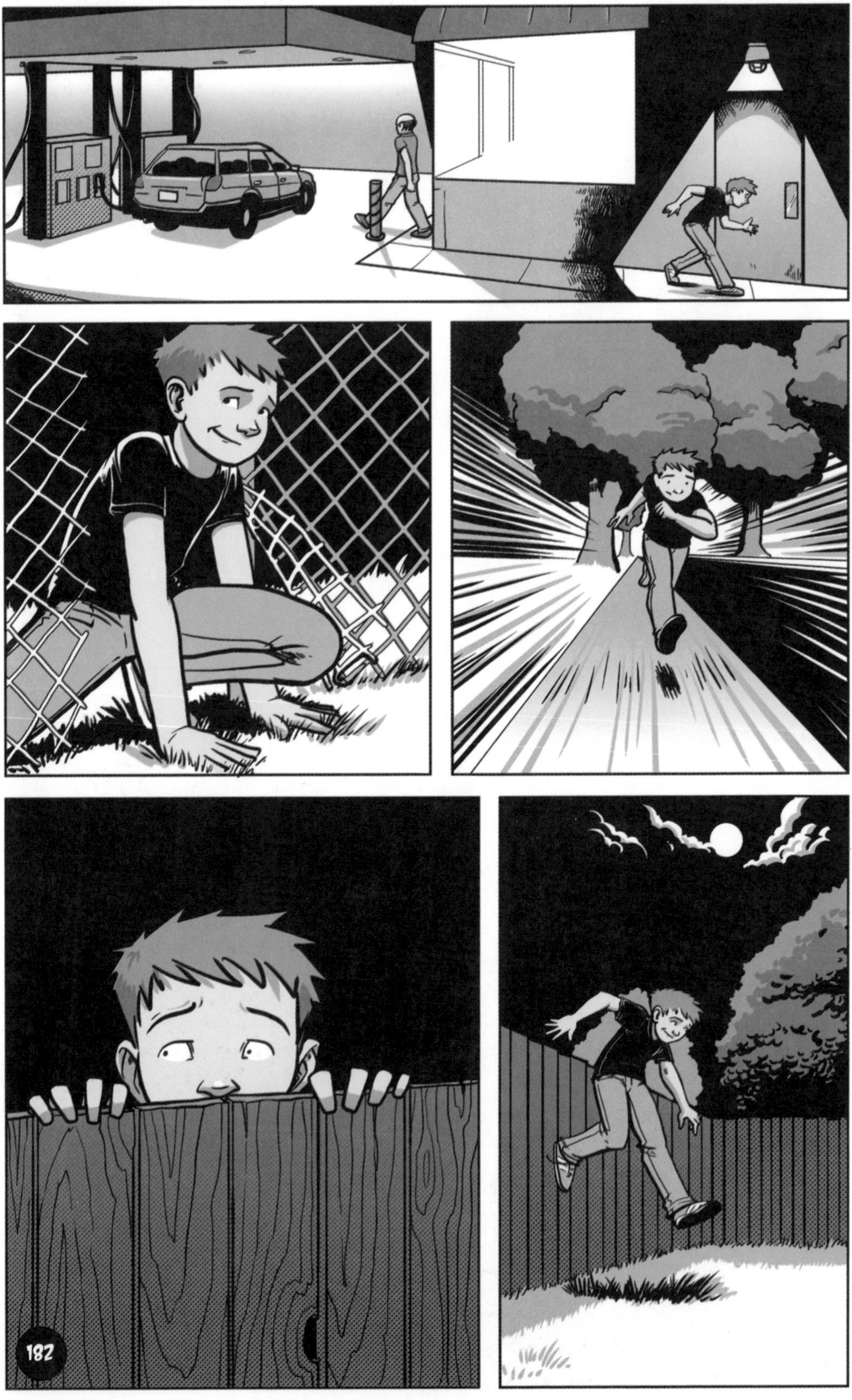

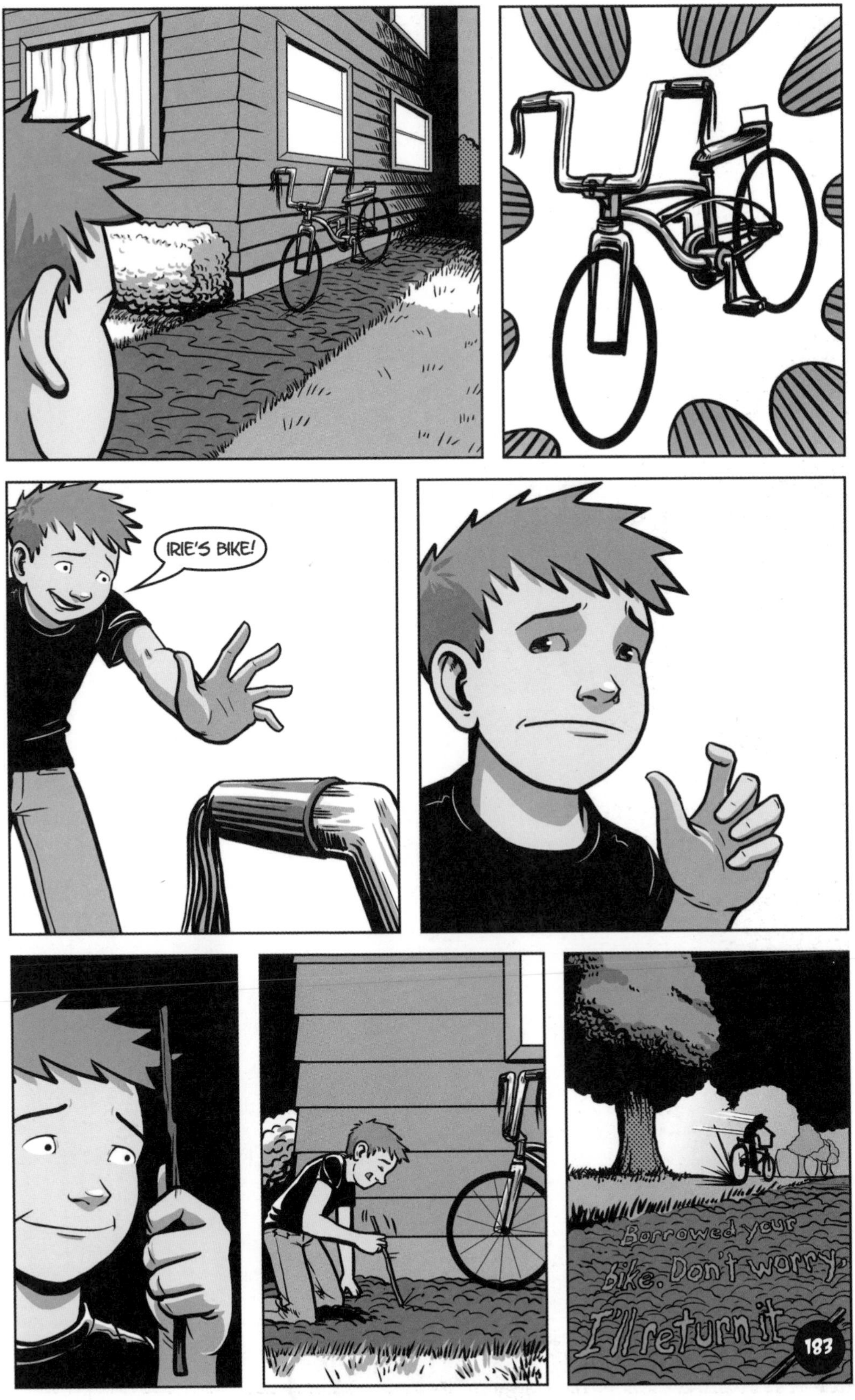
IRIE'S BIKE!
Borrowed your
bike. Don't worry.
I'll return it

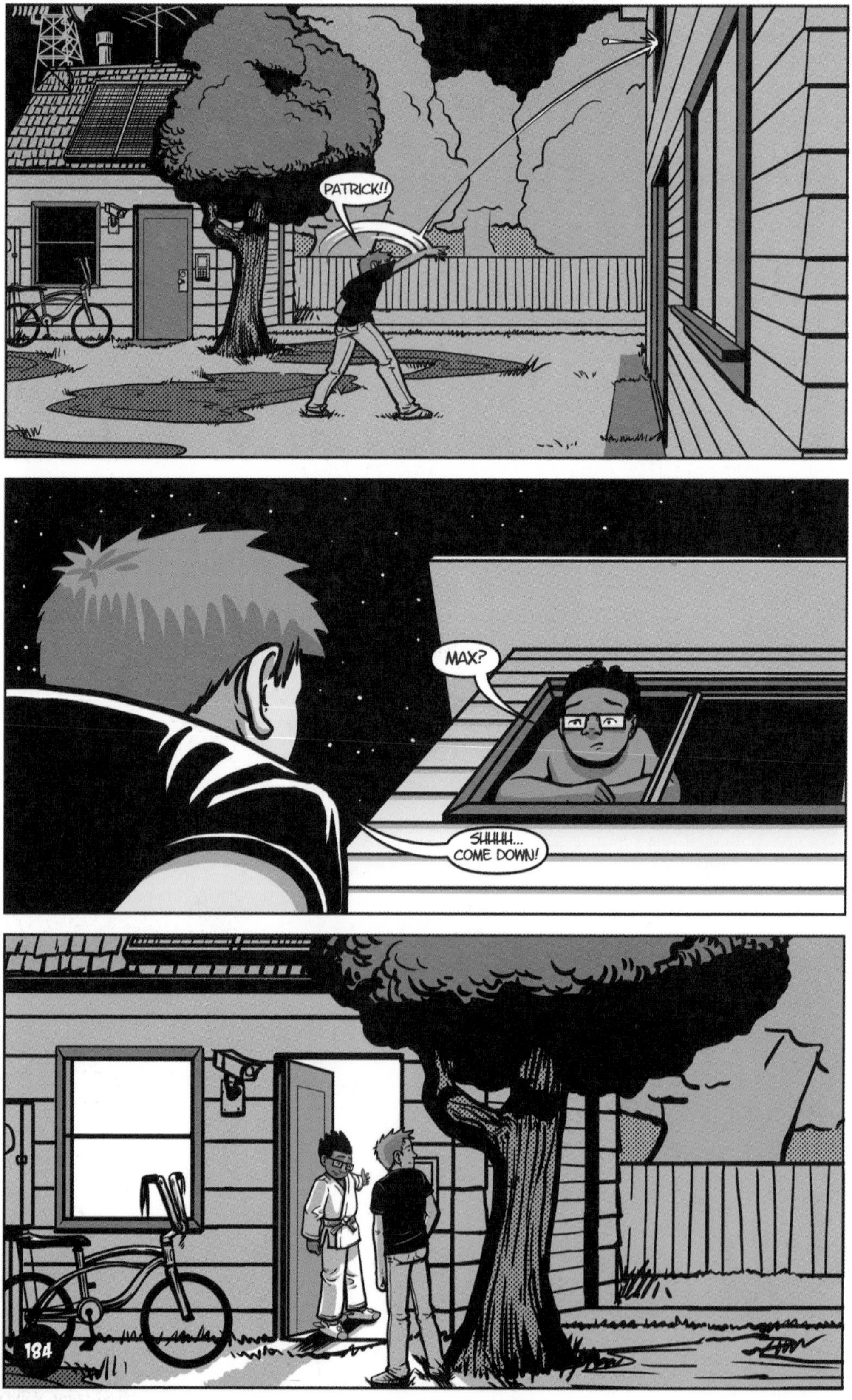
PATRICK!!
MAX?
SHHHH...
COME DOWN!

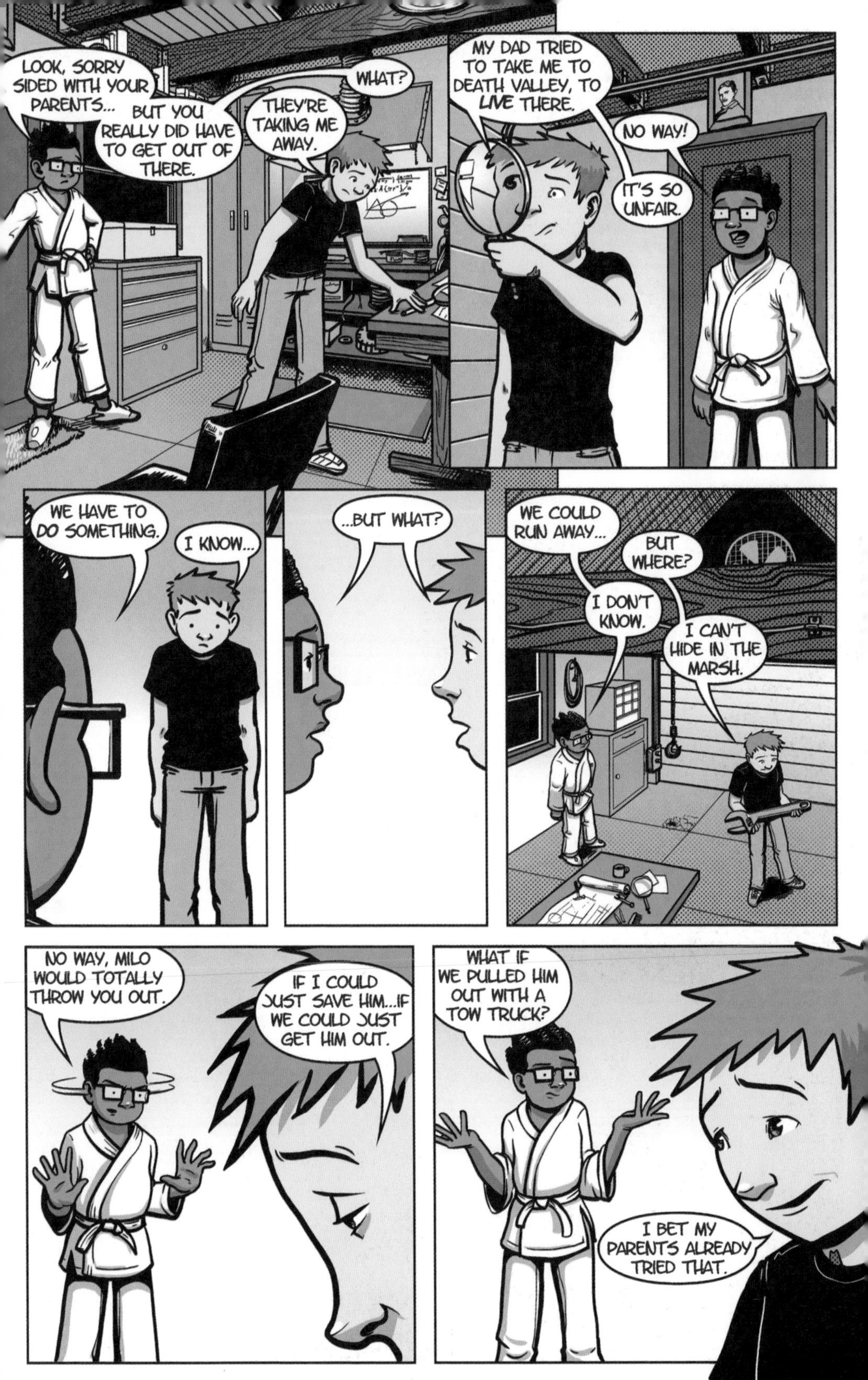
LOOK, SORRY I SIDED WITH YOUR PARENTS...
BUT YOU REALLY DID HAVE TO GET OUT OF THERE.
WHAT?
THEY'RE TAKING ME AWAY.
MY DAD TRIED TO TAKE ME TO DEATH VALLEY, TO LIVE THERE.
NO WAY!
IT'S SO UNFAIR.
WE HAVE TO DO SOMETHING.
I KNOW...
...BUT WHAT?
WE COULD RUN AWAY...
BUT WHERE?
I DON'T KNOW.
I CAN'T HIDE IN THE MARSH.
NO WAY, MILO WOULD TOTALLY THROW YOU OUT.
IF I COULD JUST SAVE HIM...IF WE COULD JUST GET HIM OUT.
WHAT IF WE PULLED HIM OUT WITH A TOW TRUCK?
I BET MY PARENTS ALREADY TRIED THAT.

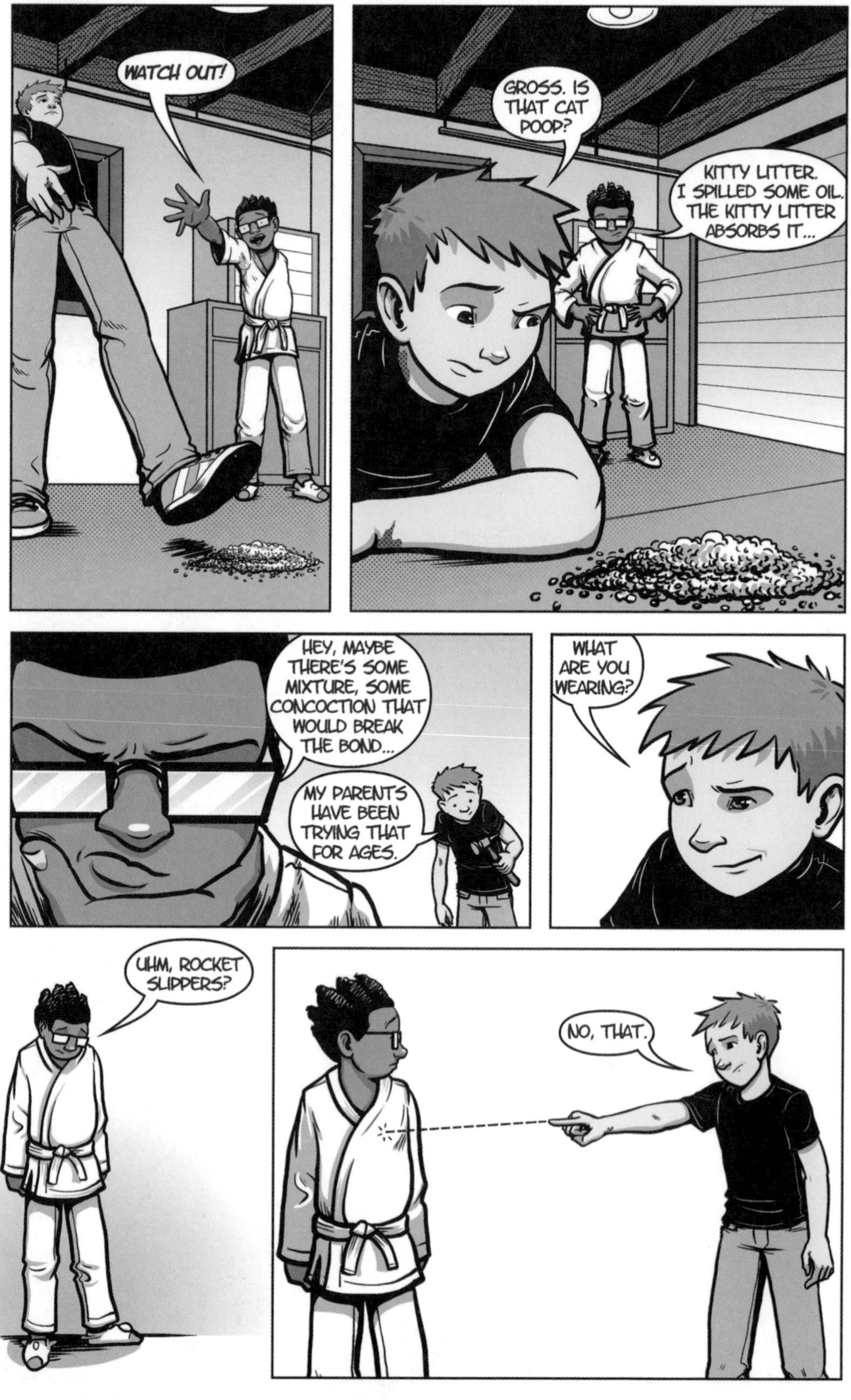
WATCH OUT!
GROSS. IS THAT CAT POOP?
KITTY LITTER. I SPILLED SOME OIL. THE KITTY LITTER ABSORBS IT...
HEY, MAYBE THERE'S SOME MIXTURE, SOME CONCOCTION THAT WOULD BREAK THE BOND...
MY PARENTS HAVE BEEN TRYING THAT FOR AGES.
WHAT ARE YOU WEARING?
UHM, ROCKET SLIPPERS?
NO, THAT.

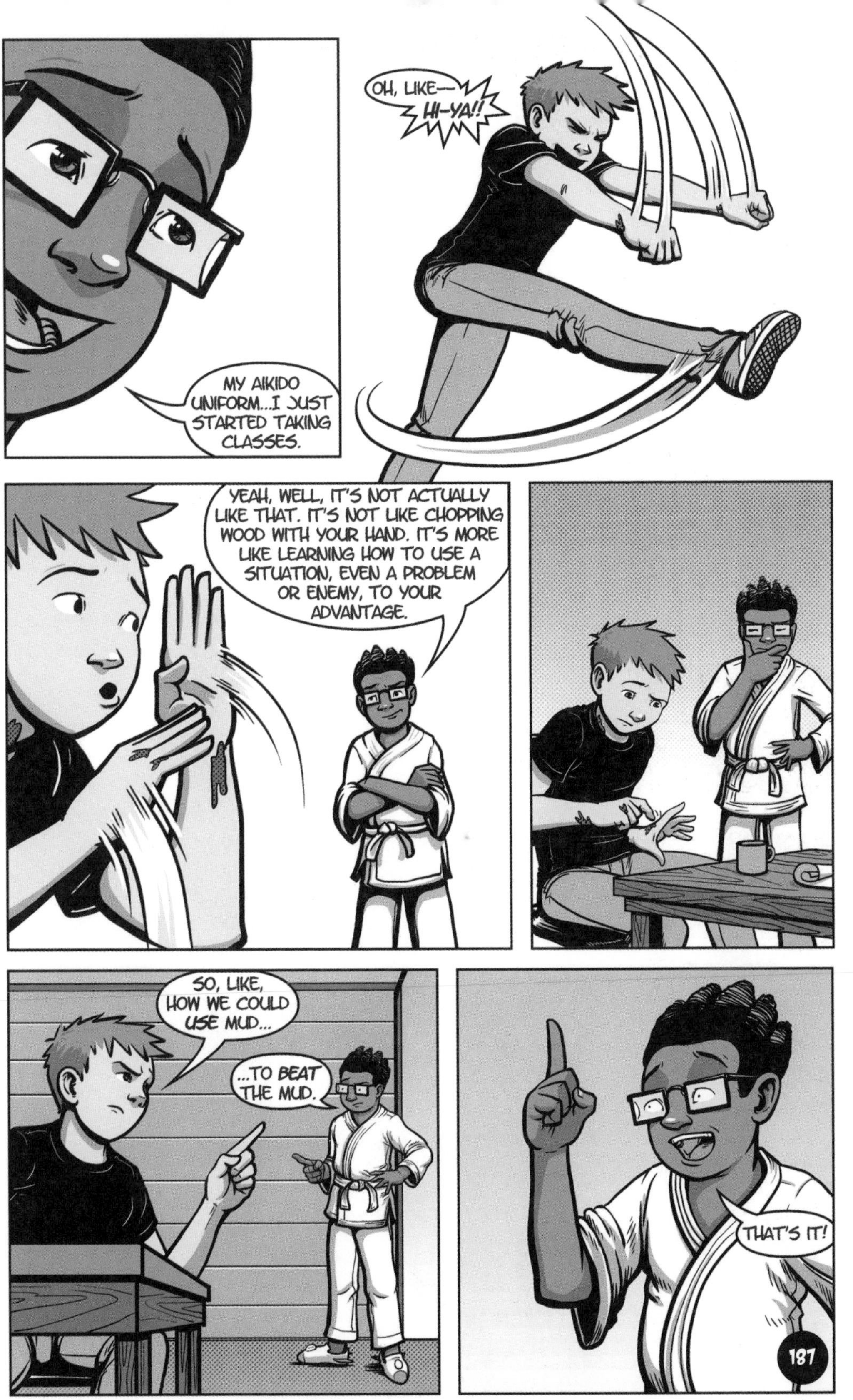
MY AIKIDO UNIFORM...I JUST STARTED TAKING CLASSES.
OH, LIKE—
HI-YA!!
YEAH, WELL, IT'S NOT ACTUALLY LIKE THAT. IT'S NOT LIKE CHOPPING WOOD WITH YOUR HAND. IT'S MORE LIKE LEARNING HOW TO USE A SITUATION, EVEN A PROBLEM OR ENEMY, TO YOUR ADVANTAGE.
SO, LIKE, HOW WE COULD USE MUD...
...TO BEAT THE MUD.
THAT'S IT!

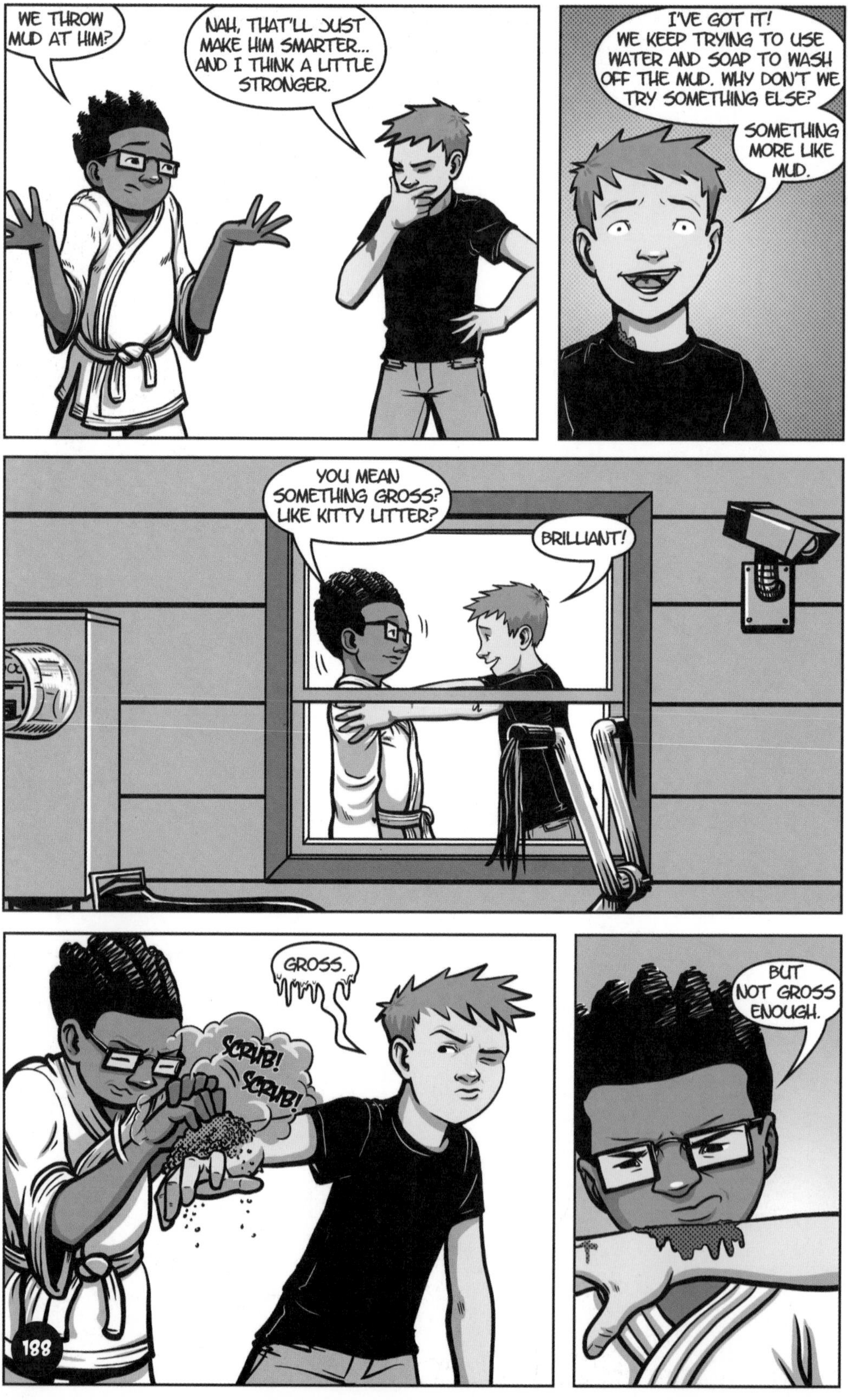
WE THROW MUD AT HIM?
NAH, THAT'LL JUST MAKE HIM SMARTER... AND I THINK A LITTLE STRONGER.
I'VE GOT IT! WE KEEP TRYING TO USE WATER AND SOAP TO WASH OFF THE MUD. WHY DON'T WE TRY SOMETHING ELSE?
SOMETHING MORE LIKE MUD.
YOU MEAN SOMETHING GROSS? LIKE KITTY LITTER?
BRILLIANT!
GROSS.
SCRUB! SCRUB!
BUT NOT GROSS ENOUGH.

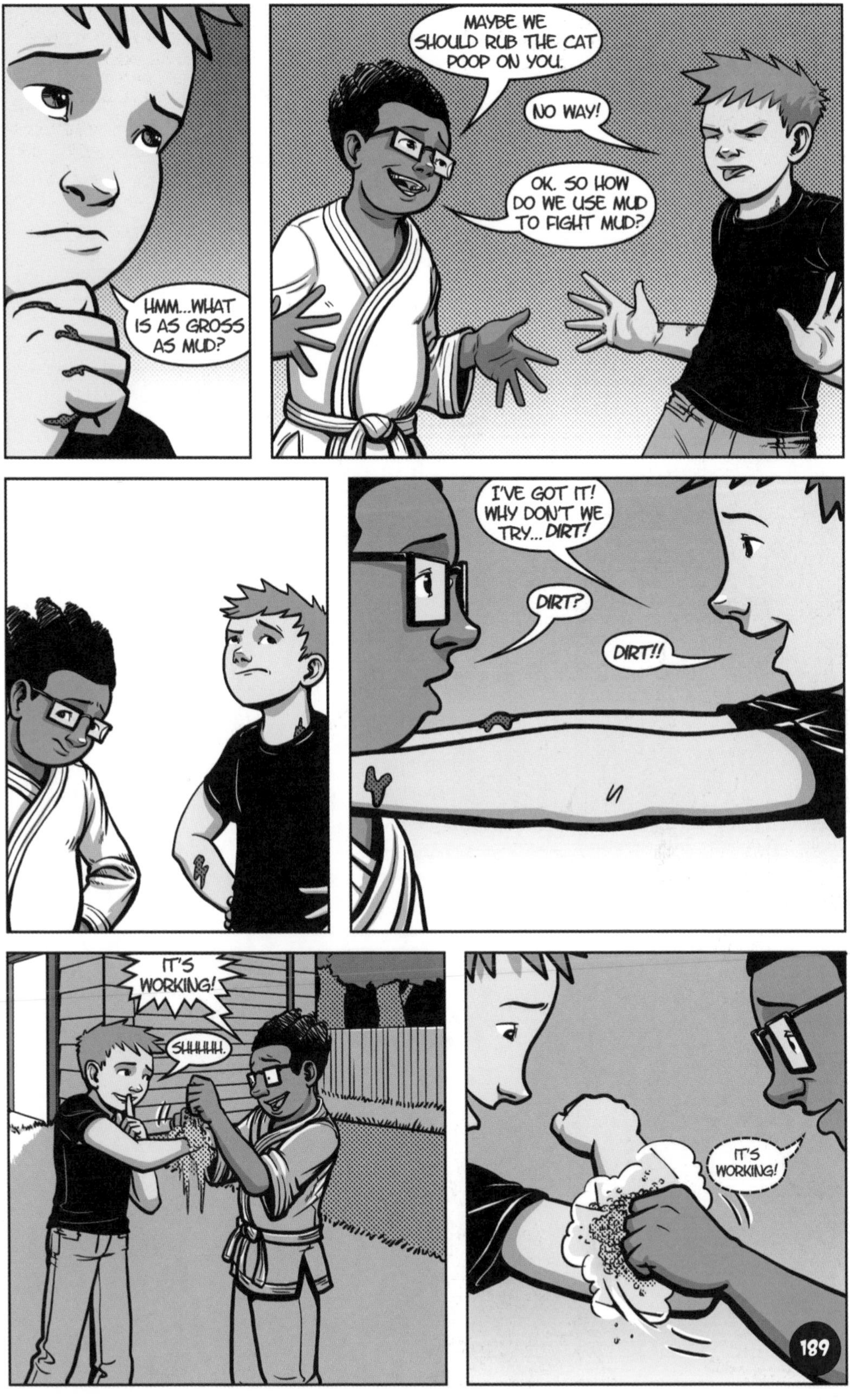
HMM...WHAT IS AS GROSS AS MUD?
MAYBE WE SHOULD RUB THE CAT POOP ON YOU.
NO WAY!
OK. SO HOW DO WE USE MUD TO FIGHT MUD?
I'VE GOT IT! WHY DON'T WE TRY... DIRT!
DIRT?
DIRT!!
IT'S WORKING!
SHHHHH.
IT'S WORKING!

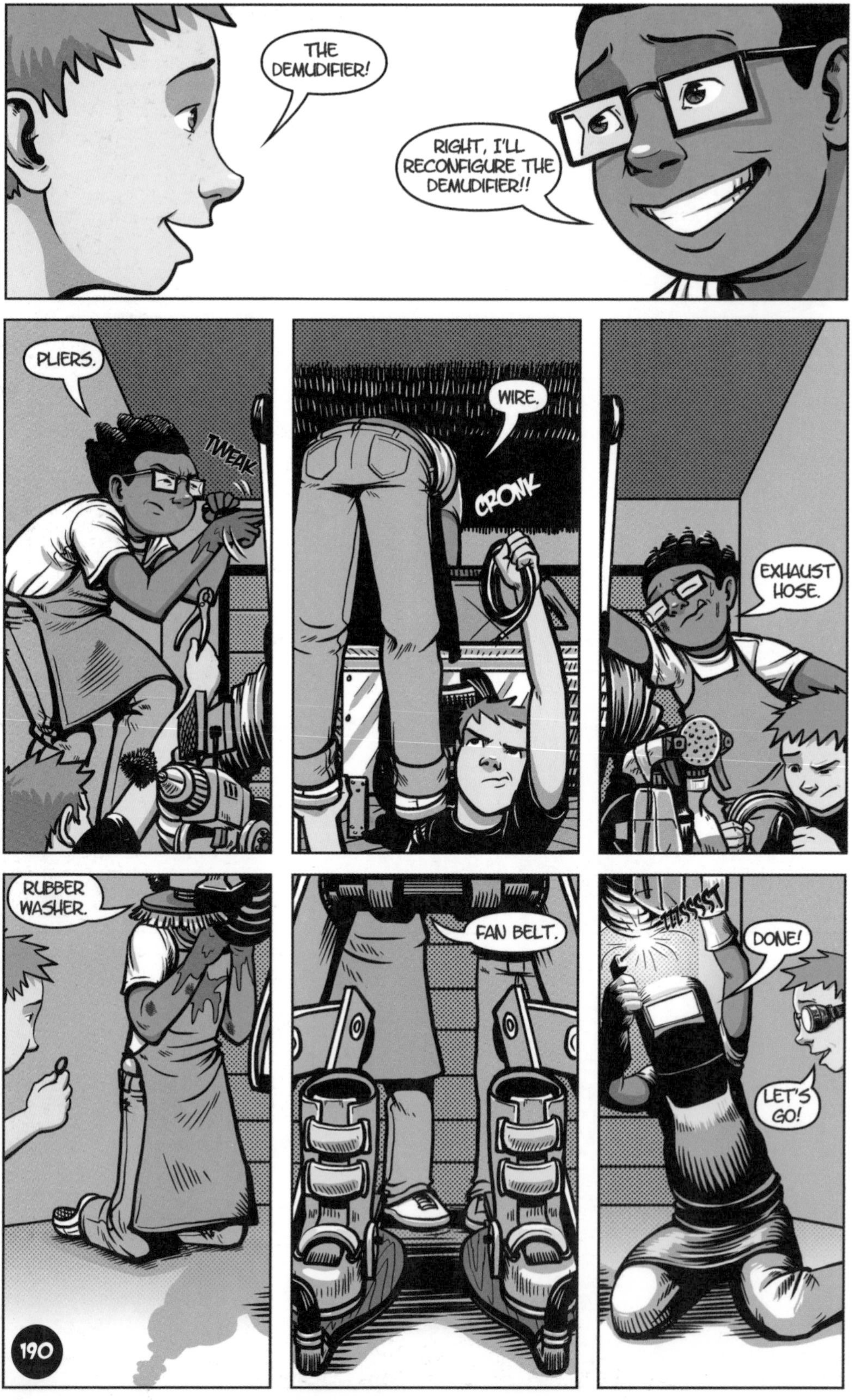
THE DEMUDIFIER!
RIGHT, I'LL RECONFIGURE THE DEMUDIFIER!!
PLIERS.
TWEAK
WIRE.
CRONK
EXHAUST HOSE.
RUBBER WASHER.
FAN BELT.
TZZSSSST
DONE!
LET'S GO!

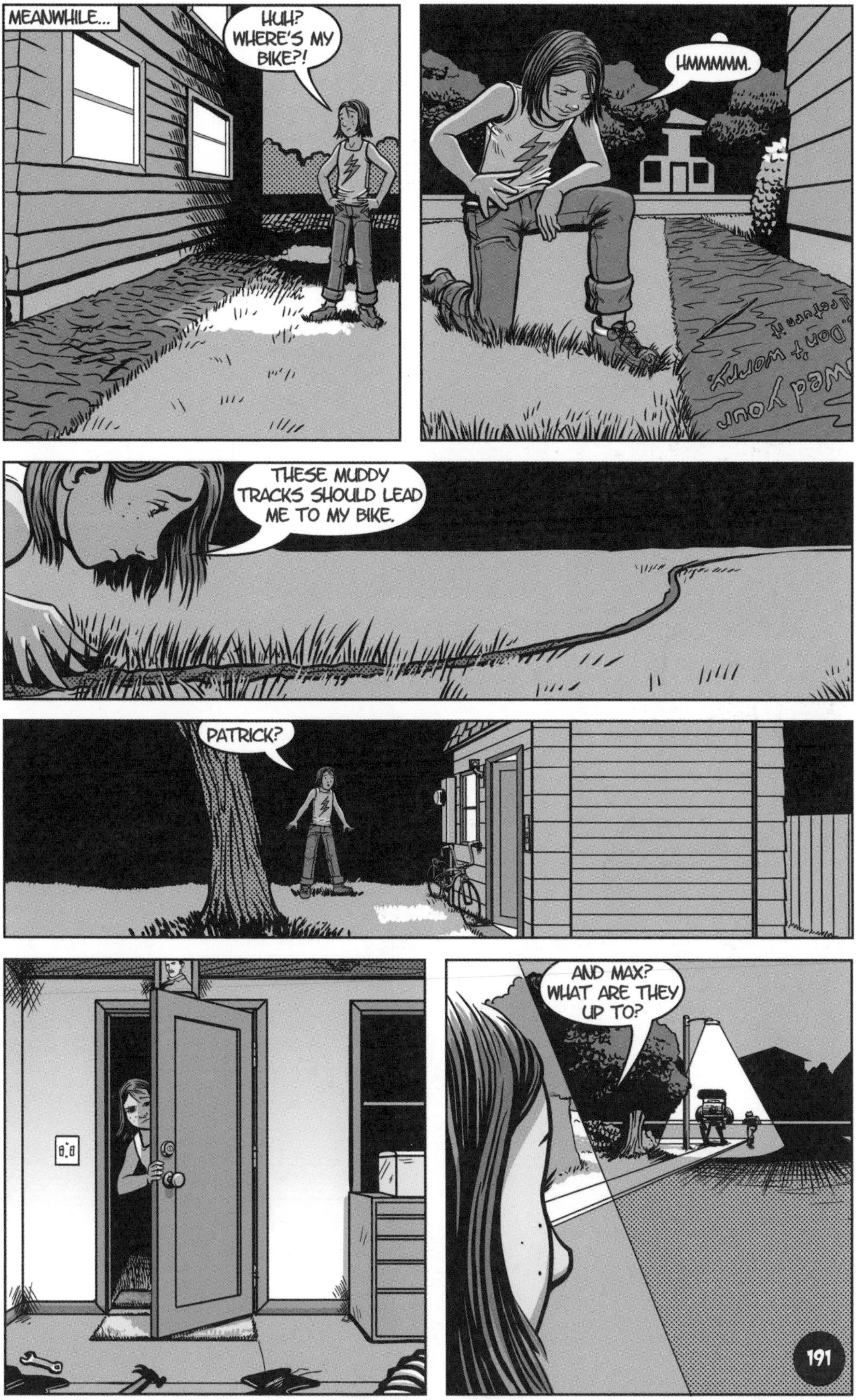
MEANWHILE...
HUH? WHERE'S MY BIKE?!
HMMMMM.
THESE MUDDY TRACKS SHOULD LEAD ME TO MY BIKE.
PATRICK?
AND MAX? WHAT ARE THEY UP TO?

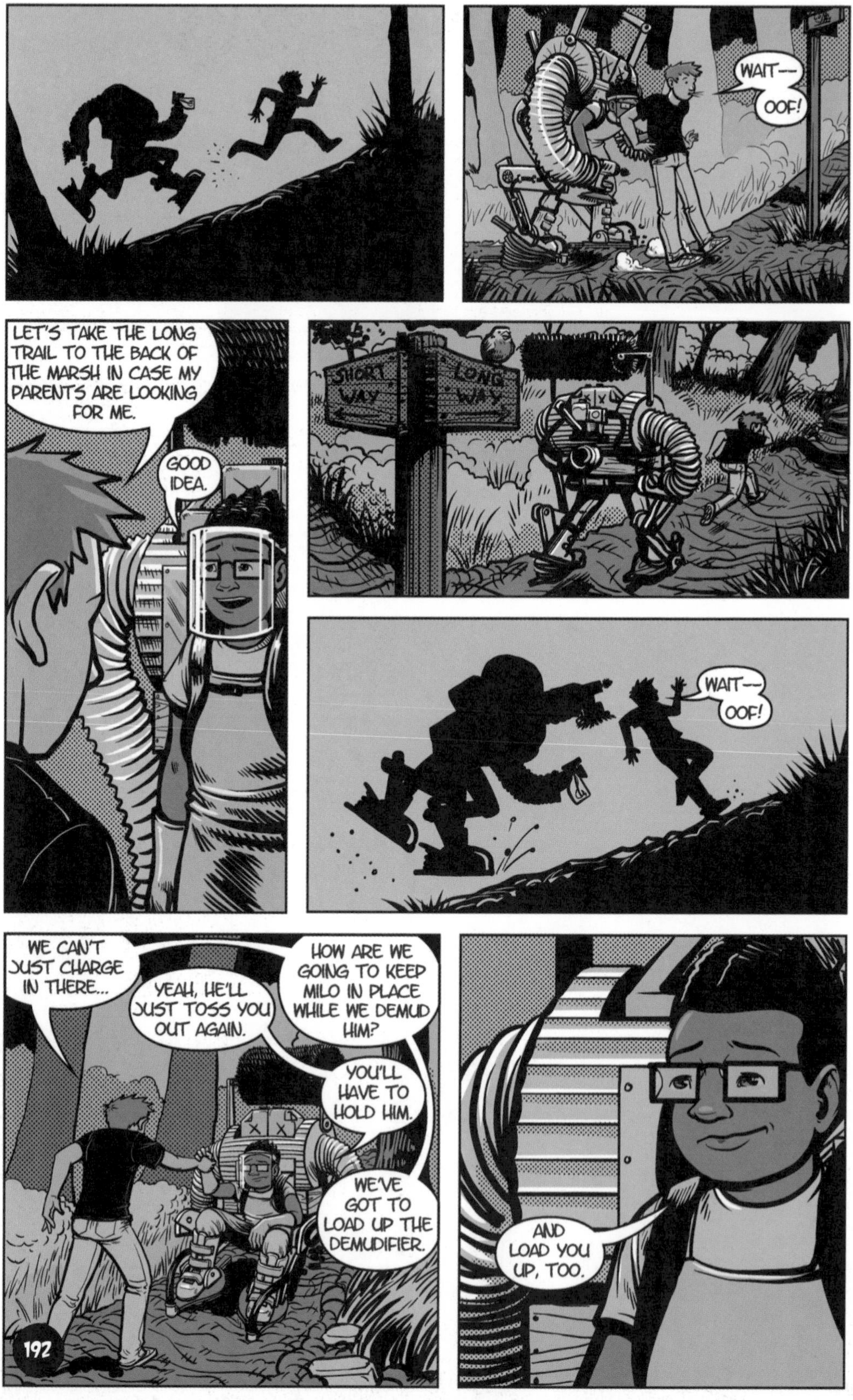
WAIT--
OOF!
LET'S TAKE THE LONG TRAIL TO THE BACK OF THE MARSH IN CASE MY PARENTS ARE LOOKING FOR ME.
GOOD IDEA.
SHORT WAY
LONG WAY
WAIT--
OOF!
WE CAN'T JUST CHARGE IN THERE...
YEAH, HE'LL JUST TOSS YOU OUT AGAIN.
HOW ARE WE GOING TO KEEP MILO IN PLACE WHILE WE DEMUD HIM?
YOU'LL HAVE TO HOLD HIM.
WE'VE GOT TO LOAD UP THE DEMUDIFIER.
AND LOAD YOU UP, TOO.

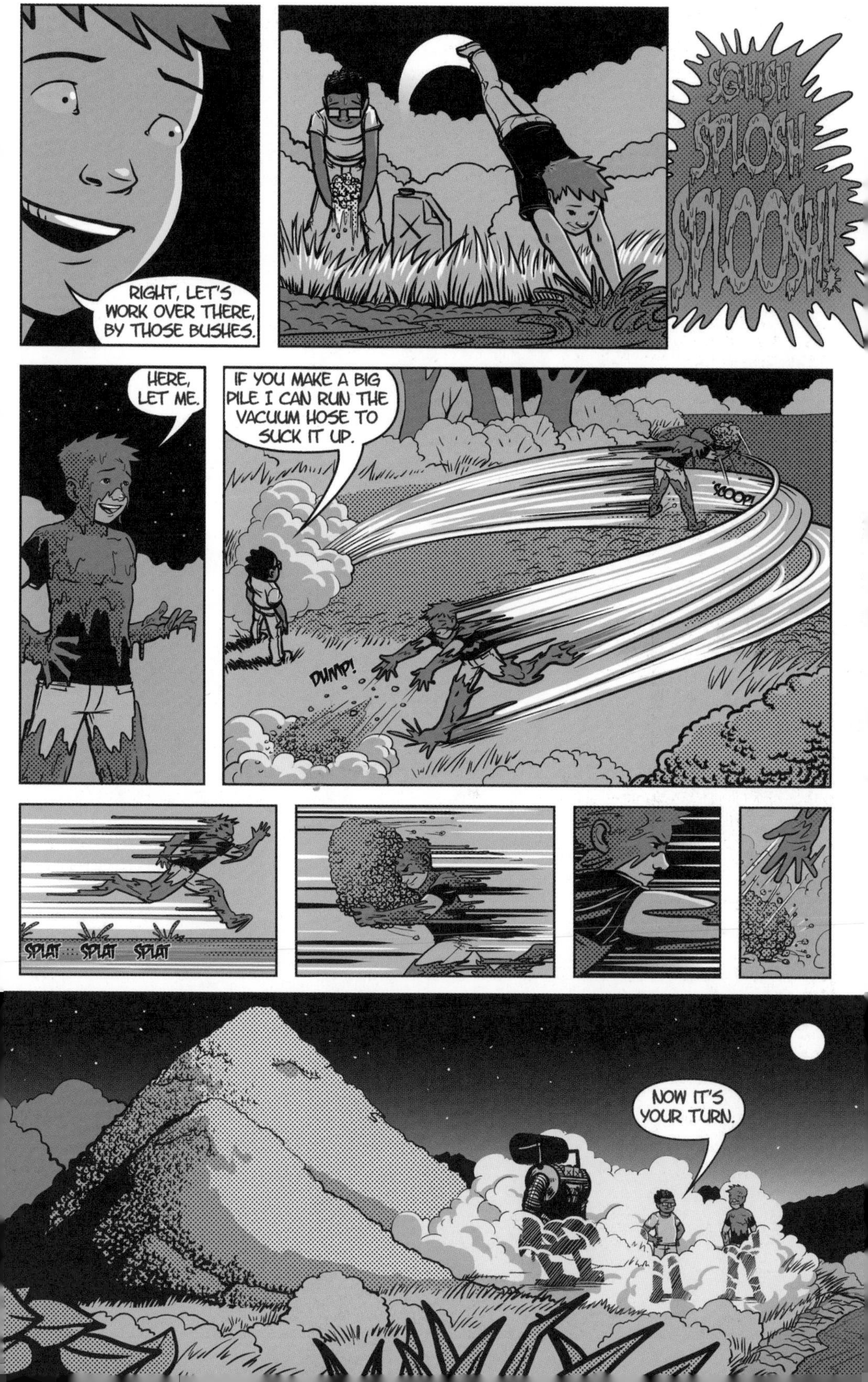
RIGHT, LET'S WORK OVER THERE, BY THOSE BUSHES.
SQUISH
SPLOSH
SPLOOSH!
HERE, LET ME.
IF YOU MAKE A BIG PILE I CAN RUN THE VACUUM HOSE TO SUCK IT UP.
SCOOP!
DUMP!
SPLAT
SPLAT
SPLAT
NOW IT'S YOUR TURN.

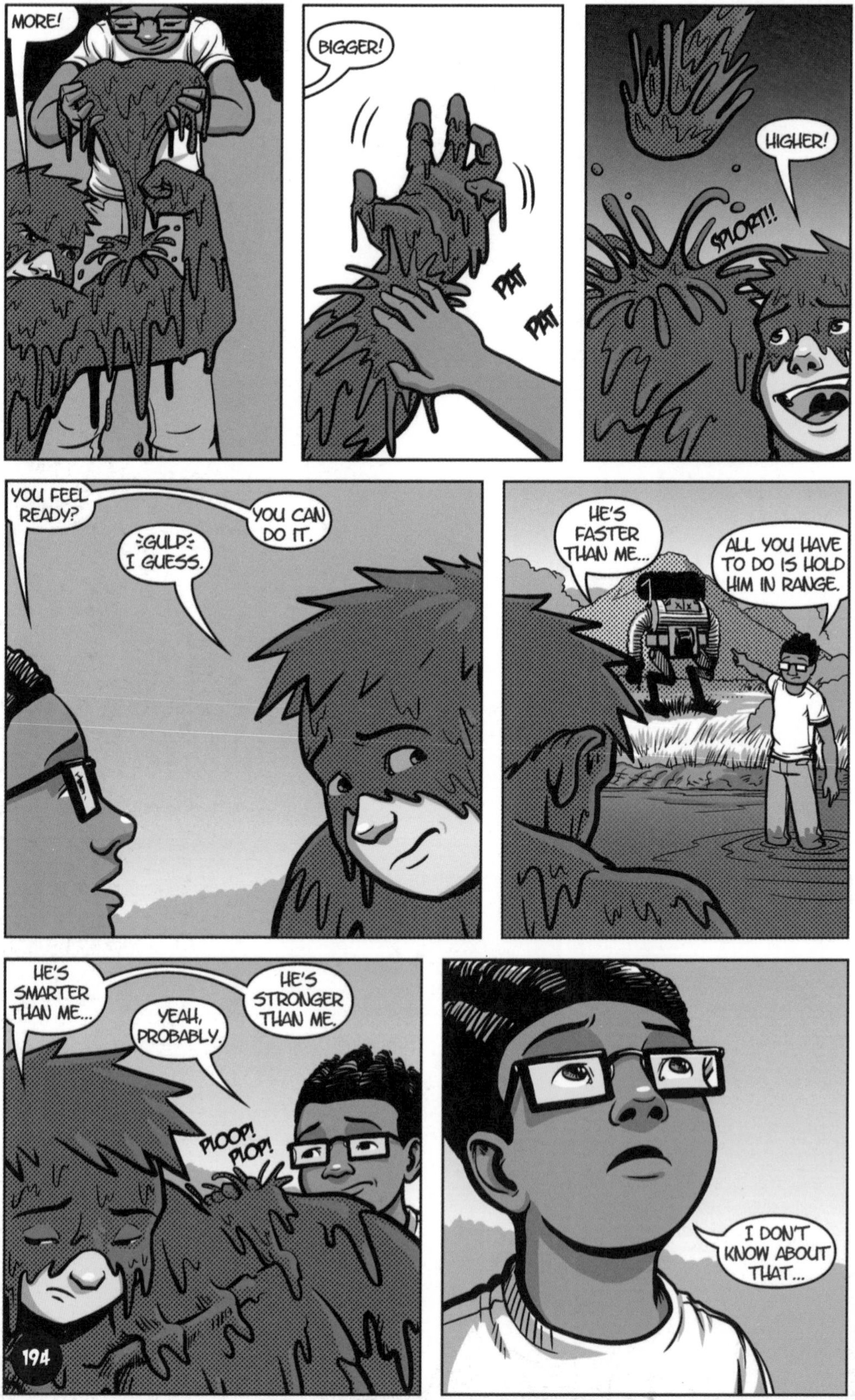
MORE!
BIGGER!
PAT
PAT
HIGHER!
SPLORT!!
YOU FEEL READY?
YOU CAN DO IT.
GULP I GUESS.
HE'S FASTER THAN ME...
ALL YOU HAVE TO DO IS HOLD HIM IN RANGE.
HE'S SMARTER THAN ME...
HE'S STRONGER THAN ME.
YEAH, PROBABLY.
PLOOP! PLOP!
I DON'T KNOW ABOUT THAT...

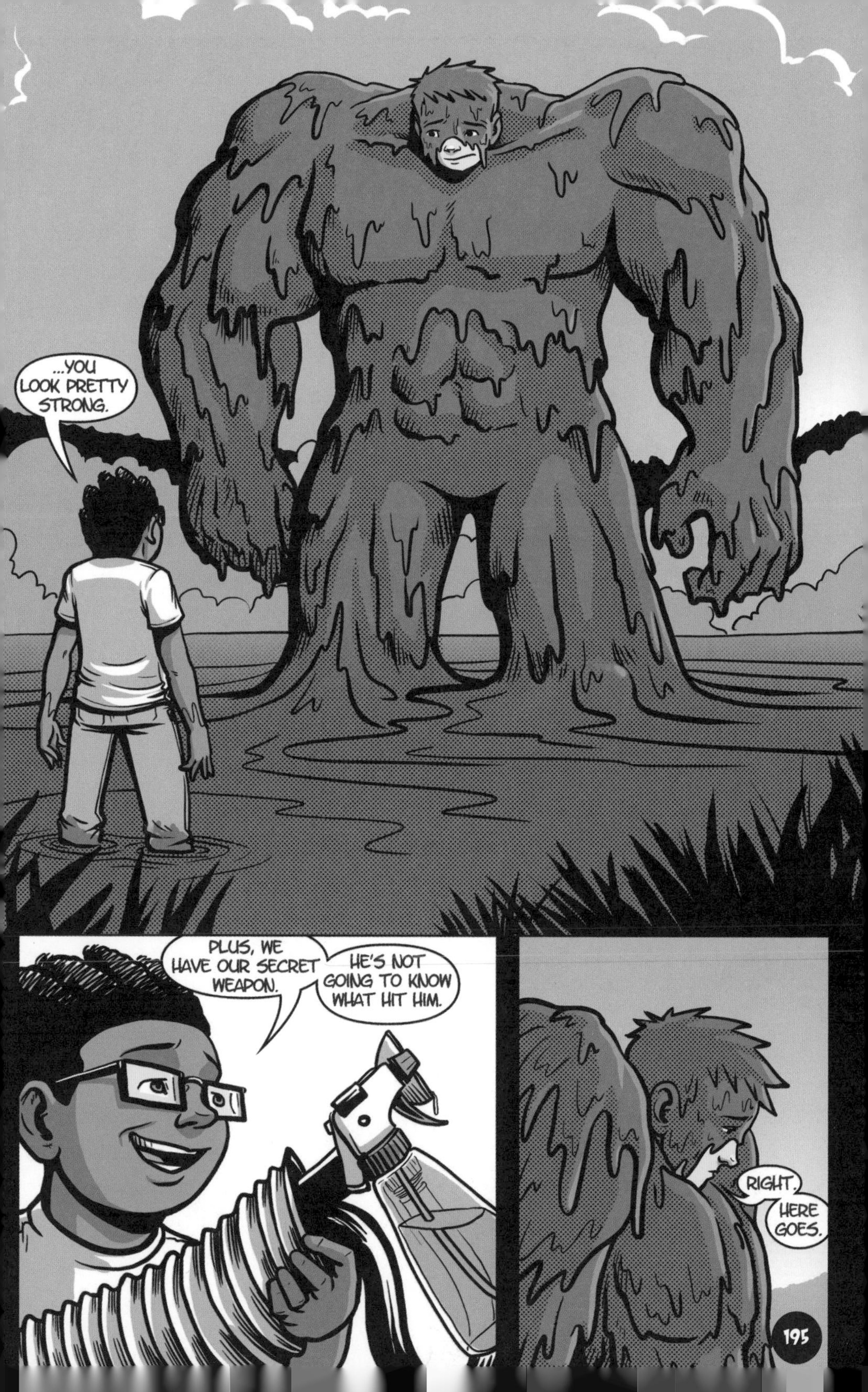
...YOU LOOK PRETTY STRONG.
PLUS, WE HAVE OUR SECRET WEAPON.
HE'S NOT GOING TO KNOW WHAT HIT HIM.
RIGHT.
HERE GOES.

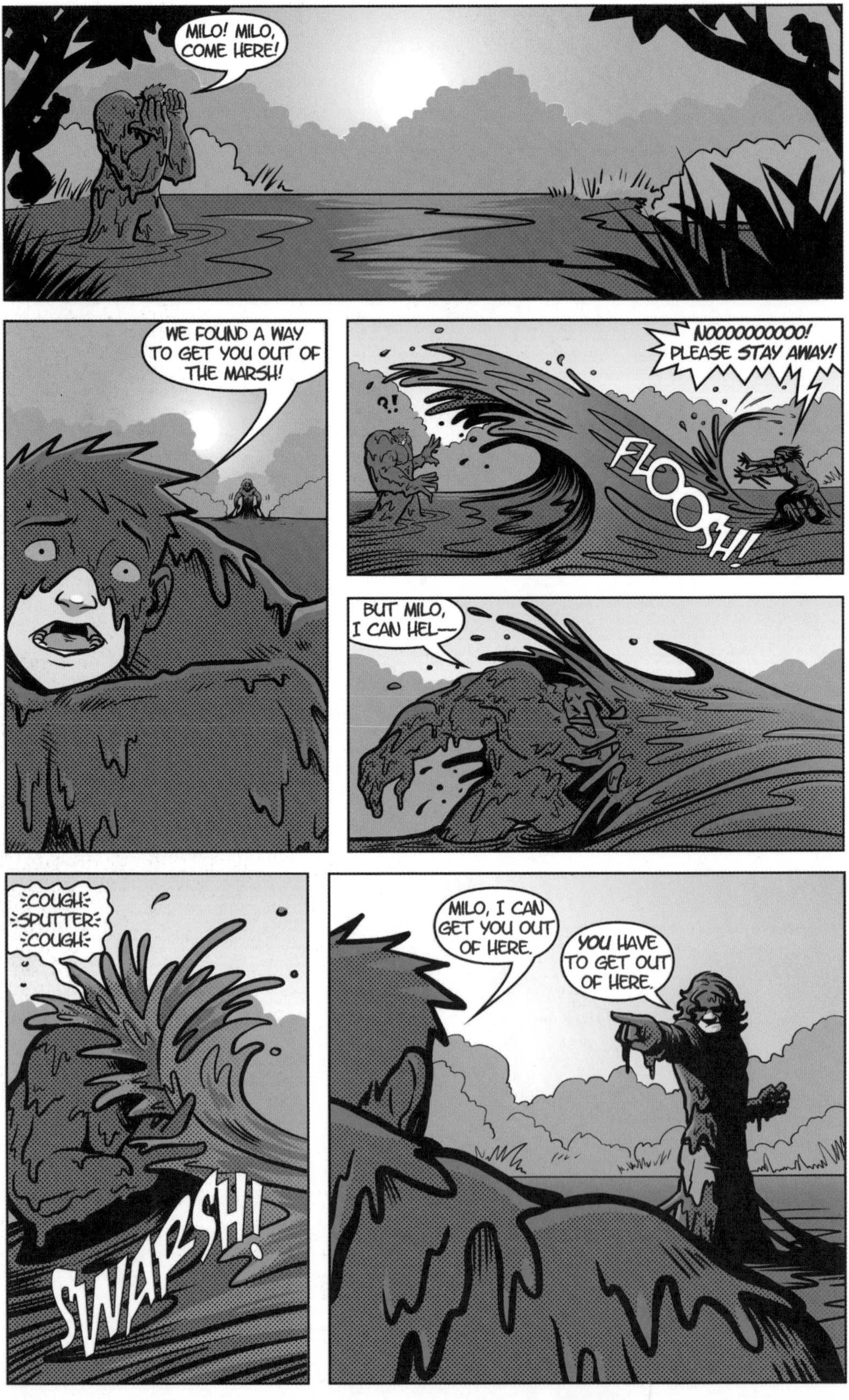
MILO! MILO, COME HERE!
WE FOUND A WAY TO GET YOU OUT OF THE MARSH!
NOOOOOOOOOO! PLEASE STAY AWAY!
?!
FLOOSH!
BUT MILO, I CAN HEL—
COUGH SPUTTER COUGH
SWARSH!
MILO, I CAN GET YOU OUT OF HERE.
YOU HAVE TO GET OUT OF HERE.

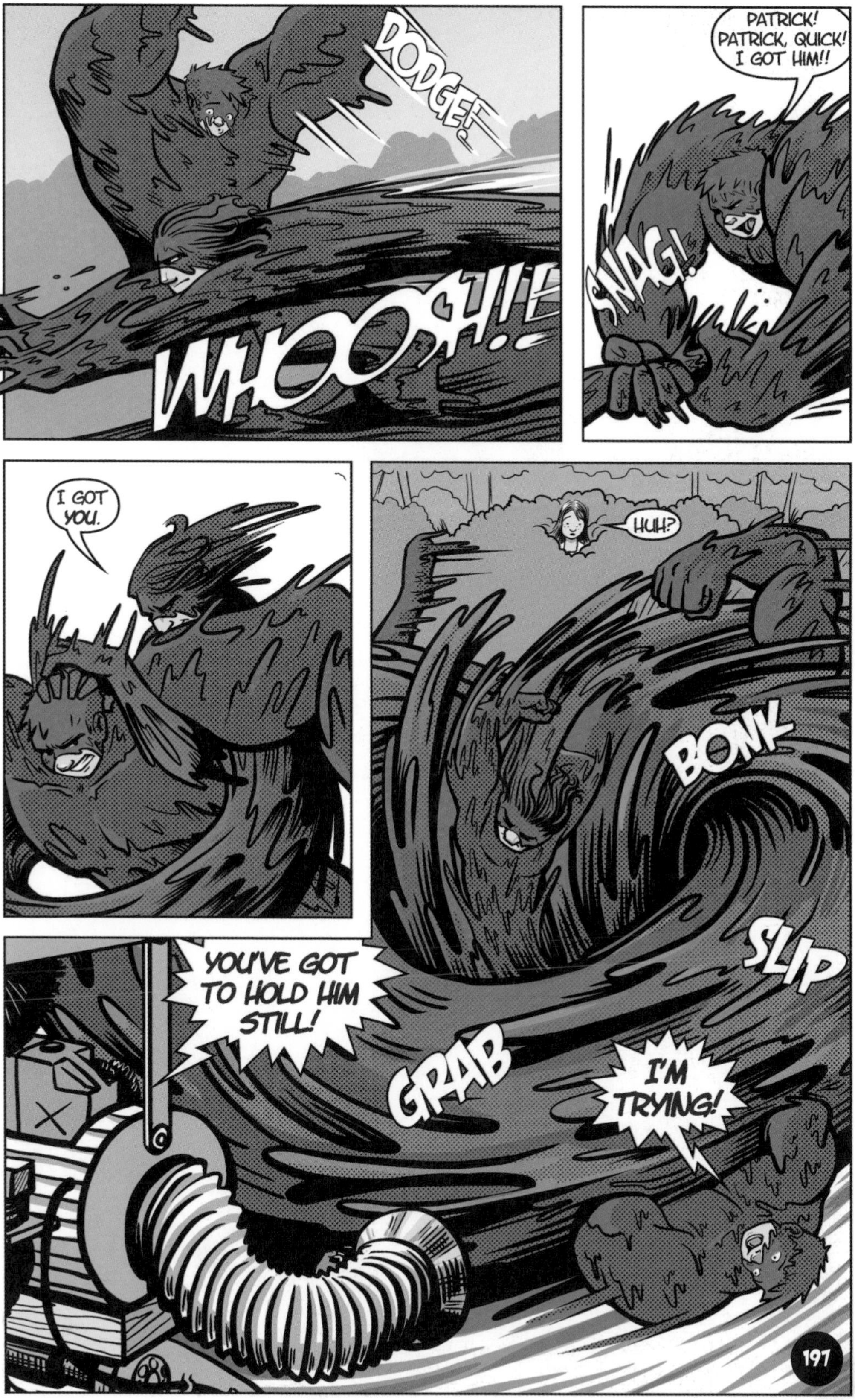
DODGE!
WHOOSH!!
PATRICK! PATRICK, QUICK! I GOT HIM!!
SNAG!
I GOT YOU.
HUH?
BONK
SLIP
YOU'VE GOT TO HOLD HIM STILL!
GRAB
I'M TRYING!

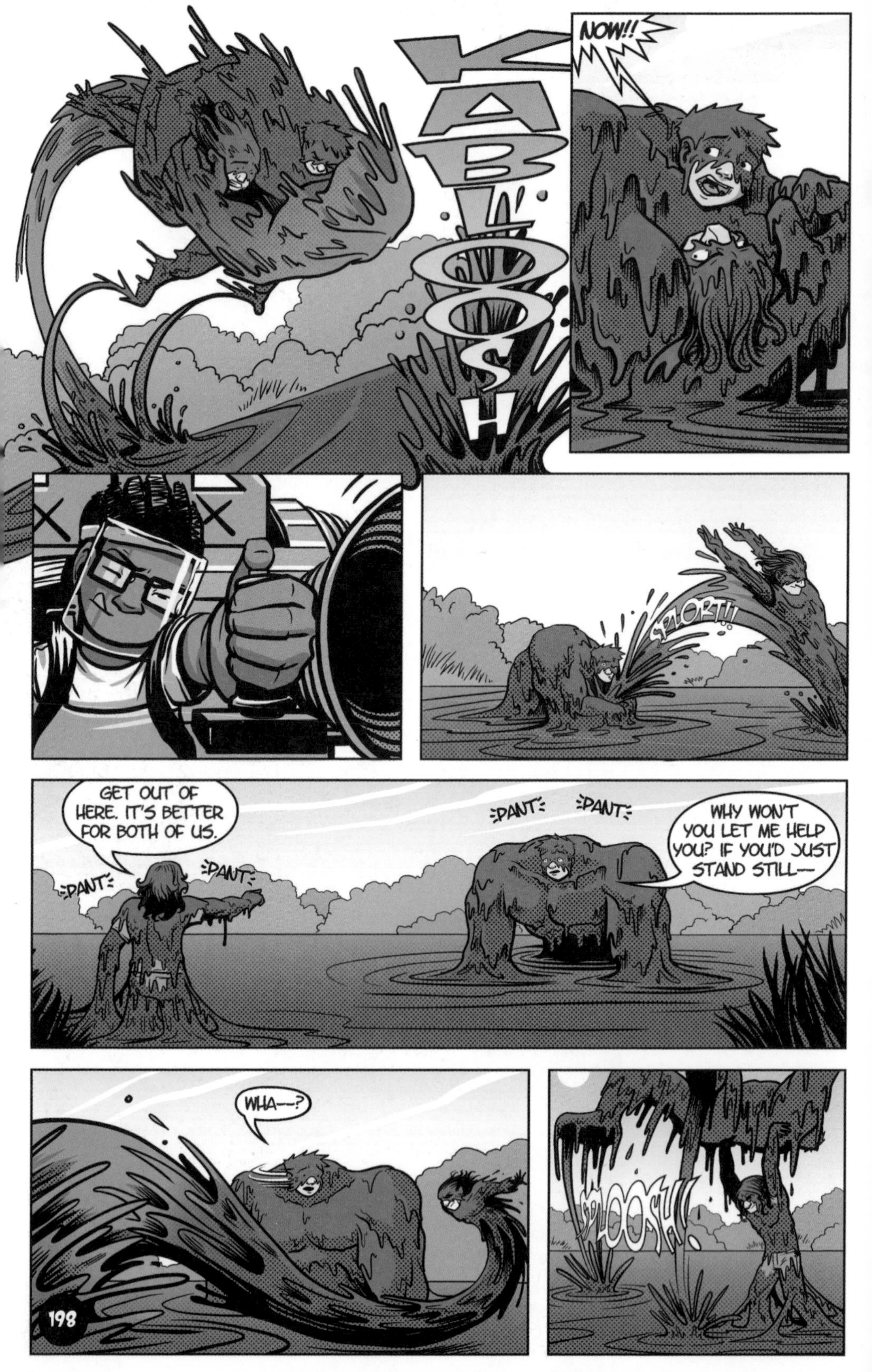
KABLOOSH
NOW!!
SPLORT!!
GET OUT OF HERE. IT'S BETTER FOR BOTH OF US.
PANT PANT
PANT PANT
WHY WON'T YOU LET ME HELP YOU? IF YOU'D JUST STAND STILL--
WHA--?
SPLOOSH!!

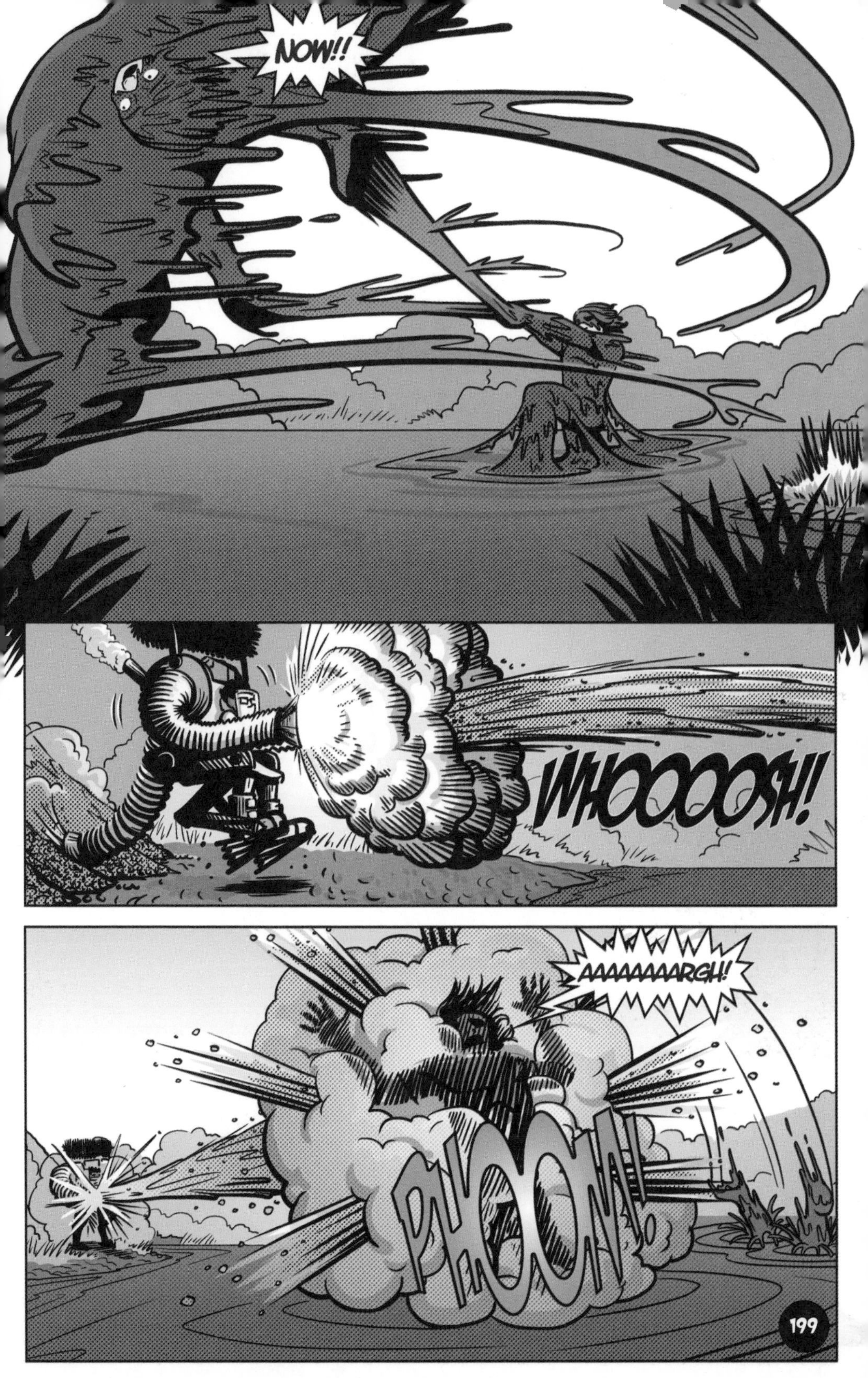
NOW!!
WHOOOOOSH!
AAAAAAAARGH!
PHOOM!

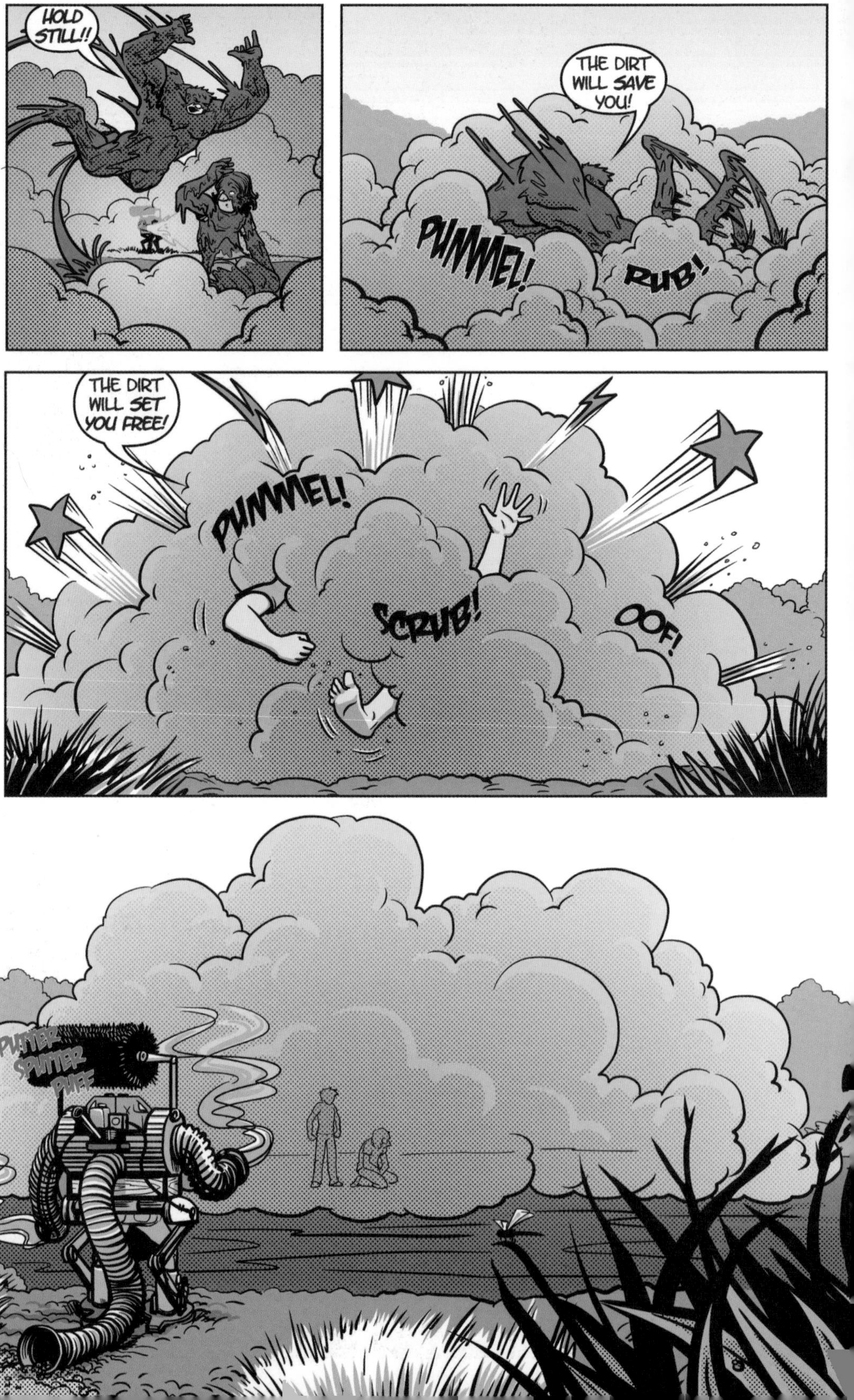
HOLD STILL!!
THE DIRT WILL SAVE YOU!
PUMMEL!
RUB!
THE DIRT WILL SET YOU FREE!
PUMMEL!
SCRUB!
OOF!
SPUTTER
SPUTTER
PUFF

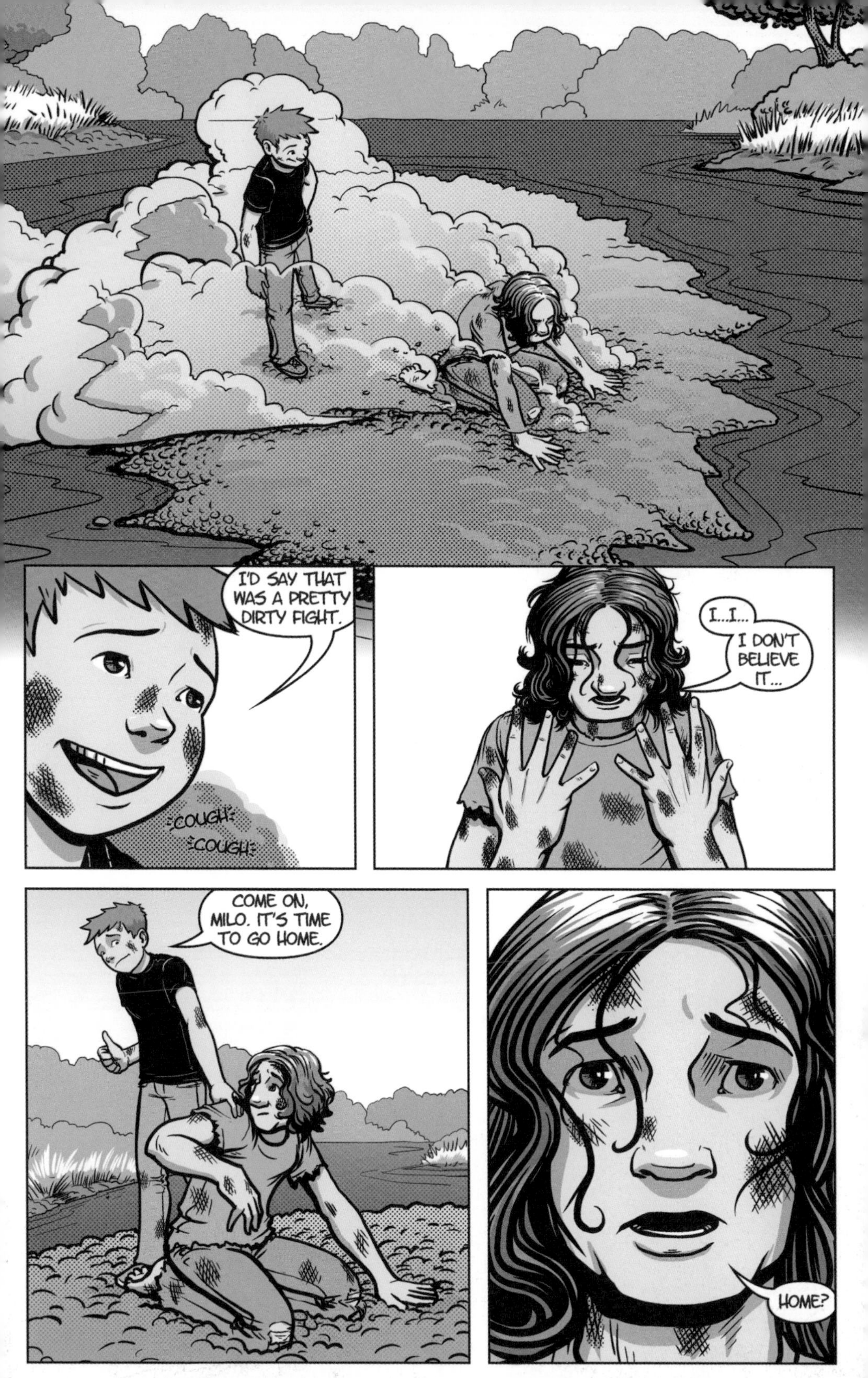
I'D SAY THAT WAS A PRETTY DIRTY FIGHT.
COUGH
COUGH
I...I...
I DON'T BELIEVE IT...
COME ON, MILO. IT'S TIME TO GO HOME.
HOME?

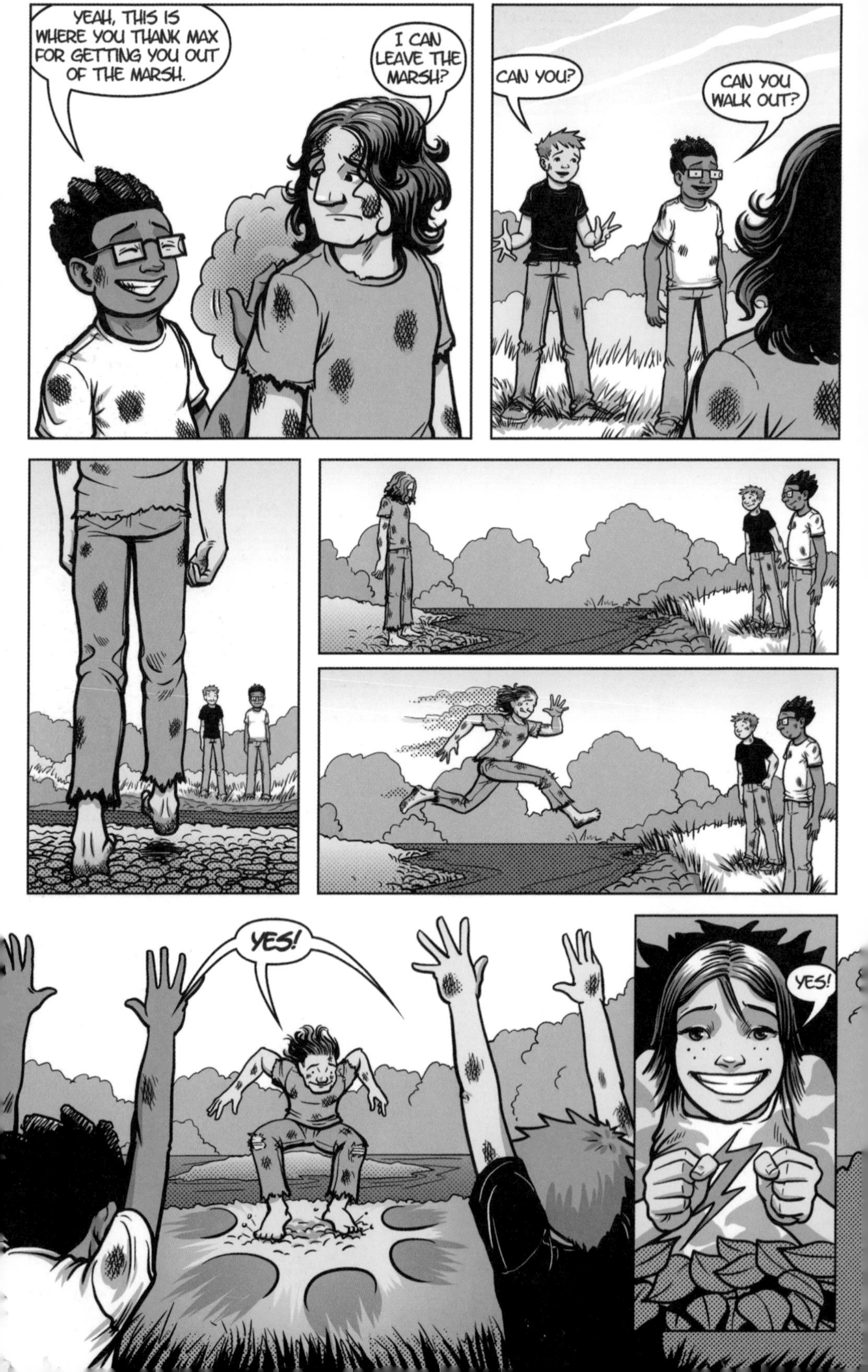
YEAH, THIS IS WHERE YOU THANK MAX FOR GETTING YOU OUT OF THE MARSH.
I CAN LEAVE THE MARSH?
CAN YOU?
CAN YOU WALK OUT?
YES!
YES!

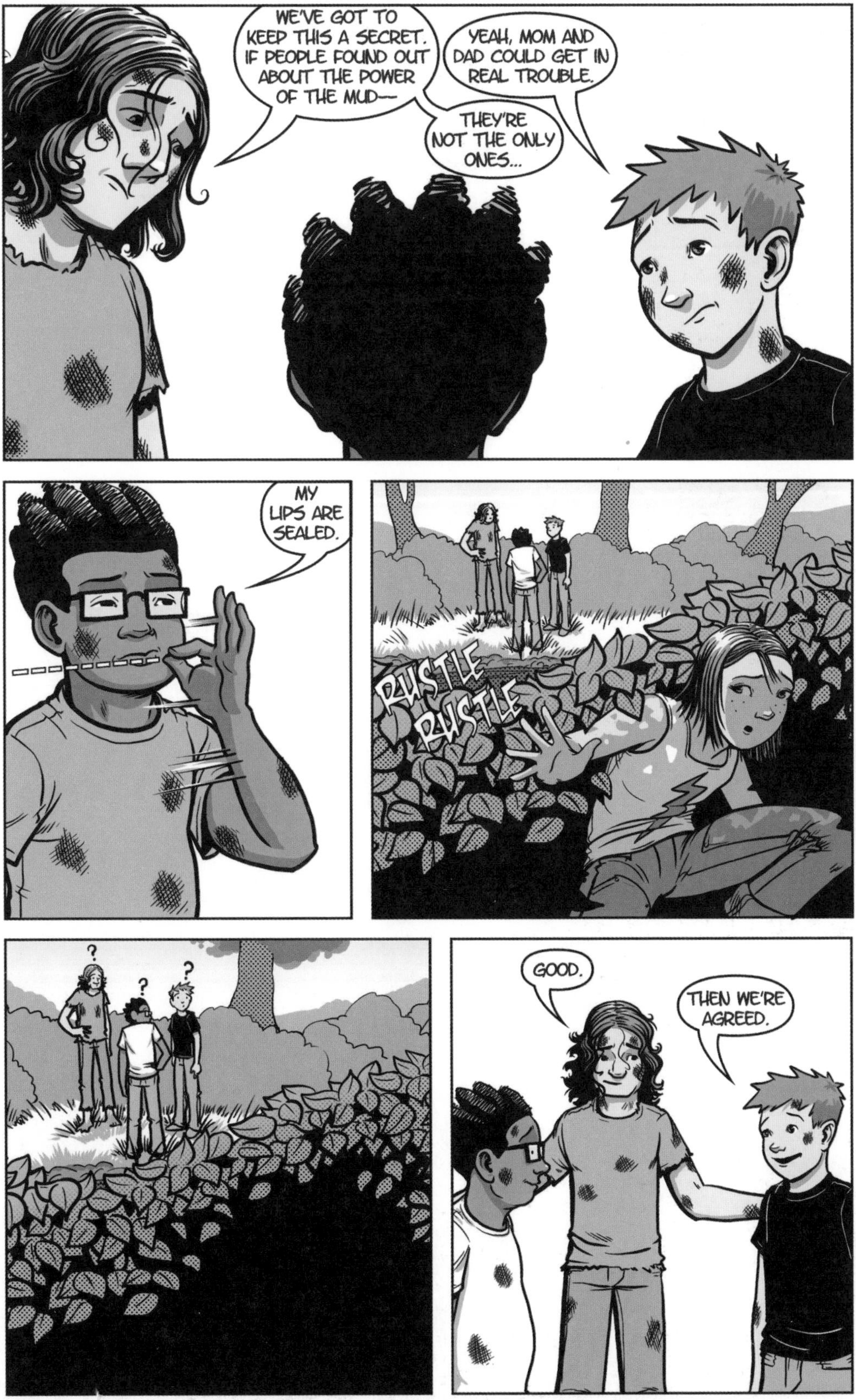
WE'VE GOT TO KEEP THIS A SECRET. IF PEOPLE FOUND OUT ABOUT THE POWER OF THE MUD--
YEAH, MOM AND DAD COULD GET IN REAL TROUBLE.
THEY'RE NOT THE ONLY ONES...
MY LIPS ARE SEALED.
RUSTLE
RUSTLE
?
?
?
GOOD.
THEN WE'RE AGREED.

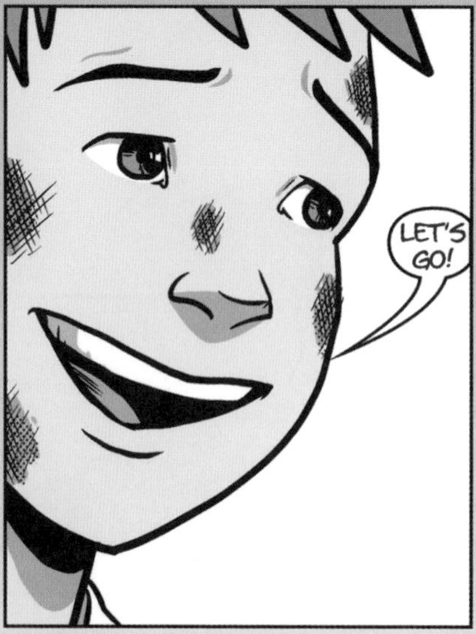
LET'S GO!

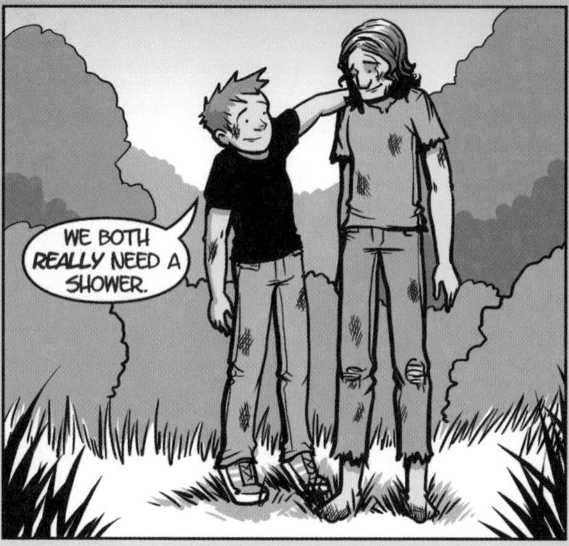
WE BOTH *REALLY* NEED A SHOWER.

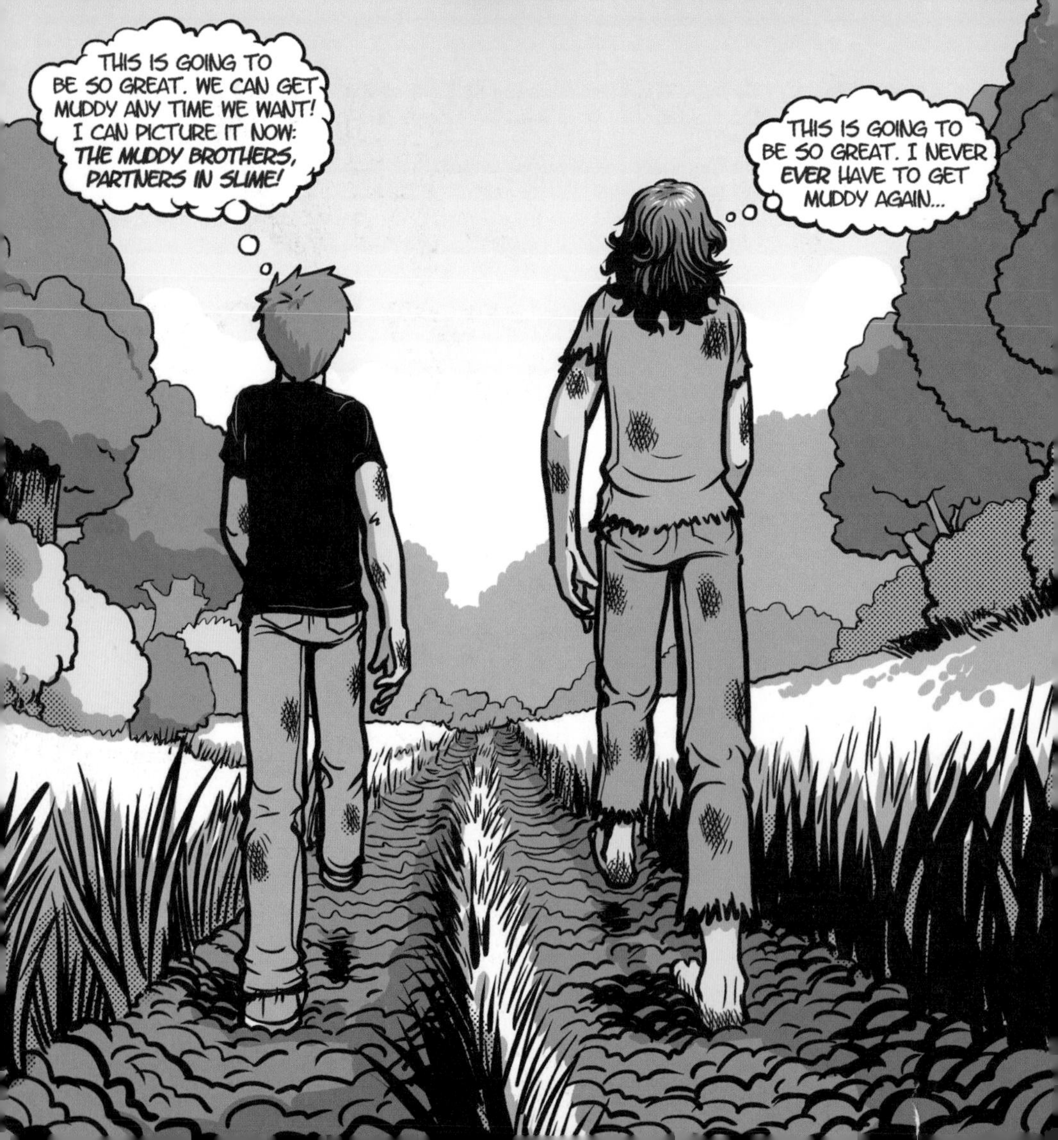
THIS IS GOING TO BE SO GREAT. WE CAN GET MUDDY ANY TIME WE WANT! I CAN PICTURE IT NOW: *THE MUDDY BROTHERS, PARTNERS IN SLIME!*
THIS IS GOING TO BE SO GREAT. I NEVER *EVER* HAVE TO GET MUDDY AGAIN...

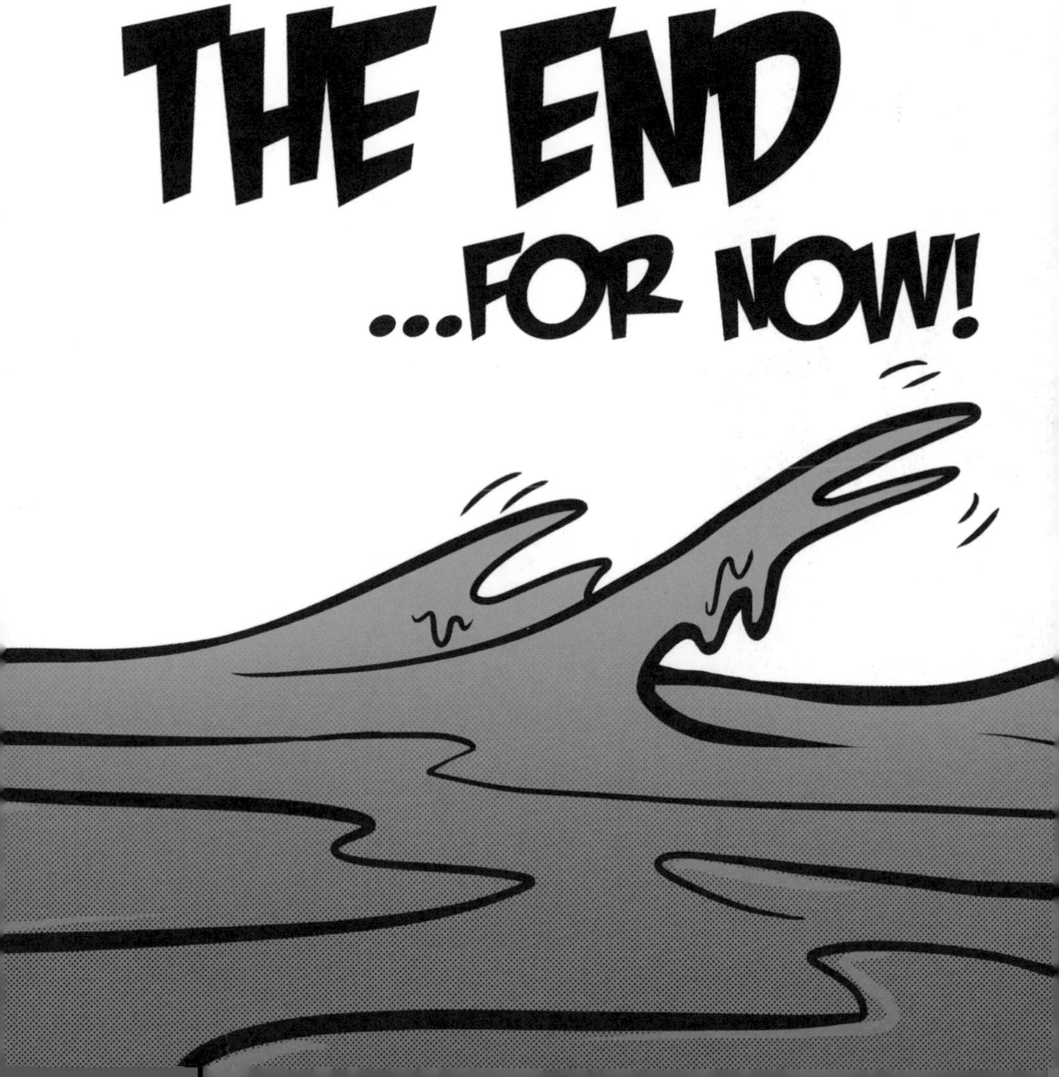
THE END
...FOR NOW!

WHAT'S IN THE MUD?

Yes, all that gross stuff that Max and Patrick learned about mud is true. It's full of earthworm poop, rotting leaves, bug carcasses, and nematodes. Find out for yourself by trying these three muddy hands-on explorations.

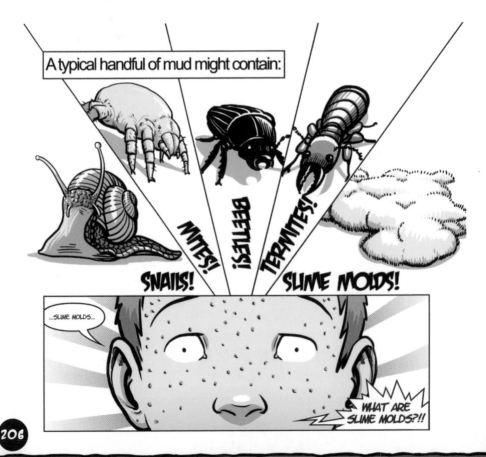

A typical handful of mud might contain:

SNAILS! MITES! BEETLES! TERMITES! SLIME MOLDS!

...SLIME MOLDS...

WHAT ARE SLIME MOLDS?!!

SOIL CLOSE-UP

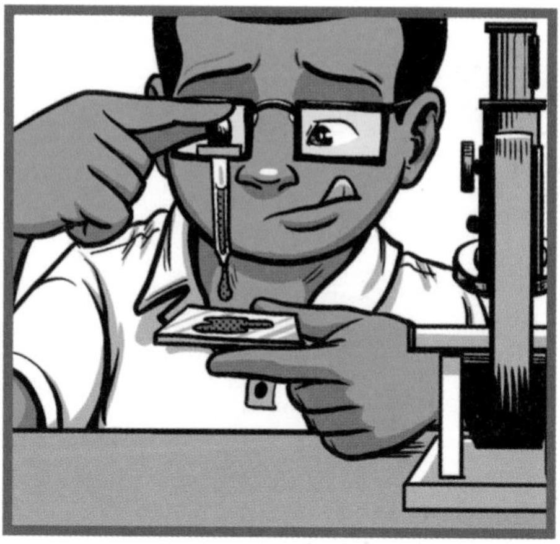

YOU'LL NEED

- Several empty yogurt tubs or small glass jars
- A magnifying glass
- Tweezers
- One sheet each of black paper and white paper

Gather soil and mud samples from a variety of places. Look for loose, dark soil; hard, dry soil; sandy or silty soil; clay; dirt from under trees and bushes; soil from the surface and soil from deeper down; soil from near creeks, lakes, or puddles; and mud. Place each sample in a container and then:

- Smell it. What does each soil sample smell like?
- Feel it with your fingers. Is it soft or hard? Moist or dry? Smooth or chunky?
- Poke through each soil sample with the tweezers and study any leaves, bugs, twigs, seeds, or other interesting material. Use your magnifying glass for a closer look.
- Place half of a soil sample on the white paper and half on the black. The backgrounds will give you good contrast so that light and dark materials really stand out. Now you can see for yourself what is really in the dirt under your feet.

MAKE SOME MUD!

YOU'LL NEED

- Water
- Your soil samples

Pour a little water into each of your soil samples.

Did adding water change the way it smells?

Which mud is the chunkiest? The smoothest? The stickiest?

Which soil absorbed the most water? The least?

Now, mix the mud together and see what you get.

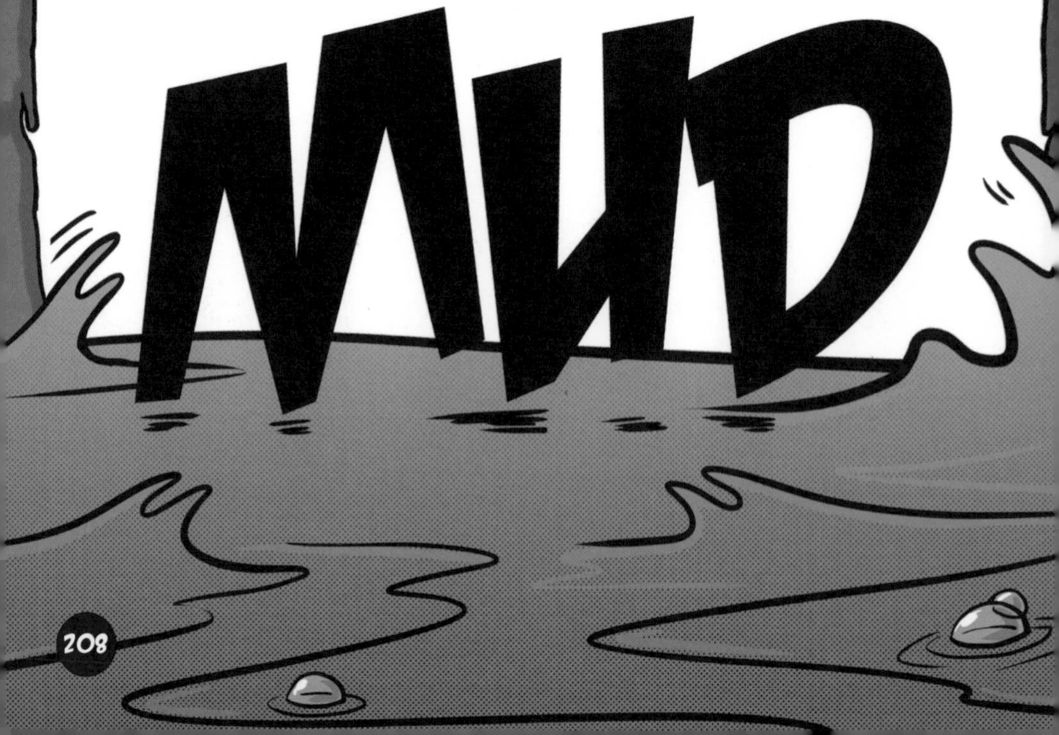
MUD

BREATHING MUD CREATURES

YOU'LL NEED

- 1 cup of soil

- A glass canning jar

- Limewater (available at pet stores), or pickling lime mixed with water (available at larger grocery stores)

- Small plastic container (like a clean laundry detergent lid)

Even if you can't see them, all kinds of creatures live in dirt. In this experiment, you can prove they are there by seeing what happens when they BREATHE! Here's how:

- Place about a cup of garden soil into the bottom of the empty canning jar.

- Fill the small plastic container with limewater.

- Place the container of limewater onto the soil in the glass jar.

- Tightly close the glass jar and leave it for a few days.

What happened to the limewater?

If it turned a milky color, that means there's something ALIVE in your soil. Creatures in the soil breathe in oxygen and breathe out carbon dioxide. The carbon dioxide from the bacteria, protozoans, and nematodes combined with the limewater and made chalk!

DIG DEEPER: Learn more of the dirty truth about mud in *Under Ground: How Creatures of Mud and Dirt Shape Our World* by Yvonne Baskin.

ABOUT ANTONI GAUDÍ

Milo's mud-fort house was inspired by the work of the groundbreaking Spanish architect Antoni Gaudí (1852–1926). Gaudí often worked with bare stone and brick. Many of his creations look more like sculptures than buildings, and seem to be carved from the ground like rabbit warrens or cave dwellings. Gaudí's style featured bulging, protruding, or wavy walls with windowsills, frames, or archways that look as if they were molded out of mud or clay. His work was wildly creative and imaginative, with thick pillars like elephant feet, ridges like the backbones of dinosaurs, and bizarre, richly ornamented chimneys, spires, and towers. Many of Gaudí's buildings, in addition to their wildly imaginative shapes, are also very colorful.

Gaudí said of one of his creations, Casa Batlló: "The corners will vanish, and the material will reveal itself in the wealth of its astral curves; the sun will shine through all four sides, and it will be like a vision of paradise."

DIG DEEPER: Check out photos of Gaudí's work in *Antoni Gaudí* by Rainer Zerbst and *Antonio Gaudi: Master Architect* by Juan Bassegoda Nonell. Learn more about his life and work in *Building on Nature: The Life of Antoni Gaudí* by Rachel Rodríguez.

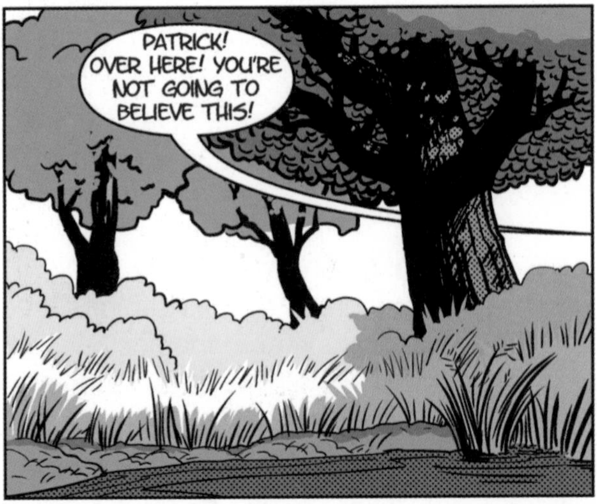
PATRICK! OVER HERE! YOU'RE NOT GOING TO BELIEVE THIS!

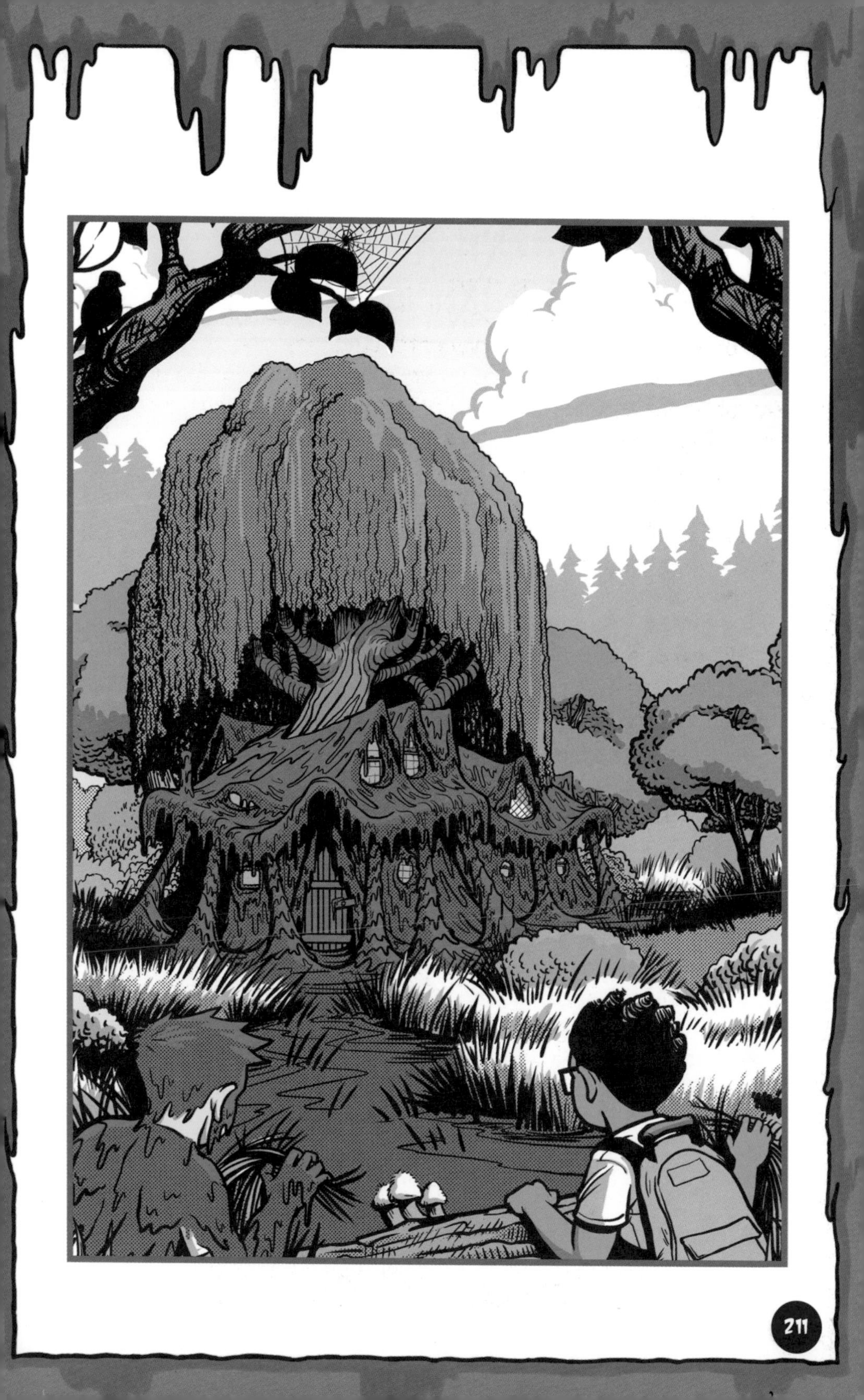

MAKE YOUR OWN MUD HOUSE

You can make a house out of mud, just like Milo's. Here are three techniques:

DRIP CASTLE

YOU'LL NEED

- Water
- Sand
- A bucket
- Paper plate, cardboard, or piece of wood (optional)

You can make a fun, drippy-looking sand castle at the beach or other sandy shore. Just try this:

- Fill a bucket half with sand and half with water, or dig a watery sand puddle near the shore. (It's important that your sand be completely saturated with water.)

- Push some sand together to make a base. You can build your base on a paper plate or a piece of wood or cardboard, or work on the flat ground.

- Scoop up a small handful of very wet sand from your bucket or puddle. Be sure to hold your fingers and thumb pointed down and closed loosely around the sand.

Quickly move your hand over the area you want to work, allowing the watery sand to flow through your fingertips in a stream. You can let the drips pile up on each other to make a tower or move your hand side to side to make a wall.

Just before all the water has dripped out of your hand, grab more drippy wet sand. Use bigger handfuls to make bigger drips on the bottom and use smaller scoops of sand to make delicate tower tops.

ANCIENT AND MODERN MUD HOUSES

For thousands of years, people all around the world have been making houses by slathering muddy mixtures onto brick or wooden frames, called wattles.

WATTLE AND DAUB `YOU'LL NEED`

- Mud
- Sticks, grass, straw, or vines

The simplest recipe is daub, a mixture of mud and grass or straw. To make a small wattle and daub house:

- Construct a wooden frame, or wattle, by weaving together small sticks, twigs, and vines.

- To make daub, mix the mud with the fibers until it becomes thick, like chunky pancake batter.

- Plaster the daub over the wooden frame and let it dry.

Can you make a house with more than one story?

COB AND ADOBE `YOU'LL NEED`

- Mud
- Straw or dried grass
- Sand
- Clay
- Buckets
- Molds

Cob and adobe are both made with mixtures of mud, straw, sand, and clay. (Adobe uses a higher percentage of straw.)

First mix mud, clay, sand, and straw into a thick paste. (For strong bricks, you need a fair amount of clay.)

Press the mixture into brick molds and let them dry (two days for small bricks; a week or two for large bricks).

Prepare more of the above mud mixture. To build your walls, lay bricks with layers of the mud mixture between them.

Then coat the walls with the same goopy mixture inside and out.

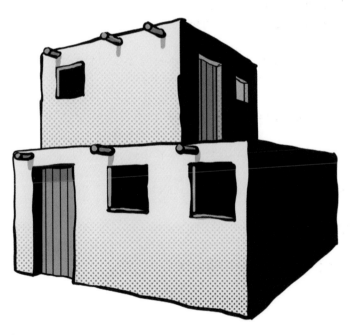

Dig Deeper: Learn more about the creative ways people use natural resources to make homes in *Sticks, Stones, Mud Homes* by Nigel Noyes and *Building: Discover the History of Buildings—Why They Were Built and the Techniques Used in Their Construction* by Philip Wilkinson.

MUD BRICKS

YOU'LL NEED

 Dirt/mud (gather a variety of types to mix together)

 Water

Dried grass, twigs, and/or straw

Buckets

Ice cube trays or egg cartons or plastic storage containers or cardboard milk cartons with the tops cut off (to make your brick molds)

Plastic wrap (optional)

Pick a sunny, warm day and an area you can get messy and then start making your mud bricks.

 Remove any rocks from your soil.

 Tear up leaves, twigs, or straw into small pieces.

Mix dirt and mud with the leaves, twigs, and/or straw and a little water until the mixture is thick, moist, and holds together, like thick pancake batter.

Put the mixture into the molds and pack the mud tightly. (If you are worried about the bricks sticking in the molds, line them with plastic wrap.)

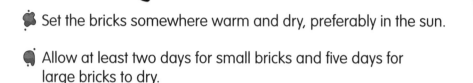

- Set the bricks somewhere warm and dry, preferably in the sun.

- Allow at least two days for small bricks and five days for large bricks to dry.

- Pop the bricks out of their molds.

- You can use them now, but for best results allow them to dry another week in the sun out of their containers. (Or you can bake small bricks in the oven at 150 degrees for a few hours.)

- To build your house, stack the bricks to make walls. Experiment with mud mixtures to use as cement to hold your bricks together.

Note: You can use just about anything for your brick molds: egg cartons, butter tubs, paper cups, small buckets, or cans. The bigger the mold, the longer you need to let your brick dry. If your bricks crumble easily, allow more drying time.

GET THE MUD OUT!

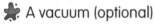 Dirty, muddy clothes

A vacuum (optional)

Liquid detergent or stain remover

A washing machine (optional)

If you don't have a demudifier, here are some easy steps to really get the mud off your clothes.

Let it dry! Rather than scrubbing the mud and rubbing it into the fabric, let the mud dry completely.

Shake, scrape, or vacuum: After the mud is dry, try shaking your clothes (outside). The dried mud may just crumble right off. You can also try picking the dry mud off with your fingernails. Or, with an adult's permission or supervision, vacuum the dry mud off.

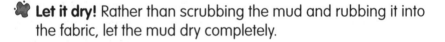 **Now scrub**: Only after removing as much of the dry mud as you can, rub liquid detergent or stain remover into the spot. Let it soak in for at least 15 minutes.

 Wash: Finally, run the clothes through the laundry, repeating the last two steps if necessary.

Your parents will be so amazed at your mud removal talents that they might even let you move into your mud fort.

AGE YOUR FACE

Police, health care professionals, and scientists really do use digital image processing of scanned photos to try to predict what someone might look like as they age. When programs age photos of children, they try to capture changes in underlying bone structure that happen as the child grows. For example, a baby starts with a very large cranium in relation to the rest of his face. As the baby develops into a toddler and school-age kid, the lower half of the face, including the nose, cheeks, and jaw, move downward and outward. Sophisticated programs that predict how adults age can even capture how things like smoking, weight gain, or sun exposure might affect how the face changes.

Two good websites to learn more are www.changemyface.com and www.ageme.com. Ageme.com includes an option to scan and age a photo for about $4. Even better, try out Make Me Old, a free age-progression app. Another cool app, Watch My Age Progression, lets you scan in lots of photos of yourself over the years and links them together into a high-speed animation so you can see how your face has really changed as you've gotten older.

3 Years Later

6 Years Later

9 Years Later

ABOUT THE AUTHOR

Elizabeth Rusch is the award-winning author of numerous fiction and nonfiction books for young readers, including *Eruption!*, *The Mighty Mars Rovers*, *Electrical Wizard*, *A Day with No Crayons*, and *Generation Fix*. Her books have been honored by the Junior Library Guild, the Children's Book of the Month Club, the Children's Book Council, the American Library Association, and the National Council of Teachers of English; and have landed on best book of the year lists compiled by *School Library Journal*, *Booklist*, *Kirkus Reviews*, *NBC News*, and the New York Public Library. Liz teaches writing at the Attic Institute and speaks widely at schools and writing conferences. She lives—and splashes around in the mud—with her family in rainy Portland, Oregon.

Learn more at www.elizabethrusch.com.

ABOUT THE ARTIST

Mike Lawrence grew up wanting to be a superhero and an artist. He never developed any superpowers, but he did become an artist after being exposed to gamma radiation while attending art school at the University of Oregon. Mike lives in Portland, Oregon, with his wife, Ashley, and their two muddy boys, Hank and Gus.

ACKNOWLEDGMENTS

I tried covering myself with mud to see if it would make me a better writer, but I found that it's really the people around me that have been most empowering. Thanks, first, to my husband, Craig Rusch, whose bedtime stories about a muddy boy inspired the book.

I want to offer my heartfelt appreciation to the fellow writers who commented on drafts: Nancy Coffelt, Emily Whitman, Barbara Kerley, Ellen Howard, Amber Keyser, Addie Boswell, Ruth Tenzer Feldman, Sabina I. Rascol, Nicole Marie Schreiber, Melissa Dalton, Mary Rehmann, and Michelle McCann. I especially want to thank the kid-readers who helped me see the story through their eyes: Maeve Kelly, Becca Zuckerman, Elliot Balmer, Haru Zemsky, Cobi Rusch, Izzi Rusch, and the members of the Northwest Library branch Comic Club. You all made the book better—and more fun.

Thanks to our agent, Kelly Sonnack, for helping to shape the story and for sharing her enthusiasm for it, to editor Andrea Colvin for taking a chance on it, and to editor Sheila Keenan for her "keen" insights.

And finally, my jolliest thanks to Mike Lawrence for all the fun brainstorming, great ideas—and even better art. I couldn't wish for a better collaborator.

—Elizabeth Rusch

This book would not have been possible without the love and support of my wife, Ashley—my greatest fan and most trusted critic. Special thanks to my sisters, Anne and Morgan Lindberg, for watching my boys, who tried their hardest to prevent me from drawing this book.

Thank you to my agent, Kelly Sonnack, and to editors Andrea Colvin and Sheila Keenan for finding a home for Max and helping make this book the best it can be.

Finally, globs of gooey thanks to Liz Rusch for sharing Max's adventures with me and being such a great collaborator.

—Mike Lawrence

Andrews McMeel Publishing, LLC
an Andrews McMeel Universal company
1130 Walnut Street, Kansas City, Missouri 64106

www.andrewsmcmeel.com

14 15 16 17 18 SDB 10 9 8 7 6 5 4 3 2 1

ISBN: 978-1-4494-3561-5

Library of Congress Control Number: 2013955462

Made by:
Shenzhen Donnelley Printing Company Ltd.
Address and location of manufacturer:
No. 47, Wuhe Nan Road, Bantian Ind. Zone,
Shenzhen China, 518129
1st Printing – 5/19/14

ATTENTION: SCHOOLS AND BUSINESSES
Andrews McMeel books are available at quantity discounts with bulk
purchase for educational, business, or sales promotional use. For
information, please-mail the Andrews McMeel Publishing Special Sales
Department: specialsales@amuniversal.com.